BY THE SAME AUTHOR

Skydancer
Shadowhunter

EAGLETRAP

Geoffrey Archer is Defence and Diplomatic Correspondent for ITN's award-winning *News at Ten* television programme. His work as a broadcaster has given him detailed knowledge of the defence systems that appear in his military thrillers – first in the bestselling *Skydancer* and *Shadowhunter* and now in *Eagletrap*.

EAGLETRAP

Geoffrey Archer

ARROW

First published in Arrow 1993

9 10 8

Copyright © Geoffrey Archer, 1993

First published in the United Kingdom in 1993 by Century

Arrow Books Limited
Random House UK Ltd, 20 Vauxhall Bridge Road, London SW1V 2SA

Random House Australia (Pty) Limited
20 Alfred Street, Milsons Point, Sydney,
New South Wales 2061, Australia

Random House New Zealand Limited
18 Poland Road, Glenfield
Auckland 10, New Zealand

Random House South Africa (Pty) Limited
PO Box 337, Bergvlei, South Africa

Random House UK Limited Reg. No. 954009

A CIP catalogue record for this book
is available from the British Library

ISBN 0 09 991910 9

Printed and bound by Firmin-Didot (France),
Group Herissey. No d'impression : 28097.

"Avoid shame, but do not seek glory – nothing so expensive as glory." –
Sydney Smith
1771–1845

Prologue

The Trans-Caucasus Military District
Early January 1992

The orders from Moscow were to make it look like a food convoy. Safer that way, the Generals thought. If the nationalists knew what the trucks were really carrying. . . .

Major Alexander Kabanov watched the uniformed drivers stamp their feet to banish the cold of the early morning. It was not yet dawn, and the sky showed no sign of lightening over the hills of Armenia.

Floodlights bathed the concrete square a dull pink. On the far side, the steel doors to the underground bunkers gaped open like hungry mouths. The men wore long, grey coats and fur hats with the gold star on a red background, their breath misty in the cold air.

It was a race against time, to tidy away the nuclear warheads before the disintegration of the Soviet Union became total. Kabanov listened to the Russian service of the BBC. He'd heard the assurances the Kremlin had given the West. They'd spelled it out – don't worry, nuclear weapons are under strict central control, and will stay that way.

Kabanov knew these words to be lies. Control would be impossible to maintain in a few more weeks. Every day thousands more Red Army soldiers were swearing allegiance to some republic or other. There'd be no Red Army soon.

That's why they were spiriting the warheads out of the

republics and back to Russia as fast as the big Antonovs could fly them there.

This was the third such convoy in ten days. The first two had worked like a dream. They'd reached the airfield fifty kilometres to the south without a hitch. Departure times had varied, so as not to set a pattern, but the planes always left in the early morning.

Time to start. Kabanov gave the signal. The drivers swung up into their cabs and backed the trucks up to the bunkers. Ordnance men pushed heavy trolleys out of the stores. The drab-green steel canisters tied to wooden pallets were lifted by mobile crane, two pallets to each lorry, two ordnance lorries to each convoy.

Four nuclear weapons.

The missiles to which the warheads belonged had been standard equipment in the artillery units of Soviet tank divisions. There were thousands in existence, and hundreds here in the Trans-Caucasus Military District. Standard procedure to plan to use them in a war with their neighbours.

The more Kabanov had learned, in the years since Gorbachev, of the real nature of the rest of the world, the more astonished he had become at the paranoia that had dominated his country's military thinking for so long.

For what, other than paranoia, had driven their leaders to invest so much in weapons that could turn the entire hemisphere into a wasteland?

He recognised the weapons had the power to deter or persuade. But that power increased little as the numbers grew. If anything it was the weapon's scarcity that made it almost priceless, a fact brought home to him in recent days.

The missile base was in southern Armenia, twenty kilometres from the Azerbaijani enclave of Nakhichevan.

It was another enclave, Nagorno-Karabakh, that had sparked off civil war between the two peoples. Now, with the break-up of the Soviet Union, national militias were expanding, aiming to take over the role and the hardware of the old Red Army.

Security at the Tochka missile base had always been drum-tight. The guards were all KGB, trained to trust nobody. The blue collar tabs and epaulettes, the letters GB on their shoulders, gave the clue. *Gosudarstvennaya Bezopasnost* – State Security.

But in recent weeks discipline had crumbled. Word was out that their unit would be disbanded in a matter of months. No jobs, no homes, no money. The effect on morale had been catastrophic.

'All right! Get moving!' yelled Kabanov. He climbed through the open side hatch of the armoured vehicle.

The striped pole was raised; the heavy gates swung open. Kabanov's BTR-80 eight-wheeled APC led the way; then came the two Gaz 2-ton covered trucks and finally another BTR-80 at the rear.

Kabanov sat in the right-hand seat behind the armoured glass screen, the young driver to his left. The boy wasn't from this area – none of them was – he came from Omsk in Siberia.

They were all Russians in the security guard. The KGB had always liked it that way – all on the same side, united against the often hostile republics where they had to operate.

Yes, thought Kabanov, his men were united all right. United in the determination to sieze any opportunity that might improve their prospects.

For much of the journey south along the Arak river valley the pot-holed road was straight and, at this hour, free from heavy traffic. As the grey dawn light began to illuminate the fertile flood-plain they could make out the patchwork of orchards and irrigation ditches that cut the landscape into rectangles.

The air was remarkably clear. Occasionally the young driver took his eyes from the road to glance to his right at the distant, icy peak of Mount Ararat.

When he was a small child, his grandmother had told him stories from the Bible. She'd talked of Noah and the Great Flood. He glanced again to the West. Could it have been true? Was the Ark still up there, somewhere?

'Keep your eyes on the road!' Major Kabanov snapped as the APC veered perilously close to the ditch.

'Yes, comrade Major. Sorry.'

The back of the boy's shaven neck flushed red. Nineteen? Kabanov wondered. Twenty at the most. What sort of life lay ahead after he was demobilised?

Back to his home village, he supposed, to drive a tractor. A grim future in the chaos of economic stagnation. But maybe the boy faced a better future than himself; if your expectations were low, you had less far to fall.

For Kabanov, home for the past fifteen years had been army married quarters. Small apartments with damp walls, and usually just a single bedroom for themselves and their twelve-year-old son.

Now the powers-that-be were promising a new flat in Moscow when he lost his job in three months' time. Fat chance of *that* happening! He thought of the thousands who'd been withdrawn from Hungary and Czechoslovakia, and were now living in tents.

A horse-drawn cart with soft rubber tyres passed in the opposite direction. He noted the sullen eyes of the two Armenians driving it. The local people hated the Russians, accusing them of siding with the Azeris. Eighty thousand men the CIS army had in Armenia and Azerbaijan. Not a conscript too many for the dispiriting task of containing the civil war.

Before, the army had had a proud, patriotic role

4

– defending the motherland against the Turkish hordes just the other side of the Arak river. In those days NATO had seemed a real threat.

The cold war had given them a sense of purpose, at least. For a moment he longed for those days to return.

What was there now to motivate them? No Motherland, no party privilege to aspire to. Nothing but their own survival.

That's why food supplies had been disappearing from the kitchens, stolen by his soldiers and sold for vodka or hashish. And, worse, Kalashnikovs and rocket grenades had vanished from the armoury, sold for dollars to Armenian militias for use against Azeris in Nagorno-Karabakh.

The officer glanced across at the fresh-scrubbed face of the driver. He looked innocent. But was he?

'Do you smoke hashish?' Kabanov asked sharply.

'Not me, sir,' the driver answered quickly, the back of his neck flushing again. 'But I've heard of it in the tank regiments. They pay with meat stolen from the kitchens.'

The officer nodded.

Drugs, alcohol. There'd always been an insatiable demand in the military. With the erosion of discipline the problem was getting unmanageable.

'Only last week I heard something,' the conscript continued. 'Tank driver got completely stoned. Drove his T.62 into the side of a house. Totally demolished it. Killed an old woman.'

'Tsch! There you are! Shows what can happen. And the boy?'

'They say he's in a labour camp . . .'

The officer smiled. The story was apocryphal. It had been circulated deliberately amongst the conscripts as a cautionary tale. He was happy to see some had swallowed it.

'And you? You must've sold things. Everyone has.'

5

The boy glanced sideways in acute discomfort.

'Comrade Major, I've done nothing wrong. . .'

Kabanov punched him playfully on the shoulder.

'It's all right. This isn't a court martial!'

The driver continued to frown, then broke into a sheepish grin.

'I once sold my hat to a girl . . .'

Kabanov laughed.

'I hope she paid you well!'

The boy flushed scarlet and nodded.

Suddenly Kabanov flinched.

Ahead of them on the road was a grubby, pale-blue truck, halted by the verge, just where the apple orchards started. Kabanov flicked off the safety-catch of his automatic. Men were jumping down into the roadway. A party of labourers? Or something else?

'Slow down!'

The driver pumped on the footbrake.

Alarmed, Kabanov made a count of heads. At least a dozen men in overalls, just fifty metres ahead. No sign of guns.

But this was how an ambush could start. A truck-load of dynamite, 'workers' scattering for cover seconds before it detonated beside the escort vehicle at the front of the convoy.

Suddenly he relaxed again. Something had reassured him.

Two of the men had begun to urinate at the side of the road. No man could afford that luxury if he was about to kill.

Labourers, that's all they were, making a reluctant start to their day's work filling pot-holes.

The major kept his finger loosely on the trigger-guard as the convoy crawled past, the road gang hardly glancing up at the trucks.

He rose from his seat and poked his head out of the command hatch to look back at the sullenly staring peasants. They would know nothing, the simpletons. But there were some who did.

What would partisans want with a nuclear warhead? Such a weapon was hardly suitable for the guerrilla warfare that would surge out of control here once the Red Army was withdrawn.

Yet they wanted one, a *serzhant* had told him. The same Armenian militiamen who'd bought guns and grenades from the guards at the barracks had been asking questions about the nuclear missile warheads, offering unspecified riches.

Crazy! Kabanov thought. They could never use the weapons, even if they got hold of them. The warheads were packed with safety systems to prevent unauthorised use; codes, switches, arming devices that only worked when the thing was fired on a missile – all this was known to anyone who handled the weapons, even the KGB guards.

Kabanov dropped back into his seat and closed the hatch.

The driver gave a nervous chuckle. He'd seen his officer ready the gun.

'Did you think they might try something?' he asked timidly.

'Maybe. Maybe not.'

Kabanov glanced sharply at the youth. Not so innocent as he looked? A conspiracy? With all of them? Had his men already been bought?

The officer placed his weapon across his knees, and watched the driver's face.

'Bastard partisans!' he exploded. 'You can't tell who they are. They could even be in our uniforms!'

The driver frowned, not understanding.

'I hate this place,' the conscript confided after a while. 'Armenians, Azeris, Kurds – they're all the same. They don't like Russians.'

Innocent, thought Kabanov. This lad's not a

conspirator. But the others? The *serzhant* had warned him; there'd been a lot of talk.

Would they do it? Turn on their officers? Shoot them and hand over the warheads to the partisans? But then what? There'd be no hiding place. The KGB would hunt them down like dogs.

Unless they could be spirited out of the country with their dollars.

He wrenched his head round, suddenly conscious of the eight, heavily-armed, well-trained fighting men sitting behind him in the vehicle. A ninth stood, manning the 14.5mm machine gun in the small turret.

No sign of revolt, just tension. But then there was always tension inside these APCs. Wheeled coffins, they called them.

'Comrade Major!'

The driver hit the brakes – Alarm sounded in his voice.

Ahead of them the road looked blocked. The engine note sank lower. A truck loaded with timber had broken down on their side, and a fuel tanker coming the other way had stopped to give advice.

An accident? Maybe. Maybe not.

'The stupid . . . !' Kabanov cursed, pushing open the hatch above his head and cocking the automatic.

'Get that bloody truck moving!'

The APC stopped. He looked round. The convoy was tight behind them.

'Hey!' he yelled, trying to raise the attention of the truck drivers.

An icy hand clasped at his heart. The cabs were empty.

As he spun round to order his men out, he caught the flash of the first missile, fired from behind an apple tree not fifty metres away.

Mesmerised, he watched its split-second flight, the eruption of flame as its warhead bored through the

8

armour of the BTR-80 at the rear of the convoy, the fountain of fire as the vehicle exploded.

Our missiles, he thought. Bought from our men!

Then the second missile struck, just below the turret of his own BTR.

Moscow, 15.00hrs the same day

Marshal Zhukov stood in the long, marble-panelled corridor of the Defence Ministry, snapping his fingers to hurry up the others. The left side of his broad chest was stiff with medal ribbons. Several members of the General Staff were out of Moscow for the day. He'd have to make do with those who were there.

At one end of the extensive red and gold runner covering the polished parquet floor, a cleaner was hustled out of the way by a guard. The suddenness of this meeting had taken everyone by surprise.

Inside the meeting room, they gathered round one end of the green-baize covered table, beneath a crystal chandelier.

'Comrades . . .' Zhukov began, his expression thunderous, heavy eyebrows jutting ferociously. 'We face a disaster. What I have to tell you is a matter of the utmost secrecy.'

Two others at the table already knew what had happened, the Commander of Ground Forces and the head of the KGB troops. The ten others looked deeply alarmed.

'Early this morning,' Zhukov continued, 'one of our transportation convoys in the Republic of Armenia was attacked by unknown assailants.

'Two *Tochka* nuclear warheads have been stolen!'

9

There was an audible intake of breath around the table. The Commander-in-Chief gestured to the KGB chief to take up the story.

'Four of the weapons were being transported – inconspicuously,' he continued flatly. 'The guard of some thirty men was led by Major Alexander Kabanov. Their armoured vehicles came under simultaneous surprise attack with RPG-22 rockets. Only two men survived; neither is expected to live.

'One of the weapons carriers was also hit, and the two warheads on board were badly damaged by fire. The other weapons carrier was driven off by the assailants. It has not yet been found.'

'Assailants? What assailants?' The question came from the Head of the Air Defence Forces.

'Armenian irregulars, we assume. But they could have been Azeris – the attack came close to the border with Nakhichevan.'

A look of horrified incredulity spread across several faces.

'Two nuclear weapons are missing, and we don't know who's got them?' The Air Defence Chief again.

'That is the situation,' the Ground Force Commander confirmed. 'But don't forget, these weapons are safe. They cannot be used without codes which have to be released from Moscow. There are safety locks; the warhead has to be launched on a rocket to activate the trigger. Whoever has the bombs is most unlikely to have the technology to deactivate those locks.'

Marshal Zhukov unbuttoned his uniform jacket and lit a cigarette.

'In an ideal world, what you say would be correct, comrade. But this disintegrating nation in which we find ourselves today is far from ideal,' he growled.

'You are all aware, I assume, of the situation at Arzamas-16? The research scientists developing the next generation of nuclear warheads have not been paid for

10

two months. Their families will be hungry by now. If the Armenian partisans were to offer enough money . . .'

'We don't intend to let it come to that,' the KGB chief cut in. 'A vigorous search is under way. The scene of the incident was detected within minutes by a helicopter patrol. The area's been sealed.'

Zhukov's raised eyebrow was noted by the others. 'Detected within minutes'? More like hours.

They all knew that the days when the Red Army controlled Armenia were over. Since it had declared itself independent, the NVD Interior Ministry troops had been withdrawn, two Red Army divisions had sworn allegiance to the new republic, and the border with Turkey had been opened to smugglers in several places.

'Comrades!' Zhukov's gravel voice called them to attention. 'I'm sure that everything possible is being done to find these warheads. The President of Armenia has assured us his own military were not involved in the ambush. They're helping in the search. We've told him the missing truck contained missile-guidance radar sets. But . . .'

He raised his finger in warning.

'There is one crucial matter we must decide at this meeting.'

All eyes turned to him.

'Should our President be told what has happened?'

His words sent a shock wave round the table. Puzzled frowns, then the Air Defence Forces Commander spoke up.

'Of course he must be told. We've sworn to support the democratic process!'

Several looked down at their hands. They had all opposed the coup to oust Gorbachev, but none had expected the collapse of the Union to follow so quickly.

'The President is at his dacha,' Zhukov intoned. 'I have to tell you that he is "nursing a headache".'

Heads shook in dismay. Some sighed. The President's drink problem was no legend.

'If I tell him that we've lost two nuclear weapons, his reaction could be . . . unpredictable, to say the least. I doubt he'll keep it to himself. He might pick up the hotline to Washington! And that could be disastrous; it would destroy the one thing that matters most to us just now – our credibility with the Americans.'

Zhukov had held a meeting in Moscow with his Pentagon counterpart just a week ago, to discuss the arrival of the Galaxies loaded with emergency food aid.

'You see, the Chairman of the Joint Chiefs is obsessed by our nuclear security. The Americans are petrified of weapons getting into the wrong hands. I reassured him. I insisted everything was under tight control. Now, if they find out how quickly I've been proved wrong . . . pouf . . .'

He threw his hands into the air.

'All the treaties we've signed with Washington to reduce nuclear weapons could be in jeopardy – that's what he told me. If we lose control, the arms reduction process goes into the deep freeze.'

'That's an idle threat,' the KGB chief retorted. 'They need to cut arms just as much as we do.'

He rubbed two fingers together to indicate the reason – money.

'Nevertheless, it's not a threat I want to put to the test.'

Zhukov brought his fist firmly down on the table.

'We must keep this secret. Only for a matter of days, I hope. Long enough to find those blasted warheads.'

He looked round, testing the opinion of his comrades.

'Agreed, then? The President should not be told?'

A few sideways glances, then one by one they nodded.

One

Lebanon
November 1993

So they were coming. That very night. Around a dozen of the best men he knew. For a military mission that broke every rule in the textbooks.

Peter Brodrick watched the sun setting over the city below. He stood back from the window so as not to be seen from outside. Pretty. Too damned pretty for a dump like Beirut.

'That bugger's blubbin' again, sir.' Sergeant Blight's soft Brummy accent a few inches from his ear. 'Shakin' his head and blubbin'.'

'Terrified at what they'll do to him for spilling the beans,' the Captain muttered.

The Arab strapped to a chair in the back room had told them what they wanted to know. Eventually.

Brodrick was still clutching the UHF radio from which he'd transmitted the single code word that gave the okay to proceed. Within a minute it had been heard by the helicopter flying twenty miles offshore, relayed to the carrier steaming near Cyprus, and an acknowledgement had come back.

One word was all they'd allowed him. Go or no-go. His decision. No chance to discuss the dangers, to question whether it was really worth the risk.

The politicians wanted the raid to go ahead if there was any chance of success, however slight. Brodrick still didn't know why. Waite and McCarthy had been held hostage for years in Beirut and the government had

13

hardly raised a finger. Why the 'big stick' this time? Why did this man matter so much?

Brodrick and Blight had flown to Beirut posing as journalists, one carrying a notebook computer, the other with cameras round his neck. Brodrick, tall and lean and with even features broken only by a small scar through his left eyebrow, was commander of the Special Boat Squadron counter-terrorist unit.

Hardy, the Embassy security man, had given them guns. He'd also told them as much as he knew.

The Brit who'd been kidnapped had arrived unannounced five weeks ago from London. Some big wheel in the financial world. Personal friend of the PM. There was a bit of a mystery as to why he'd gone to Beirut. 'Negotiating contracts for rebuilding the war-ravaged city' – was what the spokesman for Celadec, his finance company, had said. Strange that he hadn't let the British Embassy know he was coming. Still, everyone said, that's the way Richard Bicknell operated. In secret.

Bicknell had wide contacts in the Arab world. A deal he'd done with Gaddafi the previous year, to free a Briton held in Benghazi on corruption charges, had turned him into something of a national hero.

That hadn't helped him in Beirut, however. He'd got himself kidnapped by a Shi-ite gang, – 'men who did the dirty business for the fundamentalists' was how Hardy had described them. Extortionists. Drug merchants. The group, called *Mustadhafin*, had delivered a photograph of Bicknell to the British Embassy with a demand for a million pounds in ransom. Just when everybody thought the days of kidnapping foreigners were over.

'Are we on?'

Hardy emerged from the back room, sub-machine-gun in hand. In his late forties, he looked more like a PE instructor than the ex-soldier he was. His normally ruddy face was drawn and pale.

Brodrick nodded.

'Affirmative. When's the transport due?' he asked.

'In a couple of hours. Hope to God they get here. They're Druze. Usually reliable. But if they get wind of what we're up to . . .'

'You'll have to make sure they don't . . .'

Hardy shrugged. It wasn't that simple. People who came in from outside, people like Brodrick, never understood just how crazy this place was. Nobody could understand until they'd lived with it for a while.

'You gonna take another look at the house once it's dark?'

'Too bloody right! I want every wrinkle out of this plan before my men arrive.'

Brodrick pictured them, huddled, waiting to go. He could almost smell the close air of the submarine – diesel, sweat, fried onions from the galley. Billy Randal was in charge. He'd been in the batch Brodrick had instructed on the commando course at Lympstone three years earlier. He had nearly broken. Brodrick remembered standing over him as he lay on the moors, weeping with exhaustion. But he'd made it. He was Lieutenant Randal now.

Randal panicked. For a second, which felt like an age, his life was on fast-forward, out of control.

His breathing bottles had snagged against the rim of the hatch. That one moment had been enough.

They trained not to feel claustrophobia underwater in total darkness. But the fear was still there. They all felt it.

There was another fear, on this mission. The fear of not coming back.

Free now, Randal propelled himself to the surface, ten

15

metres above the casing. He broke through and rocked in the light swell. A pitch black night, no moon, no stars.

In one hand he held a limp flotation-bag attached to a line trailing down through the water to the submarine. He jerked at the toggle on the air bottle and the bag hissed full.

Two tugs on the line told the others they could come up. Within minutes they were sixteen on the surface, guided by the line. Four sections of four marines. A sergeant's soft voice called the roll.

Gas bottles roared as the Gemini dinghies inflated drum-tight. Two by two the men hauled themselves into the boats, one from each side.

They checked their kit by feel. No torches were allowed; the beams could alert a militiaman on the shore.

Lieutenant Randal unsealed the watertight pouch protecting the thermal imager. His finger found the switch, the lithium battery for the electronics, the compressed air bottle to cool the infra-red.

He pressed the eyepiece to his face, the green image ending his blindness. Switched to wide-angle, his men showed clearly around him. He counted their heads, checked the look of the Geminis and the outboards.

'We're looking good,' he told them, just loud enough to be heard above the wind and the lapping of the waves against tight neoprene.

Then he switched to telephoto and searched the shoreline. The built-in compass told him the distant blur of light to the northeast would be Beirut. Swinging right, the contrast between warm sea and cool land marked the coastline.

The Gemini rolled unevenly and balancing the imager was hard. They were about a mile from the shore. They'd need to get closer before he could see the heat beacon marking the LZ – the landing zone – that Brodrick had set up.

16

'Check your weapons. We're going in.'

Four silenced outboards purred into life. Each helmsman wore night-vision goggles. The Geminis fell into line astern, the lieutenant's in the lead. He followed a compass bearing for the shore, allowing for the wind data the submarine commander had given him.

Luck was what they needed on this mission. Too much had been left to chance. Captain Brodrick had planned it, and he was one of the best. But there'd been no time. They were having to depend on local help, but was it reliable? These were bloody Arabs they were dealing with.

They lay flat in the boats, the helmsmen the only ones with their heads up. Randal felt his way to the bows and rested the imager on the rubber prow. He could see hotspots moving, a short way back from the shore. Vehicles on the coast road. At two in the morning? Lebanese army or Syrians most likely. One of many dangers.

Where was that damned beacon? He looked for landmarks. There were precious few on a flat coastal strip planted with citrus trees.

He'd memorised every inch of the map, every detail of the photographs taken earlier through the submarine periscope. Now he searched up and down the coast for anything he recognised.

There was a shape, difficult to make out, colder than the surrounding trees. A building, its stone shell a lighter shade than the surrounding vegetation on the thermal-imager.

He remembered two buildings from the map. One was a ruined, abandoned hotel a kilometre north of the LZ, the other a house, half a kilometre south. Which was it? Either way they were off position.

It looked a big building. He chose the hotel. Must've overcompensated for the wind.

'Give it another twenty degrees. We're too far north,'

17

he breathed to the corporal on the outboard, then checked to see the other boats were following.

Where *was* that damned beacon?

Sixty-five miles west of the Lebanese coast, the aircraft carrier HMS *Eagle* was operating under electronic silence. Radars were off, radios listening but not transmitting. No clue was being given as to what the ship was about to do.

The deck boomed dully as the aft lift locked in the up position, delivering the last of the five Sea Harriers from the hangar.

Four of the fighters, known to their pilots by the acronym SHAR, each had a fat, laser-guided, thousand-pound bomb under the belly and two Sidewinders on the wing stations. The fifth carried three slim pods, holding the infra-red navigation system, a laser target marker, and jammers.

In Briefing Room 1 on Two Deck the flight crews fell silent as the lieutenant from Flight Ops held out his watch.

'In ten, time will be zero-two-thirty.'

He paused, then counted down.

'Five, four, three, two, one. Mark.'

Watches synchronised, the briefing began.

Cloud base three thousand feet, visibility good. Ideal conditions to escape from SAMs – surface-to-air missiles – if there were any.

'Two Sea King Whiskies taking off at zero-three-fifteen, then the first two SHARS at three-thirty.'

The Whiskies were helicopters with early-warning radar. They'd need a start on the Harriers to take up position ten miles from the coast, ready to yell a warning if Syrian MiG-29s got airborne.

'Target's a large house on the southern edge of Beirut. Enemy HQ. It's set back from other buildings by a

18

walled garden. There's some recce photos to look at afterwards.'

Enemy. They'd never been in action, none of them. They'd used the word in exercises, called out their 'kills', but it had just been a game. Now it was for real.

None of the pilots was over twenty-five except for the CO, and he was only thirty.

'Just remember why we're doing this. The gang you're to hit are criminals. They've kidnapped a Brit. Mr Bicknell, financier and philanthropist . . .'

The description slipped uncomfortably from his tongue, like an unfamiliar script.

'The gang's not political or religious. They're not Islamic fanatics living under the moral code of the Koran. They live on the profits of other people's misery. Drugs is their big thing. Heroin, shipped to England. Remember, it could be your kid brother or sister that gets hooked on it back home.

'Again, nothing political about the kidnap. No demands for the release of Arab prisoners in Israel, or wherever. Just money. A million pounds. Mr Bicknell went to Beirut to help them rebuild their city. Instead of accepting that help, they took him prisoner. Our government's decided it won't tolerate that sort of behaviour. It didn't tolerate it in the Falklands, nor in Kuwait. So these guys are to be taught a lesson they'll not forget in a hurry.'

The pilots looked uncomfortable. Enough of the Agincourt stuff.

'Okay, gentlemen. Lecture's over. Onto the practical details. As you know, there's a bunch of Royal Marines going ashore. They know where Mr Bicknell's being held and they're going to rescue him . . .'

The lieutenant held up crossed fingers.

'Your job's to take out the gang's HQ. You approach from the south. You're all on night-goggles so stick at two hundred feet. Bug your radar altimeters to squawk at that height. No accidents please. The SHAR with the designator is "Catseyes". The bombers are "Polecats" and "Cougars".

'Polecats make the first run. Cougars go next, but only if there's no resistance. HMG doesn't want any of you splattered all over Beirut.'

Too right! If this went wrong, there'd be questions in the House. Politics. That's what it was all about, and they all knew it.

The marines killed the outboards two hundred metres from the shore. They'd paddle the rest of the way, silently. They'd found the heat beacon.

The beach had been well chosen. It had a small, wooden jetty projecting a few feet from the shore, which a citrus farmer had built so that he could ferry his crop to Beirut and avoid the threat of gunmen on the road.

Randal cocked his Heckler and Koch MP5, and used the thermo-optic sight to search for the warmth generated by a human body. Sergeant Blight was due to meet them here, with transport.

Suddenly Randal spotted a man rise from the ground and move through the orchard towards them. Two brief flashes from an infra-red torch, then two long ones. It was Blight.

'Welcome to suicide valley, sir,' the Midlander growled. 'A soddin' nuthouse, this is!'

'Got transport?' Randal cut in. He could do without Blight's comments.

'Two pick-ups with hoops and covers over the back. And two shit-scared drivers with only six words of English between them.'

'Where's Captain Brodrick?'

'At the RV. It's an empty house just a hundred metres from the target. Interpreter's with 'im. Security man from the embassy. And the prisoner.'

'What prisoner?'

'An Arab who's told us where Mr Bicknell's being held.'

'Volunteered the information, did he?'

'After I hit 'im, sir.'

'How long from here to there?'

'Ten, fifteen minutes if we're lucky. Maybe never, if we hit a road block.'

'I saw stuff on the road, through my scope. Heading north?' Randal queried.

'Syrians. Army, the driver said. They seem to control things around here.'

'What's the odds on running into some of them?'

'Not good, sir. There's stuff in the back of the pick-ups to hide under.'

Randal shuddered. The thought of being buried under sacks in the back of a truck while 'ragheads' emptied their automatic weapons into them did not appeal.

'Okay. Let's get at it. Those boats hidden yet?'

'Sir!' came a voice from the darkness.

'Right. Blue and green sections secure the beach. Red and black, dump the immersion suits, check your weapons and report to S'arnt Blight.'

Randal lifted the cover on his luminous watch. Two thirty-five am. Just over an hour to go before their attempt to free Bicknell. Madness.

On the southern edge of Beirut the night was quiet. Nowadays the Syrian army had a tight grip on the city. The darkness that for years past had been punctuated by the flash and crack of gunfire, was silent.

Abdul Habib had slept little for the past three nights. He dozed fitfully, part of his mind alert, listening for the shout that might mean news.

The large, flat-roofed house he used as headquarters

21

for his *Mustadhafin* militia was never at rest. His men came and went at all hours. Extortion and the black-market operated twenty-four hours a day.

For Habib the past three days had been a nightmare. Ahmed Bizri, his close friend and loyal chief of staff, had disappeared. Kidnapped. Tit for tat for the Englishman he himself had seized.

For the first time for a long time he was afraid. He sensed a threat to his entire 'business' – all because of Mr Richard Bicknell.

The English cheat had walked into his hands five weeks ago. The gall of the man! Claimed he'd come to renegotiate terms. No chance! A deal was a deal.

The decision to make Bicknell his 'guest' had made sense at the time. A quick capture, a fair ransom demand, and a quick release. That was the aim. He had no political agenda like Hezbollah. No point in that – the fundamentalists had got *nothing* for their years of trouble.

For two weeks there'd been no response to the photo and the ransom demand he'd sent to the Embassy. It was as if Bicknell hadn't existed. Then word of the kidnap had leaked in the London newspapers, triggering an explosion of outrage from the British government.

London had applied diplomatic pressure on Damascus, and the Syrians had tightened surveillance of any Lebanese group that could be behind the kidnap.

Habib had covered his tracks well, but knew he was being watched.

Suddenly, three days ago, the British had taken the bait. A coded message in a newspaper had given him a name to ring at the embassy. A negotiator was coming from London.

He'd sent Ahmed Bizri to meet the man. Had to – there was no one else he could trust. But he'd been outwitted. The British had seized Bizri.

His anger had cannoned through the corridors of his headquarters. Fury at the British, fury at himself for having let Bizri go alone to meet the negotiator. Ahmed was his right hand, the man whose advice he invariably heeded. Without him, he felt paralysed.

For two days he'd sat watching for news, planning a bloody revenge against those who'd outwitted him. His younger brother, Farouk, was the only one who could still his temper.

Habib treated Farouk more as a son than a brother. Farouk had been just eight, and Habib twenty, when they fled the Israeli invasion of southern Lebanon. They left the dead bodies of their parents in the ruins of their village, and since then Habib had been father and mother to the boy. Now Farouk was just twenty.

Whoever held Ahmed Bizri would want to exchange him for Bicknell, Farouk told him. What else?

'Stay calm and be patient, my brother.'

It was unsettling to have a boy tell you what to do. But Habib took it. And there was no one else in his organisation who dared speak his mind.

But now three days had passed and there had been no word.

They'd moved their own prisoner. Every day meant another hideout for Bicknell. But Ahmed would know the places they'd chosen. Would he talk? Would he tell the men from England where to look?

Maybe the British had given Ahmed to the Syrians. Habib shuddered at the thought. He knew what *they'd* do to a man who smelled of rose-water.

If Bizri confessed, the Syrians would destroy *Mustadhafin*. They'd have to. Just to preserve the fiction that they were fighters against terrorism.

Habib lay on a rough, wooden bed in the corner of his office. He had not been home to his wife and three small children for a week. He wore only a tee-shirt and under-pants, and stank of sweat.

Suddenly he sat up. It was if a gust of wind had blown

the clouds from his mind. Heart pounding, he swung his feet to the floor.

He smashed a fist into his thigh. Exchange of prisoners? There'd be no exchange! Not now! Not after three days!

He cursed himself. How foolish to have listened to a boy!

Exchanging prisoners meant 'dealing with terrorists'; the British government had sworn never to do that. Look at the Falklands. Kuwait. What had Britain done when challenged? Resorted to the gun.

It was blindingly clear to Habib now. They'd beat out of Ahmed where Bicknell was. Question him night and day, until the words slipped from his bloodied lips. Then they'd send in the SAS to prise Bicknell free.

But what would Ahmed tell them, the wily fox? Not the truth. Something other than the truth, something they couldn't fail to believe.

Suddenly Habib knew by instinct what Bizri would say.

He pulled on the drab, green trousers that lay crumpled on the floor and stuffed his feet into a pair of grubby trainers.

Down the corridor he clattered, banging his Kalashnikov on the doors behind which his gunmen slept.

'What's happened?' Farouk emerged, tousle-haired, rubbing sleep from his eyes.

'We're going to find Ahmed!'

'How. . . ?'

'I know where to look!'

'I'm coming.'

'No, Farouk! You stay here.'

Habib had promised their mother to keep Farouk safe. And besides, he was angry that he'd allowed the boy to sway his mind and waste three precious days.

The boy protested, but Habib silenced him with a slap

to the face. Enough to put him in his place, but not to hurt.

'Whatever you say, my brother,' Farouk conceded. 'God is great!'

Lieutenant Randal felt vomit rise in his throat. The back of the pick-up truck reeked of goats and fertiliser. The marines lay concealed under sacks, behind a barrier of nitrate bags. The Arab driver was taking the corners – and there were plenty of them – at sick-making speed. From the grinding of the gears, Randal judged they were climbing the foothills southeast of Beirut.

There were ten of them in the two trucks, a raiding party of eleven, with Captain Brodrick. Enough? God only knew. Numbers had been dictated by logistics – the size of the submarine, the need for a strong guard on their beachhead, and for surprise.

Suddenly the truck lurched off the tarmac onto an unmade track and then stopped. The Arab drivers jabbered incomprehensibly in low voices.

' 'E means us to get out, sir,' the sergeant whispered into the back of Randal's pick-up. 'The trucks'll stay here. The RV's about a hundred metres further up the hill.'

'Along the road?'

'A track through the trees and along the back of a couple of other houses. It's a small village. Same way in reverse when we've got Mr Bicknell.'

'If. . .' Randal heard himself say.

'I'll lead the way, sir?'

'Do that.'

As they passed through the clump of trees, they could smell eucalyptus. Above the canopy of leaves a few stars glinted. The men moved slowly, using the image-intensifying sights on their weapons to find the way.

The houses to their left were in darkness; whether

empty, or their occupants asleep, they knew not. They came to a chain-link fence, with a section bent back to make a gap. They passed through, crossed the soft, dry earth of a vegetable garden, then climbed three concrete steps onto the veranda of a house.

Captain Peter Brodrick watched through his 'scope as the men crossed the garden, relieved to see them, but full of dread.

He'd been in Lebanon three days, investigating and assessing. He'd advised his superiors that a rescue attempt would be foolhardy. There was a political imperative, they'd said; if there was any chance of success, it had to be taken.

He suspected his superiors hadn't opposed the idea as strongly as they should've done. He could guess why; the Royal Marines had missed out in the war to remove the Iraqi army from Kuwait. Having a success in Lebanon would help secure a future for the Corps at a time of defence cutbacks.

Silently Brodrick beckoned the men into the building, whose windows had blankets pinned tightly over them. He reached for Randal's shoulder.

'Good to see you, Billy.'

In the middle of the living room, the bare cement floor was spread with a hand-drawn map, three feet square, a guttering candle at each corner.

'Welcome, gentlemen,' Broderick said in a near-whisper. 'We've not much time, so gather round and listen carefully.'

Brodrick was in civilian clothes, drab-green cotton slacks, a brown shirt and leather jacket. His team looked more sinister, all in black with darkened faces. Each man held firmly to his machine pistol as he crouched to study the plan.

'No trouble on the road?' Brodrick asked Randal.

'Just potholes.'

'Luck. Let's hope it stays with us. Now, we're here . . .'

He pointed with a garden cane to a dark square at the centre of the map.

'This house belongs to the family of one of our embassy's drivers. Building it for a son who's getting married. We won't be disturbed.'

He moved the tip of the cane across the paper and tapped at a red cross. 'The target. Distance? Hundred and fifty metres from here. That's the house where the hostage is, so we're told. The source of this information is next door, tied to a chair, and rather the worse for wear.'

He indicated the room behind with a jerk of his head.

'Name's Ahmed Bizri, chief-of-staff to a Mr Abdul Habib, who's the mobster behind the kidnap. And I mean "mobster". Drugs, extortion, kidnapping, that's what they're into, these people. Buggers don't deserve to be part of the human race.'

He was hyping it for their benefit. They'd need to hate, if they were to be ready to kill.

'We made Mister Bizri an offer he couldn't refuse! We said he could stay alive, but only if he told us where Bicknell was being held.'

Brodrick was trying humour to prick the bubble of tension surrounding his team, but failed.

'Has Bicknell been seen?' asked Randal.

Brodrick shook his head.

'No proof he's in there, then, sir?' a Scots corporal chipped in.

'No proof,' answered Brodrick uneasily. 'But the place is guarded day and night. We've been watching it for forty-eight hours. Tell 'em, Sarn't Blight.'

'Two gunmen outside. They change watches every couple of hours. Must be at least two more inside, maybe four. Armed with AK47s. No night-vision aids, so far as

27

we can see. Only one visitor in the last two days. A man carrying large boxes, probably food.'

'According to our source, the prisoner's in a cellar,' Brodrick continued. 'Not tied up or anything, but the door's got a padlock on it. Have to shoot it off. Layout? Three rooms and a kitchen on the ground floor. Unknown number of bedrooms upstairs.'

Brodrick paused to gauge reaction. None visible. The eyes above the grubby camouflage cream were steely, but expressionless.

'I know what you're thinking. And you're right. It's a heap of shit. But . . .'

He looked at his watch.

'In precisely forty-five minutes we're going to take those bastards out and free Mr Bicknell, if he's there.'

Some of the men avoided his gaze. They were Royal Marines, trained to be the toughest fighters in the world. But they knew that any military operation didn't just need guts to be successful. It needed planning, logistics and back-up. There'd been little time for any of that. They were in the middle of enemy territory, on their own.

'Okay,' Brodrick continued. 'Here's the plan. At zero-three-forty-five, there's a diversion. The SHARS attack the enemy HQ a mile down the hill, on the edge of Beirut. Thousand-pounders. Very noisy. Red section, that's your chance. Take out the two guards outside. Then, if we're lucky, the noise of the bombs'll wake the others and they'll come out to look at the fireworks.

'If that happens, take them out too. But you've got one minute, repeat ONE minute, only. If they're not outside by then, Black section goes in with me. The windows are no use. They've got metal shutters. Rollers. The only way's the door. Satchel charge. Three-second fuse. You've brought the stuff?'

A corporal nodded.

'One man with me; we go for the cellar. There's

supposed to be stairs down to it on the right of the hall. Sergeant Blight and the other three, you clear the ground floor, room by room. Lieutenant Randal and one man from Red section clear the upstairs. The two snipers stay outside, in case the enemy's got backup nearby. Questions so far?'

'Any civvies in the house?' asked a Scots voice.

'Don't know. It's possible, but we've not seen any.'

'Them trucks? Is that what's gonna get us back to the beach?'

'That's right. We bring Bicknell back here, and then down the hill to where you left the transport.'

He saw the scepticism in their eyes.

'The drivers are reliable. The embassy security bloke fixed them, and he's a man I trust.'

'And where's he tonight? Tucked up all cosy in his soddin' embassy?'

'No. He's in the next room, keeping an eye on our prisoner.'

That shut them up. It was time to crack the whip.

'Gentlemen,' he growled. 'This may sound like a raw deal, and it is. But we've been chosen to do it, because we're the best. We can do it. We've trained for this sort of job ever since we joined the Corps. The possibility of failure does not exist.'

HMS *Eagle* turned bows into the wind. Fifty miles from the Lebanese coast was close enough.

In the Flight Control Centre behind the bridge, Commander Air, known as Wings, checked the ship's heading and speed from the infotext screen, then peered through the window to the deck below. Five Sea Harriers on deck, the first pair lined up for take-off.

The Sea King 'Whisky' helicopters with their air-borne radars were already aloft, heading for a position fifteen miles short of the coast where they could loiter and control the action.

Twenty-nine minutes past three am.

'Flyco, bridge!' Wings' voice on the bridge intercom.

'Bridge. Captain.'

'Permission to launch SHARS, sir?'

'Green deck.'

HMS *Eagle* was going to war – the first time the carrier had seen action.

The red warning lights on the panel and the deck below turned green.

'Polecat one, take-off! Good luck.'

Brakes released, the first fighter sank on its undercarriage and roared down the deck. It lurched up the bow-ramp and flung itself into the void, the weight of its bombs pulling it momentarily towards the black Mediterranean as the pilot vectored the jet thrust to keep himself airborne.

'Green deck, two!'

The second Harrier hurled itself into the air, then the third and fourth. *Eagle* shuddered under the roar of the jets, lower decks echoing like a bass drum.

Finally, the fifth aircraft, with its electronic-countermeasure pods and the laser to mark the target, was away.

Wings sat back, relieved that the fighters were airborne, but knowing he couldn't relax until the eleven men in the jets and the helicopters were safe on deck again.

He'd have no communication with the flyers, unless disaster struck. The ship was in electronic silence, no radios transmitting, no radars in use.

With the planes gone, *Eagle* doused her lights and set course for the point on the chart where the pilots would expect to find her when they returned from the mission. Each side of the bridge, seamen with night-vision binoculars scanned the sea for craft to be avoided. On the bridge roof the thermo-optic weapons sight searched for danger, its images monitored in the operations room eight decks below.

The SHARS flew towards the coast at two hundred feet, radar altimeters howling whenever they dipped lower, the squadron CO in the lead. The image from the infra-red camera under the port wing appeared on his head-up display. The equipment was new, the result magical. Outside was pitch-black to the naked eye; on his HUD it was as clear as daylight. Ahead he could see the Lebanese coast, the hills behind, and the jagged concrete bulk of Beirut.

Under his starboard wing, the jammer pod was live, ready to black out the big Syrian radars on Mount Lebanon that could send guided missiles at them.

Behind the leader, the four bomb-laden 'Polecats' and 'Cougars' flew in staggered pairs, their pilots wearing night-vision goggles to hold formation. There had been no need for communication since take-off; the flight plan had been meticulously prepared.

Zero-three-forty-three.

The Squadron CO, in 'Catseyes', banked left. Below and to his right was the coast road, occasionally obscured by trees. A quarry to his right now, oil storage tanks to the left. Landmarks familiar from reconnaissance pictures he'd studied that morning. Israeli material, he guessed, though the intelligence staff wouldn't admit it.

The two 'Polecats' turned at the coast, one mile – ten seconds – behind the pathfinder. Quick checks – bombs armed, laser sensors live.

The 'Cougars' circled slowly, keeping the coast in sight, waiting for the 'go' for their turn.

For 'Catseyes' it was just like the reconnaissance video. Airport runway/taxiway junction; oil storage tank; three tower blocks on the edge of the residential area. Left ten degrees. A cemetery, then just beyond, the big house on its own surrounded by gardens.

Target cursor locked on. Laser designator slaved to the co-ordinates. Mark.

He flicked the comms switch.

'Catseyes, Polecats! Acknowledge!'

'One.'

'Two.'

They were right behind him.

'Target marked.'

'Attacking.'

The CO pulled back on the stick and banked left in a slow rising turn. From the designator pod below the Harrier's fuselage a thin laser-beam, invisible to the naked eye, reached down to the earth and painted the headquarters of Abdul Habib's militia with deadly light. As the plane turned, a gimballed 'eyeball' swivelled to keep the beam locked unerringly on the target.

In the cockpits of the two 'Polecats', green indicators showed the seeker heads on the bombs had locked on to the laser illumination of the target. Both planes climbed sharply, lofting their weapons in a graceful but deadly ellipse.

'Polecat one, away.'

'Polecat two, away.'

Relieved of their loads, the two Harriers dived for the coast and the safety of the Mediterranean darkness.

A mile away, the marines ducked at the flash. Sheets of flame lit the landscape, long enough to silhouette the Arab sentries guarding the house.

'Poor bastards!' breathed the Scots corporal.

Wait for the bang. Count to five.

The snipers held the sentries in their crosswires.

The brain-shaking boom of a ton of explosive resonated up the valley, drowning the sharp crack of the rifles.

32

Now that it was happening, Brodrick felt no terror. His body buzzed with adrenalin.

He saw the guards fall, and counted the seconds, willing the other gunmen out of the house.

Fifty-nine. Sixty. Nothing.

'Go for it!' he hissed.

Sergeant Blight ran at a crouch and flattened against the front wall. He taped the charge to the door and ducked round the corner.

The detonation of the plastic explosive splintered the timber, its sound masked by a second thunderclap from Beirut. The 'Cougars' had found their mark.

'Good timing!' Brodrick exclaimed. 'Come on!'

He hurled himself through the smoking doorway, followed by black section.

His eyes darted from side to side. Where was that bloody cellar?

Gunshots erupted within feet, showering plaster from the wall behind him.

'Left! Half-open door!' he yelled, hitting the floor.

Blight lobbed a stun-grenade through the gap, shielded his eyes from the flash, then burst into the room, firing his MP5 at the dazed gunman.

'Got the bastard!' he shouted.

Lieutenant Randal ran past Brodrick and up the stairs, followed by the Scots corporal.

Suddenly fear gripped Brodrick's gut. Not right. Not the layout Bizri had given them. The cellar. Where the hell was it?

He clicked on a flashlamp. Stairs? Just leading up, none down. Three more doors.

He turned the handle of the nearest, kicked it open and flattened against the wall.

Nothing.

Holding the torch at arm's length, he shone it inside. There, on the floor! He dropped to a crouch, first pressure on the trigger. Just mattresses! Two of them. For the guards lying dead outside.

Shots from the garden. Bullets smacked against the outside wall of the house. The scream of a man, dying.

'Bastard tried to get out the back door,' Blight snapped, coming out of the kitchen. 'Snipers got 'im.'

One more door. Brodrick booted it open. Straight-backed chairs round the walls, rugs on the floor and a TV set. No people. No stairs leading down.

Brodrick's throat was like sandpaper. He caught the smoke-blackened face of the sergeant in the torch beam.

'Where's the fucking cellar?' Brodrick screamed.

Blight stared back wide-eyed with fear.

'There isn't one, sir.'

They'd been tricked!

Brodrick flung himself up the stairs, two steps at a time. Randal and the corporal signalled they'd checked three of the four bedrooms, and found nothing.

Indicating they should cover him, Brodrick advanced towards the fourth door. He reached out, but before touching the handle, he saw it turn. Back pressed against the wall, machine-pistol on a hair trigger.

Was this where Bicknell was? In this room? Please God let it be true!

Suddenly the muzzle of a Kalashnikov poked round the door at knee height.

The shots were simultaneous. The AK47 sprayed wildly, missing him. Brodrick's Heckler and Koch pounded bullets through the hardboard panel. The Kalashnikov jerked back, clattered to the floor.

Brodrick kicked the splintered door, but it was blocked by the gunman's body. He pushed with his shoulder. Then, from inside the room, a woman's scream pierced his brain like a stiletto.

He shoved again and the door gave way. He burst through, dived for the floor and aimed at the source of the noise. At first he didn't see her. Then Randal shone

34

his torch. Cowering at the foot of a double bed, a woman with long, dark hair crushed a small child to her breast.

Randal turned the beam on the prostrate gunman by the door.

'Shiiit!'

Brodrick retched up the word.

Ten years old at the most, dressed in pyjamas, the 'gunman' was the woman's other child. He'd died protecting his mother.

'We wasn't to fuckin' know, was we?' blurted out the corporal.

Brodrick was paralysed. No cellar. No Bicknell. And he'd killed a bloody child. The kid had shot at them, but he was still a child.

Brodrick crouched before the woman.

'I'm sorry,' he heard himself say.

Stark terror blazed in her eyes.

'Where's the British prisoner?' he pleaded.

She shook uncontrollably, eyes transfixed.

'Speak English?'

The shaking grew worse.

Brodrick turned his head.

'Corp, get back to the other house and bring the translator. The man from the embassy.'

The soldier scuttled down the stairs.

'You've checked the rooms up here?'

'All of them,' replied Randal.

'Check 'em again. Cupboards. Trapdoors into lofts, anything.'

'There's nothing, sir. We've done it.'

'Oh, Christ Almighty!'

Bizri! Bastard liar who stank of perfume. He'd kill him!

But whose house was this? Whose wife? Why was she guarded by gunmen?

Still clutching her baby, she crawled to her son and pulled at his shoulder so that he rolled face up. The

35

bullets had ripped his face open. She patted his bloodied cheek and crooned to him. Didn't she understand that he was dead? Brodrick turned away, sickened.

Footsteps on the stairs. He and Randal flattened against the walls, tightening their grip on their weapons.

It was the corporal.

'Your man's dead! They've slit his throat! And the prisoner's gone!'

'What, Hardy? Dead?' Brodrick felt the earth open up beneath him. 'And Bizri's escaped?'

'It's a set-up. We've been had!'

Brodrick ran for the stairs. He'd warned them in London of the risks. Bastards hadn't listened!

At the front door, Sergeant Blight gave three short whistles to tell the snipers they were coming out.

The skyline towards Beirut was aglow with the fires started by the Harriers' bombs.

Brodrick gathered his men. Had to get back to their transport. But carefully.

Ten marines. Stuck in the middle of enemy territory, with no back-up, and no support until they got back to the beach. *If* they got back. . . .

They ran at a crouch, towards where they'd left the pick-up trucks. Every few seconds they checked with the night-sights. They passed one house where lights burned, the occupants wakened by the noise.

The smell of eucalyptus again; nearly there. The path opened out onto the rough road where their transport had left them.

Brodrick spread his men amongst the trees. Through his night-sight he could see the trucks. But the drivers? Not sure. Looked like there was a man behind the wheel of one of them.

The night was still, eerily silent. They all knew it might be a trap, but they needed that transport.

'I'll check it out,' Randal volunteered.

Brodrick and the others watched as Randal and Blight

crawled through the cover of bushes towards the trucks. Their last ten metres had to be in the open. They sprang to their feet and ran, one man to each vehicle. Then they crouched by the drivers' doors, and tried to peer inside.

Suddenly the rapid-fire crackle of rifle shots pierced the silence. Bullets ricocheted off the metal driving cabs. The windows crazed.

'Left! Muzzle flashes!' Brodrick yelled.

Out of range of his machine-pistol. Beside him the snipers opened up with their rifles.

'Our guys! They're both hit, sir!'

Through his sight Brodrick saw Randal and the sergeant slumped on the ground.

Bullets cracked overhead, splintering bark from the trees.

'On your right!'

Brodrick swung his MP5 and loosed off half a magazine at a shape he caught moving through the trees.

'Singer, stay with me and give cover. The rest pull back!'

He reached into his thigh-pocket for a smoke grenade. He pulled the pin and lobbed it a few metres ahead. They had to chance it.

'Run!' he yelled, as the smoke rose in front of them.

A few seconds of silence. Their ambushers were confused by the smoke. Then came the crack of bullets again, and a stinging thump to his left arm. Brodrick dived flat.

'I've been hit!'

The words spilled out, surprise in his voice. He felt a moment of shock, but he could still move his hand. Just a flesh-wound.

Beside him, to his left, a noise, suddenly. A strange clicking. Animal, but not human. He swung his night-sight round, then gagged. Marine Singer was prostrate beside him, half his head shot away, blood bubbling from his throat.

37

'The bastards!'

The shooting had stopped. He heard a ringing in his ears, and the raw panting of his own breath. Had to move on; had to find the others.

At a crouch again, he ran back down the path.

'Psst!' came out of the darkness to his left.

Flat on the ground he checked through the night-sight. One of his men, at the corner of a house, beckoned.

'Singer's hit,' he choked as he flopped down beside them. 'We've lost three.'

'Gotta move, sir.' The corporal wanted decisions. 'No transport, sir. How d'we get back to the beach?'

'We'll yomp it,' Brodrick growled. 'Five K's. The road's too dangerous. Have to go cross-country. Citrus and vines for the first part, then God knows. Due west, then left when we hit the coast road.'

'What about our mates? The casualties, sir?'

'Have to leave them. No chance. We've got to get to the beach and out of this shit-hole before we lose anyone else!'

The men hesitated, but they knew he was right.

'Seven of you,' Brodrick counted. 'Where's the radio? Who's got the comms?'

'Singer, sir.'

Silence. Should he go back? He hadn't seen it. Singer must've fallen on top of the set.

Couldn't risk it. The gunmen would be following to try to finish them off. But now they had no way to tell anyone what had happened. No way to ask for help.

'Okay. Let's go.'

Brodrick led them crawling across the rough yard at the back of the house, then over a low wall into a lemon grove.

On the southern edge of Beirut, open pick-up trucks swerved and squealed through the streets, horns blaring, carrying the wounded and the dead to hospital.

Some of the bombs had cratered the garden of the house, shredding the trees to matchwood. But two had hit the building directly. Nothing was left of what had once been a fine mansion, nothing left of the headquarters of Abdul Habib's *Mustadhafin* militia.

Smoke rose from the deepest crater; one bomb had penetrated to the cellar. Beside the hole, broken bricks and masonry were strewn in a jagged pile. Roof timbers pointed to the sky, burning.

Voices shouted as hands clawed at the rubble in the search for bodies that might still be living, some calling on Allah in shock and grief.

A fire pump emptied its water tanks onto the flames, shrouding the ruin in smoke and steam. The chilly light of emergency lamps flickered and died as the gas bottles ran dry. Cars were backed and turned to direct their headlights on the rescuers' work.

With a screech of rubber on tarmac, Abdul Habib's Range-Rover slewed to a halt before the scene of desolation. For a moment, as he swung open the door, Habib felt as if he had wandered into an alien quarter of the city. Nothing was recognisable. He clutched at Ahmed Bizri.

'The house! It's . . . gone! Ya Allah! Why? Who has done this?' he screamed.

He pushed through the ring of Syrian soldiers who'd sealed off the site. 'Farouk! Farouk!' he shouted.

Bodies were still being brought out. The living had all been taken away; these were the dead. He stared at the faces of the corpses; some were just mangled flesh, others he recognised as his own men.

'Farouk,' he moaned. 'Has anyone seen Farouk?'

He searched the blank faces of the rescuers. None of them knew who he was talking about.

Ahmed Bizri was beside him again, gabbling incoherently. They'd heard the explosions from the hills seen the flames, but thought it was a car bomb.

39

Habib stumbled about in the rubble. Death had been so routine in Beirut, he'd thought himself immune to it. But this. . . the sight of so many he knew. . .

This was no car bomb. The craters, the devastation; he remembered how the Israelis had destroyed his home village, with thousand-pounders from the sky.

But why would they attack him now? He was no threat to them; he had nothing to do with the Jihad guerrillas whose raids across the border were a thorn in the Zionists' flesh.

So who. . . ?

He stopped dead, as the realisation hit him. The timing of the explosions, just when the SAS attacked the house, was no coincidence!

The English! They'd done this, because of Richard Bicknell!

The British Prime Minister wanted to crow to the world that he'd freed a hostage and smashed a drug empire. So many deaths, just for one man's freedom? A bitter revenge for such a trivial offence! A bitterness the British would soon taste for themselves.

Bizri clutched at his arm. Two more bodies had been found under the rubble in the basement. Habib's heart was heavy with dread.

The first was crushed from the chest down.

'Aah,' he gasped. 'Mr Richard Bicknell! Keep him apart! Keep his filthy corpse away from our Arab heroes!'

His voice was raw with emotion.

'Send him like that to the British Prime Minister!'

The last corpse was brought up, eyes open, staring, but quite dead. The boyish face and tousled hair were grey with mortar dust.

Habib grasped his brother and laid him on the ground. He shook Farouk's shoulders, begging him to speak, then fell forward across the lifeless body and rent the air with a wail of grief that chilled the blood of those who watched.

Minutes passed, then Habib sat back on his haunches. 'Those who did this to you, Farouk, they'll be punished, a thousand times,' he whispered. 'I swear it.'

The last of the five Sea Harriers dropped onto the deck of HMS *Eagle* and taxied to the lift. In the Flight Control Centre behind the bridge, 'Wings' grinned in relief. All the planes were back – no losses.

Minutes later, the pilots gathered in the briefing room below deck, in an atmosphere of suppressed jubilation. It had been their first ever live mission, the first time they'd used their weapons in anger. Everything they'd trained for had come good in that one flight. They'd done it by the book; it had worked like a dream.

Wings listened to their de-brief, as satisfied as he could be until reconnaissance photos proved they'd hit the right target.

'Let's hope the int. brief was correct,' he mused softly.

The bubble was burst. The pilots fell silent as they remembered the other part of the operation.

'Any news of the hostage?' one of them asked. 'Did the booties get him out okay?'

'Don't know,' Wings replied. 'There's been no word yet.'

Brodrick turned for the hundredth time to check they weren't being followed. Behind them, the Chouf mountains had become visible to the naked eye. Dawn was breaking.

He'd left three of his best men dead on that hillside. It choked him. How had the bastards known where to find them? Had Habib and Bizri planned it this way? Did they guess Bizri would be taken in retaliation for Bicknell? Had he underestimated them so much?

41

And where the hell *was* Bicknell? He glanced towards Beirut, saw smoke still rising from the target of the Harriers' bombs. His heart sank as he guessed the answer to his own question. Please God, don't let *that* be true!

5.30 am. The two sections of marines guarding the beach had expected them half-an-hour ago.

How far had they come? God knew. Impossible to tell. Their trek had been painful and slow; descending a hillside of scrub and thorn, strewn with boulders, had taken its toll. Two of his men had wrenched ankles.

He had little idea where they were. His rudimentary map had ceased to be of much value. If the sun came up and caught them on an open hillside, they'd be an easy target.

The first glimmer of daylight extended the range of their image-intensifiers. Brodrick called a halt, to survey their surroundings.

The coast was visible through the sights. Somewhere out there was the submarine that could take them to safety. He was dogged by a fear that they'd never get to see it, now. Further out would be HMS *Eagle*. Oh, to be able to call up her helicopters to rescue them.

'That line of trees to the left, sir,' the corporal suggested, 'could be a road.'

'Risky.'

'We'll not make it like this, sir. We're carryin' two of the lads.' Brodrick scanned the landscape for movement. Closer to the coast, he saw a dark patch. Citrus groves, probably.

'Okay. Traverse left in pairs. We'll look at that road.'

He took the lead with the corporal. They found a goat track and followed it, the injured men hobbling, supported by their comrades.

They walked as fast as they dared, for five minutes. A hundred yards from the trees they stopped, crouched and looked. All clear.

Brodrick led them forward, to the edge of the tarmac. The road was empty. He listened. No sound of vehicles, just the first chirps from birds welcoming the dawn.

Spooky, he thought. He imagined eyes watching them through the foliage. Please, God, don't let there be another ambush. Randal, Blight, Skinner. How many more?

They'd have to run. Their time was up.

'You'll have to double with those casualties. Can you make it?' he asked softly. They nodded.

At a bend in the road Brodrick gestured to them to halt. Moving from tree to tree he peered round the corner. The sky was growing lighter by the minute.

Fifty yards further, on the right-hand side, the trees finished and the hillside gaped open. A quarry with trucks left unattended. He waved the men forward.

Brodrick ran to the nearest and tried the door. Locked. The second likewise. But with the third, the door opened. He swung up into the cab. Shading the beam of his torch he found the ignition. No key. Sod it! He looked again. There *was* a key, with the handle snapped off. The lock itself had a raised grip so the ignition could be turned on. He beckoned his men over.

'Anybody driven a truck?' he asked.

'Yes. Done an HGV, sir.'

The marine climbed into the cab and Brodrick showed him the ignition.

'Could work, if there's any diesel in it.'

It was a dumper-truck, the back half-full of granite chips. There was room in the cab for four, Brodrick, the driver and the two injured marines. The other four swung themselves over the tailboard into the back.

Ignition lights on, heater engaged. Wait ten seconds, then the starter. The engine groaned and laboured, then clattered into life.

'Brilliant!' Brodrick exclaimed. 'First thing that's gone right today!'

They drove slowly out of the quarry, without lights. The grey dawn was light enough to see by. The driver accelerated down the hill, and tested the brakes. All in order.

Brodrick recognised the road that most of them had driven up earlier that night. He'd driven it the day before, in daylight.

'About a K to the coast road, then left, and another K to the beach,' he shouted above the engine's grinding roar.

The wound in his arm throbbed. He looked at the injured men, their faces tense with pain.

'We'll make it,' he tried to reassure them. 'Not long now.'

As the driver slowed at the junction with the coast road, the headlamps of a car crossed from right to left in front of them.

The truck turned left.

'Better put the lights on. Be less suspicious,' Brodrick warned.

He strained to see the first landmark, a ruined beach club just off to the right.

'That's it. Another five hundred metres and there's a track into the orange grove. That's our beach.'

A sudden sense of elation. They were going to make it.

'Sir!' the driver yelled, alarmed. 'Trouble! Road block!'

'Shit!'

An armed man in uniform waved them down with a red torch. On each side of the road stood another half dozen bristling with weapons. Syrians? Probably. Oh, God, let them be sleepy at this time of the morning.

'Slow down as if you're stopping, then stick your boot down and smack through 'em.'

Ten yards to go.

'*Now!*'

The driver stamped his foot on the floor.

Brodrick cocked his automatic, leaned out of the side window and fired into the group to the right.

An injured marine leaned behind the driver and fired another burst from the left-hand window.

'*Go! Go! Go!*' Brodrick yelled, ducking to clip on a new magazine.

The four in the back inched towards the edge of the tailboard. As the truck swept through the roadblock, they rained fire on the men in the road.

But unseen, well back from the road, others lay in hiding, armed with heavy machine-guns. Suddenly, twenty-millimetre shells ripped through the sides of the tipper.

They flattened themselves into the chippings, but to their horror saw two soldiers raise slim, metal tubes to their shoulders.

The rockets flashed. The first grenade detonated the fuel tank, ripping open the back of the truck. Flames scorched into the air. The second blast shattered the differential, locking the rear wheels.

The truck screeched to a halt. In the front cab the four men catapulted against the windscreen.

Dazed, Brodrick tumbled out sideways, and dragged himself clear of the flames.

'Get out! Get out!' he screamed. He loosed off his last magazine toward the roadblock.

Move! Why didn't they bloody *move*?

The cab exploded, engulfing the three in fire.

His eyes blurred, as blood trickled from a cut in his forehead. He pulled himself to his feet and staggered away from the flaming truck. Suddenly he felt strong hands grab him by each arm.

'Bastards! Bastards! I'll kill you. . .' he lashed out with his weapon.

'It's us, sir! You're okay!'

A familiar voice. He'd reached the beach.

Through the orange trees they dragged him, carried

him, his feet trailing in the dirt. Behind, he heard shots, as the beach party stopped the Syrians in their tracks.

They laid him in a Gemini. He heard outboards starting.

'The others; where are they, sir?'

Brodrick wiped blood from his eyes and stared blankly at the questioner.

'The hostage, sir?'

He shook his head.

'You didn't get him?'

He found himself shaking uncontrollably. His twitching hands seemed to belong to someone else.

'Fuckin' hell!' A voice growled from further away.

'Are you – are you the only one left, sir?'

Brodrick lay back and looked up at the stars. The only one left? Oh God, he probably was.

Two

The voice was low, more of a mumble. Someone outside the room was trying unsuccessfully not to be heard.

'Not too long now, Minister. He's still pretty stressed. Obsessive, you know?'

Brodrick sat in a chair in a half-darkened two-bed ward, his left arm in a sling. They'd put him there on his own and kept him well sedated. He'd been pretty wild when the submarine docked at Limassol.

His legs felt like lead weights as he stood to receive the visitors.

'How are you feeling?' asked the doctor who'd been looking after him.

'Okay.' Silly bloody question. He wanted to die.

'This is Mr Webster, Minister of State at the Foreign Office. D'you feel up to talking to him for a bit?'

'George Webster, Captain,' said the Minister, reaching out his arm. He was a short, chubby man with rubbery lips.

Brodrick's tall frame towered above him. He shook the Minister's hand.

'Hello, sir.'

Ministers were always 'sir'. Military training.

The doctor pulled over a second chair.

'Okay? I'll leave you for about ten minutes.'

His eyes enquired if that was in order. Peter nodded and the doctor left the room.

'Shall we sit, then?' the Minister suggested. His tone

sounded like one he'd use with geriatrics at his constituency surgery.

Brodrick flopped back gratefully.

'Don't know what they've given me, sir,' he said, 'but it's knocking me out.'

'Well, I should think you need something to calm you, after what you've been through . . .' the Minister was clearly not at ease.

'How's the arm?'

'A bit sore. The bullet went straight through, but they had to clean it up.'

Webster nodded.

'I . . . I'd like to say first, on behalf of the government, how sorry we are at the way things turned out. And I can assure you we're not blaming you in any way for what happened. The decision to proceed was the Cabinet's. . .'

'Against military advice. . .'

The bitter words slipped from Brodrick's mouth.

His limbs began to tremble again. The drugs could only suppress it until he became agitated.

'Er . . . the government was certainly made aware of the immense difficulties of such a rescue attempt. But there were compelling reasons for trying to get Mr Bicknell out.'

Webster cleared his throat and fiddled with the knot of his tie.

'What was so bloody special about Bicknell?' Brodrick asked, trying to sound calm but not succeeding.

Again the clearing of the throat.

'Unfortunately, I'm not at liberty to tell you.'

Brodrick lost his temper.

'Do you *know* how many men were killed? And you're not at liberty to tell me what they died for!'

'Suffice it to say it was a matter of supreme national importance.'

'And Bicknell's dead anyway!'

Webster swallowed.

'Yes. His body was delivered to the British Ambassador yesterday.'

'Killed in the air strike?'

'Possibly. There's some doubt. He may well have been murdered earlier.'

Brodrick seized on his words, as Webster had intended. At least they hadn't wasted all those good men for an own-goal. That really would have made it a one hundred percent cock-up.

Brodrick decided he would have to calm down if he wanted to find out anything at all.

Webster fiddled again with his tie, and cleared his throat a third time. 'Now, there's something I wanted to ask you. But first I should perhaps explain that one of my responsibilities at the Foreign Office is intelligence . . .'

Brodrick noticed how dark his eyes were, staring at him steadily now. 'You can trust me', they seemed to say.

Intelligence. Spies, agents, undercover cops. Bicknell?

'Bicknell was a businessman, right? Are you telling me he was a spook as well?'

'As I said, I'm not in a position to tell you anything. Intelligence matters. . .'

'. . . are something you can't talk about. I know. But Bicknell was important enough to risk losing a dozen good men for?'

The shaking began again. If only he could stop it. If only he could stop seeing Randal and the others, their shattered bodies, their brains spilled on the flinty Lebanese earth.

Webster shifted uncomfortably.

'The answer's yes. He was that important. You must draw your own conclusions.'

Should he trust him? Better not, Brodrick decided. He had a suspicion of politicians.

'I'll say one thing more; Bicknell carried in his head

some information which, if it fell into the wrong hands, could do immense damage to our country. That's why we had to try to get him out.'

'I see.'

'And that's what I wanted to ask you about. Firstly, did you at any time see Richard Bicknell?'

'No. You know that. He wasn't in the house.'

'Just wanted to be sure. And the second question; the man you talked to – the informant who betrayed you – what was his name?'

'Bizri. Ahmed Bizri.'

'Yes. This Mr Bizri, did he talk to you about Bicknell? Did he say what Bicknell was doing in Beirut, or why they'd kidnapped him?'

Brodrick frowned. He'd been so intent in finding Bicknell that he'd never asked. He'd just accepted the official version.

'No. He just said they wanted money for him. Bizri gave the impression he thought the kidnap was a waste of time. It was Habib's idea, not his. He said that a couple of times. I suppose it made it more convincing when he eventually led us to this house in the hills and told us Bicknell was in the cellar.'

'He didn't say "Bicknell's a spy", or words to that effect?'

'Never.'

The Minister nodded. He looked relieved.

Brodrick felt desperately tired again. Suddenly he could only think of sleep.

Webster seemed to have completed the business he'd come for.

'Oh, I brought you a few newspapers. Thought you'd like to know what's being said.' He dug into his briefcase. 'The government's come in for a lot of stick, but you "booties" have had a good press.'

The nickname for the Royal Marines sounded out of place from the Minister's lips.

50

'It's this problem of not being able to reveal why Bicknell was so important,' Webster explained. 'Believe me, I'd love to be able to tell you. You, above all, deserve to know.'

He shrugged and looked at his watch.

'I've had my ten minutes. The doctor'll be chasing me out. I'll leave you to rest.'

He stood up and put the chair back on the other side of the room. Peter made to rise.

'No. Don't get up, please. Thank you for talking to me. And on behalf of the government, thank you again for all you . . . tried to do.'

He left the room. Brodrick flopped back in his chair and closed his eyes.

Tried to do. . . ? Tried and *failed*, was what Webster meant.

Brodrick took a deep breath. Marines were supposed to have skin like a rhino's. They weren't meant to feel things the way normal mortals do. So why did great sobs keep welling up from his gut?

Billy Randal. He'd taught the bugger. Bullied him to complete the commando course. Forced him to stick at being a Royal when he was all for chucking it in.

And for what? So he'd follow his leader into an ambush and get his brains blown out.

'Oh, God!'

He pressed the heels of his thumbs into his eyesockets, and heard the door open.

'I'm sorry; I shouldn't have let him in.'

It was the doctor. He picked the second chair up by its back and placed it next to Brodrick's. He'd done a lot of this in the past few days, sitting and listening.

'Look, laddie,' he soothed in the soft tones of a man from Edinburgh. 'I know what you're thinking . . .'

'I should be dead, with the rest of them . . .' Brodrick muttered.

'But you're not. And the reason for that is simple; you

51

were lucky. You just happened to escape. Not because you were a better soldier; not because you were a coward; not because you sacrificed anyone else's life to save your own. You survived through luck!

'I see the Minister brought you some newspapers. What did you make of him, by the way? You must've said something that pleased him. He had a smug wee smile on his face when he came out.'

'Really? Can't think why.' He paused. 'He was all right. Said they weren't blaming me, but I know bloody well they are . . .'

'Bollocks, man! No one's blaming you.'

He picked up a copy of *The Telegraph*.

'Look. It was the PM who got a pasting from the Opposition yesterday. Here.'

He handed it to Brodrick, and stood up.

'I'll leave you to it. Oh, they're talking of sending you home tomorrow. Feel up to it?'

Peter nodded. He had to face the world again sometime.

'See you later, then.'

Alone again, Peter began to read.

At the heart of the opposition's attack was the failure by the government to consult them before launching the military operation. The Leader of the Opposition cited the Falklands Campaign and the Gulf War as examples of the government seeking all-party support before committing troops. Why had they failed to do the same in this instance, the opposition leader demanded?

Answering, the Prime Minister said there was an issue of national security at stake. Decisions had to be taken with great urgency, and there had been no time to consult.

The Leader of the Opposition described the PM's

statement as 'balderdash'. He asked whether it was true that the late Mr Bicknell's company Celadec UK had made a major financial contribution to the Prime Minister's party during the last general election. If that was the case, he demanded, was that the real reason the government was so keen to get Mr Bicknell out of the hands of his captors? Amid uproar from the government benches, the Prime Minister replied that that was the most unworthy suggestion he'd ever heard from a Leader of the Opposition.

Surely that couldn't have been the reason. Brodrick turned to the *Guardian*.

The government refused to comment on suggestions from political sources that Mr Bicknell had connections with the Secret Intelligence Service. They gave no explanation as to why rescuing Mr Bicknell was in the interests of national security. The Foreign Office, which has responsibility for the SIS, also refused all comment.

Brodrick let the newspaper fall. His head rested on the upholstered back of the chair and he closed his eyes. He felt sleep approaching like waves up a beach.

The doctor's words came back to him. Why had the Minister had 'a smug wee smile' when he left?

What had he said to make the Minister happy?

Was he pleased that Bicknell had apparently not talked? Was that what the government had been after – Bicknell's silence, at any price?

He felt the buzz in his limbs again, the uncontrollable shaking.

Had they *wanted* Bicknell dead?

The PM had called for a sledgehammer of an operation. The Royal Marines had given dire warnings that Bicknell might be killed in the rescue attempt. Instead of putting the government off, it had seemed to encourage them.

Bicknell had certainly been silenced, but twelve good men had died!

'Bastards!' Brodrick muttered.

The two-faced, criminal bastards! Sitting in their offices in Westminster – they'd sent him and his men to Lebanon, not giving a damn whether they lived or died!

He could have stopped them. Could have said 'no' to the mission. He was the only one who could. But he hadn't!

On the VC10, loaded with airmen and their families heading home on leave, they allocated him a row to himself. An anonymous figure, not in uniform, to the families on board he was just another military six-footer in pullover and cords. The sling on his left arm was the only distinguishing feature. If they'd been able to study his brown eyes, however, they'd have seen ghosts stirring.

He was dreading his return home. He'd have to go and see the family of every man who'd died. He owed it to them. It was all he could do. What could he say to them? He'd have to tell their wives, girlfriends, mothers that they'd died heroically, and with no pain, the sort of lies that people needed to hear.

Then what? The inevitable internal inquiry.

They'd give him time off after that.

He'd call Jackie.

Would she have guessed he had led the mission into Lebanon? How could she – she had little idea what he did as a Royal Marine, and his name had been kept out of it. None of the newspapers knew his identity – yet.

He'd met her six months ago in Belize, where he'd just completed a jungle warfare course. She was a secretary with the Foreign Office, visiting the former colony with a Minister.

He had just spent six months in the jungle, in remote camps where the only women to be seen were on the pages of magazines stuffed inside his soldiers' rucksacks.

They met at the Brigadier's cocktail party. She was slim and tall. Height mattered to him; he hated having to talk down to women.

He remembered precisely what she'd worn that night; an emerald green dress formal enough for diplomatic circles, but revealing enough smooth, English skin to set his pulse racing.

His tongue had knotted in his throat. Used to the grunts and obscenities of the jungle, the refined words of cocktail party chat had eluded him. But instead of boring her, his reticence had seemed to stimulate her curiosity.

Her eyes had a look that challenged. 'Come on out! I know you're in there,' they seemed to say.

They had broken away from the party; she suggested a moonlit stroll round Airport Camp. Coconut palms and pre-fab huts. She said it reminded her of a fifties movie.

His arousal had become difficult to contain. Hers too. They made a bee-line for the deserted sick bay.

'Excuse me, sir.'

The RAF flight attendant was offering him a newspaper.

'It's today's, brought from Brize this morning. Thought you might like a look.'

'Oh, yes. Thanks.'

He took it and smiled. They knew who he was all right.

He glanced quickly at the front page, fearful of what he might see.

No mention there.

The lead story concerned the Prime Minister's meeting in London the day before with the leader of the Russian Republic. It said assurances had been given that the former Soviet nuclear arsenal was still in safe hands.

He flipped through the pages, until he found the article he was looking for. No longer front-page news. That was something.

The funeral of Richard Bicknell had been attended by the City financial community. The Government had been represented by the Foreign Minister, George Webster. There was a photo of him consoling Bicknell's widow. And in the final paragraph, the words Brodrick had hoped not to see.

The lone survivor of the failed rescue mission, a Royal Marines Captain, aged 32 and unmarried, is believed to be returning to Britain today on an RAF flight from Cyprus. His name has not yet been released.

But if the hyenas of the press had anything to do with, it bloody soon would be!

Three

London
December 19th

The door of the tube train screeched from lack of grease. Peter Brodrick flinched. Sharp noises could still startle him, though he'd never admit it to the men in white coats who'd grudgingly pronounced him fit to return to duty.

The packed carriage spilled its occupants onto the platform. Brodrick let the tide carry him towards the stairs, resisting the urge to hurry and push aside the dawdlers. Pensioners and women towing disgruntled children surrounded him.

On the first landing, a pallid youth in jeans and anorak sat dejectedly on the ground, seemingly oblivious to the danger of being trampled underfoot. Propped under his chin was a square of corrugated cardboard bearing the pencilled words 'homeless, hungry, please help'.

Christmastime.

Some pretended not to see the boy, embarrassed by the sight of poverty while on a shopping spree. Others threw coins into the scarf held open on his lap.

How much could a man make, begging at Christmas? Brodrick tossed him a pound.

In Sloane Square it was drizzling. Brodrick tugged a cap from the pocket of his Barbour and pulled it on. Loudspeakers set in the trees by Rotarians blared *Oh, Come All Ye Faithful*, while half a dozen Father Christmases rattled collecting boxes, raising money for an earthquake disaster. Parting with another pound, Brodrick lifted his collar and pressed through the throng towards the Peter Jones department store.

He'd dreaded this morning; Christmas shopping was his least favourite occupation, but this year he had a very special present to buy. He owed Jackie, after what he'd put her through in the last four weeks.

He stepped off the pavement to cross King's Road. Faces and bodies pressed from all directions. Fear lurked at the back of his mind. It always did now in a crowd. Fear that someone would know who he was, that someone would point a finger and say, 'That's the man who led the marines to their deaths in Lebanon.'

Since the 'incident', as the military had come to call it, they'd taken care to prevent his name getting out. All the men who'd been on the raid were to remain officially anonymous in the interests of security. The terrorists could be bent on revenge.

But there'd been funerals, once the bodies had eventually been recovered. Photographers by the dozen. No names in the papers maybe, but intrusive pictures of the families. Every newsdesk in the country must by now have squirrelled out the identity of the officer who'd led the ill-fated mission – and survived. How long before some editor decided it was 'in the public interest' to print it?

He couldn't escape his guilt, however often they told him the disaster wasn't his fault. What they *thought* was different from what they *said*. He could see it in their eyes; the cold glare which said, 'You should have died too, Brodrick.'

The cameramen had been out looking for him like hyenas. It was thanks to Jackie that they hadn't found him. They'd sniffed around the barracks in Plymouth and Poole, but he'd taken shelter in her flat in Fulham. Only his CO knew where he was, and he wasn't telling.

The digital clock above the entrance to Peter Jones said twelve-thirty; forty-five minutes to find Jackie's present, before he met her for lunch.

He walked through the glass and china department, the glittering displays blurring before his eyes. He'd put off thinking about what to buy until this morning.

Perfume? Too easy, and anyway she could buy it duty free whenever she went abroad. A silk nightdress? She slept naked. He wandered through the departments, looking and rejecting.

He reached the gift department at the back of the store. The shelves were full of objects that were pleasing but ultimately useless. He touched things at random, alabaster, bronze, porcelain, then left them, undecided.

It had to be right, what he bought her. It had to be special.

Brodrick disliked possessions. They acted like anchors. At heart he was a nomad. Home for him was the wardroom, or more often than not a bivouac or snow hole.

He was thirty-two. Many of his contemporaries were married with young families and mortgages. The only thing of substance he owned was his BMW.

An elderly man walking with a stick swayed unsteadily and bumped against his left arm. Peter winced from the shooting pain; a nerve, shattered by the Lebanese bullet, had sprung to life again.

There had been an official enquiry after he got back. Penetrating questions about his conduct of the mission, his assessment of its chances of success. He'd come out of it with a clean sheet, but it had done nothing to assuage his guilt, nor to moderate his anger at the men who'd sent him to Lebanon.

A week after his return to England, psychiatrists from the Navy's Medical Branch had told him he was suffering from post-traumatic stress disorder, and needed help. He'd told them to "eff off" and had discharged himself from their care.

That same day he'd phoned Jackie at work and told

her he was coming to stay. No explanation. Just put himself on the train to London. By the time he'd reached her doorstep, he'd half emptied a bottle of whisky. He still felt drenched with guilt whenever he remembered how he'd behaved.

He'd taken over her flat as if he owned it, giving her only the most rudimentary of explanations. She'd had to winkle out of him the fact that it was he who'd led the abortive raid into Lebanon.

He'd spent a week drinking and staring from the windows, while Jackie worked. The nights had been hell; he'd found himself incapable of sex – the doctors had warned him that would happen – and nightmares wrecked his sleep.

By the week's end Jackie had taken enough of his silences. She'd bullied and probed until he'd told her every ghastly detail of what he'd been through. The catharsis had shocked her deeply, and left him drained.

He examined a rosewood jewel box, its lid inlaid with copper and brass. Made in India or Pakistan, he guessed. Would she like it? It was nice enough, but would she want it? He was annoyed at his indecision.

It would have to do. He picked it up and turned to the till. Suddenly he caught sight of himself in a mirror. For a moment he barely recognised his own face. The stress lines had aged him, the brown eyes were lifeless, withdrawn.

Was that how Jackie saw him?

She'd nursed him, supported him – even loved him, so she said. And how had he responded? By closing the shutters and bolting the door, the closer she'd tried to come.

'I understand what you've been through,' she kept saying to him. Understand? How *could* she bloody understand? She hadn't *been* there!

60

She did not deserve his vicious bouts of temper and his moods. He knew that. But she wanted the impossible – for him to be the same man she'd met in Belize. She couldn't understand the metamorphosis he'd been through since then.

He knew what she really craved – for him to love her in the way that she loved him. But inside him, where such feelings should be generated, there was only an emptiness.

He looked down at the rosewood box in his hands. An empty box. Was that the sort of gift she deserved? No, it bloody wasn't!

He placed it back on the display. No more hesitation. He knew what would really please her. It would send his bank balance into overdraft, but it'd be worth it.

He strode out through the nearest door and headed up Pavilion Road to Harrods.

It was twenty past one by the time he entered L'Express Cafe in Sloane Street. Jackie saw him, and waved from her seat.

'I came early to get a table,' she called above the strident hubbub of Chelsea and Kensington. She wore a tailored skirt and a red striped blouse, and a cashmere coat hung over the back of her chair.

'I've ordered already,' she added. 'It's so crowded, I thought I'd better.'

'Good idea,' he grunted.

She noticed an unusual look in his eye.

'You're looking rather smug,' she announced. 'What've you been up to?'

'Never you mind.'

He caught the waitress's eye and asked for a bottle of Rioja, which arrived at the same time as the chili con carne and salads Jackie had ordered.

'You're mad,' Jackie giggled. 'I'll doze off at my desk.'

They raised their glasses and clinked the rims.

'To the Minister of State for Foreign Affairs!' Brodrick declared in a voice that was slightly too loud. 'May the flames of his own ambition consume him!'

'Peter! Someone'll hear.' She glanced at the neighbouring tables. 'Isn't it treason for a bootie to say something like that?'

'Probably. You know he came to see me in Cyprus?'

'George Webster? I never knew that.' She frowned, puzzled. 'I do his diary, for heaven's sake!'

He took another swig of wine and forked into his chili. 'Well, he did.'

'And what did you think?' she asked, warily. The conversation seemed to be taking a sensitive turn.

'Of – ?'

'Webster. When he came to see you in Cyprus.'

'Arsehole. Like the rest of them.'

He was stirring his food rather than eating it. Not a good sign, Jackie decided. Time to change the subject.

'So, how was the Christmas shopping?'

She peered inquisitively under the table.

'No bags? That's a bad sign.'

He stifled a smirk.

'Too big to fit under the table.'

'Oh! You've bought me an elephant. *Just* what I always wanted! You're wonderful!'

She reached across the table and squeezed his hand. More than a gesture of affection. Understanding. She knew he was still going through hell.

'I adore Christmas.' Her grey-green eyes sparkled. 'Don't you? I mean, normally?'

He shrugged.

'Too commercial.' He was sounding like a killjoy.

'But this year it'll be different,' he added, forcing a grin.

Jackie looked unconvinced.

Brodrick ate silently for a couple of minutes, then said

suddenly, 'They rang this morning from headquarters. I've got a posting.'

'Where? When?'

'Don't know yet,' he answered edgily. 'I'm to see someone at the Defence Ministry tomorrow at eleven.'

'A posting? Does that mean abroad?' She tried to disguise the disappointment in her voice.

'Could be anything. Here in London, maybe.'

'But it won't be right away? Not before Christmas!' They were to spend it together in Fulham.

'No chance.'

'And Boxing Day? You will come with me to Winchester?'

Jackie wanted to introduce him to her parents, but he had not yet committed himself.

'I still don't know.'

'It'd be a nice drive, if the weather's good.'

She hoped the chance to use his treasured BMW might tempt him.

'Look, I said I don't know!'

'Okay, okay,' she soothed.

'I'll wait and see what they have to say tomorrow.'

She gave him one of her indulgent smiles.

They finished their food in silence. Finally she looked at her watch.

'Got to go. The Minister's having another one of his briefing sessions this afternoon. Insists I take notes and type them up. Such a pain.'

'Well, try not to snore when you nod off.'

'Thanks a lot! How *was* your shopping, by the way?'

'Hopeless. Couldn't find anything you'd like!'

'You're an evil so-and-so, you know that? But I'll see you this evening. And keep your boots off the sofa, or else!'

The next morning Jackie had left the flat by seven.

George Webster started work early. Brodrick awoke to find the space beside him empty and cold.

The clock on her bedside table said eight thirty-five. He swore; he'd slept longer than he'd meant to. His morning run would have to be shorter than usual. Still, at least he'd had a night without dreams. He rolled out of bed and made a brief visit to the bathroom.

This was Jackie's home and he'd made little impression on it during the four weeks he'd stayed there. The bathroom was feminine but stylish, full of plants and antique scent bottles. It smelled strongly of lavender – the scent of the black soap that was a memento of her childhood in Spain. As he stood there naked, extracting his toothbrush from the clutter of cosmetics on the shelf above the washbasin, he felt out of place.

Back in the bedroom he reached for his holdall on the floor of the built-in wardrobe and pulled out his tracksuit and trainers. Jackie had offered him space for his clothes, but apart from a hanger for his jacket and trousers he kept the rest of his things in the bag.

He was nervous. This was a vital day; they'd already pronounced him fit to return to duty, but only today would they tell him what the duty was to be. 'Fit' meant he'd passed the physical tests; being ready for duty was another matter.

His confidence had been shattered in Lebanon. How he would cope with stress the next time, God alone knew. The men in white coats who'd signed his fitness certificate certainly didn't.

He slipped a lanyard with a key round his neck, locked the door behind him and headed towards the river at a brisk jog. The weather had brightened after yesterday's drizzle. He inhaled the crisp air deeply to expand his lungs.

A quick circuit of Bishop's Park, then a sprint across Putney Bridge, weaving between the commuters heading for the Underground. Along the tow-path south of the river, he settled into the fast pace he'd need to maintain for the whole run if he was to get any benefit from it. He had time for just four miles that morning. His normal routine was nine miles a day with a thirty-pound pack on his back.

As his feet pounded the softer ground of Barnes Common, he concentrated on the day ahead. The phone call from the appointments officer had been both a relief and a shock.

Despite the vindication of the enquiry, Brodrick was well aware of the humiliation and shame the Corps had suffered as a result of the fiasco in Lebanon. Whatever the public reassurances from his superiors, he suspected he was being blamed for things going so badly wrong.

Now they'd decided his future, but he wouldn't know how until eleven that morning.

Back at the flat, forty-five minutes after he'd left it, he showered and breakfasted, then dressed as smartly as he could for his visit to the Ministry.

Commander Nigel Pitts welcomed him into the fifth floor office at the Ministry of Defence at two minutes to eleven. The card on the door read 'Directorate of Naval Plans'.

'Glad you're on time, Peter,' he began. 'There's someone else coming to meet you in half an hour, and I wanted a chance to chat with you properly before he arrives. Do sit down.'

It was a scruffy little office; the dark-suited commander was number two in the department and merited nothing but the standard, beige walls and grey, metal desk that gave the building its depressing air of uniformity.

'Coffee? Tea?'

'Tea, thanks.'

'Molly . . .' he called into the adjoining room. 'One of each, please.'

He dropped into his chair and his face adopted an expression of concern.

'Now, first things first. Tell me how you are, Peter. And be honest. D'you feel ready for a new job?'

'Oh, yes, quite ready, sir. So long as it's not in *this* place,' he joked.

'Don't worry, they're being kind to you. This time at least. You're going to be afloat.'

Brodrick frowned. He couldn't think of any full-time shipborne postings at his pay grade. The commander read his thoughts.

'It's a new operation. Something we've not done before. I'll give you the details in a moment, but first I want to fill in a little of the background.'

He looked up and paused as the secretary placed two mugs and a plate of biscuits on the desk.

'Thank you, Molly. Now, Peter. The demise of the Russian empire has had a rather damaging effect on the brains of some of our politicians. They tend *still* to think of the forces primarily as a counter to the Soviet threat. So, take away the threat and you can axe the military! The cuts the government's ordered so far are limited, but if we don't watch out there'll be more. So, the point is this; there's a certain small, select group of people here,' and he pointed upwards to the sixth floor where the First Sea Lord had his office, 'who believe we've got to do everything possible to remind the voters how useful we are. So that we're still here the next time a global emergency pokes its head above the parapet.'

He paused to study the reaction. Brodrick was beginning to understand, but wasn't sure he would like what he was to hear.

'So the Navy's to expand its activities, Peter, and you're to play a key part in that.'

Brodrick raised a quizzical eyebrow.

'You're to intercept drug-runners in the Med. A joint operation with the Spanish.'

It was like a punch in the gut. So this was it. Let down the SBS and they bust you to the role of policeman.

'You'll be based on HMS *Eagle* with about fifty men, Mark Four Sea Kings and Whiskies. The smugglers run cocaine from South America, heroin and hashish from the Middle East and North Africa. *Eagle* will use her air assets to detect the boats and planes the smugglers are using. Your job will be to board the boats and inspect them. You'll have a liaison officer with you, from the Spanish coastguard.'

'Coastguard work!' Brodrick snapped, flushing with anger. 'Whose idea was this?'

Commander Pitts looked taken aback.

'Well, er ... As far as I know, the Commandant-General . . .'

'Anyway, why aren't the Spanish looking after their own coastline, sir?' Brodrick thumped the arm of his chair. 'Why do they need help from us? What about Gibraltar, for heaven's sake?'

The commander wasn't used to such a reaction from the officers he was posting. Had to tread carefully, though. These were special circumstances.

'Gibraltar. That's an important point. *Eagle* will be based there. The Spaniards are aware of that, so it's quite a break-through for them to co-operate with us like this. In fact, it's unprecedented. The Foreign Office are wetting themselves. They say it'll do wonders for Anglo-Spanish discussions about the future of the Rock. Even the Gibraltarians should be pleased.'

The commander's voice was just a mumble in Brodrick's mind. They wanted him out. Offer him a post that'll insult him and he'll resign his commission – that's what they were thinking.

The poisoned chalice. Drink, and his career was dead. Refuse it, and he'd have to leave the service.

'Anyway, you'll accept?'

'I'm not sure . . .'

67

'Look, I wasn't expecting you to be overjoyed,' the commander's lip twisted in embarrassment. 'It's awkward for me too, this, you know.'

He looked down and fingered the papers on his desk.

'Let me say this to you. It is genuinely important work. Both for us and the politicians. And, look – you've been through a bad time. This'll be an easy way for you to get back on your feet.'

'A good way to keep me out of sight, you mean, sir,' he retorted bitterly.

'The bottom line is this, Peter: it's the only job you're being offered. If I were you I'd accept it graciously.'

The commander's message was brutally clear.

They couldn't just sack him, of course. The inquiry had vindicated him. And the publicity, if he chose to sell his story to the press, would be devastating. But this was humiliation.

What had it all been for? The commando course, the toughest endurance test in the world; the yomping across East Falkland in 1982, fighting with his bare hands on Mount Harriet; his escape from death in Lebanon. He'd survived all that just to be paired off with some poncey Spanish coastguard to inspect pleasure cruisers off the Costa del Sol?

'Look, I'm sorry. I'm just the messenger,' the commander softened. 'I know what you've been through. We all know. And they're not putting you down, whatever you may think. Upstairs, they want to be fair to you, but you've got to be fair to yourself too. Give yourself time to get back on form.'

Brodrick pulled himself straight. The commander was getting on his nerves, with his patronising. How the hell could anyone know what he'd been through?

'I understand what makes booties tick,' Pitts tried to reassure him. 'There'll be some action, don't worry. They're tough nuts, these smugglers. Armed to the teeth. That's why the Spaniards have welcomed our offer to help. It won't be a sunshine cruise, I can assure you of that.'

Brodrick swallowed hard. Time to swallow his pride? The alternative was to resign. But this wasn't the moment. Quit when you're on top, not when you're down. And little as he fancied police work in the Med, he fancied the dole queue even less.

'I guess I don't have much option, sir.'

Commander Pitts smiled with relief and held out his hand.

'Good man! *Eagle*'s in Gib for Christmas. Lot of families have gone out to join their men. She'll be up and running again by the New Year. I suggest you get yourself out there on January the second. There's a seat booked for you on a charter flight from Luton.'

'I see. Who's her commander now?'

'Captain Dyce. Know him? He's got a few miles on the clock.'

Dyce. Quick of temper, short on judgement, one of the most disliked captains in the Navy. *Just* what he needed.

Pitts pushed a buff-coloured folder across the desk.

'All the details – and your travel warrant – are in there. And a list of the men you'll have under your command.'

There was a gentle tap at the door and the secretary poked her head round.

'Mr Packer's here,' she whispered. 'Are you ready?'

'Thirty seconds, Molly.'

Brodrick looked up from his perusal of the folder and raised an enquiring eyebrow.

'Customs and Excise. Thought it'd be a good idea for you two to meet. He'll fill you in on what the Spaniards have been up to.'

'Oh, yes. I suppose that makes sense,' Brodrick answered resignedly.

The customs officer was tall and thin, with hair that

looked as if it had been combed with a precision instrument. His complexion was unnaturally pink.

They shook hands.

'Stephen Packer. I'm a Senior Investigation Officer, and I'm head of the cocaine section at Lower Thames Street.'

'Peter Brodrick. Glad to know you.'

They stood, eyeing each other uncomfortably.

'D'you know anything about the drugs trade, Captain Brodrick?' Packer began.

'Not had occasion to . . .'

'No. It's not exactly a prime task for the military . . .'

Thanks, bastard! Brodrick dug his fingernails into the palms of his hands.

'Until now, Mr Packer,' Pitts chipped in. 'The Navy's very upbeat about the contribution it can make.'

The Customs officer pursed his lips.

'Well, you've certainly given us a lot of help in the past, tracking cargoes of IRA Semtex. But that's usually a job for submarines.' He sensed the atmosphere and began to look uncomfortable. 'Anyway, we're obviously very glad to have all the help we can get.'

Commander Pitts pointed to a chair. Packer settled into it and crossed his pinstriped legs.

'Do you want a bit of a global view first, before I talk about Spain?'

'Might as well,' Brodrick shrugged.

'Right. Well, cocaine. That's going to be your main problem. The US agencies are having some degree of success in cutting the flow from South America. Not totally, of course, but they are making things difficult for the smugglers, so the Medellin boys have found alternative markets in Europe.'

'If I can butt in for a moment . . ,' said Commander Pitts, seeing his opportunity, 'is it not correct that much of that pressure on the smugglers is being exerted by the US Navy? The military?'

'*Some* of it,' Packer corrected him. 'Extra radar's useful, and support with the odd boarding party. But it's still customs work essentially. And of course the US Coastguard is a big outfit. Oceangoing. We could do with a lot more patrol boats over here. Every European country could. That's where you chaps will be handy. Though whether a bloody great aircraft carrier is the right sort of boat is another matter. Still, the helicopters'll be useful.'

Tactless sod, Brodrick thought. Typical policeman.

'And Spain is the entry point in Europe, I suppose,' he nudged, eager to get this over with.

'Right. The main entry point, anyway. Not surprising, really; it's the nearest bit of Europe to South America, and there's thousands of Colombians living in Madrid, ready to market it and distribute it.'

'And it's too much for the Spanish authorities to handle?'

'They've two main problems. One is the length of their coastline – an enormous area to keep tabs on. Second, corruption. Most of the narcotics squad in Algeciras was arrested not so long ago for suspected complicity. They'd been reselling the stuff they'd confiscated.

'But they've had their successes, it's got to be said. They've seized nearly two tons of cocaine this past year. But it's the stuff they haven't seized we've got to worry about. And all the hash and heroin that's coming from the Middle East and North Africa.'

'So, where's it being brought in?'

'Much of it's in Galicia. That's the northwest, if you're not familiar with the geography. Rocky coastline, lots of coves, and a long tradition of smuggling. Used to be tobacco in the old Franco days. That's where the Spanish customs and police are concentrating their efforts at the moment. But there's a lot coming in down south as well. Around Gibraltar. Again, smuggling's in the blood down there. You get ships coming to the Med from South America carrying legitimate cargoes, and then they drop a few sacks of cocaine over the side to be picked up by small boats out of Algeciras or the marinas on the Costa del Sol and Gibraltar.'

'And the stuff from Africa and the Middle East? Hash and heroin, you said? Is that just for the Spanish market?'

'The heroin is, probably. But the hash and the cocaine can go anywhere in Europe. Much of it ends up here in England. You see, the border with France is one of the most open in Europe, particularly in the summer. Thousands of tourist cars cross it every hour. No checks. Get the stuff ashore at Marbella and it's as good as having it in Calais.'

'What's the intelligence plot like? Do we know who's running things?' asked Commander Pitts.

'We know plenty about the cocaine trade. The Medellin cartels and so on. The DEA – that's the US Drug Enforcement Agency – they've spent millions on intelligence, and it's paying off. But over here, governments won't cough up. Lower priority than in the States. There are some places we know very little about. Lebanon, for example. The Beka'a Valley's full of poppies and cannabis. But who the biggest producers are we've no idea. Both the Christians and the Muslims seem to be involved, but very little reliable intelligence comes out of Beirut.'

Brodrick sat very still.

'Well, of course, you know that already. To your cost.'

How did Packer know about him and Lebanon? His name hadn't been made public. Brodrick looked across at the commander, who had suddenly picked up his pen to make a note. You sod, he thought.

Sensing the tension, Packer hurried on with his exposition.

'The raw opium from the Beka'a gets sold to the

Kurds. They mix it with stuff from the Golden Crescent north of Pakistan, refine it into pure heroin and pass it on to the Turks, who pack it into the chassis of lorries and drive it to northern Europe. The trade's still flourishing despite the war between the Kurdish separatists and the Turkish military.'

'And the Turkish police? They can't do anything to stop it?'

'It's not easy. Turkey's got one of the biggest road haulage industries in the world. Short of cutting every bloody truck to pieces . . . But there's more co-operation in Europe now than there was,' Packer continued. 'Police and customs talk to each other these days, but there's no international drug squad as such.'

'Intriguing. You've got an interesting job,' chipped in Commander Pitts.

Yes, thought Brodrick. And the Marines should be leaving him to get on with it.

'Too much sodding paperwork, that's what's wrong with it.'

'Amen to that,' echoed Pitts. 'I'll be buried by it one day.'

'One more thing, Mr Packer,' Brodrick asked. 'What's the legal position? About boarding craft to search them?'

'Difficult. On the high seas you've got no right to board any vessel unless the skipper gives permission. Inside the twelve-mile limit, you're okay, so long as the Spanish coastguard is with you and is seen to be the man in authority. That's very important. Otherwise you could be accused of piracy!'

'Doesn't sound good. We can't operate independently, then?'

Packer referred the question to the commander.

'I don't need to tell you, Peter, that when it comes to dealing with the Spaniards, kid gloves are the order of the day. They're terribly sensitive. They've got their own carrier, the *Principe de Asturias*, operating in the north off Galicia. There's a bit of rivalry here. Any hint that we're trying to score points by operating outside their guidelines won't go down at all well.'

'Mmmm . . . That sounds enough to be going on with.' Brodrick felt an overwhelming need to get out of this office.

Pitts reached out his hand.

'Just remains for me to wish you good luck.'

The customs man mumbled his agreement.

'Thanks for coming in, Peter,' Pitts smiled. 'I'm sure you'll enjoy the posting. And . . . er, happy Christmas. You going anywhere?'

'Nowhere special.'

'I'll be on my way too, Commander,' said Stephen Packer.

'You can share a lift down, then. Let me sign your visitors' passes otherwise they won't let you out of the building.'

He took the slips of pink paper and scrawled his name on them.

'Molly'll show you the way.'

They didn't speak in the lift going down, but as they passed through the electronic security gate and out of the North Door into Horse Guards Avenue, Packer looked ostentatiously at his watch.

'Fancy a beer? Seems to be that time of day . . .'

'Well. . . ,' A drink was just what Brodrick needed.

'I wouldn't mind hearing what really happened in Lebanon!'

Brodrick caught his breath. I bet you wouldn't, he thought.

'Sorry, it's a bit early for me,' he mumbled. 'Nice to have met you.'

He turned and walked quickly to Westminster tube station.

*

He was lucky with the trains and arrived back at Putney Bridge within twenty-five minutes. He did after all badly need a drink and headed for the nearest pub, the Eight Bells.

.He downed one pint standing at the bar, then took a second to a table. Sitting alone in a corner, he unfolded a newspaper and pretended to read.

The meeting at the Ministry had left him seething. The job he'd been offered was even more of an insult than he'd realised. One look in the folder Pitts had given him had revealed that the Spanish coastguard liaison officer he'd be taking orders from was only a lieutenant.

As he drank, his anger grew. Anger at the Navy, but above all anger at himself. He should've refused the posting. Should've called their bluff. They'd have found him something else; and if they hadn't, he should've resigned. He might at least have preserved his self-respect.

He drained his glass and ordered a third.

When Jackie returned to the Fulham flat just before seven, she found it in darkness, which surprised her. Peter had said he'd be there.

She turned on the living-room light, and jumped with alarm.

'God! You gave me a fright! What are you doing, sitting in the dark?'

Brodrick sat slumped in an armchair, long legs extended, rigid as stretcher poles. On the floor beside him were a glass and a half-empty whisky bottle. He turned his head and blinked at the brightness.

'I'm gonna resign my fucking commission . . .' he slurred.

She put her hands on her hips. Much of the past month had been spent pulling him up from the depths of despair. She suddenly felt too tired to do it again.

'Interview went well, then?'

'It's what they want. It's what they'll bloody get . . .' he mumbled.

'Don't be daft! And what the hell's that?'

She pointed at an alteration to the landscape in the corner of the room, a sheet from her linen cupboard draped over a pile of boxes.

'Aah . . .'s a secret! Not 'llowed to touch, 'til Santa says you can.'

'How exciting.'

She hung up her navy-blue coat and glanced in the mirror. Keep cool, she told herself, yanking a comb through her hair.

Brodrick had turned on the television news; Jackie pressed the 'off' button.

'Look, before you get suicidal, why don't you pour me a nice G and T, with some ice and a slice of lemon, and then I'll issue you with a little challenge.'

She stood behind his chair and ran her fingers through the hair at the back of his neck.

'Wassort of challenge?'

'A tough one! I'll put money on it.'

'How much?'

'The price of the Indian takeaway that I've decided we're going to have tonight.'

'You're on, old thing. Now, wass the bet?'

She paused, then lowered her voice.

'I bet you can't get a hard-on with all that whisky inside you.'

Four

Armenia
December 24th 1993

Snow flurried in the streets of Yerevan. The churches
were locked and dark. It was too early for Christmas
here. In Armenia January the 6th is the date on which
Christ's birth is celebrated. It was late afternoon, and
the elderly were queuing for bread.

Colonel Yegor Papushin sat beside the driver of the
cream-coloured Volga taxi. He yawned and scratched
his craggy chin. The flight that had brought him from
Moscow had been delayed four hours.

The last time he'd been here, the old Soviet Seventh
Guards Army was still headquartered in Yerevan. Then
he'd been treated with deference and respect. Now, the
barracks had closed, the army was integrated with the
forces of the new Armenian Republic, and a Russian
intelligence officer got no official welcome. He'd had to
queue for his taxi along with a handful of new-style
businessmen.

Yerevan was not an unattractive city by Russian
standards. Today an easterly wind had thinned the
usual haze of industrial pollution so that the pink
volcanic stone of the buildings almost glowed. From the
bridge over the Razdan river Papushin caught a distant
glimpse of Mount Ararat across the Turkish border. The
mountain was a potent symbol for the Christian
Armenians. It decorated their flag, and its shape was
mirrored by the roofs of the churches.

Until the phone call yesterday, he'd thought the trail

of the nuclear warheads seized by bandits nearly two years ago had gone as cold as stone. But the Armenian security chief had talked to him of startling new information.

Immediately after the weapons convoy had been ambushed in January 1992, he'd been sent from Moscow with instructions to find the missing warheads, but to admit to no one that they were nuclear. His investigation had made little headway under such conditions of secrecy.

Papushin worked for what used to be the Third Directorate of the KGB, responsible for military security. One of the few sections of Dzerzhinsky's organisation that had remained intact after the failed coup of August 1991, it now came under the command of the military.

The cream Volga turned into the Prospekt Sayat-Nova heading for the Ani Hotel where a room had been reserved. The street was almost devoid of traffic; Armenia's fuel supplies came mostly from neighbouring Azerbaijan and were still being blocked.

There was anarchy in the air. Armenia was locked inextricably in the battle with Azerbaijan for control of Nagorno-Karabakh. The old Soviet army which had kept the two sides apart for four years was already disintegrating at the time of his last visit. Just how bad things were, Papushin had not understood until he'd come here. In Moscow, the old habit of concealing unpleasant truths died hard.

Armenian conscripts had deserted en masse in some regiments, to join the new national militias. Large stocks of guns and ammunition had been 'liberated' from the armouries and sold for food and vodka. Soviet commanders had laid minefields around some armouries to prevent further losses.

Papushin yawned again. His last visit had been fruitless. For weeks he'd interrogated men at the missile base looking for signs of complicity in the ambush, but everything had pointed to the warhead convoy being caught by surprise. If the guards had been negligent, they'd paid for it with their lives.

If it had happened a year earlier, his task might have been simpler. He could have hauled Armenian nationalists off the streets and beaten them until they talked. But the local police, with whom he'd had to work, were loyal to the new Armenian Republic, and owed no favours to Moscow.

They'd demanded to know what the missing truck had contained. 'Important technical equipments' was all he'd been allowed to say. No one was fooled. They all knew where the convoy had come from, and what sort of weapons were stored there.

The Volga bumped to a halt outside the hotel. Papushin paid the driver and stepped into the cavernous reception area. Behind the counter, two receptionists gossiped conspiratorially. They ignored him.

Little's changed, he thought.

He cleared his throat, but it was a sharp local tongue from over his shoulder that finally got their attention. He turned and recognised Major Temourian from the Armenian security service.

'Comrade Colonel! You are most welcome,' he announced in Russian.

They shook hands and the Armenian scolded the girls for their inattention.

'You must be tired and hungry,' he soothed.

'Quite true,' Papushin concurred. 'I seem to have missed lunch.'

'So did I. There's a place I know where they serve food anytime,' Temourian said. 'If you would like to leave your bag in your room, we can go there as soon as you're ready.'

Temourian drove Papushin the short distance to what used to be called Lenin Square. There seemed an abundance of cafés and restaurants. He parked the car and the smell of grilled lamb and coffee regaled them as they opened the doors.

The restaurant was small – half a dozen tables at most. It was clear from the welcome that this was one of Temourian's regular haunts. Papushin unbuttoned his greatcoat.

'You may wish to keep that on,' Temourian warned. 'There's not much heat in here. No oil, you see.'

A bottle of red wine appeared automatically. The waiter, dressed in baggy black trousers and a crumpled white shirt, filled their glasses and waited for instructions.

'I recommend the *kharput kiouftas*,' Temourian suggested. 'Lamb in a casserole of chicken.'

Papushin nodded.

'I leave it to you.'

The waiter disappeared behind the heavy curtain that kept the kitchen smells away from the diners.

'So,' Papushin began, now they were alone. 'You have something new to tell me?'

'I have. It's dollars!'

'Dollars? What does that mean?'

'One of the nationalist militias is trying to buy tanks. From soldiers in one of the tank regiments. They're offering twenty thousand dollars for a T-72. They want ten of them.'

'Two hundred thousand dollars? Where did they get that money from?'

'Exactly.'

The waiter re-emerged through the curtain, and set before them plates of vegetables and curd cheese.

'This is *tvorog*. You'll like it,' Temourian assured him.

Papushin waited until they were alone again.

'So? Where did they get so much foreign currency?' he demanded.

'We don't know. They're not responding to questioning.'

Papushin took the bottle and slopped more wine into their glasses.

'But you've a good idea, otherwise you wouldn't have got me here!'

'We think there are two possibilities. Either they've been given the money – maybe an Armenian expatriate living in America – or else they've been able to smuggle abroad something extremely valuable and sell it . . .'

He fixed Papushin with eyes that looked glassy and black.

'This "technical equipment" that was seized two years ago. . . ,' Temourian continued. 'How much would it be worth?'

Papushin stared back, his expression inscrutable. He downed the wine as if it were vodka and refilled his glass. He stared straight through Temourian.

The bombs would be worth all of two hundred thousand dollars, and much more, he thought to himself, if they got to the right customer. Suddenly he felt a fluttering in his guts that spelled the onset of panic.

As the months had gone by with no trace of the warheads in Armenia, and no intelligence reports that they'd reached another country, Papushin had convinced himself they'd been damaged in the ambush, and the rebels had abandoned them as useless. He'd pictured them dumped in a barn or buried in a trench. He knew too about the safety systems, and felt reassured the Armenian nationalists would never be able to use them in anger.

But that comforting theory had become instantly invalid, if it was true the rebels were suddenly awash with dollars. There was only one thing safe to assume: they'd sold the bombs.

Temourian was still waiting for his answer.

'It'd be worth all of that. . . ,' Papushin breathed. 'But why now? Why would it take so long to find a buyer?'

Temourian shrugged.

'I can only guess . . .' He glanced up at Papushin, wondering how open they could be with each other. To him, Russians would always be 'the enemy'.

'I'm assuming these equipments were of a highly explosive kind? We *are* talking the same language?'

Papushin hesitated for a second, then nodded.

'Highly explosive.'

'Then, this is my theory . . .'

He was interrupted by the waiter replacing the vegetable dishes with a large, steaming casserole.

'I'll bring you some more bread. . . ,' he announced.

Temourian waited until the man had finished his business.

'What you must remember, comrade Colonel,' he whispered, 'is that these extremists are simple people. They may not have had any idea what to do with the weapons. These are not people who make strategic plans. They act on the spur of the moment. Also, they're not well connected in the outside world.'

'You're saying they spent nearly two years wondering what to do with their booty?' Papushin spluttered. 'I find that hard to believe.'

'All right. Maybe they thought about it for just a few months, but once they'd decided to sell the bombs, they were faced with having to find a buyer. These are simple people, remember. Christians. Surrounded by a hostile Islamic world. It would take them time. Maybe nearly two years.'

The casserole had the aroma of allspice, but Papushin's appetite had evaporated. Temourian's theory had an awful ring of truth.

So, the weapons could now be in another country – in the hands of men for whom hundreds of thousands of dollars was chicken-feed – men ready and willing to buy the expertise to short-circuit the safety systems and make the warheads usable.

82

Papushin sensed his masters' sword poised above his head. He'd failed. The evil genie had escaped from the bottle. Would they blame *him* for it?

Moscow had ordered that the world must never know Russia had lost those nuclear weapons. What a farce! The world would find out, soon enough.

'Those rebels with the dollars – you're holding them?'

Temourian looked uncomfortable.

'Not exactly. We know them and can bring them in again. But they wouldn't talk. We tried.'

Papushin leaned forward and cracked his glass on the table.

'Major. You must find them. And you must *make* them talk!'

Brodrick marched along the Fulham Road looking for a greengrocer. Absurd to have left it so late. There were hardly any Christmas trees still in the shops.

Get some sprouts for the turkey, Jackie had said before she left for the Foreign Office that morning. He'd thought of the tree during his morning run along the river. He'd need decorations too. Crazy. Many shops had already closed for Christmas.

The tree he chose was overpriced and far from perfect. Still, he could cut the bottom off and trim a few branches. He found a newsagent open, but he had only tired-looking baubles and tinsel. Instead, he bought a pound and a half of sweets out of a tall jar. Their green and red metallic wrappers looked much more inviting.

Back at the flat, he sawed at the trunk with a bread knife and trimmed the branches with scissors. The end result wasn't bad, considering. He stood it next to the hillock of boxes that were his present for Jackie. He found a needle and thread and made loops through the twisted ends of the sweet papers, and hung the sweets on the tree. He stood back with a certain degree of self-satisfaction.

It was nearly six o'clock. He switched on the television for the evening news, and poured himself a whisky and soda.

Over the last few days, largely thanks to Jackie, he'd come to terms with his posting to *HMS Eagle* in the New Year. She'd cajoled him into half-believing his bosses really had got his interests at heart and were simply easing him gently back into military life.

Just as the television news ended, he heard Jackie's key in the door. She spotted the tree immediately.

'Oh, aren't you clever!' she exclaimed, hugging him. '*Much* nicer than horrid naff tinsel. I love it!'

She went to hang up her coat.

'You couldn't fix me a drink while I have a shower?' she called, heading for the bathroom.

'G and T?'

'Wonderful.'

Brodrick found the tonic in the fridge, dropped a couple of ice cubes into the glass, hacked a slice off a lemon, then carried the gin and tonic to the bathroom.

Through the etched glass of the shower screen, Jackie's glorious chestnut hair was a blur, flattened to her scalp by the jet of the shower. He watched, frozen in the doorway, as she turned under the stream. For a second a breast pressed against the glass, the nipple suddenly brought into sharp focus by the contact. The soft curves of her body, the dark smudge of her pubes; it was as if he were seeing her for the first time after a long absence.

He'd hardly experienced an erection since coming back from Lebanon, but he was making up for it now.

He put the gin glass on the shelf over the basin. Then he quickly removed his clothes.

As he climbed over the rim of the bath, Jackie was bending to turn off the taps. He reached past to turn them on again.

'What the. . . ? Hey!' she exclaimed, turning round, her look of surprise dissolving into a wicked grin.

'Wow! This really *is* Christmas!'

They lay on the linen-covered sofa wearing bathrobes.
She rested her head, wet hair and all, on his chest.

'I suppose you'll be wanting *me* to pay for the
takeaway tonight,' she purred. Peter had failed her
challenge a few nights ago and had had to buy the curry.

'Funny you should mention that . . .'

A tape of Elgar's Cello Concerto was playing on
Jackie's ancient music centre, Tortelier's passionate
bowing distorted painfully by the clapped-out loudspeaker.

'Peter . . .'

'Mmmm?'

Jackie was looking at the mysterious pile of boxes in
the corner, covered by a sheet.

'You know how in some countries they celebrate
Christmas tonight? Christmas Eve? Presents and all
that?'

'Yee . . . es.'

'Well, how about popping round to the Chinese,
getting us some Peking prawns and spare ribs? Then we
could sit here and eat them, have a glass of something
fizzy and . . . open our prezzies!'

She cocked her head on one side and gave him a little-
girl look, then smoothed her fingers over his leather-hard
pectorals.

'And then – if we felt like it – we could get back into the
shower!'

He rolled her onto the floor and dropped gently on top
of her, kissing her on the mouth. She turned her head
away.

'I want my present first!'

He laughed, something he hadn't done for weeks.

'It's been sitting there for days under its shroud,
tempting me! I can't stand the strain.'

'Okay. It's a deal.' He levered himself upright. 'Gimme some money and I'll get the bag rats.'

'The *what*? I said I wanted prawns.'

'Bag rats. Rations in boxes. Sailorspeak.'

Jackie reached for her bag and pulled out a twenty-pound note.

'I want some change. I take it you'll be paying for the champagne?'

She stretched up to kiss him.

Women always looked at their most beautiful when they'd just made love, Brodrick thought. He cupped her backside in his hands and pulled her close.

'Mmmm. More, more,' she murmured.

'Later, later,' he laughed.

'I can dry my hair while you're out.'

He pulled on a track suit and ran a comb through his own wavy, brown hair. Then with the banknote and a credit card in his breast pocket he set off. The houses in this street were tall, brick-built and terraced. Jackie's flat was on the top floor of one of them. Through many of the windows he could see the glow of Christmas tree lights. The night was crisp. There'd be a frost.

The shops were two minutes away, the off-licence and the Chinese restaurant next to each other. He placed the order for the food first, then went next door. The wine shop was packed with last-minute buyers. This part of Fulham was home to hundreds of singles and working couples, all too busy or too forgetful to prepare for Christmas in good time.

He chose a bottle of Laurent Perrier and queued at the till.

Back at the flat, Jackie had laid two places at the small dining table and lit a candle. She wore an enormous cream tee-shirt that ended half-way down her thighs like a nightshirt, with the words 'Wild Thing' emblazoned across it in red. Her eyes glowed, her hair shone like silk and she was barefoot.

'I'll sort the food out, darling, if you do the booze,' she smiled.

'Bet you peeped under the sheet while I was out,' Peter goaded, untwisting the wire from the bottle.

'I did not!' she retorted. 'Anticipation is half the pleasure . . .'

He popped the cork, firing it inches over her head, then splashed the wine into two glasses.

They sat and began to eat with chopsticks.

After a few minutes she stretched her leg out under the table and pushed her foot between his knees. In her eyes there was mischief. She gripped a large prawn with the chopsticks, raised it to her open lips and bit into it lasciviously.

'If you carry on like that,' Brodrick growled, 'the period of anticipation that you seem to want is going to be extremely short!'

'Spoilsport! Don't you love it when they do that sort of thing in movies? The couple have this enormous banquet spread out on a rug in a cornfield. They eat in the most sensuous way, each egging the other on. Then they start taking their clothes off piece by piece. It gets more and more frenetic, eating, kissing, then finally – ! Makes me shiver just to think of it.'

Brodrick laughed again.

'Sounds a bit complicated! I'm just a poor, humble bootie, remember? We like to do one thing at a time. "Beer, big eats, bag off and back on board." That's the recipe for a good run ashore!'

Jackie's face creased with mirth.

'Bag off! Is that what you call making love? Bagging off?'

Brodrick suppressed a grin.

'It's one of the more presentable naval terms!'

'What was it like your very first time?' Her eyes burned with curiosity. 'The very first girl you ever screwed?'

He stroked his chin. He hadn't thought about it for years. It had meant so much at the time, but so little afterwards.

'You first,' he countered. 'Truth game. How old were you?'

Her expression clouded momentarily. She mustn't let the game go too far.

'Seventeen. He was a dusky Andalusian, a year older than me. I was with my parents for the summer hols. You know they had this finca in Spain.'

'Yes. Did you enjoy it?'

'No!' she breathed. 'It was his first time too. But I didn't know that until afterwards. He never came near me again. Now your turn.'

'The first time was with my cousin.'

'Is that legal?'

'Apparently. She said so anyway. You remember I told you my parents died when I was sixteen.'

'Car crash, you said?'

'That's right. I went to live with my aunt, my mother's sister. It was her daughter.'

'Handy.'

'Mmmm. She was a year older. I think she'd been with most of the boys in the neighbourhood at one time or another. One day she decided it was my turn. Wasn't right for me to still be a virgin at eighteen, she said.'

He raised his glass to his lips.

'And? How was it?'

He shook his head.

'I wanted to try it again another day, but she decided once was enough!' he laughed.

'More fool her!' Jackie smiled. She reached across the table for his hand. 'Oh Peter, I do love you.' He squeezed her hand but said nothing. Oh dear, Jackie thought, this could get sticky.

Suddenly she jumped up from the table.

'I almost forgot! The presents! Isn't it exciting?'

She reached round the table and dragged him to his feet. Then she linked her arm in his and hustled him towards the Christmas tree. On the carpet beside it was a small package, wrapped in shiny, bright-red paper.

'It's a terribly small parcel, but I hope you like it,' she said, handing it to him. 'And now . . . Can I?'

She reached for the sheet covering the pile of boxes.

'I don't believe it!' she shouted as she pulled back the cloth to reveal a midi hi-fi. Peter grinned. He'd made the right choice.

'It's incredible! These things cost the earth! It's even got a CD! Peter, you're mad.'

She hugged him and kissed him.

'It's to thank you. For making me sane again!'

She looked as if she were about to cry, and buried her head in his shoulder.

'You must love me a bit to have given me that,' she whispered. He gave her a squeeze.

'And now I'm going to open my parcel.'

'Oh, yes.' She watched anxiously, wiping her eyes with the sleeve of her tee-shirt.

'Hey! That's fantastic. A camera!'

'You like it?'

'Terrific. Autofocus, the lot. You're brilliant.'

They sat on the floor and looked at one another.

'Happy Christmas,' he whispered.

He'd connected the hi-fi earlier that day. The Tortelier Elgar was transformed.

They made love on the floor, not with the same urgency as earlier, but with an unhurried timelessness.

When it was over, they lay apart, arms stretched wide, fingers touching.

She heard him snore lightly. She raised herself onto an elbow to look at him. The lines on his face seemed to soften when he slept.

'You've been through the wars, lover,' she thought. 'And it shows.' Some of his scars were visible, one on an eyebrow, the latest on his arm, but the deepest, she knew, were those that were hidden.

Was he like a cat, each scar representing the loss of one of his nine lives? Without being able to see beneath his skin, how could she ever know how many he had left?

He stirred and caught her watching him.

'What are you thinking?' he asked.

'I was wondering about Boxing Day,' she answered eventually. 'Wondering whether you'll come with me to Winchester?'

She felt his arm tense. She cursed herself. Now she'd spoiled it.

'Yes. I was going to tell you,' he answered awkwardly. 'I can't. I've got to go back to Plymouth.'

'On Boxing Day? The barracks'll be deserted.'

'I know. That's why I must go on Boxing Day.'

She flopped back down onto the floor.

'I've got to get back into it. Get ready for the posting. If I go on Boxing Day I can slip back in without too many people noticing. It'll make it easier. Sorry.'

She sat up, arms round her knees squashing her breasts.

'I understand.'

She looked across to the hi-fi. He'd said it was to say thank you. Had he meant 'thank you and goodbye'?

'And I won't see you again before you go to Gibraltar?'

He didn't answer immediately.

'No. It'll be a while, I guess.'

The joy and laughter that she'd seen return to his face for the first time that evening was gone again. It was as if his eyes were suddenly obscured by clouds.

He was back with the Royals. Back with his nightmare past and his uncertain future.

Five

The chill March wind that swept across the central
Anatolian plateau set the scarlet standard of the Turkish
state crackling from its masthead.

Ismet Ozkan eyed it fearfully over the top of his
newspaper. A flag the colour of blood.

He held the paper high, but it quivered in his grasp, a
feeble shield against those who were searching for him.
Terror gripped his heart, the terror of a man sentenced
to death.

He turned his wrist to check the time. Half an hour to
go. Thirty more precious minutes in which the men
who'd asked for him at the hotel might realise he'd fled.

The flight back to Istanbul had been delayed for
forty-five minutes. The bleak, concrete waiting area by
the departure gate at Diyarbakir airport had few seats,
but he'd secured one of them, facing away from the door.
Most of the other passengers stood within touching
distance, a further screen against discovery, he hoped.

He flinched as a deep roar shook the windows of the
departure lounge. A pair of Turkish Air Force F-104
Starfighters was blasting down the runway. Diyarbakir
was a military base used by only a handful of civilian
flights each day.

The Turkish authorities were at war with Kurdish
separatists and security was tight. Police with auto-
matics stood at every door. But their presence at the
airport had failed to reassure him. The men who wanted

92

him dead were desperate fanatics. His silence was all that mattered to them, even if they themselves had to die to achieve it.

The taxi journey to the airport had been a nightmare. Every car that followed, every eye that stared had seemed a threat. He wouldn't feel safe until the plane was airborne. Even then . . .

Ozkan was no stranger to fear. A senior correspondent for a newspaper on the left of the political spectrum, he'd often challenged the government in print. Over the years, the paper had faced constant threats of closure. Jail sentences, intimidation, exile, he'd known all of these during the past twenty years of Turkish so-called democracy and martial law.

The secret police, the *Milli Istihbarat Teskilati*, had a fat file on him at their headquarters. New pages would have been added in the past week – copies of his reports from southeastern Turkey, describing the abduction and killing of young Kurds by death squads. He'd named the police as being behind the gangs.

He'd also written of atrocities committed by the Turkish army in their war against the separatist PKK. Of men, women and children forced to eat their own excrement after accusations of harbouring guerrillas, of children slaughtered before their families' horrified eyes.

But the fear that now threatened to turn his bowels to water was not of retribution from the M.I.T., rather of being shot by one of those very Kurds whose cause he had befriended.

The fight between the guerrillas and the Turkish authorities had been a dirty war, on both sides. He'd been even-handed, condemning the brutal violence of the PKK campaign. He'd not made the journey from Istanbul to promote the Kurds' dream of separatism, but to judge whether their rights as a minority in Turkey were being observed.

Kurdistan was a nation defined by language and

culture rather than by frontiers, spread across Turkey, Syria, Iraq, Iran, and the former Soviet republics of Armenia and Azerbaijan. None of these countries would yield their territory to a Kurdish state; Ozkan had told them that repeatedly.

The Kurds' civil rights in Turkey had seen a dramatic improvement in recent years, with their own language now legalised. Why then was the PKK maintaining its campaign of violence? That was the question Izmet Ozkan had come to ask.

The PKK were only some five thousand strong, supported and trained by Syria in Lebanon's Beka'a Valley. Thousands of lives had been lost in more than a decade of guerrilla war.

Ozkan's mission this time had been an exclusive interview with a PKK leader at a hideout near the Syrian border – the reward of many months of assiduous contact-building. It was to be a challenging interview, and he took the granting of the meeting as a tribute to the fairness of his reporting. But in the past twenty-four hours his journalistic triumph had turned sour.

He'd learned more than he should have done, more than any man outside the movement could be allowed to know – and stay alive.

As planned, he'd met his contact in Diyarbakir, a young man he was to know simply as Salim. They rendezvoused outside a grocery shop close to the Fatih Paşa mosque. Following instructions, he asked for a kilo of tomatoes, then handed them back, saying they were unripe. That had been the recognition code. Salim had led the way to a car.

They'd driven south to the hilltop town of Mardin. The boy had given his age as twenty, clearly excited at being entrusted with bringing this distinguished journalist to see his leader.

The interview with the PKK chieftain, known simply as Nazar, had proved a sad disappointment. Held in the back room of a bakery, it had been rich in atmosphere but short on useful quotes. The guerrilla leader had talked in slogans, his adherence to the dogma of confrontation quite unshakeable. On the way back Izmet had begun to despair. So much effort to produce so little.

Halfway back to Diyarbakir they'd stopped at a *lokanta* to eat. Salim had sensed Izmet's disappointment and had taken it personally. He, Salim, had been entrusted with this mission; it was vital the journalist be impressed by his leader.

Izmet had noticed him fidgeting at the table, as if itching to tell him something, something that couldn't fail to impress. Yet the boy was holding back, not daring to take the plunge.

They began the meal with *caçik* and beans. Izmet drank beer, Salim only water. It was one of those dusty stopping places used by long-distance buses shuttling between Turkey and the Arab world. There was a regular tooting of horns as drivers summoned their passengers from the tables to continue their journeys.

As they progressed to *guveç* – lamb stew flavoured with tomato and coriander – Izmet's depression deepened at having come so far to learn so little. His conversation became snappy and dismissive.

Salim toyed with his food, unable to eat, his face flushed with anxiety.

Suddenly he leaned across and touched Izmet's hand.

'You mustn't think we're just mountain brigands! I can see it in your eyes. That's what you think of us. But you're wrong.'

Izmet was jolted from his miserable reverie.

'I wasn't thinking anything like that, my friend . . .' he blustered.

'Oh yes, you were.' He looked round nervously. 'I

95

could tell you something that would make you think differently.'

Salim hesitated.

'Oh?' Izmet sounded polite, but sceptical.

Salim leaned forward conspiratorially, his fists clenched in front of him. His eyes flickered left and right to check there was no one to overhear them.

'It's *very* secret.' He made a 'tch' sound with his tongue. 'If I tell you, it's just so that you know. So you understand the power of the PKK. You must tell no one.'

Izmet looked doubtful. Surely the boy could know nothing that mattered.

'If it's so secret, perhaps you should keep it to yourself.'

'But if I do, you won't understand why Nazar was so cautious.'

He unclenched his fists and pressed the palms together in a plea.

'Nazar is a great leader. I want you to understand that, and not to think badly of him.'

Izmet shrugged, suspecting a deception. But in Salim's dark eyes he saw no sign of guile, only fear.

'Well, tell me then,' he said casually.

Salim hesitated for a full minute. Then, in a voice so low as to be almost inaudible, he told Izmet a story that made the skin crawl on the back of his neck. It was the most terrifying piece of news he had ever uncovered.

When Salim had finished, Izmet stared in disbelief.

'You must promise to say nothing. I only wanted you to understand,' Salim stammered.

Izmet shook his head, speechless. If what the boy had said was true, then the world had to know. Immediately.

Could it be fantasy? Impossible. What Salim had revealed involved concepts and detail which must have been way outside his normal experience.

'You'll never repeat this? You swear?'

There was terror on the boy's face by now, the realisation that he'd said too much.

Izmet paid the bill and they went out to the car, Salim refusing to drive until the journalist had assured him he would not report what he had said.

Izmet Ozkan had returned to the shabby little hotel close to the Dağ Gate, a gap in the massive city walls through which buses pass on their way to Ankara and Istanbul.

He'd need corroboration, information from another source. Something that would confirm this wasn't some desperate invention.

Balancing his typewriter on his knees – the room had no table – he'd struggled to write up his interview with Nazar. But the words wouldn't come. There was only one interview that mattered – the one he'd promised Salim he wouldn't repeat.

For most of the night he'd lain awake, agonising over Salim's truthfulness. The boy had not struck him as a liar. Twenty years of listening to people had given him a certain judgement.

The more he thought, the more he knew the story had to be told. Countless thousands of lives could be at stake. But first it had to be checked.

Eventually he fell asleep, but not before he'd decided to find Salim again and cross-examine him a second time.

In the morning, after a quick breakfast of bread, cheese and black olives washed down with tea, he'd walked down Gazi Caddesi where the stall-holders were setting up their barrows of fresh vegetables, past the seventh-century Ulu Cami mosque, and turned left into the alleyway where he'd met Salim the day before.

The grocery shop was closed. Odd, thought Izmet. It wasn't a public holiday. All the other shops around were open. Suddenly he felt the hair prickle on the back of his neck. From behind the windows of the bakery opposite, eyes stared at him with stony hostility.

Alarmed, he rattled at the glass-panelled door of the grocery, peering into the darkened interior for signs of life. A boy, not more than twelve years of age, emerged from a room at the back. He shook his head and waved both hands to indicate they were closed.

'I must speak to Salim!' Izmet mouthed. The boy shook his head again and wiped his nose with the back of his hand.

Izmet repeated his message, louder this time. Another face appeared from the back, an older youth. Izmet recognised him as the one who'd served the tomatoes the day before.

He waved him away, but Izmet shook his head. Then the youth gestured with a finger to a side-alley. Izmet walked round. Behind the shop was a low house, built of earth and stone. The door was open. Izmet took his shoes off at the entrance.

The youth, probably a brother of Salim, blocked his path.

'Why are you here?' he demanded, eyes smouldering with hate.

'To see Salim. I must talk with him.'

The boy looked about to strike him.

'Is he here?'

'Yes.'

'Well, then . . .'

Izmet felt himself trembling at the menace in the air. He began to back away. Then, suddenly, the youth began to sob.

'He's dead. Salim's dead!'

Tears streamed down his sallow cheeks as he turned and beckoned.

Heart pounding, Izmet stumbled after him towards the bedroom where all the children would have slept. In the doorway he gasped and clutched at the frame for support. There, in the middle of a large bed, lay Salim, waxen hands crossed on his heart. From somewhere else in the house he heard women wailing.

On the floor a middle-aged man sat cross-legged, his chin slumped on his chest. As Izmet entered, he looked up and gestured forlornly towards the bed.

Izmet felt his knees give way. Someone pushed a chair towards him.

Salim's eyes were closed. A black and white keffiye around his neck was stained the colour of rust. His lips were swollen, blackened and caked with dried blood.

'What happened?' Izmet whispered.

'They killed him.'

'Who. . . ?'

'We were all asleep. They came in, shouting. Called Salim an informer.'

The boy's voice was flat, monotonous.

'They pulled him from the bed, onto that chair.'

He indicated the one on which Izmet was seated.

'Tied his hands behind. One man held his head . . . like this.'

He demonstrated – one hand pressed against his own forehead, the other gripped his chin, wrenching his mouth open wide.

'Then the other man used his dagger. Cut out his tongue.'

Izmet's stomach clenched into a ball. Hands clasped over his mouth, he staggered outside and vomited in the corner of the dusty yard.

He supported himself against the wall of the house to steady his spinning head. Salim's brother had followed him to the doorway, and held out his shoes to him.

'After, they cut his throat.'

Izmet shuddered.

'They spoke Kurdish, the men who did this?' he asked weakly.

'They spoke our language,' the boy answered bitterly.

So it wasn't the police or military. They'd have spoken Turkish.

'Did they say anything else?'

'They asked about you.'

'About me?' he gasped.

'Asked where you were. Salim said he didn't know.'

Izmet slipped the shoes on and dabbed at his mouth with a handkerchief.

'Go with care, my friend.'

The boy turned back inside the house.

The journalist stepped shakily into the street, then hurried past a handful of children playing football with a Coke can.

They were looking for him! The men who'd murdered Salim – they'd want to silence him too!

He pictured Salim in the *lokanta* the previous evening. The excitement on his face – he'd known of the danger all right. Yet the desire to impress had been so strong. Someone must have overheard. Just one crucial word would have been enough.

Izmet turned right at a junction, walking fast along the narrow street. He had no idea of direction, but he had to get away from that house. He sucked the cool March air deep into his lungs, to clear his head.

They'd killed Salim, because of what he'd said. So that meant that the story he'd told *had* to be true. Ozkan had the corroboration he needed. There'd be no reason for this monstrous crime if Salim's story had been a lie.

Guilt began to flood his thoughts. If it weren't for him, Salim would still be alive.

He came to the end of the street where the ancient walls, five metres thick and twelve metres high, towered above him. Ahead, through a gateway, a path dropped away sharply towards the river, fringed by blood-red patches – poppies sown by the wind.

He walked through the arch and stopped. Far below, the Tigris curled round the base of the rocky mound on which the city was built. The pale brown swirl of water flooded across the fertile silt of the valley. Beyond, the land rose, bright green with the new growth of rice and wheat. On a plateau in the distance, Izmet could see the concrete towers of the new university at which Salim had been a student.

He felt acutely vulnerable; a Turk in a Kurdish town, a wanted man. Nervously, he looked back through the arch. There was still no sign of him being followed. But his luck wouldn't hold for long. He tried to think where he was, which way would bring him back to his hotel.

He passed back through the walls and turned west, guided by the sun, which shone brightly but with little warmth. Within minutes he'd regained the Gazi Caddesi, and hailed a taxi.

'First, I need a telephone,' he told the driver. 'Do you know one that works?'

The driver shrugged and suggested the PTT a few minutes away.

There was a queue. Izmet took his turn, standing with his back to the road. He dialled the hotel where he'd been staying. The number rang interminably. When it answered, he recognised the voice of the manager.

'Hello. It's Mr Ozkan here from room twenty-two. I'm expecting some messages. Has anyone tried to contact me?'

'No messages.'

He relaxed momentarily.

'But there was someone here. Just after you went out.'

Izmet breathed in sharply.

'Did they say who?'

'I told you, no message. But I think he's waiting. I saw him walk past. Do you want me to go outside and look?'

'No! No, thank you. Just – just say that I'll be back around midday. If he comes in and asks.'

'Very well.'

Panic gripped him.

He replaced the receiver and put out his hands to steady himself against the sides of the cubicle. He knew he had to move, yet he couldn't.

An elderly man tapped sharply on the glass. The queue was growing.

'I'm sorry . . .' Izmet mumbled. He was an obvious stranger here, dressed in a light European raincoat. Many of those who jostled past him wore the *salvar*, the baggy trousers of the Kurds.

So they were waiting to kill him. He thought of his wife and children in their apartment on the banks of the Bosphorus. How would they survive without him? For a moment, that worried him more than the thought of death itself.

Escape. He had to keep ahead of them. He could do it if he thought hard. One thing was certain; he couldn't return to the hotel.

He patted his jacket pockets and felt the comforting bulk of his wallet and air ticket. The flight wasn't until midday, but he'd go straight there. Never mind his luggage and typewriter.

He climbed back into the taxi and sank low into the rear seat.

'To the airport, please.'

The flight was called at last. He stood up and pressed towards the door to the tarmac, trying to be first on board, so he could hide behind his newspaper at the back of the plane. He'd been lucky it was Thursday, one of only two days in the week when there was a direct flight to Istanbul.

Only when the DC-9 began taxiing for take-off, did he

risk lowering his paper. As the whine of the engines rose to a crescendo he looked along the aisle. He'd beaten them.

Feeling the reassuring shove in his back from the turbines, Izmet closed his eyes and tried to calm his racing brain.

But any relief at escaping from Diyarbakir evaporated immediately. This was only round one. The secret in his head was so precious to the men who'd murdered Salim, they'd surely stop at nothing to murder him too.

His instinct was to get the story into print. Once it was public knowledge, it would be too late to silence him.

But would the Kurds give up the chase when the secret was out? Maybe not, if Salim's death was anything to go by. Retribution, that's what they were after.

He began to panic again. The police. He'd need to tell the authorities, to be given protection twenty-four hours a day. He wouldn't be the first journalist to live with a police escort for himself and his family. These were troubled times again in Turkey.

But there was a much, much bigger issue at stake than the kudos of a scoop. An outrageous act of war was being planned, with unimaginable consequences for the Middle East and perhaps the entire planet.

The world had to be warned, and he was the only person alive who could do it.

He asked the steward for some paper, and began to write.

Six

Inside the back of the Sea King 'Whisky' it smelled of hot oil. The Royal Navy lieutenant in the observer's seat had an itch in his crotch which was impossible to get at through the thick, rubberised fabric of his survival suit.

The itch was an annoying distraction. It was hard enough to maintain interest in a radar screen almost devoid of 'paints', without having to worry that his genitalia could be infested with crabs. It still needled him that the young lady he'd dated on the last run ashore in Gibraltar had turned out to be quite so widely known.

A small blip crossing the outer range-ring jerked his attention back to the screen. He spun the roller-ball to place the cursor square over it, then punched the key to set 'autotrack'.

Above the screen, repeaters of the cockpit dials told him their spatial position. Altitude – 1500 feet. Radar would have a range of 47 miles at that height. Heading – northeast. Speed – 20 knots. The coordinates of the blip, now identified with a 'U' for unknown, put the boat that it represented about 50 miles southeast of Marbella.

He switched to 'Bravo Scope', which displayed a box on the screen, magnifying the square mile of sea around the target. The 'paint' was moving through the water at 24 knots, according to the computer.

Nippy little number. No more than a thirty-footer probably. Long way from the marina, too. And it was blowing a fair old gale down there. Worth a closer look.

'Got an unknown at thirty-six zero-nine north, zero-four eighteen west. Heading zero-nine-five. I'd like him nearer the middle of my scope,' crackled the observer into his lip microphone.

'Thirty-six zero-nine, zero-four eighteen. Roger,' clipped back the pilot, pleased that the monotony of the patrol was to be broken. The tail lifted and the machine banked as they accelerated northwards.

'Not too close,' reminded the observer.

'You want to drive?'

Fifteen minutes later the observer had a second, larger target on autotrack. He keyed in the profiler. On the edge of the screen a silhouette of the ship appeared. It looked like a small freighter, with the superstructure at the stern.

'Targets converging. Separation one mile.'

'That's nice.'

'Fuel state?'

'Wait.' Then after a moment's calculation, 'Thirty-five per cent. Another twenty minutes on station, then it's back to mother.'

Long enough to tell whether the tracks on the screen would become significant. The drug runners transported their merchandise in freighters, then transferred it to fast launches to be smuggled ashore. That's what the Spanish coastguards had told them, anyway. They'd yet to see it happen.

The helicopter shuddered, buffeted by the gusts of the levanter. Just beyond the side door the Searchwater radar antenna spun relentlessly, concealed inside its inflated rubber dome, known as the 'bag'.

'I do believe they're going to say hello,' the observer remarked, suddenly coming alive. Something was happening at last. On the glowing screen the two paints merged. They would have diverged again, maintaining their tracks if they'd just passed on the high seas. But the blips held like raindrops blown together on a window pane.

105

'Seven Lima Charley, this is Whisky Three.'

'Whisky Three, go,' replied the air controller on HMS *Eagle*.

'We have "cough drop" at thirty-six, zero-nine, zero-four, twenty-two. Observing. Over.'

Who thought up these code words?

'Whisky Three, acknowledged.'

No more needed to be said. No unnecessary words for the drug runners to intercept, if they were listening. On HMS *Eagle* they'd be waiting for the next signal, the one telling them the contacts had separated again, with one boat heading for the coast. They'd have the next radar-carrying Sea King airborne by now, knowing that this one was short of fuel.

The observer watched his screen. Watched the steady paint made by the two boats locked together. It was like waiting for lovers to finish and pull apart.

Thirty miles away, HMS *Eagle* lurched and rolled uncomfortably in the swell, the levanter beating against the high sides of her hull.

Peter Brodrick was lunching in the wardroom when he heard the pipe summoning the marine boarding party to the briefing room. He abandoned the remains of his salad, pushed through the curtains that served as a door, and took the steep steps of the companionway at a run. Three decks up, he wound his way through the narrow passages of the officer accommodation to reach his own cabin.

After more than two months at sea the sickening movement of the ship no longer bothered him. Boredom was the problem, the tedium of patrols and boardings of small boats that had not produced so much as a whiff of drugs so far.

They were now into their third month of steaming the big carrier back and forth through the Strait of

Gibraltar. Ten days or so in the eastern Atlantic, then a week in the Mediterranean, but so far the smugglers of cocaine from South America and of hashish from North Africa had eluded them.

With his immersion suit over one arm and gripping his green beret and pistol belt tightly, he hurried down the long walkway that ran the full length of the ship on Two Deck. The shiny grey, non-slip paint squeaked beneath the rubber soles of his boots.

Coming towards him, he spotted the ship's Principal Warfare Officer, Lt-Commander Nick Brady, recognisable from afar by his diminutive stature and by the look of anxiety permanently etched on his face.

'This the big one, then?' Brady teased.

'They're all big ones, Nick, until afterwards!'

The failure to find any drug runners had become a bitter standing joke between them.

'The old man thinks this one's real. He's fairly having himself up there.' Brady nodded towards the stairs that led to the bridge.

'Doesn't take much to turn *him* on!'

Brady snorted and hurried on his way.

Brodrick swung left into the Number Two Briefing Room. The helicopter crew were already there, zipping up their immersion suits.

'Glad you could make it,' murmured one of the pilots sarcastically.

'Right, gentlemen. Perhaps we could make a start. Time check.'

The briefing officer held up his watch and counted down the seconds.

There were five rows of padded benches, covered in green plastic. Peter sat one from the front. In front of him were the Commander Air, Percy Bradshaw, and Pepe Alvarez, the liaison officer from the Spanish Customs Authority.

'We've a reported cough-drop at thirty-six, zero-nine north, zero-four, eighteen west.'

The briefer indicated the position on the wall chart with a telescopic pointer.

'A Sea King Whisky on bandit patrol tracked a thirty-foot launch from the direction of Marbella, which made a rendezvous with a small freighter at the position indicated. The vessels were co-positioned for fifteen minutes, and the launch is now heading back towards Spain. A second Sea King W left the deck twenty minutes ago – the first is returning because of low fuel state. The replacement aircraft has already located the target and is tracking.

'Aduanas have been informed, but say they have no craft available to intercept and have asked *Eagle* to do the job. One Junglie will take off in fifteen minutes, at twelve forty-seven. Captain Brodrick with a brick of four marines, will support Teniente Alvarez in boarding the vessel. The W will guide you to the intercept position. Now the met brief.'

He handed over to the ship's meteorologist who told them visibility was clear but winds were gusting force six. Not the best weather for a boarding, Brodrick thought.

There were few questions. They'd all been through this countless times before.

'Okay, Pepe?'

Brodrick was never certain how much of the jargon at the briefings the Spanish customs officer took in.

'Sure.'

Brodrick noted the look of strain on the Spaniard's face. Pepe did not enjoy being lowered from helicopters at the end of a rope.

'This time we'll catch you a bandit, I promise,' Brodrick reassured him.

'I hope.'

They struggled into their rubber suits, then climbed

108

the companionway to the flight deck, to join the four marines who made up the boarding party.

'All set, Corporal Rees? Did you get any lunch?' Brodrick asked.

'Missed it, sir. But no matter. I'd have lost it anyway, flying about in this shitty weather. What is it this time?'

'Thirty-footer. Ready for it?'

'Your men will follow you anywhere, sir,' the Welshman replied with a grin. 'Even if only out of curiosity!'

The steel door was blown open by the wind the moment the clips were undone. A squally rain shower swept across the deck. The men leaned into the gale, and groped their way to where the Sea King waited, anchored to the deck with webbing.

The loadmaster pointed at the seats the six men should take, bare canvas stretched over an aluminium frame. The wind noise was so high that speaking was difficult.

Brodrick had found the Spanish customs officer easy to work with, once he'd got used to his manner. If he had a sense of humour, Pepe Alvarez was quite unable to communicate it in the English language. On board the British aircraft carrier he saw himself as a lone ambassador for the Spanish state. The burden of that responsibility weighed so heavily on his shoulders, that he found it difficult to relax enough to take part in the regular tomfoolery of the wardroom.

It left him an isolated figure, but Brodrick found him honest and straightforward, and an enthusiastic supporter of the efforts the British were making to catch drug-runners.

Gibraltar however was not a subject to be mentioned in his presence. Whenever the ship was due to put into the Rock to give the sailors a weekend ashore, Teniente Alvarez would be picked up from the carrier by a Spanish customs cutter on the high seas, and would not return until *Eagle* had resumed her patrol, well clear of Gibraltar's waters.

They tightened the straps over their thighs as the engines lit up with a roar. Brodrick and the Spaniard stuffed plugs into their ears, but the marines seemed unworried by the threat of deafness. The pilot released the brake on the rotors, and the machine swayed and shook as the blades gathered speed.

Brodrick looked at his watch. Twelve forty-five. Two minutes to lift off. It could take them half an hour to reach their target, depending on how fast the powerboat was travelling, and how far north it was heading.

He adjusted the pistol belt which he wore over the immersion suit, undid the flap of the canvas holster and pulled out the Browning 9mm. He checked that the magazine contained its full eleven rounds, and that the safety catch was on.

He glanced across at his squad, armed with light-weight SA80 assault rifles. They were a good humoured bunch, thank God. It had been hard enough for him to come to terms with this posting; if he'd been saddled with whingers it would have been a lot worse.

The Sea King had been airborne for twenty-five minutes when the pilot caught sight of the target. Slightly larger than expected – a forty-footer, the pilot guessed – the motor cruiser was carving an uncomfortable path through the white-crested waves.

He spoke on the intercom to his crewman in the back, and within a minute, Teniente Alvarez had squeezed himself into the gap between the two pilots and was pulling on a talking headset.

'Down there to the left, see?' the pilot pointed. 'He's doing a good fifteen knots.'

'You want I try call him?'

'In a minute. I'm going to circle low so that he knows

we're here. Then you can try to raise him on channel sixteen.'

'I wait, yes?'

'The Spaniard had only half understood.

The pilot nodded, then dived the helicopter to a point one hundred yards ahead of the powerboat and fifty feet above the water.

In the back, Brodrick strained to see the target through one of the small windows as the machine banked in front of it. They all looked alike, these boats; curvaceous plastic, with a high-flying bridge for use in better weather than this. The cabin had a long, flat roof, big enough for them to drop onto.

In the cockpit Pepe Alvarez was getting no response, calling on the radio in Spanish. He tried two other channels with the same result.

'We'll give him a burst in English, Pepe.'

The pilot flew another circuit while the navigator talked on the radio. No response.

'Not switched on, or pretending not to be,' the pilot concluded. 'I'll fly on his port beam. You'll have to wave at him, Pepe.'

Teniente Alvarez signalled his understanding with a thumbs-up. He turned back into the cabin of the Sea King and clipped on the dispatcher harness that would keep him safe when the door was opened. On his head, the gold-braided cap of the Spanish Aduanas, held in place by the talking headset.

The door slid aside and the cold down-draught from the rotor blustered through the opening. The helicopter was close to the wave tops, the motor cruiser right beside them, slicing through the water not more than twenty yards away. A wooden board bearing the name *Medina* was fixed to the side of the cabin.

Brodrick remained strapped in, directly facing the opening. He could see the powerboat helmsman looking up at them uneasily. He watched Pepe's rigid back as he

111

edged towards the void and grabbed the hand rail at the side of the doorway. Brodrick knew this was the part that terrified the Spaniard most.

Alvarez sat down on the floor, legs dangling over the edge. With his free right hand he gestured up and down, indicating the boat should reduce speed. He pointed to the badge on his cap to show he was a customs officer; the rest of his uniform was concealed by his immersion suit.

Brodrick saw the helmsman shrug and look away, concentrating on the heavy sea ahead. He appeared to be studiously ignoring them.

'He not respond,' Alvarez told the pilot on the intercom. 'But he have to stop.'

'He will. Don't worry.'

The helicopter's tail lifted and the machine accelerated forwards. Fifty metres in front of the cruiser, the pilot banked his machine across its path. He held it there for a second, then flew sideways, holding the Sea King directly in front of the boat, and only just above it.

Brodrick watched the man on the bridge swing the wheel wildly. But whichever way he turned, the helicopter could move faster.

Teniente Alvarez pointed aggressively at the helmsman, and gestured again for him to stop. He tapped his headset, hoping the boatman would switch on his radio.

'Put me on channel sixteen. I try again.'

'Switching now.'

'¡Crucero Medina! ¡Crucero Medina! Aquí el helicoptero por su serviola. Soy un aduanero español. Le ordeno que pare su motor para poder bordarle. Afirme, por favor.'

Pepe repeated the message, identifying himself and ordering the boat to stop. Through the spray-spattered windscreen, Brodrick saw the helmsman reach to his right, then hold a telephone handset to his ear.

'Helicoptero Ingles. Helicoptero Ingles. Aquí el

crucero Medina. Cambie al canal ocho por favor. Afirme.'

Pepe flicked the transmit switch to the intercom position.

'Go to channel eight, please,' he told the pilot.

'Channel eight.'

A heated discussion followed, with Pepe pointing angrily at the boat with his spare hand. Then Brodrick saw the cruiser's bow drop lower in the water as the helmsman shut off power.

'This man . . . arse'ole,' the Spaniard growled into the intercom. He'd learned some new words since joining HMS *Eagle*. 'He stopping now. We can go.'

Watching carefully from his right-hand seat, the pilot eased the Sea King gently to the right, until he placed the rear door directly over the pitching deck of the cruiser.

The crewman in the rear signalled the marines to be ready, then he shackled a rope onto the winch arm, and dropped the other end over the side.

Brodrick was the first to abseil down. His feet hit the cruiser's roof as it rose up to meet him. He stumbled clear, reaching for a hand grip. A quick look round. The helmsman had been joined on the bridge by a crewman, who stared with alarm as four more marines with guns slung across their backs slid down from the helicopter.

The abseil rope was hauled back up, and within seconds Teniente Alvarez, who'd declined to learn how to use it, was lowered to the deck in the winch harness.

Brodrick and his men spread along the deck to secure it, but kept out of the wheelhouse, despite the helmsman's surly gesture that they should enter.

The boat lurched and rolled uncomfortably in the swell, now the power was off. It was a workaday craft, not the newest nor the most luxuriously appointed that Brodrick and his men had dropped onto in recent weeks. In some the carpets were ankle deep, the interiors glittering with chrome and gold and mirrors. Floating booze cabinets, the marines called them. But this boat had a slightly grubby, used look about it and smelled of diesel and salt.

At this stage there was nothing for the marines to do but watch. Until Pepe Alvarez had completed his initial questioning of the skipper and his examination of the boat's papers, the search for drugs couldn't begin. The Spanish customs officer was a stickler for the correct procedure – everything by the book. Brodrick's instinct was to dive below and take the boat apart before anybody had a chance to flush the drugs down the head.

The helmsman who appeared to be the skipper but not the owner of the boat, shrugged his shoulders a lot, and shook his head, trying his best to look blameless. But even the totally innocent tended to assume an air of guilt when raided by a boarding party from a helicopter, Brodrick had noticed.

Finally Pepe turned to him.

'He say just two crew, one passenger below. Sick.' Pepe clutched his stomach in illustration.

'Not surprising in this swell. Did you ask him about the freighter?'

'Of course. He say this man hired him to make visit to the freighter. To see his friend.'

'Oh yeah? We going to search this thing then?'

'Sure.'

He took the skipper by the arm and beckoned Brodrick to follow. They started in the bows and went through cabin by cabin, lifting bilge covers and tapping the panelling for concealed spaces. There was a limit to what the law allowed them to do; to search the boat properly they'd have to tear it apart, but without some clear prior evidence that the boat carried drugs, they weren't allowed to do it.

There were two heads on board; there was no way of knowing for sure if they'd been recently flushed. Chances were that if drugs had been on board, they'd be at the bottom of the sea by now. That's what annoyed Brodrick most; catching the smugglers by surprise was almost impossible, the way they operated.

They entered a small cabin with a single bunk and a locker beneath it. On the floor was a 'Puma' sportsbag. A man lay on the bunk, apparently asleep, face towards the side of the hull. The cabin had a curious smell of flowers.

'Señor. ¿Permite?'

Teniente Alvarez touched the man on the arm and pointed to the holdall on the floor.

'We want to look in the bag, chum,' Brodrick added in case the man spoke English.

'The bugger's seasick,' commented Corporal Rees.

The body on the bed stirred and waved a hand at them.

'Take that as a "yes",' Brodrick decided.

The corporal crouched down and tugged open the zip on the holdall. He pulled out the contents with care and spread them on the floor; two shirts, some underwear, washing and shaving kit, and a half-empty bottle of whisky.

'No wonder he's sick if he's drunk all that,' Rees muttered. He probed the bottom of the bag, holding it underneath to test the thickness for a hidden compartment. From one of the end pockets he pulled out a passport.

'Spanish.'

He passed it to Teniente Alvarez.

'Clean, sir,' Rees concluded, neatly replacing the contents of the bag. 'What about him?' he nodded at the man on the bunk, who had not stirred.

Peter looked at the Spanish officer for guidance. Pepe snapped the passport shut and returned it to the corporal to put back in the holdall.

'Is okay.'

'May I see?' Peter reached out his hand. Rees gave it to him.

The cabin was dimly lit. Just a bulkhead light over the bunk.

'Levantese por favor, Señor. Tenemos que examinarle.'

The Aduanero had leaned over the prostrate figure to tell him he was to be searched.

Peter opened the passport and shone his waterproof torch onto the description page. Youssef Boukari was the name given to the photograph next to it, a dark print lacking in contrast or detail, produced cheaply in a photo-booth.

'Doesn't sound Spanish,' Brodrick muttered.

'Señor!'

Pepe Alvarez shook the man roughly by the shoulder to wake him. 'Boukari' turned his head and lifted himself onto an elbow.

'¡Que tenemos que examinarle!'

There was no response to the request to be searched. In the glow from the bulkhead lamp, the man looked grey, genuinely unwell.

Peter stared at him, and felt a tremble through his body.

That smell – rosewater.

The man's profile, the shape of his head. Oh, God! Peter grabbed at a bulkhead.

The crackle of gunfire in his head. The house on the hill overlooking Beirut. Singer's brains erupting from his skull.

'Sir? You okay?' The voice of Corporal Rees. Here and now.

A flashback. It had happened a couple of times. The medics had warned him it might.

Brodrick took a deep breath and forced the panic down.

'Bit queasy for a moment,' he mumbled. 'Fine now.'

Boukari. Thin strands of dark hair greased back over a bald patch. A pudgy face with a chin like a lump of dough. Just as repulsive as when he'd been tied to a chair.

Pepe's instruction in Spanish for the man to stand up met with a stare of incomprehension.

'Doesn't understand,' Brodrick stated.

Of course he bloody doesn't. That Spanish passport's a sodding forgery!

The mouth. Lips parted as if about to speak. Lips that had spilled such lies, such damned convincing, murderous lies!

Boukari? Bizri! Ahmed Bizri. That was his name last time they'd met.

'We're going to search you, Boukari,' Brodrick snarled. 'On your feet!'

The man's eyes flickered. English he understood. And at the sound of Brodrick's voice, he frowned. A muscle twitched in his cheek. The Arab had hardly ever seen Brodrick's face, they'd kept him blindfolded when they'd interrogated him in Lebanon. But he recognised the voice . . .

Brodrick's heart was pounding. Instinctively, he unfastened the flap to his pistol holster. He pulled the weapon free and slipped the safety. Corporal Rees moved fast to place himself between his Captain and the seasick passenger. Something was happening here that he didn't understand. But he knew danger when he saw it.

Boukari swung his legs over the edge of the bunk and clutched at his stomach as the boat rolled in the swell. Brodrick could see him clearly now. Oh yes! No doubt whatsoever. Ahmed Bizri, chief-of-staff to Beirut gang-leader Abdul Habib. The man whose cunning had caused the death of a dozen good men.

Brodrick felt the gun rise to his eyeline. One shot to the head, one to the heart. Who'd weep? The bastard deserved to die.

Rees turned, his look defiant and dangerous, his SA-

80 pointing at Brodrick's heart. This wasn't Beirut. There were laws to be obeyed.

'¿Hablan espanol?' The voice of Pepe Alvarez. He'd taken back the passport and was waving it at its owner.

'You speak Espanish, or no?'

'No,' Bizri replied in English. 'My wife – I have Spanish papers because my wife is from Sevilla.'

'Where are you from?'

'Algerie.'

Oh no, you're not, Brodrick mouthed silently. The urge to confront Bizri was like a bomb ticking inside him. But he held back. Rees was right. Think! Think with your head, not your guts! What's Bizri doing here? That's what matters.

Questions raced through his mind. Bizri stared at him with icy loathing. His voice had given him away, Brodrick knew that now.

Corporal Rees steadied the Arab on his feet, while Alvarez frisked him. Not much in his pockets, a few coins and some amber worry beads. Bizri submitted passively to the search, but kept his eyes locked on Brodrick's.

Why was he here with a false name and a false passport? The skipper of the boat said they'd taken him out to meet a friend on the freighter, but he was lying. The *Medina* had just picked Bizri up from the ship and was slipping him into Spain through the back door. But why?

They completed their search, and Bizri sank back onto the bed again, threatening to be sick. Brodrick beckoned to the Aduanero to follow him up onto the deck.

'Pepe! That man. I know him,' he whispered, out of earshot of the bridge. 'He's a Lebanese terrorist called Ahmed Bizri. Responsible for kidnapping a British businessman last year.'

'Ki'nap?'

'Took prisoner . . . Last year. You remember?'

'Ah . . . Aaah!' He raised a finger as he remembered the incident in which Brodrick had been involved. 'You quite sure?'

'Of course I'm bloody sure! Not exactly a face I'd forget. Now, look. What's to stop us grabbing him right away? We can take him back to the *Eagle* and put him through the wringer . . .'

Alvarez shook his head. They were outside territorial waters.

'No. Is impossible. The law . . .'

'Sod the law! This man is dangerous! Your government should be dead worried. What's he doing in Spain? Ask yourself that.'

Pepe's small, dark eyes had concentrated hard on Brodrick's words, but now they seemed to lose their focus. Teniente Alvarez was interested in smuggling, and how to stop it. International terrorism was another issue altogether, not his responsibility

'We signal the Guardia Civil from *Eagle*. They can question him when he comes ashore.'

'If we don't hang onto this guy right now, you'll never see him again until it's too sodding late. Your Guardia'll never find him.'

Pepe flinched at the insult to his national police force.

Steady, Brodrick thought. Don't alienate the blighter!

'No one'll find him. The Brits, the Spanish, nobody. I know the man. He's clever.'

'Yes, yes. I understan'. But here I can do nothing . . .'

His voice was drowned by the heavy beat of the Sea King as it passed low over the boat looking for a signal from Brodrick.

He wavered. Every sinew of his body told him that Bizri had to be held. The man on the bunk below had broken his life, and humiliated the Corps. Grab him or kill him; those were the choices, and bugger the consequences.

But he held back. 'Never underestimate the sensitivity

119

of this joint operation with the Spanish' he'd been told when he joined HMS *Eagle*. One order must always be obeyed: do nothing outside the law, nothing to upset the Aduanas.

He played his last card.

'Why don't you and I stay on board this tub, until she gets alongside?' Brodrick pleaded. 'Then we can hand him over to the Guardia.'

Alvarez's Andalusian eyes had become hard and stubborn. The harder Brodrick pressed, the stronger would be his resistance.

'We are in international waters!' he spelled out, emphasising the words with a finger pointing out to sea. 'Under emergency regulations we have the right to board a boat and search for drugs. We find nothing – we have to say sorry, thank you and go.'

'But this is a Lebanese terrorist with a false Spanish passport!'

'How you know? Maybe he has wife in Sevilla. I will ask the Guardia to check it.'

'He hasn't got a Spanish wife any more than the Pope has!' Brodrick growled in frustration. Then he had an idea.

'It'd be different if we were *inside* territorial waters, right? So let's motor a bit. Half an hour and you could arrest him and bring him ashore because of a dodgy passport.'

'But we are outside . . .'

Pepe's stubbornness had become mule-like. Brodrick stared up at the Sea King. Rees and the marines had joined them on deck.

'Okay,' Brodrick conceded eventually. 'Back in the paraffin parrot. Maybe the Whisky can track this boat to the coast.'

'Five minutes. I have my paperwork.'

Pepe returned to the bridge and began copying details

from the *Medina*'s registration documents. He also took notes from 'Boukari's' passport.

Brodrick called the helicopter on a hand-held VHF set. They could begin winching up the boarding party. He and Alvarez would be the last to leave.

The Sea King hovered over the foredeck, whipping the sea into a circular frenzy of spray. The winchman lowered the harness and the first of the marines was lifted up into the machine.

The noise of the rotors made further radio contact impossible. He was desperate to know if the radar-carrying Sea King was still around, but it would have to wait.

Pepe was finished at last. Brodrick helped him secure the harness round his chest and steadied his legs as he was winched into the helicopter. Then he put his own arms through the strop and gave a thumbs up to the winchman. As he was lifted from the deck, he saw an extra figure appear on the bridge of the Medina. Ahmed Bizri watched him being pulled inside the aircraft.

'Any sign of the "bag"?' Brodrick demanded as soon as he'd pulled on a headset. 'I want that boat tracked all the way home.'

'The AEW's gone sick,' the pilot replied. 'Hydraulics.'

'And the other one? Is that still on the deck?'

'And staying there. That's gone U/S too.'

'I don't believe it!'

Brodrick crouched at the back of the cockpit. Over the pilot's shoulder he could see Bizri's face at the bridge window as they circled the boat.

'Back to mother?'

'Not yet. Want to see where he goes.'

'Fuel's low. Five more minutes at the most.'

Brodrick cursed his luck. The situation was slipping beyond his control. Ahmed Bizri was set to cheat him again.

He glanced round at Pepe Alvarez, strapping himself in. A slim chance. If they got back fast the Aduanero's radio message to his headquarters might just be in time. Maybe the Guardia could do something.

'Okay. Back to mother. Balls out!'

Seven

Jackie closed the lid on her portable word-processor and carried it into the hall of the consulate, ready to be loaded into the van for the airport. It was late afternoon and the Minister had promised there'd be no more work.

It had been a long week; two days of meetings with the Turkish Trade and Foreign Ministers in Ankara and two days of 'cultural relations' in Istanbul – in other words, tourism. As a smokescreen for his sightseeing, George Webster had insisted on dictating more memos than usual.

The RAF VC-10 was scheduled to take off at seven. Time for Jackie to get back to the hotel, have a quick clean-up and pack her bag.

She bade farewell to the young cultural attaché who'd been so helpful and attentive during the visit, and started down the grand, marble staircase of the nineteenth century palace which housed the consulate.

'Jackie! Wait.' The voice belonged to Ann Elliott, the other half of the Minister's secretarial and typing team. 'Are you going to the hotel?'

'Yes. Come on, we'll go together.'

Ann's heels clattered on the polished stone as she hurried to catch up.

'I hate walking on my own in this town,' she confided. 'It's the way the men look at you. Sort of bestial. Like cattle.'

'Stick with me, dear! I'll look after you.'

123

'Thank you, Jackie. You're so strong!'

Ann gave a little snort as she laughed.

At the foot of the stairs Jackie turned her head and saw the cultural attaché looking down at them.

' 'Bye,' she called, and waved.

The two women stepped outside into the raw Istanbul air. The sulphurous pollution from countless coal fires burned their nostrils.

'Do I get the impression you had something going with that young man?' Ann needled.

'Mmm. Wouldn't mind. But he was awfully married. Wedding ring, snaps of babies on his desk. Not my scene.'

At the gate-lodge they weaved round the black and yellow barrier pole and turned for a last look at the enormous Anglo-Italian palazzo, built as an embassy when Istanbul was still the Turkish capital. A piece of Pall Mall dropped into an oriental city.

They linked arms, nodded at the heavily armed policemen guarding the entrance and set off for the hotel.

'Those awful machine-guns. Terrifying!' Ann whispered. 'Talking of guns, how's that soldier of yours? Or aren't you together any more?'

Jackie bristled. Ann could be irritatingly nosey.

'Oh, he's still around, swinging from tree to tree. He's away at the moment. Can't tell you where, though. State secret!'

The truth was she'd hardly heard from him since Christmas. Almost three months, and she'd received just three letters. She'd been hurt by his lack of communication, but would never admit it. Particularly not to Ann Elliott.

The intensity of her relationship with Peter during that month before Christmas had changed things irrevocably, for her at least. Before, their affair had been almost casual; he'd turn up in London and if she wasn't

124

busy, he'd stay for a night or two. No commitment had been made.

After Lebanon it had been different. For the first time she felt that he really needed her. They'd fought their way through his depressions and nightmares together. When he left her on Boxing Day to return to his barracks, her home and her heart had felt empty. She, she'd realised, needed *him* most of all.

His letters had talked of the boredom of the drug patrols, but she'd sensed his happiness at being back in a macho environment. They weren't love letters – he wasn't the type. But the way he put things was personal. Their intimacy was implied. She just wished there'd been more of them.

It was less than five minutes' walk to the Pera Palace hotel. The pavements were narrow, with loose slabs and potholes everywhere, ready to twist the ankles of the unwary. Mostly men on the streets, dark coats over dark trousers, dark hair flattened at the back of the head in a way that is curiously Turkish.

'I'll be so glad to leave here,' Ann declared. '*Look* at it!'

She waved dismissively at the cars and buses jamming the street.

'The grime! Even the people look covered with it. They need a good dusting! The place is choking to death. And the noise . . .'

'But the mosques are stunning,' Jackie insisted. 'And the ferries on the Golden Horn. Don't you think?'

'Well . . . yes. But I can't wait to get home.'

'Not long now. Then you'll be back in your own little bed,' Jackie said.

They reached the hotel, built in the nineteenth century to provide comfort for the intrepid travellers on the Orient Express. Today, with its high ceilings and ornate plasterwork, it was doing good business from nostalgia.

'I wonder if there's any hot water,' Ann queried. 'I need a shower.'

'Must be some. It's got five stars, this place. Meet you down here in an hour, then?'

Ann looked at her watch.

'Sounds about right.'

Izmet Ozkan gripped the armrest as the DC9 bounced twice before settling onto the runway at Istanbul's Yesilkoy airport. In the inside pocket of his jacket he felt the pressure of the envelope which he'd just sealed.

His pulse was racing again. He'd been safe during that flight from Diyarbakir, but now? Would they be here, waiting for him?

How long was the arm of the PKK? Did it reach to Istanbul? Of course it did – they'd car-bombed a block of government offices just a few months back. But had they guessed he'd taken this flight? Probably. Time enough to have alerted their friends in Istanbul?

In the bus to the terminal he stood in the middle, crushed on all sides by fellow passengers, concealed by their bulk.

In the terminal the crowd dispersed, heading for the carousels and the luggage. Nothing for him to collect. He was without so much as a briefcase. There was nowhere to hide now.

ÇIKIŞ.

The exit sign stared at him. Beyond those double doors would be a sea of faces, no way of knowing whether they were friend or foe. But if the Kurds were there, they'd spot him all right. He'd emerge from the hall like a target on a shooting gallery. Bam! Bam! It would be quick, at least.

Two armed policemen stood by the exit doors. He thought to seek their protection but then realised what sort of questions they'd ask.

Kurds? What were you doing in Diyarbakir? Tell us the names of the terrorists you met. And be quick, before we clip these electrodes to your testicles . . .

No point in waiting any longer. No other way out. He watched for the trickle of passengers to thicken to a stream and, heart pounding, plunged into their midst.

He was through within seconds, swept by the flow past other people's friends and relatives, towards the doors to the taxi-rank. Two men rushing into the terminal jostled but ignored him, then he was out in the foul air of the city.

The taxi queue was mercifully and unusually short. He sank into the back of the yellow Datsun and allowed himself a sigh of relief. He told the driver the address of his office in the Beyazit district close to the University and gave a final glance through the rear window.

Two men running.

The two who'd jostled him in the doorway.

They spotted him, framed by the glass, saw the fear in his eyes.

Izmet was transfixed. He wanted to shout but his voice froze in his throat.

The two men bundled into the back of a grey Mercedes, which swung out of the car park and began weaving in and out of the traffic.

'They're catching us!' Izmet croaked in terror. 'Faster! For the love of Allah!'

The driver's glance in the mirror suggested Izmet was crazy.

'What're you talking about? How can I go faster?'

He gestured at the solid line of cars and trucks heading into Istanbul.

'You must! The car behind . . . you see it? The grey Mercedes?' Izmet leaned forward between the seats. 'They're trying to kill me! If they catch up they'll kill you too.'

Fear spread to the driver like a contagion.

'Are you crazy?'

He looked again in the mirror and saw the Mercedes edging in and out, trying to jump the queue behind.

'You get out,' he shouted. 'I don't want you!'

But there was nowhere to stop, and the cars were bumper to bumper.

'Who are they? Police? What've you done?'

The driver was veering wildly in his panic.

'Not police. Kurdish!'

'Ayee, ayee!' the driver wailed and slapped the dashboard on which was a photo of his children.

Crazy to go to the newspaper office. They'd be waiting there too. The letter he'd written on the plane seemed to burn a hole in his pocket. The letter. At the end of the day it was all that mattered.

He had to get off this road. Maybe with a sudden turn they could lose them in the backstreets?

'Listen . . .' Izmet calmed his voice. 'I've changed my mind. Not Beyazit, but Beyoglu. The American Consulate. You know where?'

The driver shrugged. He was moaning with fear.

'Police! Police.'

'No police. Not here.' Izmet flapped his hand. 'Can you lose that car? D'you know a way?'

There was a turning about five hundred metres away, which would take them round by the Fatih Mosque.

'Maybe.'

Izmet craned his neck. The Mercedes was about six vehicles behind. The men inside were young, their eyes cold and determined.

The street was a main artery into the city, lined at this point with dusty shops selling car spares and electrical goods. To left and right, a maze of alleys stretched beneath a skein of power and telephone cables.

Suddenly the Datsun swerved left in front of a slow moving bus. It braked frantically, throwing forward the

128

passengers standing inside. Car horns blared, shoppers scattered as they accelerated down the side street.

The deeper klaxons of buses and lorries resonated behind them as they escaped. Traffic blocked the way into the turning; the Mercedes couldn't follow. Izmet allowed himself a nervous smile.

'Well done, my friend . . .'

The Datsun turned again, weaving its way deeper into the maze.

They drove for five minutes, the driver silent, Izmet darting frequent glances over his shoulder.

Suddenly the massive domes and minarets of the Mosque of Mehmet the Conqueror came in view, the Fatih Camii. The driver pulled into the kerb with screeching brakes.

'You! Out!'

'But . . .'

The driver reached into the back and levered up the door handle.

'Out! No money. Go, quick!'

'But I must get to Beyoglu! You must take me!'

The driver pulled his keys from the ignition and pushed his own door open.

'Another taxi. There are plenty.'

He waved towards the mosque. From the pavement he reached in and pulled at Izmet's jacket.

There was nothing for it. Izmet looked round fearfully for the Mercedes. There was no sign of it, so he hurried to the other side of the Mosque where he knew there was a taxi-rank.

The Datsun driver wiped his brow with relief, then elbowed his way into a Bufe, in desperate need of some tea.

His hand trembled as he raised the hot glass to his lips. The sweet liquid slipped down like honey. With half an eye he watched for traffic police; he'd left the car in a no-parking zone.

He wiped his hand under his nose. Tears of relief trickled down his stubbly cheeks.

Eventually he recovered enough from his ordeal to pay the café owner, who was watching him with unsatisfied curiosity.

Outside, he took a deep breath to steady his nerves, then pulled open the driver's door and slipped behind the wheel. Key in the ignition. Then he froze in terror.

The springs in the back had creaked. Someone was hidden there! A sallow-faced youth.

Their eyes met in the mirror. Stiffly, the driver turned his head.

'Yes? You want to go somewhere?'

Then he saw the gun, pointing between the seats at his chest.

Izmet had found another taxi with ease. Within minutes he was on his way again, newly confident that he'd thrown his pursuers off his track.

They crossed the Golden Horn by the Ataturk Bridge. It was nearly dark by now; to his right spotlights lit up the funnels of the Bosphorus ferries bustling to and from the jetties by the Galata Bridge. Through the open window wafted the tempting smell of fish, grilling on roadside braziers.

To his right, lights twinkled in the restaurant atop the Galata Tower. They'd be preparing tables for the evening's trade. Soon it would be busy there, with couples and families relaxing. People who felt no fear. He longed to be one of them.

The taxi began the climb towards Beyoglu. In the narrower streets the exhaust fumes seemed more concentrated. Izmet wound the window shut. Such a beautiful city, so desperately overcrowded and so ruined by pollution. The millions who'd migrated here from the spacious cleanliness of the countryside, desperate in their search for prosperity – how could they tolerate the conditions of the city? He pitied them.

The traffic slowed to a snail's pace. Pedestrians weaved round the scaffoldings and hoardings of construction projects abandoned through lack of money. Some brushed against the wing-mirror of the taxi as they squeezed past. Ahead, a bus swayed under the weight of passengers pushing through its doors.

Izmet studied his watch. It was late. The consulate might be closed already. Someone would be there surely, somebody to take his letter.

The bus lurched forward, trailing a cloud of black exhaust. Slowly, the smoke cleared to reveal something to lighten Izmet's heart: a delicious glimpse of the Stars and Stripes hanging limply above the consulate gates. He'd made it!

A cry of triumph formed on his lips. He'd beaten the terrorists – cheated the killers! Allahu Akbar!

'Is this where you want?' asked the driver. It was the first time he'd spoken on the journey.

'Yes, yes. That's perfe . . . Oh . . .'

His voice died in his throat. Disaster! What he saw on the pavement sent terror streaking through his veins again.

Two men peering into every taxi that passed. Two men whose cold and ruthless features were horrifyingly familiar.

'No! Don't stop!' Izmet howled, ducking below the level of the window. 'Drive on!'

How was it possible? How could they have got here? The driver of the first cab – they must have found him, forced him to say where he was heading and come by another route.

'I don't understand. You wanted the Americans! This is it.'

The driver turned his head, bewildered at the sight of his passenger sprawled across the seat.

'Yes. No! Don't stop. They mustn't see me.'

Izmet pressed his face to the greasy seat cover. He heard the driver grunt with astonishment, and sensed the taxi slow down.

'Don't stop!' he hissed, more urgently than ever.

There came a bang on the window and a muffled shout.

'What's going on?' exclaimed the driver. 'Look, you'd better get out. If you're in trouble, I don't want any of it.'

'Go to the British Consulate. Quick! What are they doing?'

He cowered in anticipation of a bullet in his brain.

The car surged forward, its motion controlled by the traffic flow rather than by the will of the driver.

No shots. Izmet raised his eye to the back of the seat and uttered an involuntary whisper. They were coming for him. Through the swirling exhaust he saw the two men scramble into their Mercedes. A lorry and two taxis was all there was between them.

He began to despair. They were too clever. He couldn't escape. Not when he knew their appalling secret. They wouldn't let him.

'What is this?' the driver snarled. 'Police? You'll get me in trouble. What do they want with you? You killed someone?'

'Not police. Kurdish! They want to kill me. Hey – you've gone past! Idiot!'

The Union Flag, the black and yellow pole across the entrance, the helmeted police on guard – already behind them now. His last chance of sanctuary had slipped from his grasp.

The distracted driver stamped on the brake pedal, stopping the car just millimetres from the rusting rear of a bus. The traffic stretched ahead, jammed solid.

Izmet looked back. His pursuers already had the Mercedes' doors open.

He shouldered his way out of the car and ran. Behind

him the taxi-driver screamed for his money. A single aim drove Ozkan's untrained limbs – survival.

The pavements overflowed. He collided with a tea boy bearing a tray of glasses. Curses and shouts rent the air. Above the clatter of the idling engines and the rasp of his own breath he imagined he could hear the footfall of the Kurds. Imagined or not, he knew they were there, just seconds behind him.

No police to be seen. Never there when you want them. He'd gladly beg for their protection now. Torture had surely to be better than death.

The road divided. Left? Right? A moment's in-decision. Then the neon sign above the canopied entrance to a hotel made up his mind for him. There'd be foreigners there. His only chance.

He pushed through the swing door of the Pera Palace. Blurred faces in the entrance lobby. He was conscious of a queue at the reception desk, mostly women. They appeared so orderly, he instantly guessed they were English.

Who to go to? Only seconds to decide. His eye was drawn to an olive-green shopping bag and the chestnut-haired young woman holding it. She had a sensible face. Wheezing, he stopped in front of her. She recoiled in alarm as he reached into his jacket pocket, pulled out the envelope and thrust it deep into her bag.

'For your Prime Minister,' he panted in halting English. 'You must give him. Please, please!'

Behind him, the two Kurds pushed through the swing door. Izmet moaned like a cornered animal, then ran blindly into the heart of the hotel. Stairs led to the cloakrooms. Izmet tumbled down them, slipping and sliding in blind panic.

Jackie's heart pounded against her ribs. She'd thought the wild-eyed Turk had been about to attack her. She clutched her Harrods bag to her as two more men brushed past in pursuit of the first. Ann grabbed her arm.

'Did you see that?' she squawked. 'He had a gun. One of those men had a gun!'

The shots were muffled, the sound echoing round the white tiles of the Edwardian washroom below.

'Oh, my God! What do we do?' Ann Elliott squealed.

'Let go my arm! You're hurting me,' Jackie heard herself answer, astonished at her own coolness.

A scream from someone else in the queue. A man began shouting. The undermanager emerged from behind the reception desk and pushed them towards the restaurant.

'Quickly, quickly, ladies. You must hide. In there. Under tables!'

Waiters looked up in consternation. They were setting the dining-room for dinner, and began to protest. Ann and Jackie crouched down behind a screen.

'It was you,' Anne whispered hoarsely. 'It was *you* he came up to, the first man!'

Jackie frowned, trying to recall exactly what had happened. Things had moved so fast, it was confusing. The man had been terrified. He knew they were going to kill him, whoever they were. What had he said? Something about the Prime Minister?

Her Harrods bag! That's what he'd aimed for. She'd thought he was trying to steal it. She found herself clutching it tightly, as if there was still a threat. Then she remembered; he'd actually reached into it. She peered inside. Nothing gone that she could see. Then she saw the envelope, the Turkish Airlines logo in the corner. She pulled it out, fingered it, then stuffed it down to the bottom in terror as the significance of it hit her.

'They shot him! The man who gave me the letter. He's been shot!' she gasped in disbelief.

'Maybe they'll come after you now,' Ann added fearfully.

Jackie looked horrified.

'Don't be daft!'

In the reception area there was a further kerfuffle as the gunmen fled through the main doors just as a new coach party was arriving. Desperately the desk clerks tried to restore order.

'We must get away from here immediately,' Jackie whispered, as they came out from behind the screen. 'Before the police arrive. Or there'll be a diplomatic incident. It'll delay the flight. The Minister will not be best pleased.'

She pulled Ann towards the desk. The minibus to take them to the airport was waiting outside; the rest of their party had already been on board before the incident had occurred.

'We need to go. Immediately,' she told the receptionist imperiously. 'Our bills. Quickly, please.' The room charge would be paid by the Consulate. This was just for drinks and extras.

The clerk stared at her open-mouthed. How could anyone ask for something as mundane as a checkout, after what had just happened? The clerk shook his head to clear it and addressed the computer.

The paperwork done, they pushed through the swing doors. The urgent blare of a police siren was approaching.

'Don't say anything,' Jackie warned Ann. 'Not to the rest, nor to the police if they stop us. All we saw were men running, and we heard shots. We didn't see any faces, okay?'

'Absolutely.'

They made their way to the back of the minibus; the front rows were occupied.

'What was going on in there?' a voice inquired. 'All that running about?'

'Dunno. Someone not paid his bill, probably. Shall we go? I think we were the last.'

The driver closed the door and pulled away from the kerb just as a police car came whooping up the hill behind them.

Only when the doors of the ministerial VC10 were closed, the engines running, and the plane accelerating for take-off did Jackie feel it was safe to pull the envelope out of her shopping bag.

She sat alone. The seat beside her was occupied by her portable word-processor, strapped in for take-off. For a moment she just stared at the letter, trying to divine its contents. The man could have been a nutter. Why would he want to send some message to the British Prime Minister? But if he was a nutter, whatever he had to say was sufficiently important for someone else to want to kill him for it.

Jackie looked around. Ann was sitting elsewhere. No one else was looking her way. She slit open the envelope with her thumb and pulled out a single sheet of paper filled with a neat and careful script in English.

It was an uncomfortable sensation, reading the words of a man who'd just been killed. She felt guilty, as if she were prying.

To the President of the United States of America.
Dear Sir,
I have some information that is so important, a man has died in bringing it to me. Others may also die . . .

Jackie's throat dried. She took a sip of orange juice.

As she read, her hands began to shake. It had not been meant for her to see this. After all, she was a mere ministerial secretary. If the message contained in this letter were true, it would get an instant 'Top Secret' classification.

She was trespassing, but it was too late to turn back.

Finally she lowered the letter to her lap, and flopped her head back against the rest, mouth agape.

The letter was a warning, the most terrifying, most cataclysmic warning that could ever have been written.

A man shot to death in a Turkish hotel lavatory wanted the President of the United States to know that Arab terrorists were now poised to plunge the planet into nuclear war. And Jackie Bartlett was the only person in the Western world who knew about it.

Eight

The Sea King clunked down onto the deck of HMS *Eagle*. Throughout the return flight Brodrick had sat in the shuddering machine, tense as a bow-string.

Every mile that they'd flown to the southwest, he'd pictured the *Medina* heading north, carrying Ahmed Bizri to a safe haven on the Spanish coast, where he could disappear without trace.

Bugger the law and the Spanish! Peter thought. Should have shot him there and then.

Teniente Pepe Alvarez was the first out of the side door. As he shuffled to the 'island' he'd already begun to remove his survival suit. Good as his word, he was heading straight for the communications centre on Five Deck.

He was too late, Brodrick was sure of that. By the time Pepe had sent his message to the Guardia and got them moving, Bizri would be safely ashore and blending into the background.

During the forty-minute flight back, Brodrick had taken a decision. Bizri's arrival in Spain spelled one thing – danger. Warning bells had to be sounded, loudly.

He made his way back to his quarters and stripped off the survival suit. It was a cramped cabin – just a bunk, a locker, a stainless-steel washbasin that folded down from the wall, a chair and a small desk. On a pinboard behind the desk he'd fixed a snapshot of Jackie, taken at Christmas with the camera she'd given him. Every time he looked at it he felt guilty for not writing to her more often.

He picked up the telephone and dialled the bridge.

'Officer of the watch.'

'Captain Brodrick here. Any sign of the Captain?'

'Believe he's in his sea cabin.'

'Thanks.'

He dialled again.

'Captain.'

'Captain Brodrick here, sir. We're just back from a boarding and there's something I need to report. In private, if that's okay, sir.'

'Really? You'd better come up, then.'

He pulled on his lovat-green trousers and took another look at the picture of Jackie. Before coming out here, he'd had to explain that a Royal Navy captain was two ranks higher than a captain in the Marines. She'd imagined that he and Dyce would be dining together.

The Captain's sea cabin was on the island, just below the bridge. David Dyce was known to his officers as a frustrated man. As a young lieutenant he'd been determined to reach the top, nothing less than First Sea Lord. But now as Captain of *Eagle* he was on his last sea-going post and not expected to make rear-admiral.

Some said the sense of his own failure had made his character prickly; others maintained his bad temper was natural and was the reason he'd not gone higher in the service.

Captain Dyce was always immaculately dressed, seldom if ever seen without his uniform jacket with its four gold rings on the sleeve. The politer critics on board referred to him as a stuffed shirt.

Brodrick entered his cabin and saluted. Dyce had a wan complexion and a bald dome of a head. Above silver, half-framed spectacles, mildly bloodshot eyes looked up suspiciously. They seemed to be warning not to bring trouble.

'No diplomatic incidents, I hope,' he began, pointing

Brodrick to a chair. 'You booties aren't exactly known for your subtlety!'

'Everything done by the book, sir,' Brodrick bristled, uncertain whether Dyce was joking or serious.

'So, what've you got to report, Captain Brodrick?'

Brodrick suddenly felt exceptionally nervous. Since he'd joined *Eagle*, there'd been an unspoken understanding that they'd never discuss what had happened in Lebanon. He suspected Dyce was one of those who thought he'd cocked it up. Now, he'd have to talk to him about it. A can of worms was being opened.

'I recognised someone on the boat we boarded, sir. He's a Lebanese terrorist by the name of Ahmed Bizri.'

Best to plunge straight in.

'He's number two to a man called Abdul Habib who runs the *Mustadhafin* militia.'

'Ahaa! That's the mob that slaughtered your troop?'

The bastard! Brodrick winced at his choice of words.

'Yes, sir.'

'You're sure it was the same chap?'

'No doubt at all, sir. The face, the voice, unmistakable.'

'So what did you do? Kill him?' Dyce's lips curled with sarcasm.

Brodrick felt his face redden with anger.

'Probably would've been best, sir,' he answered icily, 'But I didn't think you'd approve. Might have created that diplomatic incident you're worried about, sir. No. I followed the instructions of Teniente Alvarez who said we couldn't touch him on the high seas. He's sent a signal to alert Spanish immigration.'

'That'll take a week and a half . . .'

'Probably, sir.'

Dyce's eyes narrowed.

'So what's it mean? What's he doing here, this man? Did you find any drugs?'

'No, sir. I don't think he's into narcotics. He was very

140

seasick. I think he'd just been picked up from a freighter. Had a false Spanish passport on him.'

'Did he recognise you?'

'I believe so. My voice, I think.'

'Mmmm.' Dyce stroked his chin. 'Interesting. But if he's not smuggling drugs, he's no concern of ours, is he?'

Brodrick sat bolt upright. Dyce couldn't mean that.

'He's bloody dangerous, sir. He's into extortion, kidnapping, murder, and maybe drugs too, for all I know. You can't possibly say he's no concern of ours.'

'Of course I bloody well can!' Dyce exploded. 'You Royals think you should put the whole sodding world to rights! Let me tell you a little home truth, young man. You are paid to storm beaches, climb mountains and slide down ropes. Sending you into Beirut last year to play James Bond was by all accounts an incredibly stupid thing to do. The politicians may have taken the rap for it, but in my opinion your Commandant-General should've been hanged for letting you go in there! Bloody arrogance of the man to think that a handful of bootnecks could hack a problem that's confounded the rest of the world for the best part of a decade!'

Brodrick felt the blood drain from his face. If Dyce said any more, he'd kill him.

The Captain's face was flushed pale purple.

'Now, this man . . .'

'Bizri, sir,' Brodrick growled.

'Bizri. He may well be an international terrorist, for all I know. He may well be wanted across six continents, but it's not our job to find out what he's up to. The police have anti-terrorist squads for that. Teniente Alvarez is contacting his people, you say? That's fine. We can leave Bizri to them.'

Brodrick seethed with anger. Control. Control.

'Perhaps I might, with great respect, sir, point out one thing. This ship, in the shape of the Sea Harriers flying from her deck, inflicted a pretty heavy death toll on the

141

Mustadhafin. They bombed the shit out of Habib's headquarters . . .'

'Killing the British hostage in the process . . .'

Dyce had taken command of *Eagle* after the attack on Beirut and could afford to be scathing about the incident.

'The point is this, sir,' Brodrick pressed, gritting his teeth. 'These people live by revenge. An eye for an eye? They mean it. Now, *Eagle* moves to another part of the world since Beirut, and suddenly, what do we find? Ahmed Bizri turning up in that same area, with a forged Spanish passport. That makes me very uncomfortable.'

'What are you suggesting?' Dyce snapped. 'That he'll have a go at this ship? What with? A Kalashnikov?'

'Maybe not the ship, sir, but the people on it. There are port visits scheduled throughout the summer.'

He'd struck a nerve at last. It was a threat Captain Dyce couldn't dismiss lightly.

'The IRA tried that in Gibraltar and didn't get very far.'

'Because the SAS were waiting for them, sir.'

'Hmmm.'

Dyce pulled his desk diary towards him and flicked testily through the pages. A gun-attack on his crew would soil the record of his final command at sea.

'I have to say the whole thing sounds extremely implausible. But considering the circumstances – that total shambollocks in Lebanon – I suppose we'll have to think about it.'

'Yes, sir.'

Brodrick knew precisely what their next move should be, but decided it would be politic to let Dyce think of it for himself.

'What did you say they were called, this mob from Beirut?'

'*Mustadhafin.* I believe the word means "downtrodden".'

'Really. And are they?'

'I don't think they'd qualify for supplementary benefit, sir,' Broderick answered tartly.

Try humour on the bugger.

'They're a Shi-ite Muslim group, but not fundamentalist like Hezbollah. Religion seems to play little part in their operations. They're gangsters, really. Money, power, guns. That's what interests them.'

'I suppose you consider yourself a bit of an expert now?'

'Not really, sir. That was one of the problems. No one knew much about them before we went in. And I've been out of it since.'

'Yes, of course.'

Dyce picked up a gold-plated pen and turned it over in his fingers. He'd begun to look uncomfortable.

'I'm not accusing you of anything over Lebanon. You understand that, Peter?'

Brodrick eyed him coldly.

'If you say so, sir.'

'The fault was on the Flag Deck. Everyone knows that.'

'Glad to hear it, sir.'

'Bloody rough for you, of course. We all sympathised.'

Don't want your fucking sympathy! The words were on the edge of his lips. His insides were writhing. A dozen men dead and all they give you is patronising platitudes!

'I've got an idea. Perhaps we'll put you ashore for a bit. *Eagle*'s going into Gib for Easter. Talk to the security boys. See if they've heard anything.'

At last.

'Oh, that's an idea, sir.'

'Corporal Rees can look after things for twenty-four hours or so?'

'No problem. He runs everything anyway. And he knows how to handle Pepe.'

Captain Dyce looked at his wristwatch. It was approaching five in the afternoon.

'Have a word with Wings. Tell him I want you put ashore in Gibraltar tonight. Signal *Rooke* to find you a cabin, and to set up a meeting with the base security officer first thing in the morning. Oh, and you'd better say something diplomatic to Teniente Alvarez. Don't want the Spaniards thinking we don't trust them.'

'No, sir. Of course not. Thank you, sir.'

He stood up, saluted and left the cabin.

One deck up on the bridge, Brodrick squeezed past the charthouse and into 'Flyco'. Percy Bradshaw stood at the back of the flying control room, peering anxiously over the head of the lieutenant commander in the hot seat, who was controlling the noisy return of four Sea Harriers.

Beyond, through the panoramic window, the first pair of aircraft hovered above the waves one behind the other, thirty feet to port.

'Green deck,' announced the controller.

In perfect synchronisation the two fighter jets dipped their starboard wings, steadied themselves over the centre line, then dropped to the flight deck, sinking low on their wheels. With a sigh of relief the roar of the Pegasus engines died to a whisper.

'Spot on,' growled Bradshaw. 'Now where are the other buggers? They've missed their Charlie Time.'

'Homer says they're nine miles out,' the lieutenant commander muttered over his shoulder.

'Bloody NAAFI pilot! If he's late one more time I'll clip his wings,' snapped Bradshaw.

Brodrick leaned forward and touched him on the arm.

'Could I have a word, sir?'

'Oh, God, it's Green Death. What do you want?'

He'd spoken with the hint of a smile. It had been Bradshaw who'd sent the Harriers to bomb Beirut the previous year; he and Brodrick never spoke about the operation, but it had left a bond between them.

'A cab to Gibraltar would do nicely.'

'No bloody chance!'

'Captain says he wants me there tonight.'

'Does he now? And I suppose he knows that'll screw up my maintenance schedules?'

'Life's a bitch . . .'

'. . . and then you die. I know.'

He looked at his watch.

'Briefing room in fifteen minutes. I'll get you away before I debrief the SHARS.' He turned back to peer through the window. 'Any sign?'

Brodrick found Pepe Alvarez still in the communications centre. He'd signalled Customs in Algeciras to contact police and immigration, but to speed things up he was trying to call them direct by radio-telephone.

Pepe was trying, which was more than he'd expected. He patted him warmly on the shoulder.

'Look, just to let you know – the Captain's sending me to Gibraltar tonight. Ever since the IRA thing there, they're shit-scared about security. Wants me to talk to the Gibraltar police about the man I saw today.'

'Of course.'

He looked uncomfortable. Gibraltar always complicated matters.

'You took details of our friend's passport, didn't you?'

'Our fren. . . ?'

'Mr Bizri, Boukari or whatever he called himself.'

'Ah yes. You want to see?'

Pepe handed over his pad and pointed to the name and number that he'd scrawled down.

'Thanks. That'll give them something to start on.'

He copied it into his own notebook.

'I'll be off then. See you in a day or two.'

He held out his hand to say goodbye.

Pepe regarded him with both affection and suspicion. He felt pressure building. Mr Boukari and his forged passport were a matter for the Spanish authorities, not the British. Don't push too hard, his eyes seemed to warn. Pressure, Brodrick might discover, was something that Spaniards were quite skilled at resisting.

It was dark by the time they touched down in the grey drizzle at Gibraltar. The top of the Rock was shrouded in cloud. It had been a long day. Brodrick felt uncomfortably powerless. His instinct was to grab a car and go driving up the Spanish coast looking for the *Medina*. Daft, of course. It'd take him a week to check the marinas on the Costa del Sol. If only he had more faith in the Spaniards.

There was a message for him on arrival. Commander Camfield, security officer for the naval base, would see him at nine the next morning.

What's wrong with tonight, he thought to himself angrily. Didn't they understand the urgency of it?

A disgruntled navy driver, annoyed at having to work late, turned the car onto the road that crossed the runway and led to Spain. They headed left, into the town. Brodrick glanced through the window as they passed the garage where the SAS had shot the IRA bombers in 1988. He hoped the Regiment still had men on the Rock. They might need them before long.

The car bore to the right following the line of the old emplacements for the defensive gun battery, then turned through the gates of HMS *Rooke*, the naval residential quarters. Broderick was expected; a cabin and an evening meal had been booked.

'Can I have a look at the register?' Brodrick asked the accommodation CPO. 'See if I know anybody staying here?'

'Help yourself, sir. But the place is empty. It's the cutbacks, and there's a lot on leave too.'

Brodrick grunted and pulled the book across the reception counter. He flicked through the pages cursorily, then closed it again. No names that he recognised.

'Looks like an early night,' he commented.

'There's a video in the wardroom at eight,' the CPO offered chirpily.

'I dunno. I think I'll give it a miss. Tell you what, have you got any writing paper?'

He'd suddenly decided how to spend his evening. He'd write a letter to Jackie.

When he awoke the next morning, Brodrick pulled back the thin, yellow curtains and looked out across the harbour. A Leander class frigate had come in overnight and was tied alongside the South Mole. For some reason he suddenly thought of Pearl Harbor. Heavily armed warships might feel safe in port, but God knows they were vulnerable to surprise attack.

He re-read his letter to Jackie, then regretted doing so. He was a bad letter writer, and in the cold light of day, even he could see how uninformative his missive was. Better than nothing, perhaps? Maybe. He stuffed it into its envelope and took it down to the reception desk for posting.

After breakfast, the driver from the previous night returned to take him to Naval Headquarters. A short run along Queensway – nowhere was far to go in Gibraltar – then in through the Ragged Staff Gates.

Commander Ken Camfield, head of security at the naval base, proved to be a nervous, bird-like man. His office overlooked the harbour and that morning there was a clear view of Algeciras across the bay.

'Coffee? Tea?' he asked, head cocked on one side.

'Neither, thanks, sir.'

'Need a constant supply in this job,' Camfield twittered. 'Can't rest for a moment.'

A filter machine burbled away on the floor behind his desk.

Brodrick crossed to the window and stared at the *Leander*.

'What's to stop a terrorist swimming into the harbour and sticking a limpet mine on that frigate?' he asked bluntly.

'Plenty. We've got sonars on the bottom that can detect a swimmer at five hundred metres.'

'Hmmm.'

'Is that what you wanted to see me about?'

'No. I don't think that's what they're planning.'

'Who? Look, come and sit down and we can get on with it,' the Commander instructed.

Brodrick dropped into a low armchair. Where to begin, that was the problem.

'Tell me, sir. Are you aware of my connection with the Lebanese business last autumn?'

'I am.'

A poker face. No way to tell what he was thinking.

'Good. That saves a bit of time.'

Brodrick began by telling him as much as he knew about *Mustadhafin*. He went on to describe exactly what he'd seen on the *Medina* the previous afternoon.

Commander Camfield listened impassively, looking down once or twice to take a note.

'So we have to assume that Ahmed Bizri is alive and well, and at large in Spain, planning God knows what,' Brodrick concluded.

Camfield sat back in his chair, picked up a packet of Marlboro and held it out. Brodrick shook his head. The Commander pulled a cigarette from the packet, tapped both ends on the beige metal desk, then lit it.

'How very interesting. Not surprised you're worried. I suppose you see yourself as the main target?'

What did he mean by that? Brodrick sensed criticism, as if it was his fault there was a problem. Then he dismissed the thought. Just paranoia.

'Actually, sir, there are twelve hundred men on HMS

148

Eagle. If Bizri's after revenge, there are plenty of us to choose from.'

Was there a hint of embarrassment on Camfield's face?

'Yes of course. Anyone with a British passport would do, I imagine.'

He exhaled a plume of smoke.

'Get a picture of him?' he asked suddenly.

''Fraid not. Boarding parties may only take photographs if drugs are found. Spanish rules,' Brodrick answered bitterly. 'But I've got the details of his forged passport.'

'You're certain it was the same man?' He noticed Brodrick's irritation. 'Yes, of course you are, otherwise you wouldn't be here.

'Right. Well, first thing is to liaise with the Spanish Guardia. Have to do that through the Gibraltarian Police Chief. A bit long-winded, but it works in the end, usually. Those passport details and a verbal description from you – we can get that pinned up in the immigration office at the border. And then it's a matter of everyone keeping on their toes.'

'Is the Regiment still here?'

'The SAS? Oh, yes. Permanent fixture now. And Special Branch. They scrutinise every face that comes across that border. Have to assume the IRA'll try to get their own back.'

His eyes hardened as he thought of something else.

'How long have we got?'

He pulled open his desk diary and thumbed the pages.

'Just under two weeks before *Eagle*'s due back in Gib. Gives us time, if you're right about what Bizri's after.'

'He wouldn't know the ship's coming in for Easter, would he?'

'We don't announce it. But it's not difficult to find out. A few discreet enquiries at hotels on the Rock, and he'd soon discover that all the families staying at Easter seem to come from Portsmouth. We'll ask around; see if any Arabs have been sniffing about.'

He drummed his fingers on the desk. He'd forgotten something. The coffee. He spun round and switched off the filter machine.

'Sure I can't tempt you?'

'No thanks. The MO says too much caffeine's bad for the heart, sir.'

'Yes, but you're talking to an addict.'

Camfield filled his mug and added a spoonful of whitener.

'Tell me, what are your plans for the next few days?' he asked.

'To go back to the ship,' Brodrick shrugged.

'Can they manage without you for a day or two?'

'Easily.'

'Then I think you should go to London.'

Brodrick raised his eyebrows.

'What you've been telling me needs to get into the system fast. There are other people around who may have an angle on this. Intelligence. MOD. I can send signals to everyone, but if you can go and talk to them too it'll speed things up no end.'

He looked at his watch, then reached for the phone.

'RAF Movements?' he asked when the number answered. 'Commander Camfield here. I need one seat on the trooper to London this afternoon. Can do?'

He put his hand over the mouthpiece and looked Brodrick in the eye.

'Flight to Luton at half-two. There isn't another until next Tuesday.' He removed his hand. 'Full? You must have one cancellation, surely?'

He listened, frowning for a moment.

'Look. I've a chap here who has to be on that flight. No excuses. Top priority. He can sit in the co-pilot's lap if necessary. Just tell the airline it has to be. Name's Brodrick. Initial P, rank Captain. Got that?'

He replaced the receiver.

'It'll be all right. The crabs know me. Now, we've got work to do. You'd better signal *Eagle* and tell them what's what. Of course you won't get to see anyone in London until Monday, but it'll give you a weekend ashore. If you call Northwood I'm sure they'll find somewhere for you to sleep tonight.'

'That's all right, sir. I've got somewhere to stay.'

Jackie. He'd arrive there before his letter. Needn't have written it.

Nine

London
Friday

In Downing Street a lone television cameraman and a stills photographer from the Press Association recorded the comings and goings. Nothing newsworthy was expected today, but with an election on the horizon, the media could afford to miss nothing.

Most Members of Parliament had left London to spend the weekend in their constituencies. Normally by now George Webster would be on his way to Norfolk, so it was a surprise for the photographers to see him cross the road from the Foreign Office, and enter the door of Number Ten.

'What's that bloke's name?' asked the TV cameraman.

'Webster,' replied the 'snapper'. 'Minister of State. His boss is away at the moment. Hong Kong, I think. So Georgie Boy is in charge.'

'God help us!'

Inside, Webster was ushered into the Prime Minister's private office. The two men were old friends, despite a twenty-year difference in their ages. Both were from humbler beginnings than most of their colleagues in government.

Together they were at the centre of the crisis of confidence that confronted their party. More than any others in the government, they read their morning newspapers with fear and trepidation, dreading the headlines that might one day reveal the truth about the dead hostage Richard Bicknell and Celadec.

They both knew the newsmen were digging away at the story. They both knew, too, that if they reached their goal and exposed Bicknell's business dealings, it could spell the end of both their careers, and the chances of their party being re-elected to government would plummet.

'The *FT*'s asked me for another interview,' Webster announced, his dark eyes like pools of gloom. 'I've refused. Said I'm too busy. I feel I'm in purdah. Can't keep it up for ever. They'll start saying we're not accountable.'

'You have to, George. Until the election's over.'

Through the powerful lenses of his spectacles, the PM's eyes were sympathetic, yet calculating. Webster had a good idea what his own fate would be, and that it wouldn't be long in coming.

'Anyway, we've affairs of state to deal with. The chairman of the JIC will be here in a minute. This extraordinary letter you brought back from Turkey! You say it came from your secretary?'

'That's right. She gave it to me on the plane on the way home from Istanbul. She'd read the damned thing and was in a bit of a state.'

'Is she reliable?'

Webster pulled a long face.

'Far as I know. She shouldn't have read it, of course. It was addressed to the US President and she's not cleared up to "secret". But I've told her she'll go to prison if she mentions the contents to a living soul.'

'And the man who wrote it – it was he who gave it to her?'

'About one minute before he was shot dead. In a lavatory.'

The PM winced.

'It's appalling! Anyway, Masterton's been following it up. Ah, here he is.'

The booming voice of the Chairman of the Joint Intelligence Committee rang out in the hall.

'Better have some tea. Sir Reginald's motor runs on it.'

There was a tap at the door.

'Come in. Welcome, Reginald. You know George, of course. Tea, Alex?'

His private secretary nodded and set off to arrange it.

Sir Reginald Masterton was a diplomat of long standing, having served both in Moscow and in Washington. A down-to-earth man, sceptical of conspiracy-theories, he'd been an ideal choice to chair the Joint Intelligence Committee which acted as a buffer between the intelligence agencies and the politicians.

Within minutes the tea had arrived, and they could begin their business.

'This story is pretty nightmarish, if true,' Masterton began. 'And unfortunately there's evidence to suggest that it may well be.'

He paused to run a finger along his grey, toothbrush moustache. He had the look of a professor rather than a diplomat; a balding crown, bushy grey hair at the sides, and a pair of round, steel-framed spectacles on his nose.

'The letter, as you know, was written in English by a Turkish journalist named Izmet Ozkan. It wasn't addressed to us, but to the President of the United States. Why it was given to Ms Bartlett, heaven only knows.'

He held photocopies of the letter in his hands.

'We have, of course, forwarded the original to the White House. I'm sure you'd like to read it, Prime Minister.'

'I'd be grateful. I've not seen it.'

Masterton handed a copy to Webster as well.

To the President of the United States.
Dear Sir,
I have some information that is so important, a man has died in bringing it to me. Others may also die.

154

'Prophetic,' the PM murmured. 'Seems to have known he was a marked man.'

What I write you has come from a young man who was my contact with the Kurdish guerrilla army – PKK. He was trusted by the leader of PKK, but he broke that trust by saying me one of their greatest secrets. They discover what he do and they kill him in Dyarbakir last night.

'The letter was undated,' Masterton explained, 'but it came into our hands yesterday. The Turkish police have confirmed there was a particularly nasty murder in Diyarbakir the night before. A young student had his throat sliced and his tongue cut out.'

'Oh, God,' Webster groaned.

This is what the young man say me:
Two years ago Soviet army trucks were attacked by militia in Armenia. THOSE TRUCKS CARRY NUCLEAR WEAPONS. Only now do they try to sell them to get money to buy tanks.

'The Bloody Russian President never made any mention of this,' the Prime Minister exclaimed. 'Insisted there'd never been any problem with nuclear weapons. So much for glasnost!'

'Just a bit too sensitive perhaps, as you'll see when you read on. . .'

The militia were Armenian fighters who already steal arms from Red Army bases. The attack on these trucks is their biggest. It was a surprise. They kill all the soldiers. It was a massacre. They escaped with a truck and two nuclear missile bombs.

But they do not know what to do with the weapons; they had no use in guerrilla fighting. So they decide to sell them for as much dollars as they can.

But they had no real plan. They know the weapons were worth much money, but they not know how to sell them. For that reason they talk with the Kurds, peoples who live in mountains near and who know about smuggling weapons across borders.

It was the PKK who buy them. Not for them – they cannot use such weapons. And not for so much money as the Armenians want. But the Kurds know who want to buy such a nuclear bomb. And this person pay with something the Kurds already make much business. Drugs.

They pay for the two nuclear bombs many hundreds kilos of heroin.

'God Almighty, this is the most horrific story I've ever heard!' exclaimed the Prime Minister. 'It chills the blood.'

My contact know not who buy the bombs from the Kurds. But they take through Turkey, in trucks with watermelons or sheep. They drive to Syria – the guards take money to let them in.

Then they go on – to Lebanon.

'Lebanon! George! You didn't tell me that!' growled the Prime Minister.

'The last paragraph is the nub of it,' Masterton droned.

Mr President. The Middle East now has these bombs at its heart. I know not who has his finger on them, but the countries of the east Mediterranean may soon have nuclear war. This is a disaster, worse than anything. Please, please. I am not mad. This is true what I write. Russia is finished. Only your great country can stop this.

Yours faithfully,

Izmet Ozkan

Political Correspondent of *Millyet* newspaper.

'Until yesterday when the Kurds shot him dead,' Masterton intoned.

'All right,' the PM said briskly, taking charge. 'What's the intelligence assessment of this, Reginald?'

'We've talked to the Americans, of course,' Masterton said, removing his glasses. 'As you know, intelligence is a bit like a photograph in a newspaper – countless tiny dots. Each dot doesn't mean much, but put them all together . . .

'Well, the CIA's checked the monitoring of Armenia that was done about two years ago. Mostly SIGINT – radio stuff. Hardly any satellite. There was thick cloud over the area for most of the beginning of '92. And anyway the Russians would have timed it carefully, if they were shuttling their nukes around. They'd wait for the satellite to go past.'

'I thought those things kept a permanent watch over the Russians,' commented Webster. 'Supposed to be able to read the numberplates of the cars coming out of the Kremlin.'

'Mostly apocryphal, I'm afraid. No, the truth is that two years ago American satellite intelligence was in a mess. The birds themselves need replacing from time to time, and they'd had a couple blow up on the launchpad. So there was only one orbiting twice a day.

'But they did pick something up from a radio intercept one day. A hell of a flap on over some shooting incident. Not much detail, but it could have been the one Ozkan's referring to.'

'And what are the Russians saying now?' the PM demanded, still seething that he'd been lied to. 'Time and time again we've asked them whether all their nuclear weapons are safe. Time and time again they've assured us they are! This doesn't do much for our new relationship. Here we are trying to help them hold the bloody country together, and they're lying to us!'

'It looks that way. The Americans are working on Moscow. They're going gently on them to begin with. If we're going to sort this business out we'll need their co-operation.'

'But does anyone know who's got the bombs?' demanded the Foreign Minister. 'Or what they're going to do with them?'

'No. That's top priority, to find that out.'

'Do we have any spies in Lebanon?' the PM asked ingenuously.

'No one trained for this sort of situation,' Masterton answered regretfully. 'No. My advice is we should leave it to the Americans for now. And believe me, they are addressing the problem!'

His careful understatement was belied by the raising of one eyebrow.

'Preparing to nuke everybody in sight, I shouldn't wonder,' commented the PM cynically.

'Well, I understand that elements of the Sixth Fleet are being moved to the eastern Mediterranean – as a precaution.'

Suddenly, the PM sensed an opportunity – a way to distract the attention of the media from the Bicknell business.

'Do we have anything military in the Med at the moment?' he asked casually. 'Anybody know?'

'Well, I have made some enquiries,' Sir Reginald answered, replacing his glasses. 'There's HMS *Eagle* at the other end. Chasing drug smugglers with the Spanish coastguards.'

'That's more political than practical,' the PM remarked. A gleam had appeared in his eyes. 'Perhaps we should move her to the east, too.'

'Bit provocative, that,' Webster chipped in, concerned at the diplomatic implications. '*Eagle* and Lebanon haven't exactly had a happy association. Don't think the Foreign Secretary would recommend it.'

There was a moment's silence as they reflected on the appalling consequences of *Eagle*'s air attack on Beirut.

It needed thinking about. A fine balance of risks versus political advantages. The same balance as last autumn. Have to get it right this time.

'We'll see. If the Americans ask for our involvement, it'll be difficult to refuse,' the PM concluded.

He nodded to Webster.

'We can discuss this another time.'

Not in front of the Chairman of the JIS, Webster understood him to mean and nodded back.

'Who do you think is behind all this, Reginald?' the Prime Minister asked, finishing his tea which was by now stone cold. 'The Syrians control most of Lebanon. D'you think they've got the bombs?'

'All we have is the Ozkan letter,' Masterton answered, holding the photocopy in the air. 'And that just refers to Lebanon. If the Syrians themselves had bought the bombs, they'd have taken them straight to one of their own bases, I'd have thought.'

'So, it's Hezbollah or whatever? Islamic Jihad? The mad mullahs?'

'It could well be.'

'Jesus wept!'

'Could they use the bombs?' asked Webster. 'I mean,

these are supposed to have safety systems to stop loonies letting them off.'

'Can't answer that until we know what type they are. If they're from missiles they should have a dual-key system – needs two separate people, each with a code that the other one couldn't possibly know.

'But it also depends on what sort of friends the mullahs have. If they've been able to hire a bent nuclear scientist from the former Soviet Union, then it's possible he could by-pass the safety systems for them.'

'Doesn't bear thinking about,' said the PM. 'And I suppose they'll try to hit Israel?'

'They could put it on a ship and steam into the port of Haifa,' Masterton explained. 'Just the threat of letting it off might be enough to wring some pretty hefty concessions out of the Israelis.'

'Ozkan's letter said the buyer had paid with heroin. Does that give us a clue as to who it could be?'

'The trouble is, everybody's growing the stuff in Lebanon. Christians, Shias. The Beka'a Valley's full of cannabis and opium poppies. We've just got to wait and see what the Americans come up with.'

The Prime Minister sat back in his chair and clasped his hands in his lap. Sir Reginald Masterton and George Webster looked at him. As head of the government it was time he drew his conclusions.

'I don't need to say that I want to be kept informed of every single development, however small. Obviously, I'll need to talk to the President of the United States. There may come a point when we have to go public on this. But that can wait until there's something a bit more solid to go on.

'But I can tell you one thing. Whoever's got his hands on those warheads must be stopped before he can use them. Whatever the price.'

*

160

Jackie Bartlett's heels clattered down the stone steps, past Clive's statue. A chill wind from the north tugged at her light raincoat as she crossed Horse Guards Road into the park. It had felt like spring when she left home that morning. Now it was winter again.

She looked at her watch. Six-fifteen already. Alan was due to pick her up at seven-thirty. There'd be hardly enough time for a shower when she got home.

The path under the plane trees was lined to the right by daffodils. To the left, an old woman sat on a bench surrounded by plastic carrier bags, feeding stale bread to the pigeons. How did these bag-ladies survive the winters, with just doorways to sleep in?

She crossed Birdcage Walk at the traffic lights, and joined the other commuters funnelling up Queen Anne's Gate to the underground station. This was the part of the day she hated most. It didn't seem to matter how late or how early she left the Foreign Office, the District Line trains were always packed.

Alan. What was she doing accepting his invitation to dinner? She'd only met him that morning.

He worked for intelligence; she wasn't sure what exactly. He'd been sent round to ask questions about Istanbul. All sorts of crazy irrelevant details. At one point he'd even suggested she'd known Izmet Ozkan personally.

He'd phoned her back in the afternoon to apologise for being so aggressive. Said he'd like to take her out to dinner to make up for it.

Nobody had ever tried that line with her before, so in a rash moment she'd accepted.

She wasn't sure what to make of him, but there was a roguishness about him that was not unattractive. He'd told her on the phone that at heart he wasn't really a spook. He'd got caught in the wrong job. Should've been an antique dealer.

Original, if nothing else, she'd thought.

When the train pulled in, hundreds lined the edge of the platform to board it. If she'd had time to spare she'd have waited for the next one, but she allowed the tide of humanity to sweep her into the carriage. Pinned against a partition by a dark-suited man who smelled of old sweat, she fought to keep claustrophobia at bay.

To counter the sense of panic, she sometimes imagined doing outrageous things, like pinching men's backsides or unzipping their trousers. It helped.

At Putney Bridge she pushed her way out of the carriage and sighed with relief. People spend forty years travelling like this, she thought. No wonder some end up as bag-ladies in St James's Park.

It was five to seven when she opened her front door to find the phone ringing. Before she could pick it up, the answerphone had taken the call. Her hand moved to intercept the message, then she hesitated. Supposing it was her mother? She'd be on the phone for an age, and she'd never get her shower. She turned up the volume on the recording machine.

'Hello. It's me.'

Peter!

'I've just arrived at Luton, of all places. Had to come back for a meeting. There's a bus that'll get me from here to Victoria, and I'll take the tube from there. So, I should think I'll pitch up at your place in about a couple of hours.'

Could've given me some warning, she thought.

'Umm. . ., hope that's all right. All a bit sudden, otherwise I'd have rung from Gibraltar. Well, I'll . . . I'll see you later. Lots to tell you. Er . . . hope you'll be there.'

She grabbed for the receiver, but there was a click and the purr of the dialling tone.

Hell. Now what? Should she cancel her date with Alan? Too late. He'd be here in half an hour.

She hurried to the bedroom, unbuttoning her blouse.

She undressed quickly, throwing the clothes onto the bed, then hopped into the bathroom, still trying to disentangle her tights from her feet.

She stood in the shower letting the cascade of hot water purge her mind and body of the day's tensions. Peter could have rung earlier. He'd got her office number. He just assumed she'd be there. Took it for granted. That's what came from letting him keep a key to her apartment.

She was aching to see him again, yet she was niggled by his presumption that she'd been sitting at home waiting for him for the past three months. He needed to be taught a lesson, ever so gently.

Should she leave him a note? Rub his nose in the fact that she'd still gone out, despite his message? No. Avoid the hassle. Pretend she'd already left for the evening when he rang.

The forty miles from Luton to Fulham took Brodrick almost as long as the flight from Gibraltar.

Since his phone-call to Jackie's answering machine, doubts had crept into his mind. Maybe he should've arranged to stay at the Navy wardroom at Northwood after all.

Here he was, assuming Jackie would be waiting for him like a loyal wife. But she wasn't his wife. He'd made no commitment to her; she'd made none to him. Supposing she'd got some other bloke by now? Might even be shacked-up with him. It'd be his own fault if she had.

How many times had he written to her since Christmas? It didn't bear thinking about. On the ship they seldom brooded about their wives and women. They all knew it was pointless, being stuck at sea for months with nothing they could do about it. No point in longing for home comforts. The camaraderie of the wardroom and the messdecks was designed to compensate.

Perhaps Jackie wouldn't understand. Perhaps she'd decided he didn't care. But he did care. The closer he got to where she lived, the more he realised how much he cared.

As he handed in his ticket at Putney Bridge, he hesitated. Supposing she hadn't received his message? He didn't want to barge in if someone else was there . . .

He put down his holdall by the telephone booth and dialled her number.

That damned answering machine again. She could be away on a trip for all he knew. He hadn't spoken to her for a month. He'd called on her birthday, on the Marisat phone from the ship.

He picked up his bag and slung it over a shoulder. Nothing for it but to go and look. Soon tell if some other bloke had got his things in her flat.

In Jackie's street, cherry trees were coming into blossom. Whether they were pink or white was impossible to tell in the orange glow from the street lamps.

Brodrick fumbled in his bag for the keys – one for the house door, the other for the top-floor flat. He took the stairs two at a time. Outside her door he stopped to listen. Nothing. He rang the bell. Silence. He turned the key and entered.

He felt like an intruder. He should have telephoned from Gibraltar. He dropped his bag in the hallway.

The answerphone was still on. No way of knowing if she'd got his message.

He pushed open the door to the bedroom. Clothes were scattered across the counterpane. She'd gone out in a hurry. Must have a date.

He felt awkward, uncomfortable, as if he was reading someone else's diary.

When away, he deliberately didn't think about what she did or who she saw. But he was thinking about it now. Suddenly realised he was jealous! Hadn't felt like that for a long time. Bloody ridiculous! His own fault, coming back unannounced.

He searched the fridge for a beer and took the can to the sitting-room so he could think of what to do. CDs were scattered on top of the hi-fi he'd given her for Christmas.

Supposing she brought some other bloke home, and found him sitting on her sofa? She'd hardly thank him.

He finished the beer, found a pad of paper in the kitchen and wrote her a note. Then he picked up his holdall and slipped out of the front door. He'd ring her later from the pub.

Jackie felt pleasantly sloshed.

They'd gone first to a pub in the King's Road. Alan really did know about antiques. He seemed friends with all the people in the bar, most of them connected with the trade. It made a change from civil servants.

By nine, they were at a French brasserie, and Alan was telling her about his childhood. As he talked, she began to realise he'd never quite escaped from it. He was like a boy who'd never grown up, still trying to please his parents at the age of thirty. No wonder he hadn't found a wife, she thought.

They ate rack of lamb and drank Fleurie.

'But what I want to know more about is that letter,' Jackie announced conspiratorially. 'What's being done about it?'

Alan's eyes narrowed as his brain changed gear.

'Can't talk about that. Walls have ears.' He rotated his eyes to suggest they'd be overheard.

'Don't be daft! No one's listening. The nearest table's miles away!'

He looked over his shoulder with feigned stealth.

'Maybe. But even the existence of that letter's a

classified secret. I know you were the messenger who brought it, but you shouldn't have read it. That was out of order. You'd best forget about it.'

He refilled her glass. .

'I think you're being incredibly pompous!' Jackie retorted. 'How on earth can I forget about it? I only want to know if what it said was true.'

Alan looked relieved.

'Well, I can honestly tell you I don't know the answer to that. Above my pay grade, as they say. Look. I'm just a lowly bloke who was sent round to ask you a few questions. My bosses wanted to know all about how the letter came into your hands. And they wanted a character assessment, to see if I thought you could've written the letter yourself.'

'Oh!'

His bluntness startled her.

'Is that what this is all about?' She spread her hands to indicate the table. 'You're still assessing my character?'

'No, no, no!' he moaned. 'Much simpler than that.' He reached across the table and grabbed her hand. 'It was love! From the moment you answered my first question.'

'Fool!' she snapped, pulling her hand back. He was playing a game in which he alone knew the rules.

'Well, lust anyway! I want to go to bed with you.'

His eyes seemed to twinkle and plead simultaneously.

'That's more believable,' she smiled. 'But what would that do for my character assessment?'

'Shall I tell you what I wrote?'

'You mean it's not secret?'

'Straight as a die, I said. She's one of the finest products of the English middle-classes I've ever seen. That's what I wrote.'

'Liar!'

'It's true.'

She laughed. With this man truth and fiction must be close bedfellows.

'So what do you say?'

He grabbed her hand again.

'About what?'

'About me spending the night with you. I don't snore.'

She laughed again.

'No. I hardly know you.'

'How many dinners does it take?'

'Dozens.'

'That's quite an investment.'

'But think of the return!' she teased.

He smiled enigmatically.

'More like gambling, if you ask me.'

'What do you mean?'

He paused and withdrew his hand.

'Sex is always a gamble, isn't it,' he suggested, turning serious for a moment. 'I mean, you meet someone, have a date, get on famously. Lots of fun. Then you go to bed together. If you're lucky, it works and everything's great. If you're unlucky and it doesn't gel – then bingo! You've ruined everything.'

'Mmmm. That's life.'

She wondered how often that had happened to him. Occasionally she caught a hint of loneliness in his eyes.

The waiter came with the menu again.

'The crème brûlée with ginger is brilliant,' Alan advised.

She hesitated. Peter must be at her flat waiting for her by now. Still, a little longer wouldn't hurt.

'How could I refuse?'

The waiter swept the crumbs from the table, then left them.

'That letter . . .' she began.

Alan's expression went 'official' again.

'Okay. . . , you can't talk about it. But you can give me your opinion,' Jackie insisted. 'You know it said the bombs were taken to Lebanon? Do you think that's true?'

'God knows! That sort of info doesn't come across my desk.'

He glanced quickly around to ensure no one was near.

'I'll tell you one thing, though. Before much longer Lebanon is going to blow a hole in the Prime Minister's election campaign!'

He winked at her.

'What do you mean?'

He shook his head.

'Can't say any more. But watch this space.'

'But I don't understand! You can't just throw out that sort of titbit and then go quiet on me! What do you mean by Lebanon?'

Alan shrugged.

'You know. That stuff last autumn. The marines getting blown to bits, trying to rescue Richard Bicknell.'

'Oh.'

No one at the Foreign Office knew about her relationship with Peter. So Alan wouldn't either.

Peter! She glanced at her watch. Hope the dessert comes soon.

'You mean there's more to come out? We haven't heard the full story?' she pressed.

Alan nodded and ran a finger across his lips as the waiter placed the dessert on the table. He smiled smugly to see that he'd intrigued her.

'What do you think of it?' he asked after a few mouthfuls.

'Stunning,' she replied. The word applied both to the crème brûlée and to what he'd just told her.

She sensed he was eyeing her, preparing for the next move.

'How about coming back to my place, for some coffee? To round off a beautiful evening!'

'You don't give up easily, do you?'

'Coffee and a cuddle, that's all,' he shrugged.

'Oh, yeah?' she smiled, knowingly. 'Well, not tonight.

Thanks for the invitation. But I've got to go home. I . . . I've got someone staying with me tonight.'

'Oh? Who?'

'My sister,' she lied. It was easier than explaining.

'Like hell!'

'Well, it doesn't matter whether you believe me or not. I must go home, now.'

She gave him a smile of encouragement. She wanted to see him again soon to find out more about Lebanon.

'If it's any consolation, I like you a lot. Can we do this again? And next time I'll buy dinner.'

He shrugged. It made him uncomfortable when women offered to pay. He was old-fashioned enough to feel emasculated by it.

'So, dear Alan, could you take me home? Please.'

He called for the bill.

By the time the pub shut, Brodrick had downed four pints and several whisky chasers. He'd phoned the flat twice from the bar, to no avail. Jackie's absence depressed him. The thought of her with another man aroused in him emotions he'd seldom experienced.

With the bar closed, he had been reduced to pacing the streets – his only comfort, a quarter flask of whisky bought just before 'time' was called. It was a quarter to midnight. He'd give her another ten minutes and phone again from a call-box.

The barman had been a decent bloke and had served him a cheese sandwich, even though they didn't normally do them in the evenings. On a small television next to the till Brodrick had watched the news, only half the words audible above the hubbub of the bar.

Libya had taken a verbal hammering from the US State Department, the newscaster had said. New intelligence reports suggested Tripoli was pouring money into chemical and nuclear weapons projects. UN sanctions were mooted, and the Americans had 'not ruled out' military action.

Then came news of an Israeli raid into southern Lebanon. Helicopter gunships had killed the leader of a muslim militia and half his family.

'They don't stand no nonsense,' the barman chattered. 'Straight in. No questions asked. Not like our lot in Lebanon last year. Bloody package tour, *that* was.'

Peter gulped down his beer. If the bastard said another word, he'd have him by the throat.

Mercifully the news had switched to domestic politics, more speculation about when the election date would be announced.

Five to midnight. An icy wind cut through his light coat. He shivered and changed hands on the grip of his holdall. This was stupid. He couldn't walk the streets all night.

There was a phone booth ahead.

'Hello?' Jackie's voice answered.

'Hi, it's me.'

'Where are you? Your phone message said you'd be here, but your note said you'd ring later. What's going on?'

'I wasn't sure. Didn't know whether it was convenient . . .'

'Oh, how thoughtful!'

'Bit short notice.'

'Well I'm here. On my own. And I'd like to see you. Where exactly are you?'

'Just round the corner, actually.'

'In a phone box? You sound a bit pissed.'

'Mmmm, maybe just a little.'

'Fool! See you here in a minute!'

*

Jackie hugged him and wouldn't let go. She smelled of wine and warmth.

'Mmmm. Missed you,' she murmured, nuzzling his neck.

'Missed you too.'

'Doesn't do to deprive a girl for so long . . .'

She pressed her body against him and wriggled. Then she pulled away.

'What's happened? Why come back so suddenly? Something wrong?'

'I'll tell you later.'

He pulled her back into his embrace. After two months at sea his need for her was strong. He kissed her roughly. She tasted of garlic and wine.

'Where've you been? I've been waiting and waiting,' he breathed, as his fingers found their way to the buttons at the front of her blouse.

'I went out to dinner.'

Her grey-green eyes teased with their innocence. She ran the tip of her tongue along her upper lip.

'Who with, may I ask?'

Her back was hot and smooth to his touch. He ran an index finger down her spine.

'Hmmm . . .' Her smile was mischievous. 'My sister,' she said, and kissed him again. Sometimes it was best to lie.

'A likely story . . .'

Her blouse slipped over her shoulders and she shook it free. He lowered his face to her breasts and kissed the creamy flesh, feeling the nipples hardening under the caress of his tongue.

'Oh. . . , ohhh,' she breathed. 'You've been away too long . . .'

Fingers fumbling in their hurry, they undressed each other, dropping their clothes onto the floor. Naked, they held apart for a second, to look at each other and savour their desire. Then they clung together, hungry for the relief that was about to be theirs. He lifted her so her smooth, slim legs entwined his waist, then carried her to the bedroom.

They slept until nine the next morning.

Jackie awoke with a start at the sound of gentle snoring. She lay still, while her memory unravelled, then rolled over to check that she hadn't dreamt it.

The scar on his arm from the bullet wound had healed to a white line now. She wanted to touch it and to push her fingers through his tousled hair, but decided to let him sleep. His face looked so boyish, so untroubled. It wouldn't stay that way for long, she feared.

What had Alan meant about Lebanon?

Peter stirred and his face pulled into a scowl as men with hammers went to work inside his head.

'Oh dear! A little hungover, are we?' Jackie teased.

Peter groaned.

'I'll make you some tea.'

She rolled out of bed and stood up unsteadily. Her own head wasn't too clear either.

With the help of the Earl Grey they began to recover.

'You still haven't told me why you're back in London,' she declared, shaking some paracetamol from a bottle.

'Got to see the spooks,' he answered, swallowing the tablets.

She looked up, alarmed.

'What do you mean, spooks?'

'The intelligence people.'

He levered himself fully upright and propped his back against the pillows.

'You remember the man in Lebanon? The one who tricked me?'

'Ahmed Bizri?' she exclaimed. She'd never forget the name. He'd repeated it over and over again in the month after the mission.

'The very same. I saw him again. The day before yesterday.'

'What?'

'He was on a boat, being smuggled into Spain with a false passport.'

'What did you do?'

'Not what I'd have liked to do! He didn't know me at first. But he recognised my voice eventually. Legally we couldn't touch him. Had to leave him on the boat.'

'So, now he's in Spain? But why? What's he doing there?'

'I don't know. That's why I'm here. To see if anyone else knows.'

She sat very still. She was afraid, although she couldn't say why. Lebanon. Everything seemed to centre on Lebanon. First the Turkish letter. Then the things that Alan had said last night. And now that Lebanese terrorist turning up in the same part of the world as Peter. Coincidence? She feared not.

'You're very thoughtful . . .' Peter commented, pulling her next to him on the bed. She was naked and smelled of their love-making. He put his arm round her shoulder. If only the hammering in his head would stop.

'Mmmm. You'll be careful, won't you?' she pleaded, nuzzling her cheek against his shoulder.

'Don't worry, I'm a big boy.'

She smiled to herself, then looked up at him.

'I know,' she whispered, slipping her hand under the sheet.

Ten

London

The weekend proved as spring-like as the weather-forecasters had promised. Brodrick and Jackie took it gently on Saturday – a visit to the supermarket, a cinema in the evening.

On Sunday they prepared a lunch of roast beef and claret, then in the afternoon took a train to Kew and walked amongst the daffodils in the Botanical Gardens.

Neither of them gave much voice to their thoughts. Deep down they were both afraid. Something was afoot, but they didn't know what. Something seemed destined to involve them both, but they didn't yet know how.

Now they had a weekend together, unexpectedly. Something to savour. The calm before a storm that was still just a cloud on the horizon. But Jackie had the same sense of foreboding she'd experienced at Christmas. The same fear that when she said goodbye to Peter in a day or two, it could be for the last time.

On Monday morning Brodrick was in Whitehall before nine.

The long corridors of the Defence Ministry seemed gloomier than ever. He followed a limping messenger to the offices of the Defence Intelligence Staff. Along the way, some doors were open, revealing dusty postrooms; others were closed, their access controlled by combination lock.

Up two flights of stairs, then the messenger tapped at a panelled door, marked DIS.

'Ah, Captain Brodrick?'

He was welcomed by a short man in a grey, nondescript suit. The messenger melted back into the obscurity of the passageway.

'My name's Andrew Tapsell, and I'm the SIO to the ACDS brackets I.'

Brodrick interpreted in his head: Senior Intelligence Officer to the Assistant Chief of Defence Staff (Intelligence).

A second man rose from a chair and reached out his hand.

'This is John Donald, who works with me. He's only just joined us, so he wants to listen in.'

Donald smiled weakly and sat himself down again.

'In a minute we'll be joined by Janet Whiting, who's desk officer for the Near East at the SIS. We'll have a listen to what you've got to tell us, then add our contribution, and see what we come up with.'

'Fine.'

'As you'll remember from the . . . ah . . . "do" in Lebanon last year, our knowledge of that part of the world is not as strong as we'd like.'

'Quite,' Brodrick bristled.

'There are still gaps, I'm afraid. However, Janet'll do her best . . . Ah, here she is.'

The door opened to reveal a thin, pale woman with powerful spectacles that reduced her pupils to the size of frogspawn.

'Sorry I'm late,' she whispered, clutching a ringbinder.

'You're not, you're not,' Tapsell reassured her. He made the introductions and suggested where they should sit.

'Let's begin, then. Will you kick off, Captain Brodrick?'

175

He told them about Ahmed Bizri. As he described their encounter aboard the pitching motor cruiser, Tapsell concentrated impassively, but the woman fidgeted, opening her ring-binder and thumbing her notes. Brodrick cast hardly a glance at John Donald who was showing little interest.

'So, security in Spain and Gib have been alerted,' Brodrick concluded, 'but what we really need is hard intelligence about what he's doing in Spain.'

'Mmmm. Intriguing. He's a long way from his home territory,' Tapsell commented. 'What've we got, Janet?'

'Yes. Well, they warned me on Friday you were coming . . .'

The woman from the Secret Intelligence Service nodded at Brodrick but kept her eyes on her folder.

'So I've been in touch with the CIA at Langley over the weekend,' she continued.

'We tend to rely on America for data on the Beirut militias. I think they get it from the Israelis. Anyway they faxed me their most recent summary on *Mustadhafin*.'

She waved the document – two pages in double-spaced typing. Not much there, Brodrick concluded.

'It is rather thin,' she remarked, reading his mind. 'But what they say is that most of Abdul Habib's management team were killed in the Harrier attack last year. Habib himself only surivived because he was somewhere else at the time. They say his younger brother was one of those killed, and that's made him very bitter.'

'That's exactly what I'm worried about,' Brodrick interrupted. 'And he'll want revenge, you can be sure of that.'

'Possibly. Possibly,' the SIS woman answered dismissively. 'But there is another scenario which I find quite attractive.'

Attractive? Brodrick was getting riled at the words these people used.

'It goes like this . . . ,' she continued. 'Because most of the thugs who ran Habib's businesses were blown to bits, other gangs tried to muscle in on his territory. There were several shoot-outs in the southern suburbs of Beirut in the weeks after the bomb attack.

'The drug business was the one part of *Mustadhafin*'s activities that survived untouched. Habib controls part of the Beka'a, growing opium and marijuana. He sells the stuff through the Kurds. They process the opium into heroin, then conceal it on long-distance lorries going all over Europe.

'But unfortunately for our friend Habib, the Turks' crackdown on the Kurds is starting to cause havoc with the drug shipments. We suspect the Lebanese are finding it hard to get rid of their crops.'

She placed her notes flat on the table and glanced at Tapsell to see if he was getting her drift.

'And you think Mr Bizri is maybe trying to ship the stuff through Spain?' Tapsell chipped in obligingly.

'Exactly. And when Captain Brodrick found him, he may have actually had drugs on the boat. Just managed to flush them down the loo in time.'

'Mmmm. Interesting idea.'

'I don't believe that,' Broderick declared. 'Spain's a helluva long way from Lebanon. Over two thousand miles. Why go so far? Italy or Greece would do just as well, surely?'

'Ah, Spain's got a much better distribution network. The Colombians – well, you know all about that. Get drugs into Spain, and shipping it to anywhere in Europe is a doddle.'

'Could be a simple explanation,' Tapsell concluded.

'But the wrong one,' Brodrick snapped. 'You've missed the point.'

Janet Whiting looked alarmed and affronted.

'You don't know what they're like, these people,' he went on. 'Habib and Bizri, they're evil bastards with one basic instinct – vengeance!'

'Look, we understand your point of view. . . ,' Tapsell soothed.

'You *don't* bloody understand!' Brodrick exploded. 'You weren't there in Lebanon last November. You weren't on that boat in the Med last week!'

He noticed John Donald watching him with renewed interest.

Woken you up at last, have I?

Tapsell and Whiting glanced at one another. Brodrick sensed he'd gone over the top.

Cool it, he told himself.

'Sorry. I've got strong feelings on this one. I just know that bloke is out to get his own back.'

'We . . . sympathise with your feelings,' Tapsell replied. He'd decided not to use the word 'understand' again.

'Let me try and describe things, so you'll understand,' Brodrick continued, cautiously. 'Beirut's a cesspit. The way to win is to fight dirtier than the other bloke.

'That's why I got rough with Ahmed Bizri. We worked on him for three hours. I won't tell you what we did – it wasn't very nice. But from past experience, I've found it gets people to tell the truth.

'We thought we'd cracked it. We all did – me, Sergeant Blight and Hardy, the Embassy security man. But Bizri fooled us. And he did so in a way that was so bloody devious, it was evil.

'That villa he took us to, where he said Richard Bicknell was being held? Do you know whose it was?'

He shook his head, still bitter and bewildered that he could've been used that way.

'We hit the house hard, as you know. Took out the guards, shot a kid, nearly killed the mother. And bloody Bicknell wasn't there. Never had been . . .'

The shakes were beginning again. It was all coming back – the noise, the smell, the dead boy. Vivid images flashing before his eyes.

His hands clung to the arms of the chair. Had to finish. Had to convince them.

'The woman and her children? D'you know who they were? I found out later. They were the family of a rival gang boss. Someone Habib and Bizri had been feuding with for years!'

He leaned forward, eyeing the woman from SIS.

'That bastard Bizri – he not only tricked us, he used *us* to take revenge on their worst enemy! He's sick! Vengeance – it's in their blood.'

Tapsell let out a long, low whistle.

'Incredible . . .'

'But true!' Brodrick stressed.

Janet Whiting eyed Brodrick clinically, then closed her file and looked across at Tapsell.

'Islam's a vengeful religion,' she stated dismissively. 'But I have to say there's no indication from any intelligence sources that they're planning an attack on us. Particularly in Spain.'

'*Eagle*'s going to be in Gib at Easter,' Brodrick pressed. 'Ideal opportunity for a terrorist attack.'

'Clearly we've got to take the threat seriously,' Tapsell stepped in. 'You've alerted Gibraltar. We don't know how co-operative the Spanish'll be. They understood about the IRA, and helped with the SAS operation. But this one's vaguer. We'll try diplomatic channels. Ask for Bizri to be traced and watched.'

Ms Whiting fingered her ring-binder.

'But don't reject the drugs explanation, Captain Brodrick,' Tapsell concluded. 'It could still be the right one. Money-making – that's what *Mustadhafin* are about. Don't forget that.'

The meeting was ending. Tapsell got to his feet.

'Thanks for coming to see us. It's helped enormously.

Just one other thing – do you remember enough of what Bizri looks like to do a photofit?'

'I can certainly try . . .'

'Good. My secretary'll take you down to the police office. They're expecting you.'

Brodrick shook hands with all three and was escorted from the room.

'Whew!' Janet Whiting exclaimed, when the door was closed. 'I thought he was going to hit me at one point!'

'That's the Royal Marines for you. Fifty per cent muscle, fifty per cent aggression. It's how we got the Falklands back.'

Tapsell turned to John Donald.

'Right, doctor. Your turn to speak at last. You heard what Brodrick said. Give us a psychiatrist's analysis of that conversation. Is he imagining things, or not?'

By the time Jackie had fought her way home on the tube, it was after seven. She had no idea what to expect. Peter had said he might have to return to Gibraltar that afternoon. And of course he hadn't phoned her.

'You're still here!' she exclaimed, closing the door of the flat behind her. 'Brilliant.'

He closed the atlas he'd been studying and levered himself from an armchair.

'Hi, sweetheart.'

He mixed her a gin and tonic, then they slumped together on the sofa.

'My day was long and dreary,' Jackie announced. 'The "head teacher's" back from Hong Kong, so poor George had to spend the entire afternoon in the study, reporting on what's happened in his absence. I actually felt sorry for him.'

'Wonders'll never cease.'

'How about you? How were the spooks?'

She turned to look at him.

'Mmmm,' he mumbled.

She saw a cloud cross his face.

'I did a photofit of Bizri. Looked quite like him.'

'Is that all? You came all this way to do a picture?'

'No, no. I saw some people. There was a woman from MI6 . . .'

'Called Mata Hari?'

'Hardly. In the Marines we'd have described her as doggo.'

'I get the message. But what did she say?'

Brodrick sighed. He'd failed to convince them, he felt certain of it.

'She said Bizri was probably trying to smuggle drugs into Spain because his organisation can't sell them to the Kurds any more.'

'Drugs?' she exclaimed. 'What's this about drugs?'

Drugs. Lebanon. Kurds. A horrifying connection had been made in her brain.

'The *Mustadhafin* deal in drugs?' she repeated, aghast.

'Yes. They're like the mafia. I must have told you. They're all at it. Hash, heroin – it's where most of the Beirut gangs get their money from. The Beka'a Valley's full of poppies and cannabis plants.'

'But Habib and Bizri, they do a lot of this?'

The question surprised him. Why her interest?

'Yes. It's their main business now, according to Mata Hari.'

'Oh.'

Brodrick eyed her curiously.

'Since when have you been so concerned about the drugs trade?'

She shrugged and shook her head.

'Oh, I don't know . . .' She drank her gin and looked at her watch. 'When do you go back to Gib?'

'Tomorrow morning. I fly from Luton at nine-forty-five.'

She groaned.

181

'That early! You'll have to be up at six.'

'Got to catch a coach from Victoria at seven.'

Suddenly she pulled away from him and sat bolt upright. She stared at the ice-cube in her glass.

'What's up?'

He hoped she wasn't going funny on him, just because he was leaving tomorrow.

'You did say the Kurds? Habib sells drugs to the Kurds?'

'Yes. They process the stuff. Turn the opium into heroin.'

Odd, this interest of hers.

Jackie could suddenly see it in her mind – the Ozkan letter. She could even picture the handwriting. That's what it had said. *The nuclear bombs had been paid for with heroin!*

'What is it, Jackie? You look dreadful.'

She stood up. In her head, the warning from Minister Webster. Top secret! Say nothing to anyone.

'Nothing. I expect you want some supper. There's a couple of trout in the freezer. Suit you?'

She headed for the kitchen.

'Sure.'

He stared at her disappearing back.

He stood up and crossed to the television. Might catch the end of the Channel Four News.

. . . and new impetus seems to have been given to the dispute between Armenia and Azerbaijan. Armenian nationalist militia have been able to obtain ex-Soviet tanks and have opened up a new front in the war.

Pictures of tanks rolled across the screen. The enclave at

the centre of the Transcaucasian conflict was being progressively reduced to rubble.

Quietly, Jackie had re-emerged from the kitchen and stood in the doorway watching.

And the question of the safekeeping of Russian nuclear weapons has been raised again today. There are fresh reports that warheads may have been stolen from their bunkers since the break-up of the Soviet Union, and sold by nationalist groups to countries in the Middle East. In the Commons this afternoon however, the Foreign Secretary dismissed such rumours as unfounded.

Jackie stifled a gasp. There was the head teacher, as she'd called him, telling the interviewer there was no evidence that nuclear warheads in the former Soviet Union had fallen into the wrong hands.

'He's lying!' she breathed.

How could he sit there and say all that, when he knows about the Ozkan letter?

'What d'you mean?' Brodrick asked, startled.

'How can he say that? I mean, how can anyone really know what's happened to every single Soviet nuclear warhead? There are thirty thousand of them. And look at the chaos in places like Armenia!'

'You're right. They can't possibly know.'

There was something. He could see it in her eyes. Something she knew, but wasn't saying.

'I mean . . .'

Jackie was floundering. What should she do?

'Just supposing . . . Let's pretend for a moment that a nuclear warhead was stolen,' she blustered. 'Let's say, for argument's sake, it got into the hands of a terrorist gang. *Mustadhafin*, for example. It's as good an example as any.'

She saw his eyes narrow.

'Well ... could they make it work?' Her voice trembled. 'What could they do with it? What use would it be to them?'

This wasn't a hypothetical discussion. She was telling him something. An icy chill ran down Brodrick's spine.

Eleven

Tuesday afternoon

The Boeing 757 had begun its descent through a cloudless sky.

Brodrick looked down at the turquoise sea and the sharp outline of the Rock, the isthmus connecting it to Spain sliced in half by the runway which they were about to approach. As the plane banked tightly to keep clear of Spanish airspace he spotted the dark outline of an 'O' Class submarine aiming for the gap in the breakwater.

It wouldn't stand a chance against a nuclear weapon; no warship would. In ten days' time it'd be HMS *Eagle* down there, coming into harbour.

The night before, Jackie had told him everything, eventually. The letter from Izmet Ozkan, the shooting in the Istanbul hotel and the threat that she'd be 'sent to the Tower' if she revealed the letter's contents.

She'd had to tell him of her suspicions. If *Mustadhafin* had the bombs, the consequences for Brodrick and all on board HMS *Eagle* were too horrific for her to contemplate in silence.

The Arab thirst for revenge and the possession of a nuclear weapon was a terrifying combination that had chilled his heart.

How to defend against such a threat? The question was a routine challenge at military staff colleges, but this was different. This was for real.

He cleared customs quickly with his small holdall, pushing past the tourists and service families waiting for their suitcases. A WRN driver met him, and drove him across the broad concrete runway towards the military apron.

'Bit of a delay, was there, sir?' she asked cheerily over her shoulder.

'Air traffic. Usual thing.'

'They're hardly ever on time these days.'

A dark-green Sea King Mk 4 came into view as they rounded the corner of a hangar, its black rotor blades drooping.

'You're to see Commander Camfield before your flight, sir. He said he'd meet you at Flight Ops.'

The WRN driver stopped the car outside the cream-coloured building where pilots were briefed before their flights.

'Need me any more, sir?'

'Nope. Looks like my cab's waiting over there.' He pointed to the helicopter.

She drove off and he stepped into the building.

'I'm looking for Commander Camfield,' he told the bored RAF clerk sitting in the first office he came to. Brodrick was still wearing civilian clothes; he'd left his uniform on board ship.

'And who are you, sir?'

'Captain Brodrick, Royal Marines,' he said sharply.

The clerk stood up and began to look businesslike. He led Brodrick into the corridor and indicated a door at the far end.

'The Commander said you were to go straight in. And your helicopter crew are in the ready-room. They're getting itchy. Don't seem to like our rations here.'

Brodrick looked at his watch. It was nearly four. They'd be back on board *Eagle* in time for supper if they left soon.

Commander Camfield was on the phone, talking with the handset tucked under his chin, leaving his hands free to scribble notes.

'Sorry,' he said at last, putting down the receiver. 'So

much to do. We've got a member of the Royal Family coming in at the end of the week, and I still haven't been able to get hold of their programme. Anyway, none of my troubles, how did you get on?'

'Well, I told them what I'd told you,' Brodrick replied cautiously. 'They took the point. Said they'd treat it seriously, but seemed to think Ahmed Bizri could be in Spain to look for a new market for drugs.'

'You don't sound convinced.'

'I know the man. They don't.'

Camfield kept his expression studiedly neutral. He'd had a fax from London that morning – from Defence Intelligence. It had said Brodrick had shown 'obsessive characteristics, typical of someone suffering from post-traumatic stress disorder.' The army psychiatrist recommended Camfield bear that in mind when assessing his judgements.

'You reckon Bizri plans an attack, here on the Rock?'

'Yes.'

Camfield laid his hands flat on the table.

'Fine. We'll take no chances. Can't afford to.'

'Any word from the Spaniards? Have they found him yet?'

'No. But they're looking. Tell you what – it'd be well worth it to have you ashore here for a few days before *Eagle* comes in. After all, you're the only bloke who knows what Bizri looks like.'

'Fine by me.'

'I'll fix it.'

They'd touched base; there was nothing more to be said at that moment. Brodrick stood up, and the security officer escorted him to the aircrew ready-room.

It was a cool afternoon in Beirut. The distant Shouf mountains were cloud-capped, and after the morning's rain the film of refuse coating the streets had turned to slime.

Yegor Papushin hated Beirut. To him, it still smelled of devastation and anarchy, the legacy of fifteen years of civil war. This was how his own country was going – sliding into ungovernability.

He had driven south through the city at hair-raising speed. The political temperature of the region was rising once more; foreigners again risked being kidnapped.

He swerved to avoid potholes, but with limited success. Beside Papushin sat the Beirut correspondent of *Izvestia*. Before the demise of the Soviet Union, Belikov had been KGB resident in Lebanon. Now, transferred to the staff of the new Russian Ministry of External Security, he was complaining that he had not been paid for three months.

The trail that had led Papushin to Beirut had been long and tortuous. In the end they'd got the Armenian nationalists who'd seized the warheads to talk, but only after one of their number had died under interrogation.

The loss of nuclear weapons had shamed the military leadership. Even today, more than two years after the theft, the generals hadn't dared admit it to the Russian President.

It astonished him that word hadn't leaked out somewhere. But then, he reasoned, all those involved had a vested interest in secrecy.

As for the Armenian militias, they had no wish for the world to know how they'd come by so many dollars.

The Kurds had no desire to lose their status as the darlings of the United Nations and the Western media. If the nations who'd saved their kinsmen from starvation in snow-covered northern Iraq learned they'd been trading in stolen nuclear weapons, the charity upon which their lives depended would evaporate.

Despite the ending of the civil war, Beirut was still an evil place where one outrage spawned another, Papushin thought. People lived by jungle law. Papushin's masters had always understood that. The West hadn't.

When American hostages had been taken in earlier years, the response from Washington had been one of impotent protestation. When Soviet diplomats were kidnapped by a Shi-ite gang, the KGB had bitten back. They'd captured the nephew of the Shi-ite gangleader, sliced off small parts of his anatomy and delivered them to his uncle, saying he'd get the whole boy piece by piece if he didn't free the Russians. They were released the next day.

'There'll be a checkpoint round the next bend,' the journalist reminded him. 'Syrians. Should be no difficulties for us.'

Papushin nodded silently. His face was deeply lined for someone in his early forties. His broad forehead seemed to hang over his deepset eyes; his nose was prominent, his lips thick and sullen.

'But there'll be more,' Papushin replied eventually. 'By tonight the *Mukhabarrat* will be asking what we're doing.'

'Let them ask . . .'

When he'd first learned that the warheads were in Lebanon, Papushin had assumed that Hezbollah or Islamic Jihad had bought them. But as his enquiries progressed, a name had emerged that surprised him.

Mustadhafin.

They were not listed in KGB files as a major force. Rather, they were criminals dealing in drugs and protection rackets. They'd got out of their depth last year, demanding ransom for a British businessman, and had been all but wiped out by a British air raid.

189

So why had Abdul Habib, the *Mustadhafin* leader, bought two nuclear warheads? They'd be useless to him, if he was acting alone. Such an organisation lacked the technology to make them work.

So who were his friends? Hezbollah? Papushin had heard Habib had links with them. Was he working for them as a proxy? Providing them with a weapon with which to cripple Israel? Those fantatics might be suicidal enough to try it.

Or the Syrians? Habib was said to be friendly with them too. He'd need to be, to work his drug operation from the Beka'a. But would the Syrians want stolen warheads? It could spell the end of their arms deal with Russia if they were found out – no more spares for their MiG 29s or their T72 tanks. Papushin ruled that out.

Iran? Iraq? Libya? All were hungry for nuclear weapons.

The informant from Habib's organisation, who'd set them on this coast road south, didn't know. He'd been scared to death. But the promise of ten thousand dollars and an air ticket out of Beirut had been enough to open his mouth.

They were beyond Damour now, rattling down the road to Sidon, the verges littered every few kilometres with the rusting wreckage of war.

Habib had an uncle who grew oranges on the coast, the informant had told them. It was on his farm that the warheads had been hidden.

'These farmers we're going to see – you will write something for *Izvestia*?' Papushin asked suddenly.

They'd arranged to visit a neighbouring orchard, ostensibly to research an uplifting story of how Lebanese farmers had kept the free market operating throughout the period of civil strife. Papushin carried credentials identifying him as a photographer for the magazine.

'Of course. My readers will be eager to know how to

harvest oranges in a civil war. It could be useful to them
. . .' came Belikov's ironic reply.

Abdul Habib stepped out of the dimly-lit packing shed
and blinked in the bright sunlight. The work going on
inside the stone building involved technical concepts
that were beyond his comprehension and was being
carried out by men whose language he didn't understand.

From his trouser pocket he pulled a string of amber
beads and began to run them through his fingers. This
was the most anxious time for him, the moment when he
could go no further without the help of others.

The plan, which had been his and his alone from the
moment the Kurds had made their offer, was now no
longer under his sole control. There was no other way;
he'd had to seek help. But how could he trust them?

The technicians working with their drills and their
lathes took orders from the Libyan, not from him.

He smelled the air, mild in temperature, heavy with
the scent of orange blossom. So different from the smoke
and decay of Beirut. It made him think of his childhood
in the stony hillcountry of south Lebanon, where he'd
lived until the Israelis invaded, driving him and his
brother Farouk north.

He remembered again that terrible journey. The
panic as they'd fled their home on a sweaty June night
twelve years ago, the terror of the shellbursts and of the
Israeli tanks grinding into their villages. Thirty
thousand Israeli soldiers had invaded Lebanon that
night.

He remembered the dawn, the sky tinged the colour of
blood. Its light had revealed chaos on the coast road
north; two hundred thousand Lebanese were fleeing
their homes. Taxis, vans, tractors and trailers piled with
mattresses and chairs had jammed the coastal highway

191

to Beirut. Israeli jets had screamed overhead, driving the refugees from their vehicles to take cover in the trees.

He'd come a long way from his boyhood south of the Litani River. Just how far, the world was about to learn.

He looked up at the sky. The clouds had scattered; the night should be clear. It was as he'd hoped. Beyond the dark green of the orange groves, a line of tall silvery eucalyptus concealed the road. Beyond that was the sea. After dark a boat would steal up to a rickety jetty and take the deadly cargo on board.

He turned back towards the packing shed. Would the technicians be finished in time? The Libyan had assured him they would.

The double boom of a jet breaking the sound barrier shattered the tranquillity. Abdul Habib craned his neck, searching for the tiny fleck of silver against the blue that would be the Israeli reconnaissance fighter, making its daily sweep north, unchallenged. Habib felt himself cower; so often in the past these flights had been followed by the bombers and by death.

Not long now, he told himself, and it would be the Zionists who would bow the knee.

He felt no love for the Palestinians either; it was they who'd brought destruction to his homeland, using it as a base from which to attack Israel.

Abdul Habib had learned one potent lesson from the Israelis. A lesson about the nature of retaliation. When it came it should be massive. Not one eye for an eye, but ten. Not one life for a life, but a hundred.

And now, inside this shed, he had the means to show the world that it was a lesson he'd learned well.

Yegor Papushin lifted his craggy eyebrow from the viewfinder of the camera. The telephoto lens had produced a crisp, clear picture of the man, identifying him beyond any doubt as Habib.

A sniper's rifle with a silencer would have rid the world of the rogue, Papushin thought. However, it wasn't Habib that had to be eliminated, but the monstrous weaponry he now controlled.

Were they here, the bombs, inside that shed? Almost certainly. He'd seen the guards, pretending to be packers, holding Kalashnikovs down their trouser seams, so as to be less noticeable. With such a trophy here he'd expected heavier guns, but maybe the best security lay in anonymity; the fewer who knew the weapons were here the better.

Papushin shifted his position in the scrape he'd dug under an orange tree. He had a long wait ahead. For all he knew it could be days before he had proof that the bombs were here. The gentle breeze from the west set the dark low-hanging leaves dancing across his view.

He was on his own now.

The *Izvestia* correspondent had finished his interview with the neighbouring farmer in less than an hour while Yegor took his time with the camera. Belikov had feigned impatience at Papushin's slowness and had driven to Sidon supposedly to find them accommodation for the night. He'd told the farmer that Papushin was staying on at the farm to photograph at sunset, and he'd return later to pick him up.

Papushin raised his head slowly and looked all round to check his fieldcraft. They'd only find him if they stumbled right onto him.

The Strait of Gibraltar
17.30 hrs

The Sea King flew southwest from Gibraltar. HMS *Eagle*

was steaming through the Strait at twenty knots, driven out into the Atlantic by the ninety-four thousand horsepower of her Olympus gas turbines.

'Father won't be pleased,' the pilot told Brodrick as they lifted off from the Rock. 'Kept him waiting, you have. He won't like that.'

'What are you on about?'

'Special op in the Atlantic. All singing, all dancing. Captain's very excited. Timed the ship's transit through the Strait to coincide with your flight arriving from London, so's we could scoop you up on the way. What a dickhead! Should've known the civair would be late. Two hours!'

'Won't make much difference,' Brodrick retorted.

'Really? You can break the news to him personally in a few minutes.'

Darkness was closing in, and Brodrick could see little through the small window, but eventually he spotted the broad wake of the carrier and knew they'd be on deck within minutes.

A heavy Atlantic swell had set the ship rolling uncomfortably. The wind tugged at his survival suit as he made his way to the island. Inside the shelter the Flight Deck Officer handed him a message – to see the Captain in his sea cabin immediately after supper.

In his own quarters, Brodrick changed into the Red Sea rig, which was regulation wardroom dress in the evenings. Starched white open-necked shirt with short sleeves, and dark trousers with a maroon cummerbund.

In the wardroom ante-room, he signed for a pint of CSB at the bar and carried his glass across the room to hobnob with the Principal Warfare Officer.

'Evening, Nick.'

'Ah! So good of you to join us! Sorry if business curtailed your run ashore!'

'Piss off!'

'Hope you weren't caught in mid bag-off!'

'Bollocks to that! I've been trying to ensure you don't get your dick shot off next time you go for a bang in Gibraltar!'

'Ahh! Serious stuff. Is this the Arab you fingered last week?'

'That's the one.' Word had got around, then. 'All right. Now would somebody tell me what the hell's going on? Why are we apparently steaming balls out for the Caribbean?'

Lt Commander Brady turned to his companions and raised an eyebrow.

'Chance'd be a fine thing. This is the big one at last. The one we've all been waiting for. Captain's got some shit-hot intelligence from the other side of the pond. A sugar ship heading for the Med, carrying the biggest cocaine cargo the world has ever seen. Going to use all our assets to find it and track it. SHARS, bags, even booties, so they say.'

'Then we turn it all over to the Spaniards so they can balls it up,' Brodrick muttered cynically.

He glanced round anxiously, suddenly worried that Teniente Pepe Alvarez might be in earshot. He wasn't. He relaxed again.

'Something like that. It's called "improving diplomatic relations".'

'But seriously, what's it look like? Cut the crap for a minute,' Brodrick pressed.

'Same as usual. Just further away. Chances of our finding anything look as remote as ever. Still, nice to have a change of air. Now, swallow that nerve gas and we'll crack a bottle of claret with supper.'

Brodrick felt mellower than he'd intended as he climbed the companionway to the Captain's sea cabin. He'd spent dinner listening to his fellow officers rubbishing their mission against the drug-runners, forcing himself to keep his tongue under control. He tapped on the door-frame.

'Yes?' Captain Dyce sounded sharp and alert. 'Ah, Peter. Back at last. Just in time.'

Dyce's normally pale face looked slightly flushed. Brodrick guessed he'd also enjoyed a glass or two.

'Plane was a bit late, sir. Air traffic, so they said.'

'Never mind, never mind. Come and sit down. Glass of port?'

He passed the flat-bottomed decanter across the small table at which he'd dined by himself. Must be lonely at times as a four-ringer, Brodrick thought.

'Thank you, sir.' It would slip down nicely after the claret. He poured himself a glass.

'Anyone briefed you? You know where we're heading?'

'Only informally, sir. In the wardroom.'

'Good enough.' He looked at Brodrick with an unsettling intensity. 'You realise this is the first really hard intelligence we've had on this entire exercise? Up to now, it's been guesswork mostly, needle in a haystack stuff. But this time we know the precise identity of the ship carrying the drugs, and if we can find her early enough and keep our own presence covert, we may be able to spot all the little pick-up boats and track them back to the coast so the Spaniards can grab 'em. With a bit of luck they'll net an entire drug ring and *Eagle* will get most of the credit.'

'If it happens that way, it'll be great, sir,' Brodrick mumbled.

'But you don't think it will, eh? Now look, I want no faint-hearts on this!' There was an edge to his voice. 'Maximum effort all round and we'll *make* it work. Total concentration. This one must *not* slip through the net. Okay?'

'Absolutely, sir.'

Pompous bastard! Treats his officers like school-kids, Brodrick thought.

'Good. Now, tell me about your trip to London. What did the experts have to say?'

'Not a lot, sir. They still don't know much about the Lebanese militias. What the intelligence guys did say was that *Mustadhafin*'s concentrating on drugs. Heroin and cannabis. And apparently they're having problems distributing the stuff. Trouble with the Kurds. They suggested Bizri could be in Spain looking for a new way of shipping the drugs to northern Europe.'

The Captain's eyes lit up.

'That's interesting! New route, or new drugs maybe? Perhaps he's planning to trade in cocaine! A bit of business expansion. Timing's perfect, with this massive cargo heading our way.'

'I'm not so sure . . .'

'Come on, it's a neat explanation. It's got some logic to it.'

'It's possible, sir. But I still think Bizri's in Spain because we're in the area.'

'Sticking to your revenge theory, are you?'

There was a caustic edge to his voice. Dyce's eyelids lowered minutely. He doesn't believe me, Brodrick thought. The bastard thinks I'm paranoid. Anger began to boil in his gut.

'If you only knew the man. . . , sir,' he growled.

'Quite. Your personal assessment is obviously invaluable.'

His eyebrows arched so they matched the curve of his domed head.

'Anyway, I'm sure the security people in Gib will take no chances,' Dyce concluded neutrally.

'Oh, that reminds me, sir,' Brodrick said. 'Commander Camfield suggested I go ashore a few days before *Eagle* docks at Easter. Since I know what Bizri looks like.'

The Captain shrugged.

'Fine. Can't do any harm. So long as we've got these smugglers in jail by then. If the Spaniards do their stuff, they might have your Mr Bizri locked up too!'

'Now you'd better go and organise your team. We're flying reconnaissance missions from dawn and I'll want your boarding parties standing by round the clock from then on.'

Brodrick stood up and saluted.

'Good night, sir.'

His men were accommodated in a block built into the end of the aircraft hangar. Most of them were watching a Rambo video when he got there.

'Sergeant Dennis?'

Brodrick beckoned his senior NCO to come into the passageway to talk to him.

'Tommorow, at oh-crack-sparrowfart. Boarding parties on twenty-four hour standby. You know that already?'

'I'd heard, sir. Not official, like.'

'Captain thinks we're onto the biggest cocaine-bust of all time. Wants us to get the credit, right?'

'I believe you, sir.'

'But there's another thing.'

'There always is . . .'

'Firearms drill. We're out of practice. I'm going to ask for a splash target. We need to get all our weapon firing up to scratch.'

'They'll like that, sir. You know how they get, watching Rambo . . .'

'Time they had their cocoa, sergeant! See you in the morning.'

Darkness was Yegor Papushin's friend. It enveloped him with a cloak of security. On the hilltop in front of him lamps were still burning in the packing shed with its blacked-out windows. Every so often a door opened letting out a shaft of light.

The night was still; only the occasional breeze rattled the brittle leaves of the eucalyptus trees. There'd been little traffic on the road since sunset. Only those who really had to ventured abroad here at night.

Papushin had spotted no more than a dozen men guarding Habib; whether there were dozens more within hailing distance he was unable to tell. But there was nothing here that a good Spetznaz detachment couldn't deal with in minutes.

It was bitterly disappointing; if he'd been an Israeli, they'd have had a boat load of commandos offshore ready to seize the bombs and slaughter the men who controlled them. Instead, Papushin was alone; he could only watch and wait.

At one time he'd considered suggesting the Israelis be warned. After all they were the most likely target. But these were Russian weapons; it was Russia's responsibility to get them back.

A diesel engine erupted into life and accelerated Papushin's heart-rate. It was somewhere to his right, but he couldn't see it. He detached the image-intensifying night-sight from his AKS-74 assault rifle and switched it on. Allowing a few seconds for warm-up, he scanned the telescope sideways. Suddenly, the glint of starlight reflected off a moving vehicle. A farm tractor, an earth-moving scoop attached, emerged from the trees.

He clipped a reflex camera to the sight, checked the

focus and released the shutter. As the tractor approached the packing shed, the loading doors slid open and light spilled into the stony yard.

Papushin cursed. It was impossible to see inside from where he was lying. The tractor drove through the doors, its scoop held out like a begging bowl.

Minutes later it emerged again.

There was something in the scoop! Drum shaped, covered in a polythene shroud. Papushin clicked the shutter.

Damn! The tractor drove behind the trees, bumping down the track to the road. Was it one of the warheads? He couldn't be sure, but what else would it have been?

If it went far, he'd be stuck. He had no transport, no means of following.

He raised himself to a crouch, steadied the sight and swept a full circle, looking for sentries. There didn't appear to be any.

Running at a stoop, his rucksack on his shoulder, he moved from tree to tree for cover. Twenty metres from the road, he stopped to look and listen.

He heard the diesel grind and stutter. Driver's avoiding the potholes, he thought. Hope the bastards haven't given that weapon a hair trigger!

He powered up the sight again for another sweep. Halfway round, he froze. The outline of a ship had filled the viewfinder.

He swore foully. A small ship was tied up to a jetty, about a hundred metres beyond the road. Where had that come from? It hadn't been there earlier. So that was it. The warhead was to be put on board a boat. Then what? To some Israeli port, to continue the holocaust?

A terrible sense of powerlessness paralysed his limbs. He was just one man, armed only with a rifle. He couldn't stop them. Help was on its way, but wouldn't reach him for hours.

This was too soon! They were moving too fast!

The trail had been long and hard. Now, with the weapons in sight, he was impotent.

From the north, from the direction of Beirut, came a new noise, the sound of a car approaching fast, but slowing down.

From the trees by the road, he heard the crackle of twigs. He swung the lens. Ghostly green figures, picked out by the image-intensifier, rose up from the roadside ditch.

Damn their eyes! He'd nearly run straight into them. So Habib wasn't a fool. He had sentries after all.

Four of them were rolling something into the middle of the road. It looked like a tree trunk. Bastards! If the car hit that at speed . . .

Habib's men scuttled back to their ditch.

The tractor, carrying its delicate and devastating load, had reached the road and turned north. No co-ordination! Why don't they tell it to get off the road? Papushin pressed himself flat to the ground. Any second now, there'd be a collision . . .

The diesel note changed. The tractor had swung down a track to the jetty. Papushin breathed again.

Suddenly tyres squealed. The approaching car had seen the roadblock. Too late. The shattering of glass, the crunch of metal, then silence.

Voices, soft but urgent. Papushin clipped the sight back onto the AKS-74, and watched through the cross-hairs. The front of the car was crumpled, the wheels buckled. Both doors were wrenched open and the occupants dragged out. One, his face bloodied, stood slumped against the car with Habib's men frisking him. On the other, a pistol was found. A kick to his groin and the man buckled, groaning.

There were shouts in Arabic, harsh, cruel sounds that Papushin couldn't understand. More kicks, then sharp questions from the interrogator. The replies were feeble and fearful.

Why weren't they answering? Who were they?

A gunman pulled some documents from the car and held them in the air. Looked like passports. The kicking stopped. A torch was shone on the pages. Then the click of a bolt pulled back.

Two single shots.

The man on the ground twitched, then lay still. His companion still stood, blinded by the blood from his head wound, his hands reaching out in vain to stop the bullets he knew were coming.

Two more shots. Then a burst. He crumpled backwards to the ground.

Papushin lay just twenty metres distant, hidden by a tree. His heart pounded. First pressure on the trigger. How many? Four of them. He could take them all if he was quick. But how many more were there?

Finger off the trigger. Breathe out slowly. Then in again. Time to retreat.

Slowly, noiselessly, he got to his feet, and backed away one step at a time, his firearm to his shoulder, eyepiece pressed against his face. Thank God for a night-sight. Habib's men didn't seem to have any. He doubled the distance from the road, then crabbed to the side, heading north. He had to get closer to that boat.

He moved in a curve from tree to tree, arcing round to the road. Then he spread himself in the dust and aimed his scope towards the south.

He was a hundred metres from the wreckage of the car. He counted six men now, gripping the back of the vehicle, bouncing it on its springs to move it to the side of the road.

Papushin took his chance. Rubber soles silent on the tarmac, he darted to the other side. Then down in the dirt again and up with the scope. They hadn't seen him.

He crawled across the disused coastal railway track and made his way to the water's edge. The westerly breeze pushed small waves gently, rhythmically onto the shingle beach.

He was two hundred metres north of the jetty. Against the starlit sky, he could make out with the naked eye the vee of the fishing-boat's mast and derrick.

He clipped the scope back onto the camera body. Now, with night-vision, he saw the proof he needed. The trail he'd followed for three months *had* been the right one. The drum-like canister of the nuclear missile warhead, as it was winched from the scoop, was unmistakable.

The shutter clicked. He'd have to find out the name of the ship. But first he had to report.

From the bottom of his rucksack he pulled a small R-392 VHF transmitter. He screwed together the three parts of the aerial and plugged it into its socket.

Turning on the power he held down the transmission and call-tone buttons to test the battery. The indicator glowed. He checked the frequency and began to transmit.

Twenty kilometres to the south, in a hotel room in Sidon, Belikov would be listening. As well as the VHF set, he'd have beside him a bigger, high-frequency radio to relay Papushin's frantic messages to Moscow.

Wednesday
00.45 hrs

The Nimitz Class aircraft carrier USS *Carl Jackson* was steaming at an easy eight knots, just south of Cyprus, ninety-five thousand tons of war-fighting machinery powered by two nuclear reactors.

Her schedule specified she should've been heading

west to Gaeta in Italy for maintenance and shore leave, following the spring exercise. But a signal from CINCUSNAVEUR in London had turned her massive bows east again.

On the Flag Deck, Rear-Admiral James D Bock slept fitfully. The orders he'd been given were clear, yet obscure: to position his Carrier Battle Group within striking range of Lebanon, but with no explanation as to what their mission might be.

The instructions had come direct from the White House.

Above the grey, steel island that housed the bridge and flight control, the skeletal communications mast reached up, its black paint and jumble of antennae giving it the look of a tree scorched by fire.

Amongst the radar and satellite dishes, a UHF rod aerial downlinked data from the ES-3A Viking aircraft conducting its ELINT mission over the eastern Mediterranean. The plane was like an airborne vacuum cleaner, sucking up radio transmissions in the military frequencies. It filtered out the routine and relayed anything in Russian back to the carrier.

The SIGINT section on board the *Jackson* was deep in the citadel below the island. The large spools of multi-track tape decks turned slowly, and the two Russian-speaking signals analysts hopped from channel to channel, listening for the unusual.

For twenty-four hours now they'd been on full alert. A Tango class submarine had passed from the Black Sea to the Aegean two days earlier. Any Russian naval activity was unusual now, since the disintegration of the Soviet Union. It had headed east, travelling on the surface to maximise its speed. South of Cyprus it had finally submerged, to escape detection.

The US Navy had tried to track the boat on sonar as it sped towards the Lebanese coast. A hard task in the

Mediterranean, where the density of shipping and the water conditions give the submarine the advantage.

A couple of hours ago they'd struck lucky. A British Nimrod maritime reconnaissance plane from Cyprus had detected the Tango's radio mast raised above the water. Listening, presumably. So far they'd not heard the submarine transmit.

Commander Norman Tracy paced about in the half-darkness of the Combat Direction Centre, the central nervous system of the USS *Carl Jackson*. As Operations Chief he could have left things to the lieutenant on watch, and gotten his head down. But he was uneasy. Why had the Battle Group been sent east? What was the big secret?

Something was up. They'd listened to Voice of America and the BBC World Service for hints, but there'd been none. No news of an impending crisis in Lebanon; no orders yet for special missions; no reconnaissance flights in preparation for bombing raids. They'd simply been ordered to build up the surface and sub-surface picture within a hundred miles of Lebanon.

The surprise appearance of the Russian Tango had produced a little excitement. It was a diesel-electric boat, quiet, with a shallow draught, ideal for working close to the coast, or for putting commandos ashore. Were the Russians planning some special operation in Lebanon or Israel?

Tracy patrolled the Combat Direction Centre like a stray dog in a pound. This was his kingdom, womb-like at times with its soft red lights on the ceiling, green and amber from the displays.

He peered over the shoulder of the operator at the surface plot. The screen displayed an area of sea one hundred and fifty miles across. Cyprus in the top left, Lebanon and Israel bottom right. Across the screen were over a hundred amber flecks, denoting vessels from supertankers to fishing boats criss-crossing the sea. 'White traffic', they called it.

It'd be like looking for a needle in a haystack trying to find a specific ship in that lot, Tracy thought to himself, praying they wouldn't be asked to do it.

He turned to the sub-surface plot behind him. A red triangle denoted the last known position of the Tango, a yellow line projected the course they guessed it was following. They'd have a blue symbol to plot within hours. One of their own submarines was hurrying east to join in the search for the Russian boat.

'Ops Officer, EW!' A voice crackled from an intercom box.

Tracy leaned forward to press the key.

'EW, Ops!'

'If you're feeling bored, sir, we got something to wake ya up!'

'On my way.'

The Electronic Warfare suite, where they could analyse any emission in the electronic spectrum, was in a separate area adjoining the CDC.

'The ES-3's reporting an "indecipherable" at four-zero, point six meg.,' the EW operator told him. 'That's one of the VHF frequencies used by the Soviets. The Viking's trying for co-ordinates. Said it's somewhere on the coast of Lebanon.'

'You got it patched through?' Tracy asked.

The operator passed him a set of headphones.

Static and hiss were all that was audible now at 40.6 MHz. Then suddenly a voice. Soft, almost whispered, and quite indecipherable at first hearing.

The operator talked to the SIGINT plane on a separate circuit.

'You betcha! They got the transmitter right on the shore line, at thirty-three, thirty-eight north,' the operator grinned.

'Any of you Tolstoys make sense of that?' Commander Tracy asked.

'Give us a little playtime and we'll see what we can come up with,' the Russian-speaking signals analyst replied.

They listened for more, but the frequency was dead.

'Gimme a shout when you've worked something,' Tracy said, turning back to the CDC.

'Sure.'

For fifteen minutes the analyst played with the sounds on the tape, filtering, slowing and examining them syllable by syllable. Then he had his answer.

'Not much, Commander. Just three words is all I could make out.'

'Which were?'

' "Israel", and "two packages". Crazy, huh? *Dva pachka*. Those were the words, but don't ask what they mean.'

'Two packages?' Tracy scowled.

Must be code. But it was Russian, transmitted from the Lebanese shoreline. And there was a Russian sub heading for the same co-ordinates.

Time to shake the Admiral out of his beauty sleep.

01.10 hrs

On board the Soviet patrol submarine *Korund*, tension was high. The commander, Captain 2nd Rank Nikolai Bonderenko, faced an action for which he felt singularly unprepared.

Their departure from Sevastopol had been rushed. Time was all-important, they were told. The *Korund* had been the only patrol submarine at the Crimean naval base ready fuelled and provisioned. Half the crew had been at home on leave and had had to be rounded up. They'd sailed the moment the marines had come aboard, little more than ten hours after the alert.

Their initial orders had been to head for the coast of Lebanon at maximum speed. The *Korund* could move at twenty knots on the surface, but only at sixteen submerged. So, to maximise speed, they'd pitched and rolled like a trawler for most of the voyage, to the acute discomfort of the crew.

The Americans had dogged their progress every nautical mile. Eventually, however, Bonderenko had decided it was time to make it less easy for them. They were close to their designated area of operations; concealment was essential for the submarine to do its work. Also, if his men were to fight they must recover from their seasickness. South of Cyprus, he'd dived into the bliss of the still depths.

Now, fifty nautical miles from the Lebanese coast, Moscow had given them instructions. Clear, precise orders.

To commit an act of war on the high seas!

Bonderenko had never fired a shot in anger. None of them had. One thing was clear in his mind; if he was to sink a ship, precise identification was essential. And so far he'd not even been given its name.

The message from the KGB officer ashore had been clear as far as it went; a fishing boat was about to leave the coast of Lebanon, carrying two 'packages' – the codeword for the 'objects of military technology' that had been stolen from the former Soviet Union. Bonderenko had not been told what the 'technology' was, except that it was vital that it never be used. Moscow believed the fishing boat to be destined for an Israeli port; it mustn't reach it. The fishing boat, they insisted, had to be sunk.

Bonderenko was no fool. He knew there was only one

type of military technology whose loss would strike terror into the hearts of his high command. A nuclear weapon.

Bonderenko seethed with anger. Why couldn't his commanders trust him with that information? Torpedo the fishing boat, they'd ordered! 'Commit suicide' was what they'd meant! He was no nuclear expert, but surely a torpedo could detonate the bomb if it was on board, and destroy them all.

He had a plan, to do it his way. He had no wish to die for a nation that no longer existed. But first he had to find the right fishing boat.

The co-ordinates he'd been given marked the point on the coast from where the boat was expected to sail. It showed on his chart as a small spit of sand and rock, three hours away even at full power. And running flat out, in a straight line, they'd risk being tracked by the Americans.

In addition, he had to come up to periscope depth once an hour to listen for further instructions from Moscow. But he had no choice.

01.30 hrs

In the dimly lit Combat Direction Centre of the USS *Carl Jackson* the men had adopted an appearance of alertness. The Battle Group Commander, Rear-Admiral Bock, had descended from his night cabin to take up residence in the Flag Plot, adjoining the CDC.

The combat plot had changed little in the past hour. There'd been no further sighting of the Tango. The sea between Cyprus and Lebanon was a mile deep. The

Russian captain was making good use of the temperature layers to avoid detection.

Commander Tracy had ordered the Viking ASW aircraft to lay barriers of sonobuoys across the boat's predicted course, but with no contact so far.

'Ops Officer to Flag Plot!'

The crackling command from the intercom sent Tracy to the far corner of the CDC.

'Sir?'

Inside his own small command centre, Rear-Admiral James Bock had repeaters of the main screens in the CDC. He'd told the operator to offset the radar picture from the centre, to concentrate on the Lebanese coast.

'See this here?' The Admiral pointed to the display. 'I want every shipping movement logged from now on.'

His lugubrious voice seemed to imply there'd be hell to pay if it wasn't done.

'Aye, sir. Just along the coast there?'

'That's it. And can we get a better plot?'

'We got a Hawkeye flying up and down the coast, twenty miles out. I guess most o' these tracks are his. But he won't pick up the inshore stuff. Too much clutter.'

'I know that, Commander.'

'Sir.'

'Just do what you can.'

'What are we looking for, sir?'

Admiral Bock narrowed his eyes the way Bob Hope did it. He had been told he bore a certain facial resemblance to Hope, but no one had ever suggested he had the same sense of humour.

'Can't tell you that, Norman. No one's told me, either. I'll let you into a secret. I have no goddam idea why we're here! I guess they'll tell me one day; I just hope it's not too late!

'And I'll tell ya something else. The Cold War may be over, but that doesn't mean we have to trust the Russians. They're up to something out there.' He jabbed a finger at the screen. 'We gotta keep our eyes open.'

'Yes, sir.'

Tracy returned to the CDC and looked round to see who was least occupied.

'Kopinski!' he called to the sub-surface operator. 'You been having it easy. Come here and give Roberts a hand.'

He stood behind the surface plot and explained what he wanted done.

'Log everything, sir? To thirty miles out?' Leading Radarman Kopinski protested. 'There's maybe fifty paints on that screen, and half of that's clutter.'

'Just do what you can, Kopinski,' Commander Tracy ordered. 'Anything big moving through. Anything to or from the shore. Anything you think matters.'

The radarman shrugged and slipped a transparent plastic sheet over the screen.

Every few minutes the radar plot changed, as a new picture beamed back from the E-2C Hawkeye. And each time it changed, Kopinski made a fresh chinagraph mark on the overlay.

A guy'd need to be psychic to see any significance in it, Tracy told himself. He paced across to the air picture on the far side of the CDC. This was the easy part. Nice clear symbols on the screen – airliners following the invisible lanes that criss-cross the sky. Amongst the white symbols, two blue ones, the Viking and the Hawkeye aircraft, which were the long-distance eyes and ears of the carrier.

'Uh – oh; looks like these guys know each other.' The voice was Kopinski's.

Tracy hurried back to the surface plot.

'See this guy, here?' The radarman pointed to an amber blip in the centre of the screen.

'Ain't moved. You can't see it now, but that's two paints there. One of them was there, all along. Could be at anchor. The other was real small. Couldn't track it half the time. Now they're alongside and not going anyplace.'

'Kopinski, if we were looking for smugglers, you'd get a citation for that!' Tracy clapped him on the shoulder.

'Jeez, sir! What are we looking for?'

'I don't know. But put it in the log. It'll look good.'

It was well over an hour since the last confirmed fix on the submarine, which could be anywhere within a thousand square miles of sea by now. More than likely it was close to where they thought it was. Just that the sonobuoys hadn't picked it up.

Radarman Roberts punched up the wider chart of the eastern Mediterrean. With the island of Cyprus at the top of the screen, the positions of the US aircraft carrier and her escorts appeared in blue.

He tapped the screen where the Tango had last been detected.

'The *Stevens* is close. No more'n thirty or forty mile,' Tracy mused.

The *Stevens* was an Oliver Hazard Perry Class Frigate with a towed-array sonar, able to detect submarines up to a hundred miles away in ideal conditions. It was far from ideal here, and the *Stevens* had had no luck.

That radio intercept troubled Tracy. *Dva pachka*. 'Two packages'. He looked down at Kopinski's overlay on the radar screen. Two ships, Kopinski'd said.

'Two ships' – 'two packages'? The same thing?

No. Couldn't be. Too improbable.

Fifteen minutes later the amber traces on the surface plot had separated again. The larger one began to move, heading west. The smaller boat, so small it kept disappearing from the display, turned south.

Captain Nikolai Bonderenko checked the chart. He'd turned his boat towards the southeast. If the vessel he was to sink was bound for an Israeli port, they'd be hard pressed to catch it in time.

He looked at his watch. A few more minutes and they'd get an update on their orders.

'Periscope depth! Revolutions for five knots!'

Stealth. Almost silent at that speed. The Americans would need to have hydrophones within metres to hear anything.

It took a couple of minutes for the fore-planes to bring them up from the deep. The *Korund* was large, three thousand tons and ninety metres long. One of the last of her class to be built, she was less than ten years old.

Bonderenko was proud of his crew, more professional and with better spirit than most in his navy.

'Sonar reports no surface contacts within visual range, Comrade Captain!'

'Up periscope!' ordered Bonderenko.

He unfolded the grips and rotated the sight to scan the horizon.

'Surface clear! Down periscope.'

Too quick for any American radar plane to detect them. Even if the Viking's screens had registered a blip, it would be gone so fast the operators would dismiss it as clutter from the sea.

'Steer one-eight-zero. Maintain revolutions for five knots.'

Thirty seconds before 02.15 hrs, their scheduled communications slot. If there was nothing this time they'd listen again in an hour.

'Raise radio mast!'

The hiss of hydraulics as the shiny steel slid upwards.

'Mast locked, Captain!'

Bonderenko strode to the wireless cabin and leaned in. Almost immediately the teleprinter began to chatter. The signaller nodded; it was for them.

The moment the transmission ended, Bonderenko ordered the mast down. The sensors at the base of the antenna confirmed that they had not been detected by airborne radar.

He tore the page from the machine and told his executive officer to dive the submarine deep again.

Back in the privacy of his cabin, he twisted the combination lock on the wallsafe and took out the codes for the day.

Five minutes later he'd completed his decoding and stared dumbfounded at the message. It confirmed his worst fears.

Target identified as fishing boat '*Joun*'. Estimated one hundred fifty tonnes. Departed Lebanon 33 deg 37 mins N at 01.47 hrs. Initial course southwest. Present course unknown. Believed proceeding south.

Your orders: to intercept if target passes south of latitude 33 degrees.

Following rules of engagement:

1. Positive identification of vessel's name.
2. Vessel appears bound for an Israeli port.
3. It is in international waters.
4. It can be attacked in darkness.
5. There are no other vessels within visual range.

Torpedoes must NOT be used. Cargo contains nuclear weapons materials. THIS FOR YOUR EYES ONLY!

Essential not to damage cargo in attack. Suggest boat is sunk by machine-gun fire below water line. Expect fire to be returned.

No survivors and no trace of vessel to be left on the surface.

Mark location of wreck with sonar beacon. Cargo is to be recovered later by salvage vessel now en route.
The Commander-in-Chief salutes you, comrade. Your actions will serve the Motherland well. Our thoughts are with you.

Bonderenko leaned back against the cold steel wall of his cabin. Motherland. How wayward that mother had become. She'd ordered him to kill.

His throat dried. He swallowed to moisten it.

He'd trained for this. The manuals had made death a clinical business, an academic matter of course and speed, torpedo accuracy and warhead lethality. Buzz-words. But to do it with gunfire, when you could see the fear in the eyes of the men whose lives you were about to end?

And to do it in the knowledge that one bullet out of place could detonate an atom bomb and vapourise the lot of them.

His thoughts turned to his only child, a girl, brought into the world with such pain and difficulty by his pale, young wife. His eyes moistened.

Enough!

He raced back to the chart table.

'How far south are we?' he demanded.

The navigator checked.

'Thirty-three degrees and twelve minutes north, Comrade Captain,' he answered smartly. 'And about thirty-five nautical miles from the coast.'

To the left of the chart table was the combat plot.

'Three surface contacts, Captain,' the Michman at the sonar panel told him. 'To the northwest we have a bulk-carrier. South, a ferry, bound for Haifa probably. And here,' he pointed to his display, 'a general cargo ship, maybe two thousand tons, between us and the shore.'

'We're looking for a fishing boat,' Bonderenko breathed.

'Nothing at the moment,' the Michman shrugged.

Back at the chart table, the Captain pointed to the thirty-third parallel.

'That's where we need to be. On the edge of the continental shelf. What's the name of that headland?'

The navigator read from the chart.

'Ras enn Naqoura.'

'Lay a course for it.'

He moved to the centre of the cramped control room and stood there, arms folded. They had less than two hours to prepare.

The machine-gun! When had it last been fired? Months ago. Would it work? There was a bracket for mounting it on top of the tower; when had it last been greased? Hell! There was much to do.

Leaving the navigator in command, he summoned his officers to the wardroom to give them orders which would shake them to the core.

04.45 hrs

The faded paint on the prow of the fishing-boat *Joun* made her name difficult to read. In the narrow wheelhouse, the grizzled skipper kept the bows due south, far from certain that the money he'd been paid was sufficient to justify the risks he was now taking.

Down in the cramped and smokey cabin sat his two regular crew, sharing the space uncomfortably with the two gunmen Abdul Habib had left on board.

Nobody had told him what was inside the two heavy canisters they'd loaded into the hold, but the feeling

216

deep in his gut told him that Allah's wish was that he should have nothing to do with them.

Too late now. Habib's men had made an offer he couldn't refuse; if he did what they wanted, the two gunmen sitting in his meagre home, keeping his wife and children 'company', would depart in peace.

Habib's men hadn't told him where he was heading. Just south, and that meant one thing to him: Israel, and the aggressive little patrol craft that zipped out from Haifa at thirty knots to interrogate every Arab boat that came near its coast. He'd encountered them twice, fishing, and he had no wish to encounter them again.

The five-hundred horsepower diesel shook the wheel with a steady rhythm. The log had long since ceased to work, but he knew they were doing eleven or twelve knots. The wheelhouse clock said ten minutes to five. To the east the sky was lightening and he could just make out the dark headland at Ras enn Naqoura, which marked the southernmost point of Lebanon. From this point, the land to their left was Israel.

The door to the wheelhouse opened, letting in a cool, damp draught. One of the gunmen pushed inside, clattering his Kalashnikov down onto the chart table.

'Show me!' he barked, pointing to the chart.

The skipper obliged, then demanded suspiciously 'Where are we going?'

'Just south. For a few more hours. Then we go home again!'

The skipper didn't believe him. The gunman gripped him by the shoulder and laughed at his fear.

'You'll see . . .'

He unhooked the binoculars, focused them on the headland, then scanned south and west, searching for navigation lights.

'If the Zionists come, get your nets ready. And say nothing about us. Understand?'

The skipper understood all right.

'Just a few hours,' the gunman repeated, and left the wheelhouse.

04.55 hrs

'Periscope depth! Revolutions for five knots!'

Bonderenko checked that the helmsman was responding, then glanced down at the chart to where the navigator was pointing.

'Shallow water, Comrade Captain. We're crossing the edge of the shelf. The bottom's sloping up. It'll be fifty metres soon.'

The Captain turned back to the periscope which was now locked in the 'up' position. His executive officer swept the horizon, then moved aside for Bonderenko to look.

He turned the optics to the east. A dark headland silhouetted against a pale sky, Ras enn Naqoura.

'Mark the bearing!'

The navigator read the figures from the periscope and entered the data on the chart.

'Confirms our position, Comrade Captain.'

Bonderenko switched on the image-intensifier, then swung the periscope in a slow circle. All the way round, then back again.

Suddenly he stopped in mid-swing. A boat. Inshore. He checked the range. Two thousand metres.

'Depth under the keel?' he demanded.

The navigator checked the echo-sounder.

'Sixty-five metres.'

'Steer zero-nine-five. Five knots. Navigator, keep your eye on the depth.'

'Yes, Comrade Captain.'

Slowly they closed with the boat. A fishing vessel. Bonderenko switched the optics to high-power. He could see a figure on deck, adjusting the net cable. They'd have to take care not to get fouled. The last thing they needed.

'Sonar! Any sound of nets on the starboard bow?'

'No contact,' came the instant reply. 'But cavitation on the port beam.'

Bonderenko swung the periscope round to the north. Nothing. Whatever the sonar had detected was too far away.

Back to the fishing boat. How the hell to make a positive identification in this light?

'Ten metres under the keel!' the navigator shrilled.

'Full astern!'

The sea bed must have sloped up sharply. Or else the lieutenant hadn't been watching. Bonderenko took his eyes from the periscope to glare across at the chart table. The navigator kept his eyes glued to the depth-sounder, as the boat juddered to a halt.

'Stop revolutions!'

Time to take stock.

'Fifteen metres, Comrade Captain.'

This was a fool's game. Too close inshore for safety, trying to identity a boat that was clearly fishing. This one couldn't be the *Joun*. And even if it was, they'd never get close enough to read its name.

'Sonar! Report contacts!'

'One contacat. Single shaft, three blades on port beam, Comrade Captain! Range closing.'

Still no sign through the periscope.

'Steer zero-zero-zero. Revolutions for three knots. Navigator, shout depths every ten seconds.'

The deck of the *Jackson* thundered under the thrust of the steam catapults. The twin turboprops of the Hawkeye clawed at the air to gain height, the radar plane with its large circular antenna looking like a flying saucer in the half-light of early dawn.

Two F-14 Tomcats, armed with photo-reconnaissance pods beside their missiles, queued up to launch.

Four decks down in the Combat Direction Centre, Commander Tracy had decided to call it a night. The Admiral had returned to his cabin; his 'eyes-in-the-sky' were changing shift, and there was nothing new to report. Time to leave it to the watch officer.

A few hours' sleep, then the fighters would be back with some visuals on the ships they were so painstakingly plotting on radar.

He walked the long passageway back to his quarters; some of the men were turning in; others were just waking up.

Norman Tracy undressed to his boxer shorts and flopped onto the bunk. He was asleep within minutes.

05.28 hrs

Bonderenko aligned the periscope cross-hairs on the wheelhouse of a second fishing boat. It was coming steadily towards them, the sonar beat of its propeller turning suddenly to steel and timber, an identifiable shape.

The *Korund* was positioned to the west of the target, on the dark side. The fishing boat was just fifty metres from their periscope, but Bonderenko could see that the hunched figure in the wheelhouse was quite unaware of their presence.

It was an elegant little boat with a high prow and a stem stern. Not much more than fifteen metres in length. The bow wave sparkled through the image-intensifying sight.

Maximum magnification. There was a name on the prow, a short word. Bonderenko strained to read it.

It was in Arabic! He should have thought of that. None of his men spoke the language. How the hell was he to identify it? The first rule of engagement: identification must be certain.

But the boat was slipping away from them.

'Revolutions for twelve knots! Steer two-one-zero!'

The submarine accelerated sharply.

Periscope crosswires on the stern. Oh, yes, there was a name all right, written in Roman lettering. He'd learned English at school. Would he be able to read it? Closer, closer. He urged the boat forward. Fifty metres again.

His heartbeat quickened.

Four letters. Last letter N.

J-O-U-N.

Joun.

He pulled back from the rubber eyepiece.

'Eight knots.' His voice was hardly audible.

'Captain?'

'Revolutions for eight knots,' he announced more strongly.

So this was it. This was the little boat with the nightmare cargo, the one he had to attack with surgical precision to stop his Motherland's carelessness plunging the Middle East into nuclear war.

He ran through the rules of engagement in his mind.

The boat looks bound for an Israeli port – yes.

It can be attacked in darkness – yes, if they were quick.

No other surface vessels within visual range –

221

'Sonar! Report contacts!'

Eyes to the periscope again, for a careful all-round look. Nothing but the target five hundred metres ahead of them.

'No other contacts on sonar, Comrade Captain!'

One more rule:

Sink the boat in international waters – No! They were well inside the twelve-mile limit.

What should he do? Pull back, raise the mast and ask Moscow for clarification? That'd take too much time. The *Joun* would be almost in Haifa by then.

A marine in a rubber suit stood at the base of the conning tower, waiting for instructions, a heavy machine-gun resting on the deck at his feet.

'Revolutions for ten knots! Prepare to surface!'

Faces turned to him, strain showing on every one. None had been in combat before. None had been allowed to know the reason for this attack.

Mustn't let them see the fear in his eyes. It was contagious. He looked through the periscope again.

They were two hundred metres astern of the *Joun*.

'Surface! Surface! Revolutions for maximum speed.'

Air hissed into the ballast tanks. As the tall fin broke the surface the valves on the snort tube snapped open, and the three diesels cut in to whip up the speed to twenty knots.

'Marines – action!'

Two men in black rubber clattered up the conning tower ladder, manhandling the heavy gun. There was the clang of the clips being eased. A sudden drop in air pressure made their ears pop as the upper hatch was opened.

Bonderenko realigned the periscope. One hundred metres ahead of them, the fishing boat was wallowing in the light swell.

He searched the deck of the *Joun*. One man with an assault rifle was leaning against the wheelhouse. Was that all? Probably not. They'd probably have RPGs that could blow a crippling hole in the *Korund*'s pressure hull.

The two marines slipped and slithered on the wet grating at the top of the conning tower, finally clunking the NSV machine-gun into its mount. They'd attuned their eyes to night vision and easily made out the shape of the man on watch. The first bullet would be for him.

They clipped in the belt of 12.7mm ammunition, every third round a tracer shell. One man swung the barrel and aligned the sight on the target. The other straightened the belt.

The submarine came up fast on the fishing boat's starboard side.

Trrrrrrrat!

The six-round burst went wildly high. There'd been no time to adjust the sights.

Trrrrrrrat!

Inside the *Korund*'s hull, the hammering of the recoil virtually deafened the crew.

Trrrrrrrat!

Bonderenko watched horrified through the optics, as tracer shattered the wheelhouse roof and ricocheted crazily into the sky.

'Lower, you idiots! Lower! Below the waterline,' he hissed through clenched teeth.

Bows and stern! Not the hold! Please God, not the hold!

For a full two seconds he closed his eyes and prayed. Any moment now! He cringed in anticipation of the blinding flash that would spell the end if the shots went wide.

Trrrrrrrrrrrrat!

He looked again. At last, a long lethal burst into the stern. Black smoke erupted through the splintered planks. The engine was hit! Two men with Kalashnikovs were peering into the dark, to see where the shots had come from.

Trrrrrrrrt! The *Korund*'s shells tore through the pair, felling them like saplings.

The *Joun* began to sink by the stern. The sea spluttered and boiled as it engulfed the hot machinery inside.

Trrrrrrrt! A burst into the bows, below the water.

Thank God, Bonderenko thought. They missed the hold.

The *Korund* pulled ahead of the devastated *Joun*. The marines let the gun barrel droop over the rail, assessing their work with sickening satisfaction.

'Starboard thirty!' the Captain ordered.

The job was done. They had to get away as quickly and silently as they'd come.

The submarine heeled sharply as it turned, the exhaust from its diesels drumming from the pipe at the back of the fin.

They swept round in a full circle, Bonderenko's eyes clamped to the periscope. The sea was ablaze. Fuel leaked from the fishing boat's ruptured tanks, and the gunwales were awash at the stern.

The marines on the fin watched the black smoke turn to steam, as the burning timbers were sucked under by the weight of the foundering boat.

Suddenly one of them pointed. An elderly man clung to the edge of the half-submerged wheelhouse, trying to beat out the flames on his back with a life-jacket.

The marines looked at one another uneasily. No survivors: those were their orders.

They raised the barrel.

Trrrrat!

Below, the crew of the *Korund* heard the short final burst, then the sound of the heavy gun clanging against the sides of the tower as the marines brought it down the ladder and closed the lid.

Bonderenko watched transfixed as the last traces of the *Joun* disappeared.

'Release the beacon!' he ordered hoarsely.

Through a narrow tube in the pressure hull the sonar transponder slipped into the water and dropped to the sea bed, close enough to the wreck for the recovery vessel to retrieve the deadly cargo whose sting they'd drawn.

'Dive! Maintain periscope depth. Maintain starboard thirty. Revolutions for five knots.'

He nodded to his executive officer to take over.

His knees felt like jelly. The last seconds of the *Joun* seen through the periscope, and the tracer shells blowing out the brains of the old man in the water, would be etched on his mind for ever.

Twelve

Sir Reginald Masterton had been awake since four, when the first signals came in from Washington. He'd left it until seven before telephoning the Prime Minister.

He strode up to the door of Number Ten. The policeman on duty saw him coming and tapped on the famous black panelling so they'd be ready for him inside.

'Thank you for seeing me at such short notice, Prime Minister,' Masterton began as soon as they were alone. The Chairman of the Joint Intelligence Committee was always meticulously polite to politicians.

'Didn't have much option, by the sound of it.'

He'd been shown up into the private flat. A pot of tea and two cups were ready in the breakfast room.

'You'll have heard Radio Four this morning, Prime Minister? Two corpses dumped outside the American Embassy in Beirut late last night?'

'Yes. CIA? The BBC's Middle East man seemed to think so.'

'He was correct, unfortunately. They were the two sent to find the nuclear weapons. They'd got a lead it seems, but in following it, they took one risk too many.'

The Prime Minister removed his spectacles, blew on them and polished them with a handkerchief. He felt weary. At sixty-seven he was getting a little old for this sort of drama.

'How much do we know?'

'Langley say their men had been tipped off that the

warheads were near Sidon and were being shipped out of the country on Tuesday night.'

'Shipped? Where to?'

'God knows. That's what they were trying to find out. Somewhere along the road they must've been intercepted.'

'Poor devils!'

The Prime Minister shook his head and replaced the spectacles.

'So what do we know, Reg?'

'A lot more than we did twenty-four hours ago. Firstly, we know who bought the weapons. The name, I'm afraid, is painfully familiar. Abdul Habib, the leader of *Mustadhafin*.'

'Habib!'

The name sent a shiver up the PM's spine.

'What a tragedy we didn't bury him in that house in Beirut.'

'Quite. Anyway he's very much alive. And his number two turned up in Spain the other day. They think that's to do with drug shipments.'

Masterton paused to observe a trace of discomfort on the PM's face.

'Which makes one wonder why Habib bought two nuclear weapons,' he went on. 'What would he want with them? There are theories, I might tell you, and they've come from a rather unexpected quarter.'

'Really? Where from?'

'The former Soviet Union.'

'Good heavens.'

'Moscow's been talking to Washington, at last.'

'And they've admitted losing the weapons? After all this time, after all their denials?'

'Yes. It's the military who've finally confessed. Until yesterday they hadn't even told their own politicians! That's what my friends in Washington believe, anyway!'

Masterton smoothed the grey tufts at his temples.

'Bloody hell!' the PM exploded. 'What lunatics! Totally unaccountable!'

The intelligence chief studied his fingernails. Un-accountability wasn't exactly unknown in Downing Street, according to the papers that had recently crossed his desk.

'What have they told us? And why are the Russians suddenly co-operating?'

'They had an agent in Lebanon, a former KGB chap. He'd been on the trail of the bombs for months, apparently, and got a lot closer than the Americans did.

'He says the warheads were being worked on in a fruit-packing shed. He has photographs of people going in and out. One of them was our friend Habib; another was indentified as a Libyan colonel trained in missile technology by the Soviet Union.'

'A Libyan! We should have known!' the Prime Minister exclaimed.

'The Russians says the bombs were loaded onto a Lebanese fishing boat called the *Joun*. Habib and the Libyan also went on board. They've pictures to back all this up, which they've faxed to the Americans.'

'I still don't understand why the Russians are sud-denly telling us all this.'

'I'm coming to that. Anyway, the boat sailed from a little jetty north of Sidon, and about four hours later it was detected by a Russian submarine, heading straight for the Israeli port of Haifa.'

'Oh, Lord!' exclaimed the PM.

'Now we come to why the Russians have told us all this. Because they ballsed it up. Their submarine attacked the fishing boat and sank it, killing all on board. Needless to say they believed the weapons were still on the boat.'

'But they weren't. . . ?'

'Unfortunately not. A Russian deep-sea recovery ship was heading their way, but because the wreck was inside

Israeli waters, Moscow ordered the submarine to put out divers and examine it. They found the hold to be empty. . . .'

'No explanation, I suppose?'

'The assumption is that the bombs were transferred to another ship somewhere off the Lebanese coast. The reason the Russians are talking is that they want our help in finding it. The trouble is, we don't know the name of the ship and it could be three hundred miles away by now. The Russians certainly don't have the resources to look for it. But the Americans, with a bit of help from us, probably do.'

'It's heading for Libya, yes?'

'That's a strong possibility.'

'So all we need to do is blockade Libyan ports and inspect every ship that tries to enter them,' the PM suggested.

Politicians always tended to oversimplify matters in Masterton's experience.

'May I?'

Masterton indicated the tea pot. He didn't mind if it was cold by now.

'Of course. Help yourself.'

'Blockading ports would be fine, Prime Minister, if we knew for certain that the bombs were heading for Libya. But for all we know, the ship could be going round in circles in the Med, waiting for the right moment to steam into Haifa. It'd make the most devastating suicide bomb the world has ever known.'

'Mmmm. I take your point. So what do the Americans say?'

'The President's going to ring you in an hour. They've outlined his proposals to me, so that I could brief you beforehand.

'The Americans have already activated the Sixth Fleet and a Marines unit. The carrier *Carl Jackson* is off Cyprus. They detected some of the activity the night before last, but didn't know what it meant. Nobody told the Fleet anything about nuclear weapons being in Lebanon.'

'Sounds like a bit of left-hand, right-hand.'

'The fact that we knew about the bombs was still top secret. Anyway, that's history now. After today, one hell of a lot of people will have to be told.'

'So, what's the plan the Americans are proposing?'

'Well, they've had one bit of luck. As a precaution, the battle group commander had ordered a log to be kept of shipping movements off the Lebanese coast. And at just after the time the Russians say the *Joun* put to sea, the *Jackson* logged a very small vessel, like a fishing boat, coming alongside a freighter anchored off the coast. After a while, the ships parted, the fishing boat heading south and the freighter west. Could be coincidence but it might be a vital clue. The radar operator remembers that the return for the bigger vessel, the blip on the screen, was small. Under five thousand tons, that was his estimate.

'So the Americans want to locate every ship in the eastern Mediterranean. It's a colossal task. You're talking of thousands of ships, Prime Minister. They'll ignore anything over five thousand tons, but actually identify everything below that size. Then, with the help of Lloyd's, they'll eliminate those that are obviously innocent. The rest'll come in for closer inspection.'

'Whew! That's a tall order. How much time have we got?'

'Three days. Maybe four.'

'Sounds impossible to me.'

'It may turn out that way, but they're going to give it a go. They want Britain to give every assistance it can. After you've spoken with the President, the Pentagon will call the MOD with a wish-list.'

'And what about the buggers who lost the damned weapons in the first place? The Russians,' the PM demanded, irritated.

'They've come up with something, a sort of aerial geiger counter. They say that if they can fly it over the deck of a ship, they can tell whether there are nuclear weapons on board. I don't know how well it works. But a few years back, the Americans and Russians did a joint experiment with it in the Black Sea. It was all to do with arms control. Verification.

'The Soviets have got two sets of this kit, and they want to fly them into RAF Akrotiri in Cyprus, so they can be shuttled out to the *Carl Jackson*. The Americans'll fit them to their own helicopters.'

'No problem about that. Can't possibly object. And the Americans have agreed?'

'Instantly.'

'Astonishing. They never used to talk to each other except through clenched teeth, and now we've got the CIA and the KGB arm in arm over this.'

'They know the consequences if they don't co-operate.'

'Quite.'

They both fell silent for a moment.

As a young officer in military intelligence in the nineteen fifties, Masterton had witnessed one of the British H-bomb tests in the Australian outback. The sight had terrified him.

'What sort of help is Washington going to want from us?' the PM asked.

'Oh, maritime reconnaissance. Nimrods. That sort of thing. And they mentioned HMS *Eagle*.'

'She's still catching drug runners for the Spaniards. Could be tricky to pull her off at short notice.'

Masterton pushed the round steel spectacles back up his nose.

'I believe the President plans to phone all his NATO allies after talking to you, Prime Minister. So the Spanish'll know about the bombs later today.'

'Then I'm sure they'll understand.'

'There's one thing I should warn you about.'

'Oh?'

Masterton frowned, wondering how best to phrase it.

'If it does turn out the bombs are bound for Libya . . .'

The Intelligence chief paused to see if the politician was getting his drift.

'. . . then I suspect the Americans will take advantage of the situation.'

'Meaning?'

'Like doing to the Libyan leadership what they did to Saddam Hussein in Iraq back in 1991.'

'Ahhhh. I see.'

The PM's eyes narrowed.

'Obviously any decision as to how far Britain should get involved with such an action would be a political judgement, sir. There was a frightful bloody hoohah last time the Americans tried it, if you remember.'

'Quite so, Reg. Quite so.'

'The Americans will be playing politics too. They'll want us aboard, to help shoulder the blame if things go wrong.'

'I'm sure they will. I'll need to consult on this one.'

The PM stood up and crossed to the window that looked out over the garden. The view was partially obscured by the heavy net curtains designed to contain shards of glass if a terrorist bomb should shatter the panes.

He thrust his hands in his pockets and hunched his shoulders.

'I'm confused, Reg.' Without turning round he asked, 'Who's the guilty party? Abdul Habib, or the Libyan leader?'

'That, Prime Minister, is a bit of a mystery.'

His political antennae sensed he was at a turning point. The decisions he faced in the coming hours could make or break his whole career. Great danger lay ahead.

The pilots of the two Sea Harriers saw a small break in the cloud and dived their fighters towards it. Somewhere below the 'clag' was a banana boat, the prime suspect in a search which had by now lasted for forty-eight fruitless hours.

The Spanish Aduanas knew everything about the ship, down to the exact position of every locker and duct on board, where cocaine might be concealed. The one thing they didn't know was where the ship was.

The tip-off had originated with the US Coastguard. The ship was the *Lobitos*, registered in Panama with a displacement of 3,600 tons. According to the Americans, it was a certainty that she had cocaine on board. Agents had watched her loading bananas in Venezuela and had spotted known drug dealers joining the crew. She was due to dock at Algeciras in two days, with her most valuable cargo – cocaine with a street value of six million dollars – probably already off-loaded at sea.

Spanish P-3 Orion aircraft had scoured the eastern Atlantic with radar, matching the superstructure profile of the ships they detected with the picture they'd been given by the Americans. Early this morning they thought they'd found the *Lobitos*. Now it was the job of the Royal Navy Sea Harriers to prove they were right.

The co-ordinates of the banana boat provided by the P-3 were twenty minutes old. If her course hadn't changed, the Harrier pilots calculated their navigation computers would bring them over her stern in about three minutes' time.

The fighters dropped to two hundred feet. The video image from their photo-reconnaissance pods appeared on a small screen in the cockpit.

The pilots' task was tricky. They had to get close

enough to the ship to see her name, but avoid alarming the crew into ditching the cargo.

The pilot of the lead aircraft lifted his sunvisor and looked down at the Blue Fox radar screen, scanning the sea five miles ahead.

There, to the right. A mile south of the prediction. Not bad, if it was the *Lobitos*.

He banked for the turn, knowing his wingman would follow half a mile behind. He touched the toggle that armed the countermeasures ejector. They had not only to photograph the banana boat, but to deceive it as well.

He slaved the camera to the radar target. At two miles he saw the ship emerging from the mist. He pressed the record button, and locked the camera to follow the target automatically.

The radar altimeter screeched. Too low. He eased back on the stick. Hold at two hundred feet, three hundred and fifty knots. It'd be easy to fly into the sea on a grey day like this.

A black hull, cream superstructure, yellow bands on the funnel – that was all his eyes could absorb as the Harrier screamed over the ship. Now for the firework display.

He banked hard left and fired the countermeasures. Brilliant balls of fire pumped from the Harrier, flares to deflect heat-seeking missiles. The crew on the banana boat's bridge would see them, as the second Harrier roared over their heads. Just two fighters on a training exercise – that was what they wanted the sailors to believe.

Back on the stick, up through the stratus to the clear air at five thousand feet. A glance over his shoulder to confirm his wingman was still there. He waggled the wings in greeting, then circled right looking for another clearing. The breaks in the cloud were infrequent, but he wanted to see his way through; some of that cloud reached down to the sea.

They found a hole and tumbled through, then weaved their way across the horizon ahead of the *Lobitos*, in a simulation of combat.

Enough. Hope to God someone was awake on the bridge to watch their efforts. Up through the cloud again. Time to go home to mother.

HMS Eagle
14.25 hrs

'This is the picture faxed by the US Coastguard,' explained the Operations Officer. 'The one on the right is from the recce sortie this morning. It's the same ship. Only difference is she's painted out her name.'

Peter Brodrick sat in the second row in *Eagle*'s briefing room, behind Captain Dyce and next to Teniente Alvarez of the Spanish customs.

'The Spanish P-3s are keeping a twenty-four hour watch. At fourteen hundred Zulu today the *Lobitos* was three hundred and thirty miles westsouthwest of Cape Trafalgar. If she maintains her present course and a speed of twelve knots, she should be off the Cape at seventeen-thirty Zulu tomorrow. But she's not due in Algeciras until noon the following day, so she's got about fifteen hours spare in which to meet her contacts and off-load the drugs.'

'She may not meet anyone at all, of course,' Captain Dyce interjected.

'Sir?' the Ops Officer queried, uncomfortable at being interrupted in mid-brief.

'She might drop the stuff over the side attached to floats.'

'Indeed, sir.'

'How will we know if she does that?'

'We won't, sir. Without constant covert observation, and we don't have the assets. A submarine would be best, but the Spaniards don't have one available.'

'Hmmm.'

'May I carry on, sir?'

Disgruntled, Dyce nodded. For once Brodrick agreed with him. Here they were, twenty thousand tons of warship with a thousand men on board, unable to keep a round-the-clock watch on a bloody banana boat!

The door to the briefing room opened suddenly. The Ops Officer looked up, annoyed at the interruption. It was the communications chief.

'Signal for the Captain.'

He entered the room and placed the folded sheet in Dyce's outstretched hand.

Dyce opened the typewritten page, noting the word 'immediate' at the top.

As he read, the tendons in his neck began to twitch.

He stood up.

'Gentlemen,' the Captain announced, 'there may be a change of plan.'

His voice grated, his eyes blazed with anger.

'I shall adjourn this briefing for thirty minutes.'

And he walked briskly from the room.

'World War Three?' Brodrick quipped.

'At least.'

'Well, nothing for it.' The Ops Officer looked at his watch. 'Back here at fifteen hundred, gentlemen.'

Brodrick found himself walking the length of Two Deck with Pepe Alvarez.

'What you think?' the Spaniard asked.

'Search me. Maybe the government wants us home again, so they can sell the ship to Argentina!'

'Escuse me?'

'Forget it. A bad joke. I really don't know. But I'll tell you something – he didn't look happy.'

Brodrick lay on his bunk, fantasising about what had
been in the signal to the Captain. A face kept floating
before his mind's eye. The face of Ahmed Bizri.

Suddenly, the whistle of a 'pipe'. Brodrick stuck his
head out of the cabin to listen.

'Do you hear there? This is the Captain speaking.'

The voice on the loudspeaker sounded tense. Brodrick
felt the ship begin to shake as the engines wound up power.

'I've just been sent new orders by the Commander-in-
Chief Fleet It's a complete change of plan, I'm afraid.
We've been ordered to turn back into the Mediterranean
with all speed. I can't tell you why at this stage. I know
the reasons of course, and I can tell you that the task
we've been given is of enormous significance.

'The downside of it is that we're having to abandon
our support for the Spanish coastguards. This is deeply
disappointing, particularly as we were just about to take
part in a raid on some drug runners, which showed every
sign of being immensely successful. The Spanish government is being contacted at this moment by our own
government, and I hope they'll understand the reasons
for this.

'As you'll have realised from the way the ship's
shaking, we're building up speed now. We'll have to stay
at about twenty-five knots for the next two days. It's
going to be a hard slog I'm afraid, but at the end of that
two days, we've got to be somewhere near Malta. Can't
tell you any more than that at the moment. Just one
service message. The ops briefing due to reconvene at
fifteen hundred is cancelled. That's all.'

'Shit!' Brodrick hissed. His phone rang, and he
grabbed it.

'Father wants to see you right away,' said the voice of
Nick Brady, the Principal Warfare Officer.

'Where?'

'In his sea cabin.'

'On my way.'

He hurried back down Two Deck and bumped into Pepe Alvarez coming down from the bridge.

'I leave. In one hour,' the Spaniard stammered in astonishment.

'What's it all about?'

'I don' know. But I think is crazy. Tomorrow anyway it is finish and we catch them. Now . . .'

'Crazy! You're right. They flying you ashore?'

'To Rota. In one hour. I must call my headquarters.'

'Pepe, I'm sorry it's ended like this.' Brodrick stuck out his hand. 'We were getting there, I really believe it. But good luck for tomorrow. You'll still catch your smugglers, believe me.'

'I hope. Well, goodbye.'

'See you. One day soon.'

'Adios!'

Captain Dyce was flushed and clearly agitated.

'This is a right bugger's muddle! The culmination of the whole Spanish operation and we get pulled off it at the last minute! Bloody coitus interruptus. Poor Alvarez! He just couldn't believe it when I told him we were abandoning his coastguards and sending him back to Spain.'

'I just saw him, sir. He's in a state of shock.'

'I know. Couldn't tell him why we're doing it, that's the trouble.'

Dyce looked uneasily at Brodrick over the half-moons of his reading glasses.

'There's a hell of a flap on at the other end of the Med,' he began, turning to a chart on the wall. 'And what I'm about to tell you is highly classified and must not be discussed with anybody who's not already privy to this information.

238

'It seems that the Russians have "lost" two nuclear weapons, and the Libyans are about to take delivery of them!'

'The Libyans? How come, sir?'

This wasn't the reaction Dyce had expected. It was almost as if Brodrick already knew about the missing weapons. He eyed him suspiciously.

'Two years ago, a Russian nuclear weapons convoy was ambushed. God knows how, eventually the warheads ended up in Lebanon. Then early yesterday morning they were loaded onto a ship believed to be bound for Libya. The combined resources of the Soviet, American and British navies have been pooled to try to find it.'

'That's incredible!'

'Yes. Totally unprecedented! RAF Nimrods are already involved, and they want us down there as fast as possible. Only, you're not going to be with us . . .'

'*What?*'

'I'm sending you on ahead. The Americans are flying a plane to pick you up from Gib. It'll take you straight to the *Carl Jackson*. That's where they're running things from. The US Marines have got an Amphib Unit down there too – just finished a training exercise in Turkey. They've got some plan – don't know what, exactly – and they want to drag us into it. Partly political, I gather. They want another NATO ally involved. I think they're planning something against Libya.'

'I see. And that involves the Royal Marines?'

'Apparently.'

Dyce shrugged and rolled his eyes.

'There's a whole lot more of your chums heading for Cyprus this afternoon. Led by a Colonel. You're to report to him, when he gets his feet on the ground. He'll let you know where he is. In the meantime you're to liaise with the US Marines, a Major Seymour Hoddle . . .'

'Ah, I know him. We were on an instructor's attachment at West Point together.'

'Good, good! Should make things easier. Find out what the Americans want you to do, and evaluate it so you can give your Colonel a head start. Talk to Wings about your transport. He's well into it. But you'd better move fast. The Americans were airborne half an hour ago.'

Brodrick felt railroaded. There were too many questions, and not enough answers. In the pit of his stomach he felt a knot of foreboding.

'Sir? These nukes – they ended up in Lebanon, right?'

'That's what I'm told,' Dyce growled, knowing what was coming.

'But who? Which faction, sir?'

'*Mustadhafin.*'

'Shit!'

The scenario Brodrick had treated as no more than a suspicion, was a nightmare coming true.

Dyce glowered over the steel frames. Don't push me too far, his eyes warned.

'I don't get it, sir. Are you saying *Mustadhafin* had the bombs and then gave them to the Libyans?'

Dyce peeled the reading glasses from his face.

'Apparently. There's a limit to the amount of detail Northwood can put in a signal,' he answered tartly.

Peter opened his mouth to speak, but Dyce forestalled him.

'Look, young man, if you're going to remind me about Mr Bizri, and if you're going to suggest those weapons could be used to take revenge on this ship, then I must tell you that it does not fit in with the information I've been given.'

The expression in his eyes was that of a nanny being firm with a fractious child.

'The intelligence assessment is that the nuclear weapons were just another bit of business for Habib. He struck lucky. They came on the market; he was in the right place at the right time. Bought them relatively cheaply, sold them to the Libyans for a fortune. That's it.'

That's it? Brodrick struggled to stifle his anger.

'Since when has the intelligence community known anything about *Mustadhafin*, sir?' he demanded icily.

'What d'you mean?'

'I spoke to them in London three days ago. They said sod-all about nuclear warheads. And last year their briefings were as much use as an ashtray on a motorbike. I was on my bloody own in Lebanon!'

'Look Peter, I understand why you feel strongly . . .'

'That's the trouble, sir, you don't understand. Nor do the spooks. You can't understand, because you weren't there! You don't *know* these men. You didn't *smell* them!'

Dyce sat bolt upright, not used to such effrontery from his officers.

'I see. So, with this special insight that only you have, what is your professional advice, Captain Brodrick?'

Brodrick realised he'd overstepped the mark again.

'What I'm saying, sir, is that with *Mustadhafin* nothing is quite what it seems. If Habib really has sold the bombs to Libya, fair enough. But until we see proof of it, I think we should assume he hasn't.'

The Captain looked down at his signal file. Beneath the orders which had sent them speeding eastwards, was another message from Fleet HQ at Northwood. A confidential note, passing on, for guidance, the assessment by the army psychiatrist in London that Brodrick was still suffering post-traumatic stress disorder. It warned him to expect the occasional irrational judgement.

In the light of that, he'd questioned whether it was wise to send Brodrick to liaise with the Americans. However, he did have one unique qualification. He was the only man in either navy who'd ever had direct dealings with *Mustadhafin*.

'Thank you for your advice, Captain Brodrick.'

Dyce picked up the file and thumbed through the sheets of paper, studiously avoiding Brodrick's eyes.

'The safety of my ship is paramount, of course. But I think you've assessed the situation the wrong way round. I intend to assume that the intelligence experts are correct about Libya, until you or someone else *proves* that they're not.'

For a moment Brodrick sat motionless, stunned by the snub. Then his anger began to boil again.

Innocent until proven guilty! A good rule for civilised society, maybe, but bloody pointless when dealing with terrorists. Ulster had taught them that.

Still, what could an over-the-hill ship's captain know about such things?

Dyce was still ignoring him. The interview was over. Brodrick stood up.

'Good luck, Captain Brodrick.'

'Thank you, sir.'

Thirteen

Marshal Zhukov glanced round the green-baize table. His uniformed commanders avoided his gaze. They'd watched their nation disintegrate during the past few years, powerless to prevent it. They'd saluted the flag of democracy, even while believing that freedom would be a poison to their people. Now their military impotence had been exposed for the world to see.

'Gentlemen! We must decide our strategy ...' Zhukov sighed.

His own position as Commander-in-Chief hung by a thread. The President had sacked him on the spot for failing to tell him about the stolen nuclear weapons. It had been the deepest of humiliations for the Russian leader to learn about the missing bombs from the White House, two whole years after they had disappeared.

Only the threat of a mass resignation by the General Staff had brought about Zhukov's reinstatement.

'We are, as you know, "co-operating" in the search with our American friends . . .'

Zhukov's gravelly voice was heavy with irony.

'The President insisted we accept their offer. We do need their help, it's true. We can't find the weapons alone. But they're asking a price which is too high, politically and militarily.

'They have not confided in us, of course. But our intelligence services are not totally defunct. We know much of what they plan, and we can guess the rest.'

'It's obvious,' the Ground Forces Commander snorted. 'They want the bombs for themselves, to dismantle them and learn our secrets. All their offers to "help" us dismantle warheads, withdrawn under the START Treaty – it's the same game. An excuse to get our technology.'

A murmur of agreement rippled round the table. Everyone present knew that the weapons, though highly effective, were obsolete, but pride prevented them saying so.

'Comrades, that's only half of it,' Zhukov growled.

His words prompted nine pairs of eyes to look his way.

'They plan an invasion! To attack Libya. To stop the regime becoming a nuclear power.'

'Aaah,' sighed Admiral Shokin. 'They've been looking for an excuse; now it's fallen into their laps. And there's nothing we can do to prevent them.'

His Black Sea Fleet had ceased to function as a fighting force; the dispute over how much of it belonged to Russia and how much to Ukranie rumbled on, and many of the crews were close to mutiny.

'We must stop them!' Zhukov thundered. 'An American attack might set the whole Middle East ablaze. And besides . . .'

He lowered his voice to a mumble.

'There are some aspects of our past relationship with Gaddafi which could be . . . embarrassing . . . if the Americans were to uncover them.'

'But how?' the Admiral sneered. 'When they have the entire Sixth Fleet there, and the Marine Corps?'

'We must deprive them of their excuse for an attack,' Zhukov countered. 'We must get at the missing weapons before the Americans do.'

A snort of ironic laughter ran round the table.

'All we have is the *Korund*, Grigoriy. We'd need to be clairvoyant to get her in the right place at the right time.'

'Not quite, Pyotr,' the Marshal replied. 'Don't forget it is we who control the neutron detectors.'

Admiral Shokin looked sceptical.

'Stopping them attacking Libya is a political matter,' he insisted. 'The President should use his influence with the Americans.'

'He has as much influence with Washington as I have hair on my head,' retorted the totally bald Marshal. 'Every day the White House expects him to be out, pushed either by the parliament or by us. The Americans owe us no favours. They'll do what they want, unless the *Korund* can trip them up.'

The panelled walls of the meeting room were hung with portraits of dead heroes from previous General Staffs, men who'd felt themselves masters of their fate. The present occupants had become the slaves of theirs.

The Admiral turned again to his old friend.

'You've discussed this with the President?'

The Marshal nodded. His broad chest seemed to sag.

'He said that if we let the weapons fall into American hands, he'll make us answerable to "the people". He was drunk, of course.'

'The man's intolerable,' exploded the Commander of Ground Forces. 'Answerable to the people? Who the hell does he think he is?'

The Marshal restrained them with a gesture of his hand.

'This is not the time for confrontation with the politicians,' he cautioned. 'We'd lose. In time we may be forced into it, but the moment must be chosen with great care.'

'Then we put our fate in the hands of one solitary submarine commander,' the General concluded rue-fully. 'Who is he, by the way?'

'Nikolai Bonderenko,' the Admiral informed them. 'He's a good man. Not the best, not the worst. He's a Russian, so he'll understand what he has to do.'

Marshal Zhukov scanned the faces lining each side of the table. The same thought had occurred to all of them.

'Let us hope enough of his crew are Russian too . . .'

The Mediterranean
37 degrees 22' N, 30 degrees 22' E

Abdul Habib hated the sea. A vicious northerly wind was blowing, whipping up a swell that had set the *Baalbeck* rolling relentlessly for the past twenty-four hours, slowing the progress of the small freighter.

For much of the first day, Habib had been confined to his bunk, but when daylight entered his porthole for the second morning, he'd decided the combined stench of diesel oil and cooking smells would do nothing for his seasickness. Since then he'd stayed on the bridge, or clung to the guardrail at the stern.

His eyes scanned the skies constantly. He knew the chase could only intensify. Short-wave radio messages from Tripoli had told him that someone, Russian or American, had taken his bait, attacking the boat he'd sent towards Israel as a decoy. He felt no remorse that everyone on board had been killed; they would be rewarded in heaven.

And they were hunting for *him* now, America and Russia, the two great sources of evil in the world. America had poisoned the Middle East by pouring money into Israel to the detriment of the Arab nation, and Russia had poisoned the region with godlessness and guns. The Russians had intended the guns to be turned against Israel; instead, the Arabs had turned them against each other.

Habib was philosophical about the destiny life had

awarded him. The chaos in Lebanon was the work of outsiders; left to their own devices, the Arabs would have lived in harmony, he believed. God had seen fit to bring the wrath of the foreigners down on his head, and to make it his destiny to strike back at those who'd hit his people hardest.

They'd destroy him if they found him, he knew that. But he wasn't afraid; after all, the British had tried once and failed.

They couldn't have detected the weapons being transferred from the fishing boat to the *Baalbeck*, or they wouldn't have attacked the fishing boat. But when they found that wreck empty, they'd guess and come looking.

He and the Libyans had been careful to leave no clues; the owner of the freighter was in Malta, happily counting the money which had bought the use of the ship and his silence. The Libyans would 'look after' him until the mission was over. And the ship's master? His family were receiving the same firm treatment.

Did those hunting him know about his deal with the Libyans? Possibly the Soviets had found out; they still had close connections in Tripoli.

Habib looked round at the sound of boots on the steps up to the bridge. A full head of curly black hair appeared, and below it the unsmiling yellow face of one of Colonel Ellafi's guards. Metal clanged against metal as he knocked the back of his SA-14 missile launcher against the handrail.

Abdul Habib's instincts told him not to trust these Libyans to fulfil their side of the bargain, yet he had no choice in the matter. There were at least a dozen of them on board, and only three of his men.

Colonel Ellafi was a weapons specialist who'd trained for a year at the Soviet nuclear missile centre of Kapustin Yar. But the delicate work of removing the barometric fuses and permissive action links from the warheads had been carried out by two civilians whose language Habib had recognised as Russian.

They'd worked for two days and nights in that orange-packing shed north of Sidon, converting the weapons from ones that needed the insertion of two secret codes, into devices detonated by a simple time switch with the force of ten thousand tons of TNT.

He shuddered at the thought of the explosive power beneath his feet, and the ease with which it could now be released.

He sensed the two Russians were aboard the *Baalbeck*, but keeping out of sight. One of the cabins stayed locked day and night. He'd seen food being taken in at mealtimes.

The Libyan guard laid his weapon on the deck and checked the safety catch. Without a word, he took the binoculars from around the neck of the helmsman and began to search the sea and the sky for signs of danger.

Habib sensed new tension. The Libyans had spent little time on watch up to now.

'Has there been some news?' he asked.

The guard looked coldly at him and shrugged. He wasn't being paid to talk.

'In the name of the Arab nation, can't you speak?' Habib demanded. The rasp to his voice could not be ignored.

'Maybe there has been word,' he answered grudgingly. 'I have to watch.'

With that he pressed his face to the rubber cone covering the radar screen and adjusted the range to its maximum.

Habib had done all this himself just a few minutes before. He knew there'd be nothing to see. They could only wait. All was prepared.

He looked down from the bridge window, noting again the special equipment draped in tarpaulins and bolted to the deck beside the hatch covers. It would need just seconds to bring it to action once the radar warning receivers on the bridge roof told them the hunters were getting close.

Habib turned back towards the helmsman to find the Libyan guard staring at him with contempt.

Habib was unnerved. He was used to seeing hatred in men's eyes, but this Libyan considered him a nothing, an irritation, a boil that would soon be lanced. Habib's instinct was to kill the man, but not yet.

The guard turned away, pretending the look had never been meant. Habib felt his fears confirmed. His enemies were not just those who would come in warships and fighter planes, but the very men he was in league with, men who called themselves his friends.

24.00 hours
135 miles northwest of the Baalbeck

The flight deck of the USS *Carl Jackson* dwarfed that of HMS *Eagle*; it was twice as long and five times as wide. Brodrick had landed on the deck of these giant American flat-tops many times, yet they never ceased to impress him. He stepped off the rear ramp of the Grumman Greyhound, dizzy with exhaustion after a five-hour flight from Gibraltar in appalling discomfort.

All around him was blackness, but the flight-line was lit up like a small airport. It was half-past midnight Greek local time, two hours ahead of GMT, or 'Zulu', to which his watch was permanently set.

Mechanics crawled over the machines, crammed together along the deck, while pilots strapped themselves into cockpits and made their final checks before take-off.

'Welcome to the *Jackson*, sir,' a deck officer shouted above the turbine roar of an E-2C Hawkeye, warming up for departure. 'Would you follow me, please?'

The American's cap was held in place by bulbous ear defenders. Brodrick pulled off his beret and held it tight as the strong wind, generated by the ship's speed, blew them towards the island and shelter. His camouflaged combat jacket flapped like a sail.

'Flying round the clock?' Brodrick asked when they'd escaped the wind and the noise.

'Sure. Captain's ordered extra training sorties. I guess we might be seeing some action.'

'Have they told you what it's about?'

'Not yet.'

No need to know and this man wasn't going to speculate.

'How was your flight, sir? Guess you refuelled at Sigonella, right?'

'Right. In Sicily,' Brodrick replied. 'Quick turn-around. Just thirty-five minutes. We've been airborne for about five hours altogether.'

'Sooner you than me, friend. I hate those mothers. The noise and vibration – makes you feel like you've done ten rounds with Mike Tyson!'

As they headed down and down into the depths of the ship, the hum of air-conditioning fans replaced the noise on deck. They entered a long passageway where the lighting was dimmed and the air smelled of sweat.

'They've given you a cabin with the aviators, sir. Ship's pretty full just now. Most of the guys who aren't flying are sleeping.' He kept his voice low. 'They're doing reconnaissance missions in the morning and their briefings start at six.'

'Is Major Hoddle on board?' Brodrick asked. He'd half expected his US Marine counterpart to be here to greet him.

'No, sir. Major Hoddle's with his MAU. I guess they're fifty miles north of us. You're due to fly up there, first light.'

'Oh, right.'

'I er . . . guess he hopes you get a good night's sleep, sir,' the deck officer added almost apologetically. He checked the number above the sliding door.

'You're in here, sir. Heads are just along on the left. I'll come by at around seven and show you to the wardroom for some breakfast, if that's okay?'

'Sure. That sounds fine. Oh, I didn't catch your name by the way.'

'Lieutenant Steve Harbin.' He grinned and nodded awkwardly. 'Well, goodnight, sir.'

'Yep. See you in the morning.'

The American hurried away down the long corridor. Brodrick grinned ruefully at the realisation that there were five and a half thousand men crammed into this massive ship, and he knew the name of just one of them.

He pushed open the door to the cabin. Grey walls, a narrow bunk with lockers under, and a small folding table. Even less space than he was used to on board HMS *Eagle*. He swung his small holdall onto the bunk and looked for the light switches.

He sat on the edge of the bunk, puzzled by the lack of formality in his welcome on board. He'd expected something more. After all, he *was* the representative of an allied navy whose support for this operation had been eagerly sought. Instead of a handshake or a briefing from someone in authority, he'd been bundled into a cabin and put to bed like a child.

Oh, well. No point in thinking about it.

He checked the number above the door so he'd find his way back to the right cabin and made for the heads. Eight decks above him a steam catapult thundered, propelling the Hawkeye radar plane into the black Mediterranean sky.

Four decks above, in the flight operations office, the Commander Air Group, known as CAG, leaned over the large-scale chart of the eastern Mediterranean taped to the worktable. Two of his staff were checking latitudes and longitudes from a list, and locating them on the chart with coloured markers.

A blue box between the islands of Crete and Cyprus marked the area where the *Jackson* was currently steaming. The markers represented ships located by the umbrella of maritime reconnaissance aircraft that had been up for the past twelve hours.

'Have we got to take a look at every goddam one of these?' the Commander howled. 'Jeez, how many you got on that list?'

'About eighty, sir.'

'You sure they haven't left in some of the big guys by mistake?'

'Yessir. They say there's nothing here over five thousand tons.'

The Commander scratched his head. The ships farthest from the *Jackson* were over five hundred miles away – near Benghazi to the west, near Port Said to the east. Every one of these vessels had to be photographed by a low-flying aircraft during the coming hours of daylight. It was his task to provide the Intruders and the Tomcats, and to divide the targets into groups so that all could be visited within the shortest time span possible.

'Why are we doing all this, sir?' the lieutenant asked, stifling a yawn. Like the rest of them he'd been on the go since early that morning.

'Answer's the same as it was this morning – I have not been told. And if there's no need for me to know the reason, lieutenant, then there is surely no need for you to know!'

The Commander realised he'd snapped at his junior and immediately regretted it. They were all dog-tired.

'There's probably no more than half-a-dozen people on this ship who know what this is all about. Our job's to identify every one of those tubs so's the people in the right pay grade can decide what to do next. Now let's group these markers so we can brief the pilots when they've finished their beauty sleep.'

Brodrick lay restlessly on his bunk, still dressed in his lovat-green sweatshirt and trousers, his half-open, un-focused eyes locked onto the dim, red lamp in the ceiling.

The noise of ventilation fans and distant machinery drummed in his ears, seeming to grow louder, closing in.

He seldom suffered from claustrophobia, yet there was something happening to him that had set his heart pounding as if he were on a route march. He knew what it was, all right. He'd felt it last on the hills above Beirut.

Panic.

He was buried deep in the bowels of a bloody aircraft carrier. How the hell would he get out if he had to? He tried to remember the way the lieutenant had brought him, but couldn't.

How many decks above him? How many below? How many walls of steel on each side cutting him off from the fresh sea air?

What if they were torpedoed?

In his mind he heard the clang of the shockwave resonating through the decks. The tearing of metal. The screams of men trapped, men dying in darkness.

He shook his head like a dog, trying to clear his brain, angry at his own weakness.

Marines weren't meant to panic. He turned on the main overhead light, hurled himself from the bunk and wrenched open the door. The passageway stretched away from him in the soft, red glow of the night-vision lightning.

He walked a little way; more passageways led off in all directions. He listened. Sounds of snoring came from the cabin next to his. Further away a man moaned in his sleep, deep in some carnal dream. Brodrick tried to regulate his breathing, to control his heart rate. God, the air was foul down here!

He went back to his cabin, leaving the door open. He wiped the sweat from his brow with his forearm.

Concentrate on something else! Think of the pain of a thirty-mile run with a pack on your back.

Think of something good. Think of Jackie.

What would he give to have her with him now!

She'd be asleep. Alone? What day was it? What time?

Friday. 2 am. Zulu. The same time in London. It was the weekend. Maybe Jackie was out, or in bed with some bloke. No! He didn't want to think of that. But why shouldn't she be? He didn't own her.

He lay back on the bunk.

Close eyes. Mind in neutral. Erase all thoughts.

Jackie asleep. Keep that. Don't wipe that one away.

Soft hair on the pillow. Tranquillity.

Every time the nightmares had wrecked his sleep in those weeks after Lebanon, he'd sat up in bed and looked at her, then felt the calm return to his body.

Whenever his howling blood-smeared comrades pointed their accusing fingers, she'd woken up, her soft warm body there for him to cling to like a raft.

But he was alone now. The ghosts were all around him and there was no Jackie to save him from them.

Concentrate. Fight sleep. Think of something else. Think of the task ahead.

Abdul Habib. Where was he? What monstrous evil was he planning?

Brodrick couldn't visualise the man. He'd never met him. Yet he *knew* Habib, knew what drove him.

There could be only one reason for Abdul Habib to procure nuclear weapons; to make those who took the lives of so many of his men pay a similar price.

And Habib had chosen his weapon well. Only with a nuclear bomb could he destroy HMS *Eagle*.

Peter knew it with an awful certainty. He knew, too,

that he was alone in his certainty. The Americans, with all their intelligence apparatus, had convinced themselves it was a Libyan plot. Even Captain Dyce on HMS *Eagle* had swallowed that concept.

He lay awake, fighting off the ghosts, until morning.

Fourteen

Brodrick stood at the edge of the flight deck and looked with relief at the broad expanse of blue. Air had never smelled so fresh; open space had never looked so inviting.

His ears protected from the noise by small foam plugs, he watched a flight of A-6 Intruders take their turn on the steam catapults and hurtle into the air in pairs. The fixed-wing aircraft were using the angled flight deck, leaving the forward third of the main deck free for helicopters.

'Your cab'll be here in ten minutes, sir!' the deck chief shouted above the roar of a dozen gas turbines.

Brodrick nodded and adjusted the strap of his life-jacket which was uncomfortably tight under his crotch. There was a brisk wind across the deck and he was glad of the rubberised survival suit. He was to be flown to the USS *Nashville*, Flagship for the Marine Amphibious Unit attached to the Sixth Fleet.

Behind him he heard the heavy beat of rotors and turned to see two Sea King helicopters with Royal Navy markings position themselves over the port side, ready to land.

In this totally American environment it gave him a thrill to see his own team turn up. But what were the Brits doing here?

Deck crew with fluorescent yellow paddles guided the Sea Kings to their landing spots, then ran forward to attach the leads which earthed the static.

256

The rotors slowed, then stopped, flapping up and down in the wind. The side doors slid back and the loadmasters helped four men out of each machine. They were clad in bright dayglo orange once-only suits. Their awkward movements suggested they were civilians.

From a doorway on the bridge island, a quartet of smartly dressed officers stepped out towards the new arrivals. One, Brodrick noticed, had four gold bands on his sleeve – the Captain.

The quartet reached the helicopters and stopped a few yards short. A junior officer strode forward and introduced himself, then brought the visitors across to meet the Captain. They shook hands, but didn't address each other directly, turning instead to speak through the junior officer.

He's translating!

Brodrick's curiosity grew. The visitors had flat, high-cheekboned faces. Slavs. They're bloody Russians! On an American carrier!

The Brits must've flown them here from Cyprus.

The American deck crew stared with more than usual curiosity. No wonder the Captain had come out personally to greet the visitors.

A fork-lift truck wheeled up to the Sea Kings, and the Russians turned to supervise the unloading of their palletised equipment. The loadmaster from the helicopter helped them strip off their survival suits.

Brodrick was tempted to walk across and ask his fellow Britons what was going on, but the arrival of a twin-rotored Sea Knight marked 'Marines' told him it was too late.

'Straight on board when I signal, sir! They're gonna stay whirling and burning!'

The helicopter's wheels touched the deck and the ramp cranked open. Brodrick ran across to it and was pulled inside. He'd hardly strapped himself in before the machine lifted and banked sharply away.

*

After twenty minutes' flying at two hundred feet, the machine began to sit back on its heels. Brodrick looked through the circular window behind him and saw the broad beam, high forward superstructure and long landing deck of the *Nashville*.

As the wheels touched, Brodrick spotted a broad-shouldered Major, his black face taut with anxiety.

The handshake was as vice-like as Brodrick had remembered.

'Hi, Seymour. How're you doing?' Brodrick shouted above the engine roar.

'Good. Yourself?'

'Great. Nice to see you again.'

'Come on down. See if we can get some coffee.'

Inside the hangar Brodrick stripped off his survival suit, then followed Hoddle down three decks to a small neon-lit briefing room.

A bull-necked, shaven-headed enlisted man poured them coffee, pointed to a plate of blueberry muffins, then left them to it.

The US Marine Major had a Hollywood quality about him, razor-sharp crease to his dark-green trousers, immaculately-pressed fawn shirt and skin the colour of dark coffee beans. His eyes glowed with almost evangelical virtue.

Now they were alone, he allowed himself a fleeting grin.

'You look real fine, Peter,' Hoddle began, a furrow of concern momentarily disturbing the smoothness of his brow. 'I heard about your rough time last year.'

'That's old history,' Brodrick replied defensively.

Hoddle noted his sensitivity. Both stood hands on hips, two military elitists trained never to acknowledge weakness.

'Sure, sure. Hey, did we get muffins like this at West Point?'

'Certainly did. That's where I acquired the taste. What is it? Three years since we were there?' Brodrick asked. 'You haven't changed. No grey hairs!'

'Nope. Still all black!'

They laughed a little awkwardly; small talk didn't come easily to either of them.

'So, are you going to tell me what's going on, or not?' Brodrick goaded, finally.

'Sure, sure.' Hoddle's eyes hardened. 'How much do you know?'

'That there are two stolen Soviet atom bombs on a ship heading for Libya, and that we're teaming with the Russians to find them. I saw a couple of RN helicopters deliver what looked like Russians to the *Jackson* just now.'

'You did? Oh boy! I sure hope somebody checks these guys out before they show 'em around.'

'They didn't look like spooks.'

'Russians? They're *all* spooks. What else d'you know?'

'Okay. The crazies who got hold of the bombs belong to *Mustadhafin* – the same guys I ran up against in Lebanon. But there's this Libyan connection.'

He shrugged to indicate that he didn't understand that part.

'And you've got me all the way out here because you can't handle this thing on your own,' he concluded with a grin.

'You got it.' Hoddle nodded without smiling. He had a way of nodding which involved rocking his whole torso.

Brodrick heard the resentment in his voice. It was politics that had brought them together again, not military need, and they both knew it.

'So give me a sitrep. Where are the nukes now?'

'As of an hour ago, we don't know. We believe they're on a ship. The Sovs are gonna try and locate them with radiation detectors. In five hundred thousand square miles of ocean! Can you believe that?

'And the Libyan connection? Well, that comes from the Russians. They say they identified one of the guys who was working on the bombs in Lebanon as a Libyan colonel. A weapons specialist.'

'Really? I hadn't heard that.'

'And the assessment by our own intelligence is that these guys in the Lebanon wouldn't know what to do with a nuclear warhead. *Mustadhafin* – you know them and I don't – but we think nukes are out of their league.'

Hoddle looked at Brodrick for confirmation, but got none. He went on, 'Number one: in the past they've been racketeers, not political. A nuclear weapon? What the hell would they want one for? They're not goin' to be stupid enough to take on Israel. Lebanon would be wiped out if they did. And we don't see that guy Habib as a suicide case – he's a survivor.

'And number two: even if they did have some crazy idea of using the bombs themselves, they couldn't make them work without a lotta outside help. Those nukes are fused to airburst at one thousand feet, and there's a Permissive Action Link, so they can't be used without two sets of codes. And those codes are locked up in the Kremlin.'

'But you said the bombs were being worked on in Lebanon,' Brodrick interjected. 'By this Libyan. Maybe others, too. Suppose they had the technology to de-activate the safety systems? Suppose they could turn them into simple terror weapons?'

'Okay, Peter. That's maybe possible. But what for? Why would they want such a powerful weapon?'

Brodrick swallowed hard. This was the moment of truth when he'd learn whether his old friend took him seriously.

'Last year the Royal Navy wiped out most of Habib's men, including his younger brother. He wants revenge.'

'With a nuke? You're crazy!'

'No. But he may be. Crazy with rage. If he wants to hit

back at HMS *Eagle* a nuclear weapon is about the only way he can do it.'

Brodrick picked up his cup and drained the watery coffee.

'That idea stinks!' Hoddle declared eventually. 'Why would the Libyans help Habib blow up your navy? They got enough trouble right now with the United Nations. If they're ever goin' to get those sanctions turned off, they've *gotta* renounce terrorism.' He shook his head in disbelief. 'Giving terrorists the know-how to use a nuke! They couldn't be *that* stupid!'

Brodrick felt the back of his neck prickle. Hoddle's scorn was unsettling. *Could* he be wrong?

'Look, the spooks in the Pentagon say Libya's desperate to speed up its nuclear weapons programme. Getting hold of a couple of Russian warheads could give it a kickstart. Once they look inside, they can maybe get enough materials to copy them. With Iraq out of the nuclear game, it's Libya that wants to lead the race for the Arab bomb.'

'But why is Habib involved?'

'Money. Big bucks. The bombs just fell into his hands. The Armenians wanted dollars and were desperate to sell. The Kurds had the money and saw a bargain. They knew Habib through the heroin trade and guessed he could find an Arab end-user who'd pay a top price. You can bet the Libyans paid ten times what the Armenians got. They all made on it.'

The American's explanation was plausible, even logical, yet Brodrick still wasn't convinced.

'So what's the plan if you find them?' he asked coolly.

Seymour Hoddle interleaved the fingers of his massive hands and pressed them out at arm's length until the joints cracked.

'It's "flexible" . .

To military men the word meant 'undecided'.

'. . . but there is a plan.'

'Go on.'

'We're gonna seize the ship and make the bombs safe. Then, if the link with the Libyans is proved, we're gonna bomb the shit out of them. Finish off what we started in eighty-six.'

'I guessed as much,' Brodrick nodded. 'But seizing the ship isn't going to be easy. If there are Libyans on it, they'll have SAMs, heavy machine-guns, God knows what.'

'Sure. We'll do it at night. First we cripple the ship with a missile, cause lots of confusion. Then you abseil onto the deck, or come up the side. You choose.'

'Whaddya mean "we" choose? You want the Brits to do the boarding?'

Hoddle shook his head.

'The White House does. If it were up to me, I'd prefer to do that job myself.'

So that was it. The Royals were to be on this operation, just so the American government could tell the world they weren't acting alone. No wonder he'd been received with so little ceremony on the *Jackson*.

'I see. So what's your role going to be?'

'To take out the Libyan leadership if the bombers miss again. We go in after the air strike. The whole goddam MAU. Amphibs up the beaches, choppers into Tripoli. Hell on wheels, man.'

Hoddle rolled his eyes upwards.

'You could take a lot of casualties,' Brodrick warned.

'The President knows. He thinks the American people will understand it's a price that has to be paid to stop Libya getting the bomb.'

Brodrick leaned back in his chair, arms folded. Hoddle's words had left a bitter taste in his mouth.

They did things in strength, the Yanks. Sending in a whole Marine Amphibious Unit; thousands of men, armoured vehicles, helicopter gunships. They might achieve something with that lot. Not like the handful of men the British government had sent to Lebanon.

'You want us to seize that ship on our own, or are you giving us support?' Brodrick asked abruptly.

'You can have whatever you need. I guess you'll use your own assault helicopters, but we could give you some Cobras to fly shotgun. As I said, first in is the precision air strike. Then you gotta go in fast to secure the nukes before they can use them . . .'

'Shit! You reckon they might try to let them off?'

'It's possible. Arabs are big on suicide.'

So the Royals had drawn the short straw again.

'You volunteered us for this job, did you?'

Hoddle raised his hands in a gesture of innocence.

'No, sir! That was decided at the top. And I mean the top! My President, your Prime Minister.'

'It figures,' said Brodrick bitterly.

'But we'll have weapons specialists in a chopper five minutes away. As soon as you've secured the ship, we'll get 'em on board,' Hoddle reassured him. 'They'll make the goddam bombs safe.'

'American specialists? Or Russian?' Brodrick asked pointedly.

Hoddle smiled wrily.

'Good question. The Sovs don't know our plans. We're co-operating in the search for the ship, but that's it. They say the bombs belong to Russia, so they should reclaim them. We don't see it that way!'

This'll end in tears, Brodrick thought to himself.

'Are you happy with the plan?' he asked flatly.

' "Happy" is not the word. But we're going to give it all we've got. B52s, F-111s – Libya won't have a military installation left standing once we're finished. By the time the Marines go in, the guards round the leadership will have been turned to jello.'

Pinned to a board on the wall was a large-scale chart of the Mediterranean. Brodrick measured off the distance from Gibraltar.

'It'll be three days before *Eagle* gets anywhere near

263

here,' he commented. 'If you find the ship with the nukes on, we may have to move sooner than that.'

He was thinking of the Commando helicopters, which were on board *Eagle*.

'We can give you deck space, if you can get the machines over here,' Hoddle answered, reading his mind.

'And the helos'll need mods. Countermeasures, flares. The Libyans'll be bristling with missiles.' He was talking to himself as much as to the American. 'What's the earliest this thing could start?'

'Well, the radar plot was finalised last night. Today they're doing photo-reconnaissance. Tomorrow they'll check the ships with those Russian geiger counters. If they strike lucky, we could be ordered to seize the ship tomorrow night. If you guys aren't ready, I guess we'll just have to do it ourselves.'

Hoddle was grinning, but Brodrick wasn't in the mood for jokes.

'We'll be ready.'

'Oh, we had a signal from your Colonel Guthrie this morning. You know him?'

'He's in Cyprus? Must've arrived there last night. Yes, I know of him. He's Comacchio Group, from Arbroath. They specialise in throwing terrorists off ships and oil rigs.'

'Sounds just the guy. Wants you to contact him. You can use the satcom.'

'Okay. But first, show me on the chart where you reckon the Libyan ship'll be when we have to hit it.'

'If she's a small freighter and she's been steaming west since Wednesday, then I guess she could be anywhere between Benghazi and Tripoli by tomorrow night.'

He pointed to the coast of Libya.

'We're still five hundred miles too far north and east. Here.' He indicated a spot southeast of Crete. 'But we're heading to close the gap.'

'Are you carrying war stocks?'

'Some. The supply ships are in Souda Bay. They'll be leaving Crete tonight. We'll have to tranship the stores at sea.'

'It'll be a week before your MAU is ready for the assault.'

'They gave us four days. We've just finished an exercise in Turkey, so they think we're good 'n ready.'

'Even that's too long if you're hoping to surprise them.'

'They're not going to be surprised when we turn up. We'll just have to surprise them by hitting them hard, harder than they ever expected.'

The first of the F-14s smacked onto the deck of the *Carl Jackson*, returning from one of the biggest reconnaissance missions the US Navy had ever mounted.

No sooner had they taxied to the flight line and shut down, than a technician rushed forward to remove the video cassettes from the camera pods.

Down in the intelligence centre, the tapes were spun through – pictures of suspect ships superimposed with time of day and position.

Intelligence officers guessed the tonnages, then keyed the vessels' names and co-ordinates into a computer, so they could be matched with the blips on the airborne radar plot.

They listed over three hundred ships, far too many to be screened by the helicopters with the radiation monitors. The field had to be narrowed drastically. So ships of over three thousand tons were eliminated as too large.

Still frames of smaller ships were made from the video; one picture of the stern, showing the name and port of registration, and two profiles to help future recognition.

The names of these 'possibles' were faxed by satellite

to Lloyd's Maritime Information Services in Colchester, England.

Within minutes a fax came back listing where the ships had come from and where they were bound.

With some vessels, Lloyd's held no information, or it was out of date. That in itself was suspicious and it was upon these ships that the Navy was to focus its attention. As the hours passed, they pieced together a hit list for further investigation.

In the Combat Direction Centre of the *Jackson*, the Operations Officer, Commander Norman Tracy, watched the picture build. From the known course and speed of each vessel, a computer calculated where they'd be the next morning. Painstakingly he entered these positions on a chart and began dividing the targets into groups so he could plan the next day's missions.

In the Flag Plot off the CDC, he could see the lurking figure of the Carrier Battle Group Commander. Rear-Admiral Bock had finally learned what their mission was about the previous evening, but had only briefed Tracy that morning. The tension throughout the ship was almost tangible.

Below them in the vast, grey helicopter hangar, two Sea Kings were being readied for the final search. Mechanics bolted the Soviet radiation detector heads to the underside of the fuselages, and secured the bulky control boxes to the cabin floors.

The Russian technicians, feeling awkward, were supervising the work. They were not used to uniformed men who displayed great technical proficiency, but little military discipline, or enlisted men who talked to officers as if they were equals.

They felt anxious too. They knew their American hosts wanted to exploit their technology for their own ends. Their orders from Moscow were to prevent them doing so. But there were just eight Russians on this ship, and over five thousand Americans.

The crackling roar from the tailpipes of the F-14 Tomcats jolted Abdul Habib from his half-slumber on the bridge. Wrenching himself from the stool, he propelled himself to the window.

'You saw that?' he barked at the Libyan, Fahd, who was guarding the helmsman. 'Where's Ellafi? Get him up here.'

Fahd began to move, then remembered it wasn't Habib he took his orders from.

'You tell him. I've got a job to do.'

Habib tensed his muscles to strike the man, then thought better of it. He'd have to deal with this troublesome one, but not yet.

At that moment Colonel Ellafi appeared at the top of the companionway, alerted by a lookout on deck.

'You saw them? American jets. F-14s,' Ellafi announced excitedly, fingering his pistol belt.

'I thought you had equipment to give you a warning of planes,' Habib growled.

'They weren't attacking,' Ellafi yelled, a dangerous anger in his eyes. 'If they had been we'd have known about it. Their radars would set off the alarm.'

Ellafi looked down at the deck and hissed. The canvas covers were still on the launchers for the missile countermeasures.

He strode onto the bridge wing and yelled to the lookout on the deck below.

'Get those covers off. Now!'

Ellafi was dressed, like his subordinates, in jeans and a leather jerkin. From a distance they'd pass as ship's crew, if they kept their firearms well hidden.

'They were looking for us,' Habib insisted, when the Colonel came back inside the bridge.

267

'Maybe! Maybe not! The Americans – they use innocent ships for target practice! You won't see them again.'

The Colonel swung himself down below to kick awake the lieutenant in charge of the electronic counter-measure systems. He suspected Habib was right. They should have known about the approaching aircraft.

The radar-warning equipment had been installed in the same evil-smelling cabin as the powerful radio that kept them in touch with Tripoli.

'You expect too much, Colonel,' said the lieutenant defensively. 'Those fighters aren't using radar. They take directions from the Hawkeyes and the P-3s. We've picked up those emissions all day. Look. Here.'

He pointed to the flickering LEDs. The vertical display showed the frequencies of the airborne radars detected, and a circular one the bearings.

'Well, keep alert! They have tricks up their sleeves, the Americans.'

Ellafi leaned over the chart and fingered the pencilled cross, fifty miles due south of Malta. They'd be there by the middle of the next morning, insh'Allah. The other boat had better be on time, or Habib would be swimming for it, he thought to himself.

The Libyan had developed a profound dislike for the leader of *Mustadhafin*. He'd be glad to be rid of him. The man was a hornet's nest of anger, of bitterness at the world at large. But whatever fiery emotions Habib exhibited now, they were nothing to the rage that would erupt when he learned he was being cheated of his prize.

Under the deal struck between them, Habib was making them a gift of one of the warheads. In exchange, the Libyans had found and hired the Russian tech-nicians with the skills to convert both bombs into terror weapons. Since they'd been at sea, however, a signal had come from Tripoli, ordering Ellafi to renege on that deal.

Supported on his outstretched hands, Ellafi stared

blankly at the chart, no longer absorbing its details. His mind was preoccupied with his own survival. To be entrusted with this task had been an honour; to fail in it could result in his early death.

His leaders would show no mercy if he failed to bring the two Russian nuclear weapons to Tripoli.

The handling of Habib presented the greatest danger. The man was always alert, always suspicious.

Some time in the night, that's when he'd have to move .

Up on the bridge, Abdul Habib sensed the rising tension. Long years of gang-warfare in Beirut had taught him to recognise the smell of treachery.

It was time to take stock, time to plan his move. At the far end of the bridge stood Samir, one of his most trusted men, the scar across his throat a memento of the knife attack that had nearly cost him his life.

Down in the hold were his other two henchmen, Ali and Rashid, one sleeping while the other watched over the fat canisters encased in plastic sheeting.

Four men, including himself, against a dozen.

They had one advantage, however, that was sure to lead them to victory. The Libyans were a rabble without a cause. But the men of *Mustadhafin* shared a commitment to avenge the slaughter of their kinsmen.

The means of achieving that lay in the hold of this ship. They weren't going to let it slip from their hands.

Fifteen

Above the Mediterranean the blue sky of day had turned into the black of night. Deep below the surface, few on board the Soviet submarine *Korund* were in any frame of mind to notice.

As the boat slipped almost noiselessly through the water at fifteen knots, her crew changed watch. Men weary with fatigue slipped into the warm, fetid bunks just abandoned by the comrades who'd taken over their duties. Sleep would not come easily; their minds were occupied with the dispute which had set one man against another in the past few hours.

For much of her journey westwards the *Korund* had travelled on the surface, using her diesels for speed. But she was on batteries now, running deep to avoid the attentions of the American Carrier Battle Group.

When night fell, Captain Second Rank Nikolai Bonderenko had brought the *Korund*'s three thousand tons of black steel to periscope depth. Through the image-intensifier, he'd observed the US Marine Task Force meet with two supply ships and begin the transfer of supplies by helicopter. They must be in a hurry to be cross-decking in the dark, he thought. A mission that couldn't wait?

Moscow had acknowledged his report and ordered him west with all speed. No details, just a chart position north of the Libyan coast.

Nikolai Bonderenko was Russian, but half his officers and most of his seamen were Ukrainian. National

270

rivalries which strict naval discipline had managed to suppress for decades erupted that evening into the threat of mutiny. Only the personal respect which his crew felt for him kept them obeying his orders.

For the past two hours the boat had been a hive of rumour as to the purpose of their mission. As the watch changed, those who'd come on shift had been drawn in to the debate.

'The men have no respect for politicians, Comrade Captain!'

The voice belonged to Ivanov, his executive officer, a Captain Third Rank, from the Ukraine. Four of the most senior officers were squeezed into Bonderenko's cabin.

'Orders from the General Staff must be obeyed,' Bonderenko replied stolidly.

'Russia's General Staff! Not mine?'

The Ukrainian's eyes betrayed his unease. The issue was a crucial one, but he considered Bonderenko a friend and didn't want this conflict with him.

'The fleet still comes under joint command,' Bonderenko insisted. 'Russia and Ukraine.'

'But it was Moscow the orders came from,' Ivanov insisted.

Their faces were flushed, only inches apart in the tiny cabin.

The security officer, Captain-Lieutenant Amelin, intervened to try to soothe matters.

'If I may suggest it, Comrade Captain, we should signal Sevastopol and ask them to reconfirm Moscow's instructions.'

'And withdraw from operations until they do,' insisted Ivanov the Ukrainian.

'We can't,' Bonderenko stated bluntly.

'We must,' retorted Ivanov. 'You haven't told us everything, Captain. That is your right, of course. But from what I can judge, the orders from Moscow could put us in danger. We're heading for Libya. So are the

Americans, maybe. Are we on opposite sides again? I thought all that was over. So why is this happening?'

Bonderenko knew only too well, but his orders were not to tell his men.

'The real question is this,' Ivanov persisted, 'who is giving the orders in Moscow? The General Staff, you say. But who are these men? Are they democrats? Are they responsible to the politicians? Or are they acting alone? Maybe there's been another coup, and perhaps this mission is part of their crazy plans.'

The others nodded. Ivanov had voiced the fear they all shared.

'We are intelligent thinking men, Comrade Captain. We must not allow ourselves to be used for some dark purpose that could throw the world into new conflict.'

They all looked to Bonderenko for his response. It was desperately hot in the tiny cabin. Sweat glistened on their faces. The only illumination came from the red nightlight above their heads.

'We must continue the mission,' Bonderenko declared sombrely.

From their sullen response he knew he'd have to tell them why.

'It's not to throw the world into conflict; it's to keep it out of one. Please believe me.'

Their eyes remained doubtful.

'Look. The fishing boat we sank . . .

The officers shifted in their seats. That incident had never been explained to them.

'Those big canisters our divers went to look for in the hold, and couldn't find. . . ? They were nuclear weapons.'

Bonderenko had their attention now.

'Russian nuclear missile warheads, stolen, and now in the hands of the Arabs.'

'I don't believe it,' the Ukrainian whispered. But he knew Bonderenko wouldn't lie.

'You *must* believe it. If you don't, there'll be a catastrophe. That fishing boat – they thought it was taking the bombs to attack Israel. That's why we were ordered to sink it. But the Arabs had tricked us. The bombs were already on another ship.'

'Those men we killed . . .'

'A mistake. Don't think about it. There may be more to come.'

His officers glanced at each other uneasily. Bonderenko knew he'd won.

'They still haven't told me what we'll have to do. But they're sending us close to Libya. Maybe that's where the nuclear warheads are destined.'

He let them think about it for a moment. They all knew how dangerous and unpredictable was the Libyan regime.

'Those are Russian warheads. It's not a problem for Ukraine . . .' Ivanov muttered defensively.

'If Libya uses them, who knows what'll happen? Soon, there might not be a Russia or a Ukraine to argue about,' Amelin, the security man, added sombrely.

'So, we all agree, the mission must go on?' Bonderenko checked.

More glances, then they nodded their assent.

'But we should ask Moscow for more information,' Ivanov pressed, 'in the interests of democracy. We need to be certain their orders are just.'

'I'll ask,' Bonderenko agreed. 'Now, it's time for the officers to restore discipline on board. See to it please.'

'What shall we tell the men?' Amelin asked.

'The truth. What you've just told us,' Ivanov declared.

Bonderenko hesitated. It defied all the rules. Classified information never normally went below officer level in their navy. But at such times it was for individual commanders to set the rules.

273

'The truth,' he affirmed. 'But informally. No broadcast, just word of mouth.'

One by one they squeezed out of the cabin and spread through the boat to reunite the crew.

Nikolai Bonderenko returned to the control room.

There were seven contacts marked on the tactical combat screen.

'The American carrier's moving faster, Comrade Captain,' the lieutenant told him. 'Bearing two-three-five.'

He pointed to the largest of the noise sources on the screen.

'Any sign that their task force has detected us?'

'No, sir. Unless there's a submarine close by, which we've missed. But in these waters detection is difficult. We should be safe.'

The boy was just out of the academy, speaking with the authority of the truly inexperienced. Bonderenko patted his shoulder. He'd been the same at his age.

Time for his rounds. He ducked through the hatchway heading for the bows, passed under the ladder that led up to the fin, then swung himself onto the rungs that would take him to the deck below. Oil on the handrail – someone deserved a tongue lashing for that, but not today.

The smell of garlic and cooking fat wafted from the cramped mess for the *glavnyy starshini* – the petty officers whom he relied upon to keep his conscript crew in order. They stiffened as he peered through the entrance. He could tell from their eyes that they'd learned the truth about their mission. He grunted and moved on.

In the weapons compartment two crewmen slept on the pallet beds clamped to the torpedo racks. Bonderenko was tall for a submariner and had to duck his head to avoid hydraulic pipes fixed to the roof.

Ahead, he was faced by the tube hatches and the rails for loading the torpedoes into them. To the right was a closed-off armoury separated from the main torpedo stacks by a wire grille, secured with a padlock. Inside were two very special weapons, Type 65 nuclear-tipped torpedoes, designed to destroy American aircraft carriers.

The codes to activate them were in the safes in his own cabin and that of the security officer, Captain Third Rank Amelin.

He looked at the sleeping sailors. What had it done to their bodies to share this space with nuclear warheads? Officially, the weapons were perfectly safe. But no one wore radiation monitors, so how could they know? In Murmansk they joked that you could tell a Russian submariner by the way he glowed in the dark. He shuddered.

The ordinary torpedoes on which his crewmen slept were the teeth of this submarine, the fangs that could tear open the enemy's flesh. Before long, his gut told him, they would be ordered to use them.

He looked again at the men who'd have to load them into the tubes. They were tired, slack from too long at sea.

Let them lie there for another few hours. Then he'd bully them from their bunks and drill them until their shoulders ached with fatigue.

MV Baalbeck
23.37 hrs

Abdul Habib pretended to sleep. On another bunk in the small cabin, Colonel Ellafi was doing the same.

Nearly time, Habib thought. He couldn't see his

watch without revealing that he was awake. His heart thundered in anticipation.

Suddenly, he heard running feet in the passageway outside. A prayer to Allah that it was his man, not Ellafi's.

The door burst open. It was Rashid.

'Habib! Quick!' he breathed, loud enough for Ellafi to hear as well. 'Come to the hold. The weapons. Something's happened. There's gas . . .'

Abdul Habib sprang to his feet, thrust his pistol into his belt and propelled himself out of the cabin after Rashid.

Colonel Ellafi sat up, startled. Gas? What was the Lebanese talking about? How could there be gas? He looked at his watch. A quarter to midnight. Two more hours before his men were due to make their move.

Uneasy, he checked his weapon, then pushed into the next cabin to rouse Fahd. Maybe they'd have to act sooner.

Running along the deck to the forward companionway that led to the hold, the two Libyans smelled smoke.

Shouts came from below.

'Water! Get water,' they heard Habib splutter.

They started down the ladder. Black fumes billowed along the short passageway to the hold.

Covering his mouth and nose with a shirt-sleeve, and with the pistol gripped firmly in his right hand, Ellafi ducked forward to see what had happened. Inside, the smoke enveloped him.

Suddenly a baulk of timber cracked onto his skull and felled him to the deck. His pistol clattered against the steel and was seized by waiting hands.

Six feet behind him in the passageway Fahd froze, thighs tensed to spring, his Kalashnikov barrel probing for a target he couldn't see.

'Colonel?' he yelled into the choking, black smoke.

Then his jaw racked open in a rictus of agony, a silent scream, as a long steel blade pierced his rectum and ripped into his gut.

The force of the knife thrust toppled him. His assault gun spattered bullets into the void, the shots hammering in the confined space.

Habib's man Samir stamped on Fahd's wrist, and the gun fell silent. Then with a pistol, he fired a single merciful shot into the Libyan's temple.

'Allahu Akbar!' he yelled.

'Allahu Akbar!' came the answering cry – Habib's voice, muffled by a gas mask.

There was a hiss of carbon dioxide, extinguishing the flames in the bucket of oil-soaked rags they'd used to create the smoke.

'Is it Fahd?' Habib demanded. He had a profound wish for the man who'd defied him on the bridge to be dead.

'It is,' Samir confirmed.

'Bring him into the hold.'

Habib's other two men, Rashid and Ali, switched on fans in the ventilation shafts. The smoke began to clear.

They heard shouts on deck. The rest of the Libyans had been alerted by the shots.

'Stay on deck!' Samir yelled as a foot appeared on the top rung of the ladder. 'Any further and we'll kill Colonel Ellafi!'

He fired a single round, aiming to miss. The foot disappeared in an instant.

Habib splashed water on Ellafi's face to revive him. A gash on the Colonel's scalp oozed blood.

There was blood, too, on Habib's sleeve. A ricocheting bullet from Fahd's Kalashnikov had grazed his arm.

Ellafi coughed as he recovered consciousness. He looked about, dazed and bewildered, then began a futile struggle. His hands and feet were already bound.

'Fahd!' he yelled.

Habib pointed to the body, with its dark smear beside the ear.

'You Lebanese son of a whore!' Ellafi cursed.

Samir cracked his pistol butt across the Colonel's mouth, splitting his lip.

Habib raised his hand to stay a second blow.

'Enough! No one else needs to die!'

He crouched in front of Ellafi and searched his eyes for fear. All he saw was defiance.

'Traitor to the Arabs!' Habib hissed. 'You were going to break the bargain, steal our weapon!'

Ellafi didn't deny it.

'You do what I tell you now. Forget the orders of the madmen in Tripoli.'

'To hell with you!' Ellafi snarled. 'Kill me if you wish.'

'No.'

Habib's eyes were icy cold.

'You are going to live, so I can see the fear in your eyes when I give you to Samir . . .'

Ellafi blinked, as Habib's henchman crossed over to the prostrate body of Fahd.

Samir's hand reached down. Something projected from the seat of the dead man's jeans.

'Aaaagh!' Ellafi cried in horror, as the long crimson knife was slowly pulled from Fahd's intestines.

He turned away and began to retch. Habib grabbed his hair and twisted his head to face him again.

'You will do what I tell you?'

Ellafi shook uncontrollably.

'Yes,' he sobbed.

Habib nodded to Rashid, who seized the Libyan under the armpits and hauled him to his feet.

'You and me, we go to the bridge,' Habib told him. 'Tell your men to stay on deck and throw down their weapons. Shout from the ladder. And convince them! Samir is behind you!'

They cut the ties round Ellafi's ankles and pushed him towards the ladder. His hands were still bound. As he stepped up the rungs, Samir held him against the metal with a fist to prevent him toppling backwards.

'Tell them!' Habib ordered.

The Colonel stood high on the ladder, his head above the deck. He felt the point of Samir's knife against his thigh.

'Get on deck!' All of you,' Ellafi shouted. 'That's an order!' he screamed as he saw their hesitation.

'Tell them to get the deck lights on so we can count them,' Habib barked from below.

'Lights. Lights on! Hurry, for God's sake!'

The knife pressure increased.

The working lamps came on. Samir pushed Ellafi onto the deck and into the pool of light cast by the bulb on the forward mast. He wanted the Libyans to see their Colonel's terror.

Behind them Habib emerged from the hold but remained in the shadows.

'Put down your weapons and move away. Do as they tell you and no one else need die,' Ellafi choked.

He saw some of them hesitate. Would they disobey and open fire? Part of him hoped they would, part prayed desperately that they wouldn't.

There was a clang of metal against metal as one by one they dropped their guns on the deck. Habib counted.

Two were missing.

'The Russians,' he hissed at Ellafi. 'Get them out of their cabin and into the hold.'

The Libyan Colonel began to hyperventilate. The Russian technicians were his last card. On his orders, they'd installed a safety device on the bombs. Codes were needed before the weapons could be fused. He'd kept this to himself, and the Russians' presence secret, but again Habib had the measure of him.

'The engineers,' he ordered wearily. 'Bring them up here. Mr Habib has a use for them.'

Sixteen

Brodrick awoke the moment the marine lieutenant shook him by the shoulder. Years of military training meant catnapping was second nature.

'They want you back on the *Jackson*, sir. With Major Hoddle.'

'Why? What's happened?' he mumbled.

'Don't know, sir. They just asked me to wake you.'

'Okay.' He looked at his watch. 'When are we flying? Do I have time for breakfast?'

'Take-off's in one hour, and there's coffee in the wardroom, sir. Major Hoddle said he'd see you there.'

He'd slept well in the spacious two-man cabin. No more nightmares.

The previous afternoon he'd made contact with Colonel Guthrie in Cyprus. First thing that morning, the US Navy was sending Greyhound transport planes to Akrotiri, to collect him and his Comacchio Group commandos.

He'd also contacted HMS *Eagle* and warned them of the technical modifications they'd need to make to the Commando Sea Kings. Receivers to warn of missile attack, flare dispensers to deflect the heat-seekers, and heavy machine-guns.

The helicopters would fly to the *Jackson* as soon as *Eagle* got within range. But it would be late afternoon before they could begin to ferry across, mid-evening before they linked up with Comacchio Group. Touch-

281

and-go whether they'd be ready in time. He knew that Hoddle was preparing his own assault team, just in case it was needed.

Fifteen minutes later, Brodrick was shaved and dressed and had found his way to the large refectory. Seymour Hoddle was already there, dealing with a pile of ham and eggs.

'What you wanna eat?'

'Same as that'll do nicely.'

'Coffee and juice are to go. Over there.'

He pointed to a pair of urns on a sidetable. Brodrick filled two plastic cups, and sat down opposite him.

'So, what's it about?'

'They've got seats on the two search helicopters. One for you, one for me. The boss thought we should take a look, just in case they find this goddam ship.'

'Makes sense.'

The smell of the grilled ham made him realise how hungry he was. He glanced towards the galley.

'Do you know what it does, this kit the Russians have?' Brodrick asked.

'Nope. What I do know is that they showed it to our guys a few years back and it does work.'

'A few years back? Glasnost already.'

The steward placed a steaming plate in front of him.

'Arms control. Moscow wanted to show it could check which ships carry nuclear warheads. We said it'd be impossible to verify. They said they'd got special helicopters that had been checking on our ships for years!'

'Bet that went down like a lead fart!'

'You got it! The Pentagon sent a scientific team to take a look. The Russians demonstrated with one of their own ships, the *Slava*, in the Black Sea. It worked pretty good.'

'Really?' Brodrick was intrigued. 'How close does the helicopter need to be?'

'Now that's technical. Below my pay-grade. Finish those eggs, and we'll go see the guys who do know.'

The assault ships of the US Marine Task Force had finished cross-decking war supplies from their support vessels, when the Sea Knight took off for the Carrier Battle Group twenty minutes' flying time away.

Five amphibious vessels, and another dozen missile ships with the *Jackson* – a strike force of awesome power – were now heading southwest towards Libya.

As Brodrick looked back through the round side window, the warships, with their herringbone wakes, looked like darts homing on the bull.

Opposite him, Hoddle's black face was almost invisible in the half-darkness of the helicopter, identifiable only by the buff-coloured, hemispherical ear-defenders clamped to his head. His eyes seemed to be closed, dozing.

Sleep whenever you can – the motto of a soldier.

Brodrick closed his eyes too, but didn't sleep. All around him the American war machine had a look of unstoppability, which filled him with unease.

In their determination to prevent Libya from obtaining a bomb, he feared the Americans were overlooking a much smaller player, one whose desire to possess such a weapon was based not on power politics, but on a pressing wish to use it.

A change in engine pitch told him they were about to land. Seymour Hoddle heard it too and stretched.

With a shake and a shimmy the machine settled onto the vast, steel deck of the USS *Carl Jackson*. The rear ramp hissed open. The crewman collected the ear-defenders and signalled them to disembark. Brodrick glanced at his watch. Nearly 6.30 am.

'Welcome on board, sir. See those two SH-3s? Cap'n Brodrick, you're in the first one. Major Hoddle in the second. Mission's the same – just searching different sectors.'

Bolted below the side door of each Sea King were panels, two metres by one, that looked like solar cells, but weren't.

Brodrick waved as Hoddle walked to the second helicopter, then pulled himself into the cabin of the first.

The engines fired immediately. The crew-chief pointed to a seat and handed him a talking headset. Brodrick pulled it over his ears.

'Do you hear me okay?'

The voice was the aircrew's. Brodrick signalled a thumbs-up.

'We're behind schedule. We'll explain everything when we're airborne.'

Brodrick nodded and buckled his seat belt.

It was an anti-submarine version of the Sea King, a bulky winch for the dipping sonar filling the forward part of the cabin. In the cramped rear, much of the usual acoustic processing equipment had been removed to make way for the boxes of specialised electronics.

There were four other passengers apart from Brodrick, all dressed in survival suits; one had the look of a naval officer, the other three he took to be Russians.

The blades bit into the air and the machine, heavy with fuel, men and machinery, heaved itself off the deck, and settled at a thousand feet and one hundred and ten knots, heading southwest.

A hand touched Brodrick's shoulder. It was the man he'd taken to be a naval officer. He smiled a greeting and searched for a socket for his headset jack. The noise in the helicopter wouldn't allow normal conversation.

'Okay. Can you hear me now?'

The clean, east-coast accent came clearly through Brodrick's headphones. He gave a thumbs-up.

'Jim Ackerman. Lieutenant-Commander. I'm an EWO from the *Jackson*. Welcome aboard.'

Brodrick shook the outstretched hand.

'Peter Brodrick.'

'D'you want to unbuckle, and I'll show you what we got on here.'

They moved to the back of the aircraft and found new sockets for their headsets. The three Russians looked preoccupied with their equipment.

'Got their own comms,' Ackerman explained. 'They talk to their own guys on the *Jackson*, and *they* talk to Moscow. First time I've been on a flight that's reported to the Kremlin!'

'It's weird,' Brodrick answered, flicking the 'talk' switch on the headset lead. 'I've spent ten years training to kill these buggers!'

One of the Russians looked up. Brodrick wondered if he'd heard what he'd said.

'Don't worry. They're on a different net,' the American reassured him, tapping the lozenge-shaped microphone pressed against his lips.

'So how does all this stuff work?' Brodrick asked. 'Those panels outside? That's the detector?'

'Sure. They're Helium-3 counters. They detect neutrons. D'you know much about nukes?'

'Not enough!'

Ackerman had only learned the technology himself that morning.

'The core of the particular weapons we're looking for is Plutonium-239. That stuff's always contaminated with Plutonium-240. What you get in Plutonium-240 is spontaneous fission – atoms splitting and releasing neutrons. Okay?'

Brodrick nodded.

'Well, that's it. This gear counts the neutrons.'

'Simple as that?'

'The processing is complex.'

285

He gestured to the racks of dials and oscilloscopes.

'The neutron release is minute. So these guys also have to measure background radiation, to compare it with what they're getting. Only then do they know if they're onto something. And there's another problem. We have to get the detector to within fifty yards of the neutron source.'

He pointed at a bulky tripod set up by the side door.

'See that? It's a laser rangefinder, so we know we're close enough. Bolted to it is a camera to show us which part of the ship the detector's looking at when it sniffs the neutrons. All that data gets recorded on a multi-track.'

'Sounds dodgy. D'you think they'll really know when they've found something?'

They glanced at the Russians. There was a look of resignation on their Slav faces. The day was going to be long and uncomfortable.

'I sure don't know,' Ackerman breathed. 'Personally I've always thought Soviet technology was a heap o' shit!'

'Which one of them's the boss?' Brodrick asked.

'I'm not sure. Could be the guy with the face like granite. The other two know about the gear, but they seem scared of him.'

'Probably KGB,' Broderick conjectured. 'One of them's bound to be. Do you know any names?'

Ackerman pulled a notepad from the knee-pocket of his survival suit.

'Papushin. Yegor. That's the guy.'

Brodrick noted the man's cold gaze.

'Wouldn't want to meet him on a dark night,' he commented. 'How long until we reach the first ship?'

' 'Bout ninety minutes.'

Brodrick's eyebrows arched. That wouldn't leave much search time before they'd have to fly back to refuel.

'There's an Italian frigate somewhere that we can get a drink from,' Ackerman explained, reading his mind.

He pulled a chart from his other knee-pocket.

'We've got sixteen ships to look at. All under three thousand tons. These were the fixes at six this morning. We'll get hourly updates from the P-3s.'

The chart had been marked by hand. A symbol for each ship, with an arrow showing its heading, then a box beside it with the ship's name and tonnage.

'Impressive detail,' Brodrick conceded.

'Lloyds have been great!' Ackerman grinned.

'So, which is our first?'

Ackerman pointed to the most easterly of the symbols.

'Starting here and working west. She's general cargo – two thousand tons. Last reported in Iskenderun two weeks ago.'

He tracked his finger through a succession of symbols, then made a circular gesture on the chart.

'Italian frigate's somewhere here. Hope we find her. Else we'll be swimming.'

Brodrick looked at the grey ocean below. White flecks showed that the wind had strengthened. Sea Kings could float – but not in a sea like that.

He glanced at the Russians. Papushin's face looked ashen. Was he too imagining what it would be like to ditch?

He crossed and shook the hand of each in turn. It'd do no harm to be friendly.

Then he dropped into a seat and tried to doze. It would be another hour before they got busy.

09.57 hrs

The US Navy P-3C Orion maritime patrol aircraft out of Sigonella in Sicily flew a box pattern at fifteen thousand feet. Its radar gave a 360 degree picture of the sea to a distance of one hundred and fifty miles.

The crew expected an uneventful flight. The positions of all surface ships in their sector were already known and logged. It was a matter of tracking them, so they could guide the search helicopters to their targets.

Their sector touched Malta in the northwest, and to the south and east the coast of Libya from Tripoli to Benghazi.

A new blip entered the plot from the east, faster moving than the ships. This was one of the Sea Kings. The radar operator watched the paint pause beside one surface ship after another, like a slow-moving bumble-bee pollinating buttercups.

At the forward end of the cabin, the mission commander sat at a large, circular display of the search area, the raw radar returns processed by computer into easy-to-read symbology.

'Do I have a go for the turn, commander?'

It was the pilot's voice on the intercom. He'd reached the southern end of the patrol box.

'Affirmative for the turn.'

The plane banked to the right, the four turboprops biting into the cold, thin air to pull them north again.

The radar operator switched to ISAR mode to check the profile of one of the closest targets. On a separate screen appeared the fuzzy, but unmistakeable outline of a ferry. He marked the confirmation in his log. This was the same vessel that had left Valetta ten hours earlier.

He switched back to maximum range; for a few seconds the screen was a blur as the closer images faded and the long-range paints took their place.

He frowned. There was something odd in the north-west corner of his display. An outbreak of clutter.

He reached up to reduce the sensitivity, but it made no difference.

He switched to the processed display which the

mission commander was seeing. Unable to interpret the clutter, the computer had retained its earlier picture. In the area where there was now a proliferation of returns, it revealed that a few minutes ago there'd been just two ships there, one heading north, the other south, a few miles apart, on the route from Malta to Libya.

The operator switched back to raw radar. Still the explosion of returns.

'Commander? Could you come take a look at this?' he called on the intercom.

The mission chief eased himself from his swivel chair, relieved to stretch his legs.

'We had just two tracks there a moment ago. Now look what we got,' the operator said, tapping his screen.

'Crazee! What's the range?'

'One hundred forty.'

'Must be somebody's navy on exercise. Those returns are from countermeasures. I'll call the *Jackson*, see if they know anything.'

10.10 hrs

In the back of the SH-3 it smelled of hot oil. Spirits were low. So far the Russian equipment had detected nothing suspicious. Until it did, there was no way of knowing whether it was even working.

The two Soviet technicians looked agitated. They'd overflown eight ships. Not a flicker.

Circumstances were far from ideal, one of them kept saying, in broken English. In the Soviet Union they had their own purpose-built aircraft, where everything was carefully calibrated. Here it was all . . . he couldn't find the words.

'Heath Robinson,' Brodrick suggested, but the Russian was none the wiser.

'We've less than thirty minutes' fuel,' Ackerman told him through his headset. 'We're going to look for our Italian mama! They've given us a fix. Hope they know how to navigate.'

'Christopher Columbus was an Italian,' Brodrick reminded him gently.

Ackerman gave him a withering look.

The Sea King climbed to three thousand feet and flew due north for fifteen minutes. Then, precisely at the position they'd been given, the Italian frigate appeared out of the haze.

It was on occasions like this that regular NATO exercises paid off. The Italian frigate's landing deck was too small for a Sea King, so they'd have to refuel in flight, a technique the two navies practised routinely.

The frigate swung bows into the wind, moving slowly. The Sea King eased into the hover, just above the port safety-rail of the frigate's flight deck. Below, the Italian seamen had the fuel hose ready. Down went the winch cable, then back up with the fuel nozzle attached.

The crew-chief leaned out of the open side door and plugged the hose into the filler pipe below the sill. Thumbs-up to the Italian deck officer, and fuel began to flow.

'Thank God for that,' Ackerman babbled in Brodrick's earphones. 'Just hope we don't get a gearbox failure.'

'Cheerful sod, aren't you?' Brodrick retorted.

'I hate these machines. There's so much can go wrong.'

From his pallor, Brodrick could see that Ackerman meant what he said.

'Anyway, we'll have the door shut again when the tanks are full, then we can eat. Hungry?'

'Not really,' Brodrick answered. 'But if I'm going to die, I might as well do it on a full stomach.'

12.30 hrs

In the Combat Direction Centre of the USS *Carl Jackson*, Rear-Admiral James D Bock strutted in and out of his Flag plot, getting on the operations officer's nerves. Things were moving.

The first alert had come early that morning when the towed-array sonar on the USS *Stevens* had detected an unidentified submarine heading west at speed, two hundred miles southeast of Malta.

A NATO submarine? Commander Norman Tracy had signalled SUBMED at NAVSOUTH HQ, Naples, where the NATO navies coordinated their undersea operations. The answer had been negative.

Was it Libyan, Egyptian, even Israeli? Checks with the last two countries were being made through diplomatic channels. Reconnaissance flights over Libya would soon reveal whether any of their submarines had left port.

But as far as Tracy was concerned the boat was almost certainly Russian, probably the same Tango that had sunk the fishing boat *Joun* earlier in the week.

Time to test how serious Moscow was about co-operating in the search for the nuclear bombs. On the hot-line to Moscow, the Pentagon had asked the Soviet Defence Ministry if the boat was theirs. No straight answer so far. Just the same old prevarication from Moscow that they'd experienced during the cold war years.

'How can they still be checking, goddammit?' Bock

exploded at the most recent signal from the Pentagon. 'Don't the Russians know where their submarines are? Of course they goddam do!'

An hour ago, there came a second alert. The signal from the P-3C, reporting a confusion of surface contacts fifty miles south of Malta. They suspected a warship firing decoys – clouds of aluminium chaff to confuse radar. But again, there was no NATO ship in the area.

The Admiral had despatched a pair of F-14s to take a look. By the time they got there, the chaff had dispersed. No military vessels to be seen, just a couple of small freighters and a trawler winding out its nets.

Something strange had been happening there none-theless, so Bock had ordered the Sea King that had just refuelled from the Italian frigate to cut short its list of ships and head straight for the scene.

Nothing to do now but wait.

That submarine worried them most. If there was a fight coming, a lone wolf submarine could cause them havoc.

13.07 hrs

'Target's at five miles. Overhead in three minutes,' said the cool voice of the Sea King pilot. He had the ship on radar. Nothing visual yet because of the haze, which had cut visibility to a mile.

Brodrick watched the Russian technicians flick the switches to power up the neutron detectors. Their methods were familiar to him now; this would be the ninth ship they'd overflown.

The aircrew slid back the door and the technicians braced themselves against the buffeting slipstream.

'Target visual. Fishing vessel. Heading two-seven-zero.'

'Not listed,' Ackerman clicked in. 'I guess they considered it too small to worry about.'

'Heading west,' added Brodrick. 'Would it be fishing? Out here?'

'Not my subject.'

'Nor mine.'

The tail dipped as the pilot lost speed. Brodrick grabbed the handrail and peered round the edge of the doorway. The down-draught drove the smell of burning kerosene into his nostrils.

There was a light swell. He guessed the wind was force three to four. The boat was very small. A hundred tons at most with a fishing gallows on each side. As they drew into the hover fifty yards astern he could see a trawl wire strung out from the port side.

The camera and laser-rangefinder were live and registering. A thumbs-up from the Russian technicians. The aircrew told the pilot they were ready, and the helicopter dipped forward until it was in line with the trawler's stern.

They advanced slowly; the neutron detectors needed thirty seconds to scan the length of the deck. Brodrick searched the superstructure, first with the naked eye, then with binoculars.

It was a sturdy craft, steel hulled and well found. Atop the small wheelhouse were antennae for radar and satellite navigation. He tried to read the name on the stern, but it was obscured by dirt or rust. He made out the letters E-T-T-A, and guessed the home port was Valletta, Malta.

On the foredeck a crewman in blue denim paused in his securing of the hatchcover to stare up at the helicopter. He waved at the wheelhouse and pointed up at the sky. Then Brodrick saw the face of the helmsman press against a side window and look up.

Seemed innocent enough.

The Russians had registered nothing on their instruments. No need for a second pass.

Ackerman told the pilot to fly on. The nose dipped; the machine banked to the right, then climbed to a thousand feet so the radar could locate the next target.

'Range fifteen miles,' the pilot called.

'This one could be the *Baalbeck*, registered in Malta,' Ackerman read from the target list supplied that morning. 'Last known port of call Limassol.'

'One of the ones that got lost in the radar clutter?' Brodrick checked.

'I guess so.'

He glanced behind at the Russians. Papushin, the man he'd guessed was KGB, was prodding questioningly at the dials. Probably reckons the equipment's duff, Brodrick thought.

'Range five miles,' the pilot intoned. 'Target has turned right, through sixty degrees.'

The heading had been northerly, the direction of Valletta. Now the *Baalbeck* had swung to the east.

Thirty seconds later the pilot came on again.

'Turning back to the north. Maybe there's a dog at the wheel!'

A minute later the machine began to sink towards the sea.

'We have visual contact. Range – a thousand yards. Getting hazier.'

Brodrick steadied himself against the door-frame, holding on with one hand while raising his binoculars with the other.

A general cargo vessel. Superstructure at the stern. Hatchcovers along the deck. A kink in its wake, where it had turned and then thought better of it.

Slowly the helicopter pulled level with its rudder.

Behind him the Soviet technicians concentrated on their dials, and signalled they were ready for the scan.

Brodrick focused on the bridge. He saw one face looking up at him, and several darker shapes inside.

He panned the binoculars along the deck, then paused, puzzled.

Grubby, green canvas covered two pieces of machinery just forward of the superstructure, one on each side of the ship. Winches? Odd place for them. He adjusted focus and continued his pan along the deck.

All the usual fittings were there, just where he'd expect them to be – and none of them was covered.

A movement caught his eye. For a split second a face peered from behind a companionway cover on the foredeck. Dark, curly hair and frightened eyes. Gone again.

Then, something else which sent a shiver down his spine. Instinctively he reached for his weapon, but realised he had none with him.

Something on the deck, just where the face had been. A pipe, a few inches in diameter. Inside it, just visible, a shiny hemisphere.

'Scram! Scram!' Brodrick yelled into his lip microphone, hoping to God the pilot could hear.

Ackerman stared incomprehendingly.

'Tell him to scram! They've got SAMs!'

The lieutenant commander flicked the intercom switch and barked at the flightdeck. The machine lurched to the left.

Brodrick stole a last look at the *Baalbeck*. He knew now what was under those covers. He should've known instantly. Rocket launchers for the chaff that had confused the radar on the American P-3C.

'Hey, you sure about those SAMs?' Ackerman checked.

'Bloody sure!' Brodrick insisted. 'And they've got countermeasures. That's the ship that fogged the radar. Look.'

He pointed at the tripod by the door.

'Check the tape. The camera must have seen what I saw.'

They turned from the door and realised the Russians were in a huddle. Yegor Papushin stood behind the technicians, gripping the back of their seats and staring at the dials.

'They've found something!' Brodrick growled. 'The bastards have found something!'

Ackerman pursed his lips, stepped towards the Russians and rested a hand on Papushin's shoulder.

'What did you get?' he demanded. 'Looks like they had missiles on that ship. Could be the one.'

Papushin shrugged.

'Too quick. Not enough time. . .' he answered in halting English.

He gestured at the instrument panel. The two technicians had their heads down, ignoring Ackerman's enquiry.

'You got something, for God's sake. Some reading?'

Papushin shrugged again.

'You see, they can't be sure.' His voice was heavy with accent. 'We take the data to your ship. They have better equipment. Maybe they give an opinion.'

Ackerman suddenly noticed one of the technicians was already speaking on the radio to the Russian support team on the *Jackson*.

Shit! Those guys could talk direct to Moscow!

Maskerovka! Concealment! The Russians had detected neutrons all right, and they were trying to keep it to themselves.

Disaster loomed in Ackerman's mind. The Kremlin would hear what was going on before his Admiral did.

He pushed forward to the cockpit to use the secure radio link to the ship.

*

On the bridge of the *Baalbeck* Ellafi yelled at the helmsman.

'Turn! Turn south. For Tripoli!'

They'd been discovered! No point in pretending to head for Malta.

The smudge of jet exhaust from the disappearing Sea King was still visible through the binoculars. They should have shot it out of the sky when they had the chance.

He knew about the Russians' technology for detecting warheads from the air; he'd guessed that's what those panels under the Sea King were for, guessed they'd asked for American help to find the bombs.

The instant the lookout had spotted the helicopter approaching, he'd ordered his men out of sight. Damn the fool in the bows who'd been unable to restrain his curiosity!

From the bridge Ellafi had watched, as if it were all in slow motion; the fearful face revealing itself, the missile tube sliding into view, the helicopter jinking left and diving low.

There could be no doubt. They were finished. The combined wrath of the superpowers would descend upon them.

'Get everyone up here,' Ellafi yelled from the bridge window, his voice raw with panic.

His men despised him now. He could feel it.

He, the commanding officer of a dozen trained men, had fallen for the tricks of a quartet of brigands. In the hands of Habib they'd seen cowardice spill from his mouth like bile. He'd let them murder Fahd and had set the saving of his own miserable life above the preservation of their honour.

A traitor to their country. That's how they saw him now. He read it in their eyes.

Ellafi smarted at his treatment. How could they understand the terror he'd faced, threatened by ritual mutilation? A bloodstained bandage bound his head. Samir had sliced off the tip of an ear. He'd expected disembowelment to follow. One day, God willing, his people would take their revenge on *Mustadhafin*.

When would the Americans move?

They'd know the *Baalbeck* could dock in Tripoli by noon the next day. They'd come within hours, in the dark of night.

How would they do it?

He shuddered at the thought of the firepower the Americans commanded. But he had one trump card – the cargo in the forward hold. They'd surely want to recover that intact.

Nine of his guards clattered up the companionway onto the bridge. Wisely, the bow lookout had stayed where he was.

The eyes of his men showed fear and loathing.

'The Americans will come tonight,' he barked at them. 'No one may sleep. We must watch every second of the night, in every quarter.'

'What will they do, Colonel?' a sullen voice demanded.

'They want our cargo. To get it they must put men on board, from the sea or from the air. We shall not make it easy for them. Our brave air force will send fighters to protect us. The Americans will pay a heavy price. Now, make ready your weapons. Take up your positions.'

They knew he was lying. They'd be on their own. Martyrdom would be their fate.

Ellafi couldn't face their accusing eyes. He elbowed through their ranks and slid down the ladder to the communications cabin below.

He pulled the code-book from the shelf, then clutched his head in his hands. What was he to tell the leadership?

Should he confess he'd let Habib hold him to the

bargain he'd been ordered to betray? Tell his unforgiving masters that Habib had gone and that one of the two nuclear weapons was no longer on the *Baalbeck*?

He daren't tell them that. They'd kill him; they'd kill his sons.

Death might come for him anyway, this night. But he could face that, as long as his children were spared.

He kept the message simple – that they'd been discovered and expected an attack. He jotted the Arabic onto a notepad, one sentence at a time, then encrypted it into numerals and Roman letters.

Help from their air force? Impossible, and he knew it. For the leadership to send fighters to defend a Maltese registered freighter would be to announce to the world that Libya was secretly buying stolen Russian bombs.

And in practical terms, his country's fighters were no match for the Sixth Fleet's F-14s.

He handed the completed signal to the wireless operator to transmit.

He checked the time. Ten minutes to two in Tripoli. The signal would go straight to the Revolutionary Command headquarters, where the leader would be waiting for news in his tent.

The wireless operator played with a VHF set while they waited, switching around the bands used by the US military in the hope of catching something they could understand.

It was an age before the print head on the teletype exploded into life, and zipped back and forth, hammering dots onto the page like coffin nails.

It stopped as abruptly as it had begun. The operator tore off the page and handed it to the Colonel.

Deciphering was slow. Ellafi was ill-practised. But gradually the message emerged.

It was just a single line.

'IF THE ATTACK PROVES IMPOSSIBLE TO
RESIST – DETONATE THE BOMBS. ALLAHU
AKBAR.'

Seventeen

The Sea King pilot squeezed every last knot out of his machine. Brodrick sat strapped to the canvas seat behind the cockpit, hunched forward, his hands clasped between his knees. They were hurtling northwards; within minutes they would be landing on the deck of HMS *Eagle*.

He had no idea his own ship was so close. She'd made remarkable speed. Her tanks must be almost dry. Her Olympus turbines burned nearly five hundred tons of fuel a day at full power.

Brodrick sensed that his role had undergone a radical change in the split second when he'd spotted the missile launcher on the *Baalbeck*. No longer was he just an observer in the search operation; events had propelled him into the very heart of the mission to neutralise this nuclear threat.

His euphoria was tempered by a fear which gnawed at his insides. Within hours he'd be face to face with those men. In the battle that would ensue, only a few could survive. Maybe none at all.

He felt powerless, stuck up here in the Sea King. The decisions were being taken on the *Jackson*, decisions he needed to influence. Major Seymour Hoddle would be back on the carrier by now, talking with the commanders.

They were boxed in by time. The *Baalbeck* could be in Libyan waters by dawn. Comacchio Group had been earmarked for the boarding. But Brodrick realised they were in the wrong place. The men were on the *Jackson*; their aircraft were five hundred miles away on the *Eagle*, beyond helicopter range. And the fixed-wing Greyhound transports couldn't land on *Eagle*'s short deck.

They'd been caught short. Vast assets, but not where they were needed. Typical bloody cock-up!

Could the Italian frigate help? She was the closest warship to the *Baalbeck*. Brodrick doubted it; the government in Rome would never make up its mind in time.

Brodrick ground his teeth with the tension. There was only one way the *Baalbeck* could be seized: by himself – with his men from the *Eagle*.

He unclipped his seat harness, stood up and leaned into the cockpit, plugging his headset into the pilot's net.

'How're we doing?'

The pilot turned nonchalantly to see who'd spoken. He was a big man who lounged in his seat as if driving an old Chevrolet.

'Hi, there. Think we're goin' to make it. But we could be in free fall for the last mile.'

He tapped the fuel gauge which looked perilously close to empty.

'Have you had contact with *Eagle*?'

'Sure. And they've got a 'Whisky' up there, keepin' an eye on us. You'll be home with momma soon!'

Brodrick forced a grin and looked beyond the instrument panel into the haze ahead.

'Ten miles to go. Ten minutes of fuel,' the pilot drawled.

Captain David Dyce occupied a big swivel chair in the centre of *Eagle*'s operations room. To his left and right, table-top radar screens showed the air picture and the surface and sub-surface plots. In the dim glow from the cathode tubes, his bald, pale head took on a ghostly hue.

Eagle's dash eastwards had put them out on a limb,

with no escorting frigates, no tanker nearby to top up their dwindling fuel reserves. He'd rely on the Americans, both for protection and, more immediately, for an urgent supply of kerosene.

From first light, his ship had come under the command of the US Sixth Fleet. Their arrival off Malta was in the nick of time, the Battle Group Commander had told him. He'd ordered *Eagle* southeast at full power, to provide a deck for the American Sea King that had located the weapons. Only in the last few minutes had Captain Dyce learned that Peter Brodrick was on the helicopter.

Signals had come thick and fast in the past hour, both from the USS *Carl Jackson* and from Dyce's own headquarters in London. Unfortunately the two sets of orders he'd received were in direct conflict with one another.

It wasn't for him to resolve it; he'd batted it straight back to CINCFLEET at Northwood. It was the old problem; the military men had one plan, the politicians another.

But they'd need to make their minds up fast, if he was to know how to handle Brodrick.

'Homer's got the Sea King on finals, sir,' the Principal Warface Officer announced.

'Good news, Nick.'

Dyce glanced up at the digital clock. Fifteen-thirty, Zulu.

If the Prime Minister stuck to his guns, Peter Brodrick would have a quiet night tucked up in his bunk, before heading back to Gibraltar after sun-up. But if the American Admiral had his way, in a little over eight hours, he'd be leading his men in the attack on the *Baalbeck*.

'I'll be in my seacabin,' Dyce informed Lt. Commander Brady. 'As soon as Brodrick's feet are dry, tell him to come up and see me, would you?'

*

The engines of the Sea King wound down with what sounded like a sigh of relief. Brodrick unclipped his harness and stood up. Weariness was etched into the faces around him. Eight hours of vibration and noise had taken its toll.

The side door slid open and he dropped onto the deck.

'Welcome home, sir.'

The flight deck officer greeted him with a grin.

'Thanks. Look after these guys, will you?'

'Of course. And what about the Russians? Wardroom or chiefs' mess?'

'They're officers. KGB probably,' Brodrick added in a whisper. 'Watch 'em like a hawk.'

'Yessir!'

'Captain asks you to go to his sea cabin, right away, sir,' the movements chief shouted as he passed through the airlock.

He dropped down to Two Deck, walked towards the bows, then climbed the companionway to Zero-Three Deck where the Captain had his sea cabin.

'Come!' Dyce's voice answered his knock. 'Ah, Peter! Good to see you. Well, what a surprise! Come in and sit down.'

'Thank you, sir.'

'I send you off to do a bit of quiet liaison with the Americans, and what happens? You find the bloody bombs! Well done!'

'Team effort, sir,' Brodrick grinned. 'I spotted the SAM-7s or 14s, couldn't tell which. But I'm pretty sure the Russians detected neutrons. Have they confirmed it?'

'Not to us, the sneaky buggers. But they did to the Kremlin. The *Jackson* intercepted their comms.'

'What are they playing at? They're supposed to be co-operating. They kept shrugging when we questioned them in the helicopter.'

'Quite. Now look, Peter, what happens next is not

entirely clear. There's a lot of chatter going on between London and Washington. What is certain is that the *Baalbeck* has to be nabbed tonight. The question is, who does it? It seems to me there's only one real option. This ship's the only one in the right place. So my guess is it'll be down to you.'

'I'd already reached the same conclusion, sir,' Brodrick answered grimly.

'But that's a military judgement, Peter,' Dyce cautioned. 'The politicians may decide something else, and they're our masters.'

'I'm painfully aware of that, sir.'

It was happening again, he thought.

'So proceed with your planning, but don't talk to the Americans until I say. Is that understood?'

Dyce looked shifty and embarrassed.

'Sorry for the embuggeration. But this is not a straightforward matter. Decisions are being taken right at the top. Give them an hour or two. Should be clear by then.'

Dyce's reticence alarmed Brodrick. Something was going on that he didn't understand.

'Can't do much on my own, sir. It's got to be tied in with the Yanks. Intelligence, surveillance, close-air-support – all that comes from them. If I don't talk to Major Hoddle before I start work, we could get in a right mess!'

'Well, you mustn't. And I can't explain at the moment!' Dyce snapped awkwardly. 'Look, just plan what you can. As soon as I've got the final okay from London, I'll let you know. By the way, do you think you're up to it?'

The question startled him. Then Brodrick guessed what lay behind it. Dyce had the grace to look embarrassed.

'Wouldn't have minded a week's training first,' Brodrick declared.

Dyce looked down at his hands. Maybe the PM was right; perhaps it was unfair to put Brodrick through the mill again. But as far as he could see, they had no choice.

Dyce nodded.

'You'd have liked seven days? Well you've got seven hours! Make the most of them.'

Eighteen

Jackie had got up late. It was Saturday, and the previous night she'd been to the theatre with Ann Elliott. She hadn't heard the radio before doing her weekly shopping, so when she read the headlines at the newsagents' it had been a shock.

Why hadn't she known about it? She was his secretary, for God's sake! Must have happened after she left the Foreign Office last night.

She stared again at the bold print in the right-hand column of the *Daily Telegraph*.

MINISTER RESIGNS
WEBSTER WAS A DIRECTOR OF TROUBLED COMPANY
George Webster, Minister of State for Foreign Affairs, resigned last night, citing personal reasons. Mr Webster had held the post for over a year and was a member of the Prime Minister's inner circle of trusted advisers. It emerged yesterday morning that before attaining office, Mr Webster had been a non-executive director of Celadec UK, the financially troubled trading company owned by Mr Richard Bicknell, who was taken hostage in Lebanon last year and who lost his life during an abortive rescue attempt by Royal Marine commandos. In recent years, the company had provided considerable sums of money for the political funds of the Prime

Minister's party. Since Mr Bicknell's death, company auditors have been unable to explain how that money was raised.

Sources close to Mr Webster claimed that the former Minister's wife was suffering from an unspecified illness, and that he wished to spend more time with her.

The Leader of the Opposition, however, suggested there could be other motives for the resignation.

'This Celadec business stinks,' he told the *Daily Telegraph*, 'and if the Prime Minister thinks he can take the heat off by ditching George Webster, then he's got another think coming!'

Jackie flopped onto the sofa and gathered the pages together. She'd never heard mention of Lavinia Webster being ill. She had looked perfectly healthy at a Foreign Office reception the week before.

She turned to an inside page, to an article which had disturbed her even more deeply. Ever since reading it she'd been gripped by premonition.

Peter, she believed, was in mortal danger. She read the words one more time.

ROYAL NAVY IN DASH TO JOIN 6TH FLEET
The Royal Navy aircraft carrier HMS *Eagle* (20,000 tons) rushed to the eastern Mediterranean earlier this week to join an American naval task force assembling south of Crete. A Royal Navy spokeswoman in London last night refused to give details of the operation, saying simply that *Eagle* was 'somewhere in the Mediterranean'.

Sources in Gibraltar, however, report that the British carrier broke off joint manoeuvres with the Spanish coastguard on Thursday morning, abandoning an exercise designed to crush a major drug-smuggling operation. Pentagon sources hinted that the Anglo-American manoeuvres were designed to put yet further pressure on Libya.

But another report from a Washington source, so far unsubstantiated, claims that HMS *Eagle*'s emergency dash could be connected with recent rumours in military circles that nuclear weapons have been stolen from arsenals in the former Soviet Union, and are now circulating in the Middle East. Questioned about this last night, a Foreign Office spokesman said, 'It's the first I've heard of it.'

Like hell it was, Jackie thought to herself.

So the secret of Izmet Ozkan's letter was slipping out.

And HMS *Eagle* had sailed straight for the hornet's nest!

She felt a sharp pain in the pit of her stomach. Better eat something, or she'd end up with an ulcer.

If only she could talk to Peter! She had to know if he was safe.

She wandered into the kitchen. Two days' worth of washing-up cluttered the sink. She pulled open the fridge. Half a pizza – that'd do. She put it on a plate, poured a glass of apple juice and returned to the living room.

How could she stand a weekend here without knowing? She bit into the cold pizza. It was foul. No matter. She needed to eat something.

She had George Webster's home number. She could ring him in view of the *Daily Telegraph* article. That was quite in order. But he'd never talk about HMS *Eagle*.

A brainwave! Alan worked in the intelligence section! *He'd* know what was going on!

What was it he'd said to her about Lebanon?

'Before long Lebanon's going to blow a hole in the Prime Minister's election campaign' – she remembered those cryptic words clearly. There was more to come out, he'd said.

Was this what he'd meant? Was Webster's resignation part of it?

Where'd she left her Filofax?

She pulled the phone extension to the sofa, dialled Alan's number and got his answerphone.

'Hello,' she began, after the beep. 'It's Jackie. How are you? I was just ringing to say hello, and er . . . to see if maybe you were free this evening. You remember I said that next time the dinner would be on me? Well, how about it? Could we make it tonight? Hope so. Will you ring me? Thanks. Byee!'

She put the phone back on the rest, suspecting she was on the point of making a fool of herself.

10 Downing Street
16.00 hrs

The Prime Minister had cancelled plans to go to Chequers for the weekend. The election was just a month away and there were crises to be faced.

Webster was a sad loss, but he'd had to go. The misjudgements of his past had caught up with him. To keep him in government any longer risked the accusation that Downing Street was condoning what he'd done.

There was a danger someone might yet uncover the truth about the funds Richard Bicknell had given to the party. But so long as the accusations stopped at

Webster's door, the government could survive. George would get his reward – in time.

This afternoon he faced another decision, which if misjudged could wreck his political career.

The Chief of the Defence Staff was on his way over from the Defence Ministry with the military assessment that had to be the final one.

If HMS *Eagle*'s participation in 'Operation Barricade', as the Americans had dubbed their mission, was a success, it would boost the prestige of Britain, and of his government. But any failure could be crippling.

And failure now appeared to him a fearful possibility. All their efforts to get the right men in place had been negated by the speed of events. More than that, luck had turned sharply against him.

To have Brodrick at the centre of things – the man who'd bungled Bicknell's rescue in Lebanon – what an appalling mischance!

The moment he'd heard it was Brodrick who'd been sent to liaise with the Americans, he'd ordered him back to Gibraltar. But too late.

A knock at the door.

'Come in.'

'The Chief of the Defence Staff, Prime Minister,' his secretary announced.

'Come in, CDS. Do sit down. Cup of tea?'

The Field Marshal looked at his watch.

'No thanks. And it's too early for anything else, much as I feel in need of a Scotch.'

'Are you sure?'

'Quite, thanks. It's going to be a long night, by the look of it.'

'So what's the latest?'

'Comacchio Group pressed hard to be allowed to seize the *Baalbeck*. Wanted to drop into the sea next to her by parachute. But it's too bloody risky.'

'Really? They're the best men for the job, you said.'

311

'Indeed, but paradropping into the sea at night is no joke. The Americans won't agree to it. And time is pressing. At midnight the *Baalbeck* could be fifty miles off the Libyan coast. Any closer, and there's a risk of Libyan warships or planes coming to help her. The Americans say fifty miles is as close as they'll let her go.'

'And they're happy that Captain Brodrick leads the attack?'

'Perfectly. He's a fine officer, Prime Minister. He just had one bit of bad luck.'

The Prime Minister took off his glasses and polished them on a tissue.

'Let's hope it *is* only one.'

He stood up and crossed to a Queen Anne sideboard.

'Malvern water?'

'Why not? Thank you.'

The Prime Minister carried the Waterford tumblers back across the room.

He sat down thoughtfully.

'What I'd like to know is what the Russians are up to. When the White House called the Kremlin an hour ago, the Russian president couldn't be found. Gone AWOL again, apparently.'

'God help us!'

They raised their glasses to their lips.

'Well, only a few more hours and it'll all be over, one way or another,' the Prime Minister sighed. 'The President's expecting the press at Camp David in the morning. I suppose I'll have to go out into the street and say something too. Pray to God it'll be "rejoice, rejoice"!'

'Amen to that.'

The PM fell silent. The Field Marshal felt it was time.

'Leave it to Brodrick then?' he asked casually.

The eyes behind the spectacles were ringed with worry.

'Leave it to Brodrick.'

312

The pub was half empty – it was too early for most drinkers – and there was no sign of Alan.

Jackie walked up to the bar and asked for a lager. He'd phoned her forty minutes ago. Love to meet for an early drink, he'd said, but he was due at a dinner party at nine.

So where was he, then? Jackie was nervous. She flicked her chestnut hair aside and looked around. She hated going into pubs alone. It looked as if she was out for a pick-up.

At last, Alan bustled through the door, sweating. He wore a maroon velvet jacket and bow tie.

'Wow! How elegant,' Jackie smiled.

'The dinner's at my sister's. They're awfully posh,' he replied, pecking her on the cheek. 'Now, what are you having? Oh, you've got one.'

'It's on me, remember?'

'Well, in that case, a large Scotch!'

The barman appeared at her shoulder and she ordered.

Alan spotted a friend on the other side of the bar and waved.

An oddity, Alan was, Jackie thought. Tallish, slightly flabby, with tousled hair and a wicked smile. How on earth had they let him into the Foreign Office? Intelligence branch, too!

'Well, this is a nice surprise,' he grinned, raising his glass. 'I was worried I'd disgraced myself last weekend!'

She sipped her beer, wondering how to come to the point.

'So, what's new with you? Any excitements?' he asked, reaching for the crisps the barman had placed beside them.

'Well! Extraordinary goings-on! Did you read the

papers this morning?' she exclaimed, concealing her nervousness.

'Your ex-boss, you mean?' He nodded. 'I've been at work all day preparing a brief for his successor. They'll announce the name on Monday.'

'It was so sudden. I knew nothing about it.'

He pressed a finger to his mouth.

'My lips are sealed.'

'They weren't last weekend! You were dropping all sorts of hints about funny goings-on!'

A cloud seemed to cross his face. He picked up the bowl of crisps and led her to a table where the barman couldn't overhear.

'Look, I don't think I did say anything indiscreet when we had dinner. But if I did, then forget it. Please?'

He looked pale and scared. But why, she wondered?

'You just talked about the election campaign,' she reminded him, 'and how Lebanon might . . .'

He waved his hand dismissively.

'Absolutely not. Never mentioned it!'

His eyes blazed defiantly.

'Now why don't we talk about something really interesting.'

He spoke as if the previous sentences had never been uttered.

'You and me.'

He reached over and clasped her hand, a little too tightly for comfort.

'I know why you rang this afternoon. You can't sleep at night! You've been lying awake thinking about me. There's a simple cure, you know . . .'

'Alan! There's something I've got to ask you.'

Things weren't going the way she'd intended.

'About me? Do I practise safe sex? Undoubtedly. King of the condoms, that's me!'

'Oh, for God's sake!' This was a mistake. She pushed away her glass still half-full of lager.

He watched her for a moment, startled at the realisation she was about to leave.

'Okay, sorry. I got it wrong. No more bad jokes.'

He held up his hands in mock surrender.

'Look, you know what my job is. There are things I can't talk about.'

This wasn't going to be easy. But she had to try.

'Alan ... that letter from the Turk – about the bombs. . . ,' she whispered. 'The one I brought back from Istanbul?'

His eyes were full of warning again. He leaned forward.

'Not here.'

Jackie leaned forward too.

'No one's listening,' she whispered.

'Your interest in that little matter should've ended when you handed over the letter,' he growled.

'Well, it didn't.'

'Why not?'

She saw suspicion in his eyes. This was the most difficult part. She'd have to tell him. She took in a deep breath and sighed.

'Because. . . , because someone I love is on HMS *Eagle*.'

His lips parted into a silent 'aaah'.

'So there is a man in your life. You women are so devious!'

He spoke lightly but two thoughts boiled in his head.

First, the girl wasn't interested in him; she was just here to pick his brains.

The second thought chilled his blood. This boyfriend of hers – what had she told him about the letter? Had there been a security leak?

'Who exactly is this friend of yours?' he asked angrily.

The hardness in his eyes alarmed her. She could see now that he had the mettle of an intelligence officer.

'He's a Royal Marine.'

'I see.'

The alarm bells in his head rang louder.

'Does he have a name?'

She was in it up to her neck by now. No way back.

'Brodrick. Captain Peter Brodrick.'

'Ahhh.'

Stony-faced, he stared at her for a full ten seconds. Embarrassed, she turned her eyes away.

'I think perhaps we should go for a little walk,' he declared flatly.

The way the words came out, she knew it was an instruction, not a suggestion.

He swallowed the last of his whisky. She left her own drink unfinished.

Without another word, he led the way outside.

'Told him about the letter, did you?' he asked.

'Yes. I know I shouldn't have done, but . . .'

'They could send you to prison . . .'

A few yards down the road, he turned right, through a pair of wrought iron gates, into Brompton Cemetery.

'Know this place, do you? One of my favourites. Makes me think of nineteen-seventies spy movies.'

'Alan!'

She grabbed his arm to stop him.

'Don't go all official on me! Look, if I've offended you – I mean, by not saying anything about Peter, then I'm sorry.'

'That's not the point. You were sworn to secrecy about that letter. It's the most incredibly sensitive issue. And for all I know, you've blown it wide open.'

'Alan, that's absurd!'

There was a quaver in her voice. She looked about her. They were surrounded by cracked tombstones and crumbling mausoleums. Suddenly she was very scared. Why had he brought her into this place?

'Peter's security-cleared, for heaven's sake! He's handling classified stuff all the time. And I had to

316

tell him. The letter said the bombs had gone to Lebanon . . .'

'So?'

His aggression was frightening, but there was no turning back.

'Peter was the one who led the rescue attempt last year . . .'

'I know that!'

'Well, he thinks *Mustadhafin* want revenge, and if it was they who'd got hold of the bombs, then HMS *Eagle* could be in danger . . .'

They stopped in a small circle of gravestones. Alan spun round slowly, taking in the scene, checking they were alone.

'Known him long?' he said.

'It feels like it.'

'Has he told you about Lebanon?'

'Yes. He stayed with me when he was getting over it.'

'Ah. I see.' He paused. 'You think he's okay now? Recovered?'

'Yes.'

He gave a little snort, which sounded almost derisive.

'That's not what they think.'

'What do you mean?'

'Still suffering from post-traumatic stress disorder – that's the official verdict!'

'Oh. . . ,' she answered, defensively. 'He's a bit up and down at times . . .'

'Unreliable. That's the word they use.'

'Who? Who's been saying these things?'

He shook his head. He'd already said too much.

'Tell me something,' he asked, looking her straight in the eye. 'Why did you ring me?'

She took in a deep breath.

'I read in the paper that *Eagle* has sailed east to help the Americans. And that it might be because of the nuclear weapons.'

His stony face confirmed nothing.

'I. . . , I'm scared stiff, Alan!'

Her eyes blurred with tears. She turned away so he wouldn't see.

'That man Habib wants Peter dead!' she gulped.

He put his arm round her shoulder and gave her a hug.

'Okay. It'll be all right. Don't worry. Let's sit down for a minute.'

They sat on a bench with several slats missing.

'Look, I'll personally strangle you if you tell another soul, but there is a huge operation underway in the Med. They think they've found the bombs .., on a ship controlled by the Libyans, not by that gangster from Beirut.'

'I see. . . ,' she breathed. 'And Peter? He's involved?'

Alan hesitated.

'Has been up to now, yes.'

'What. . . , what does that mean, "up to now"?'

He sighed.

'Last I heard. . . , mid-afternoon. . . , was that the PM had ordered your Peter to be kept well away from any action.'

'What?' she gasped. 'I don't understand.'

Alan shrugged. He'd said enough. Surely she'd got the message.

'Why, Alan? Explain!'

'I told you. They think he's unreliable.'

'Oh God!'

'But he'll be safe. Isn't that what you want?'

He frowned at her fickleness. A moment ago she'd feared for Brodrick's life.

'Look, sweetheart, it's just politics. Try to understand. The Marines have got a big role in this operation. If it went wrong, and word got out that the man in charge was the same one who'd come unstuck in Lebanon – Jesus! The outcry! The press would cut the government to ribbons . . .'

'Bastards!' she exploded. 'Absolute bastards!'

Her face flushed crimson.

'Come on, it's perfectly understandable,' he soothed.

'Is it?' she snapped. 'To kick a man when he's down, and to tread on his face! That's okay is it?'

'Oh, for heaven's sake! You're overdoing it,' Alan countered. 'They'll be tactful. They're sending him back to Gibraltar. HMS *Eagle*'s due there next weekend for Easter. He'll be supervising security.'

They'd need more than tact with Peter. She knew what it'd do to his confidence. *She'd* have to pick up the pieces.

She stood up and shivered. The wind had turned chilly.

'Thank you for being frank, at least,' she said, bitterly. 'I'd better go. You'll be late for your dinner party.'

He grabbed her hand as she made to leave.

'What're you doing for Easter?' he asked casually.

She raised one eyebrow in astonishment. The man was incorrigible.

'Gibraltar's nice at this time of year. . . ,' he added softly.

Nineteen

Inside the massive hangar of the USS *Carl Jackson*, activity was concentrated on a pair of A-6E Intruders. The design of the planes was thirty years old, but inside their bulbous noses, state-of-the-art electronics kept these squat fighters the Navy's most effective night bombers.

Maintenance crews checked engine states and electronics boards, while armourers, crouched below the wings, prepared to attach the AGM-123A Skipper II laser-guided anti-ship missiles. Five hundred pounds of high explosive to be delivered with pin-point accuracy into the stern of the *Baalbeck*.

From the flight deck above came the thump of vulcanised rubber on steel as a quartet of F-14s returned after hours on combat air patrol, the arrester wires drumming with tension as they jolted the aircraft to a halt.

Major Seymour Hoddle wound his way through the maze of grey passageways to the lower decks. The British Marines of Comacchio Group had taken up temporary residence in a seamen's mess.

He'd already faced the wrath of Colonel Guthrie when he'd told him his team had been written out of the script. Now he was fulfilling a promise to brief them on the final plans.

'Good evening again, gentlemen,' he announced, walking briskly into the mess. 'I trust you're being looked after okay.'

320

'As well as can be expected, in the circumstances,' the Scottish Colonel growled. His cropped grey hair stood up from his head like bristles.

'Sure.'

He knew there was nothing he could do to make these men happy.

He unrolled a chart of the eastern Mediterranean on which he'd marked the latest positions.

'The *Baalbeck*'s heading for Tripoli like there's no tomorrow,' he told them innocently.

'Perceptive of them,' Guthrie answered drily.

'Oh, sure,' Hoddle chuckled. 'Okay, we're still back here, one hundred fifty miles northeast of Benghazi, about five hundred miles from where the *Baalbeck* should be when we hit.'

He pulled a ten-by-eight print from a folder and laid it on top of the chart.

'She's general cargo, about fifteen hundred tons. Crew? Believed to be Lebanese and Libyans. The nukes? In the forward hold, we guess. Defenses? Radar counter-measures, shoulder-launched SAMs, and presumably heavy machine-guns.

'At 00.20 tonight an A-6 from the *Jackson* will hit the *Baalbeck* with a missile. The purpose is to disable the ship, not to sink her or damage her cargo.'

Hoddle noted the murmur from the Marines. He too knew what a risky strategy this was.

'We guess they have night surveillance equipment and'll be expecting us. We want them in shell-shock by the time Brodrick and his men attempt to get on board.

'Assuming they're successful at taking down the ship, we'll have two nuclear specialists parachute into the sea close by. Once in the water, they'll light flares so as your Sea Kings can pick 'em up and drop 'em on the *Baalbeck*. Gentlemen, that's the plan.'

Guthrie glanced at his second-in-command, then nodded.

'Not ideal,' he commented. 'But then, neither are the circs. Brodrick's team don't have the same training as us, but they'll do. Tell me, Major, after all this are you going ashore in Libya?'

'If what we find on the *Baalbeck* confirms our suspicions, then the answer's yes. The CIA's identified a nuclear weapons research site inland from Benghazi.

'Our mission's to seize it intact. We want to know who's been supplying Libya with the nuclear technology.'

'There'll be plenty of glory for you, then. . . ,' snapped Guthrie. 'Hope somebody remembers the Royals played the toughest role in the whole mission.'

Hoddle saw the bitterness in the eyes of Guthrie's men.

'I'm quite sure, Colonel,' he answered curtly, 'that neither you nor any other Royal Marine will ever let us forget it!'

23.00 hrs

The cat's-eyes on the centre line guided the A-6 pilots to their launch positions. A big Warrant Officer, muffled against the cold night wind, swaggered about the deck, waving them into line.

Behind each catapult a blast deflector protected the other aircraft awaiting take-off. As each one went, it dropped flat to let the next take its place.

Maintenance men made final checks, then pulled the red-flapped safety pins from the weapons under the wings.

Locked onto the catapult, each pilot waited for the twirl of the WO's fingers signalling it was time to spool up the engines. Final adjustments to the steam pressure, then the fighters hurtled from stillness to flying speed in two and a half seconds.

Behind the A-6 bombers came the F-14s. For the next couple of hours six of them would patrol like eagles north of Libya's coast, watching for fighters braving the skies in defence of the *Baalbeck*.

Already aloft were the E-2Cs which would guide and direct the coming mission, and an EA-6B Prowler, sucking the airways for radio transmissions from the *Baalbeck*, ready to jam them.

In the Combat Direction Centre, Commander Norman Tracy watched over the screens on which the night's activities would be played out like a computer game. Beyond, in the Flag Plot, he could see the brooding figure of Admiral Bock.

There was nothing ideal about this operation. Much as he admired the British, to have the most crucial part of the whole plan run by some other man's navy did not make him comfortable.

He got up from his chair and scratched his crotch. This would be a long, sweaty night.

The big, multi-coloured air-picture screen was filling with symbols, as his assets took station over the southern Mediterranean. He was comfortable that he had enough in the air for now, and could scramble a helluva lot more within minutes if it was needed.

Then he crossed to the surface and sub-surface plots. Radar and sonar returns from aircraft and ships had been combined to show a detailed, three-dimensional map of the sea.

But as Tracy looked at the symbols on the screen, he knew there was one critical omission – one joker in the card deck that might yet spring a dangerous surprise.

Somewhere, between his carrier and the *Baalbeck* there was a submarine, not yet located, not yet identified, but believed to be the Tango.

The Russians had denied it was theirs, but he didn't believe them. They were up to something; their attempt to hide the data from the neutron detectors proved that.

His prime concern was the safety of the *Jackson*. The Viking tracker planes had sown their sonobuoys around the carrier to ensure there'd be no surprise attack. The Libyans had submarines too, though none had been seen leaving port.

'Signal from the *Eagle*, sir,' the comms officer reported. 'Tigers one and two are airborne.'

His heart skipped a beat. It had started. The Royal Marines were on their way.

A dozen young men, flying to a rendezvous with two atom bombs, each five times as powerful as the one that destroyed Hiroshima.

MV Baalbeck
23.40 hrs

At sundown, the Colonel and his men had prostrated themselves on the deck and prayed to Mecca. As ever it was Allah alone who had the power to say whether they should live or die. Tonight his decision would be revealed.

Down in the hold, it still smelled of the smoke Habib had used to bait the trap into which the Colonel had so disastrously fallen.

Ellafi was left alone in the half-darkness. The bulkhead light had fused, and the battery in his black rubber torch was beginning to fade. He knelt on the dusty, steel floor, shining the yellowing light onto the single, grey-black canister that remained here. It was still strapped to the softwood pallet which the Soviet army had used to facilitate its transport.

He ripped off the thick polythene protective sheet and exposed the modified firing controls. The dual-key combination locks for the four-digit access codes were the originals, but only one of them needed setting now, with a figure that Ellafi carried in his head. Next to the dials was the liquid-crystal display of an electric timer, and an on/off arming switch. Exploding this nuclear weapon would be as simple now as priming a car bomb.

He felt a paralysis in his brain. His orders were specific, but amounted to suicide for all on board and anyone else within a radius of two kilometres.

He thought of the lifeboat they'd lowered over the side two hours ago. The two Russian technicians had gone with it, preferring to take their chances adrift. They'd primed this bomb as they had Habib's; would they die too, swamped by the tidal wave that would follow the blast?

Beneath his knees, the steel deck throbbed from the pounding diesel, driving them towards Tripoli in a race against time, which he felt certain they would lose.

In his mind he saw the faces of his sons. Allah be praised, let them at least still live. One day, perhaps, they would help his country make amends for the past and become a nation revered and respected in the world.

He reached forward to touch the combination dial. It clicked satisfactorily under the pressure of his fingers. It would be a matter of seconds to set the code and the timer, and to press that fatal switch.

It looked so evil sitting here on its pallet. Perhaps it was after all God's will that it should never reach its intended destination.

*

In the pitch black rear of the Sea King, the stench of hot oil was oppressive. Brodrick's mouth was dry, his palms sweaty. Three marines sat beside him, three more on the canvas seats opposite. Invisible in the dark, they were all as terrified as he was.

He could see the twinkling of green and red from the cockpit controls, the bulky shapes of the pilots, silhouetted against the silver-grey of partial moonlight. When they turned their heads, the infra-red goggles attached to their flying helmets made them resemble bug-eyed monsters of science-fiction.

They flew slowly, no more than thirty knots, so as to minimise the risk to the essential cargo suspended from the underside of the helicopter. Surprise was the key if they were to succeed; to achieve that, the helicopters were sweeping south, well wide of the *Baalbeck*, and would put them in the water ten miles from the target.

The marines had brainstormed their procedures, but it was the worst of scenarios; intelligence on the enemy's strength was limited to one fleeting glimpse of a curly-headed gunman and a SAM tube.

It had to be done; there was no-one else to do it.

Brodrick had drummed that into his men during the past seven hours. They were fit. They'd trained hard on the boats and boardings in recent months. But were they ready? Was anyone ever ready when the time came?

Pulse racing, Brodrick took long, deep breaths to steady himself. He was going into action again.

Visions of Lebanon came out of the darkness to haunt him. He battled them back by concentrating on the nightmares which were still to come.

Two helicopters in the first wave, each with a Rigid Raider slung underneath. At midnight, ten miles south of the target, directly in its path, they'd launch the boats and board them. Twenty minutes later, the *Baalbeck* would have halved the gap, and with their outboards they'd have closed to a mile. Then they'd watch for the Americans to do their bit, with the air strike on the *Baalbeck*.

They were operating in electronic silence. No radar, no radio, except in an emergency. But with their night goggles the pilots of the two helicopters could see each other's machines clear as day.

What would they find when they scrambled up the sides of the *Baalbeck?* Would Brodrick at last come face to face with Abdul Habib?

He lifted the cover of his luminous watch. Five minutes to go.

23.57 hrs

On the bridge of the *Baalbeck* they'd removed the shade from the radar screen so that several could look at it at once. Ellafi pointed to the two small blips moving south, ten miles to their west.

'Maybe smugglers,' the Maltese skipper opined in his broken Arabic. 'Speedboats. I see them often here at night.'

'Or helicopters,' Ellafi whispered. 'If Allah wishes it.'

The *Baalbeck*'s navigation radar couldn't differentiate between a slow-moving, low-flying aircraft and a power-boat.

Two minutes to midnight.

Ellafi had set the weapon timer for sixty seconds. All it needed was for him to dial in the code which only he knew, and press the arming switch.

There'd be time for a final prayer, then the

hemisphere of conventional explosive would detonate, compressing the plutonium core to a critical mass – and oblivion.

But when? When would he know it was time to take the final, irrevocable step? If he waited too long, it could be too late.

He slid down the companionway to the wireless room. 'Well?'

'Nothing. The Americans must be in radio silence.'

The operator raised an eyebrow. They both knew what that meant.

'And still the Hawkeye radar?'

The operator nodded.

'It will be soon,' Ellafi croaked.

He climbed back up to the bridge. His men were positioned at the four corners of the deck with their heavy machine-guns and SA-14 missiles.

One man on the bows and one on the stern had image-intensifiers. It would not be easy for marines to get on board.

When they began to fire, that would be the signal for him.

He'd make his way to the forward companionway, and at the first sound of shooting drop into the hold and carry out the orders of his leader.

Midnight

The winch whined. The Rigid Raider dropped thirty feet to the water. Half a ton of glass-fibre and steel, the unsinkable boat smacked onto the waves and danced under the down-draught of the rotors. The coxswain gripped the line hanging from the side door, abseiled into the boiling sea and pulled himself into the boat.

Brilliant! Brodrick shone a torch to locate the shackle so the winch line could be freed. Next down were the flotation bags filled with grappling gear and weapons, then the six of them slipped into the icy water and hauled themselves into the dory.

The Sea King dipped its nose and banked away, removing its whirlwind from the men in the water so they could gather their wits.

'Rees, Banks. . . ,' Brodrick counted out their names. All were there, all breathing.

The coxswain worked on the engine, removing the seals that had protected it from immersion. Fuel line on. Throttle open. Contact.

Instant life.

'That's a bloody miracle!' exclaimed the coxswain.

Brodrick powered up his infra-red binoculars and strapped them to his helmet.

'Checked the kit?' he asked.

Each man had his SA-80 and a beltful of grenades.

'Checked.'

He felt strangely calm now they were on their way.

'Give the green light to the paraffin parrot.'

Two quick flashes from a torch were answered in turn from the helicopter. The machine would hold off, five miles away, and wait for orders.

The coxswain slipped the clutch and swung the wheel until the compass pointed north.

Brodrick looked round for the second boat. It should've been half a mile ahead of them by now. Salt spray blurred his night-sight. He pulled the glasses from his head.

'Useless bloody technology! Better without.'

A small problem, but it had fazed him.

The moon emerged briefly from behind a cloud. Its light sparkled on the gentle ripples of the calm sea.

Blessedly calm. But further away, the black of the sea merged with the black of the night. He'd need the thermal-imager to see anything at a distance. He polished the lenses with a finger.

'Position check?' Brodrick asked, his voice just audible above the thrumming of the 140 horsepower Johnson.

The coxswain consulted the Magellan GPS satnav receiver strapped to the driving console. Using signals from outer space, it updated their position every second, and was accurate to twenty-five metres.

'Spot on, sir. This is where the others should be.'

He slowed the boat.

'Cut the engine,' Brodrick ordered. 'We'll listen.'

As the dory steadied, he aligned the glasses on the horizon ahead, the thermo-optics showing the warm sea as dark grey, the cold sky as near-white. He swept right and left, then right again.

Found it. The *Baalbeck*. It had to be. A black smudge of heat from its funnel. It looked the right size, maybe five miles away, closer than expected.

He felt a hand on his shoulder.

'Behind us, sir. We've got the other Raider.'

He could hear it now, slowing down as it came alongside.

'Where've you bin?' he growled to the other crew.

'Boat went arse over tit,' yelled back Sergeant Dennis who was in command. 'Had to get the chopper to winch it straight.'

'Lost anything?'

'GPS kit. Lucky we found you.'

The sort of trouble they could do without. Brodrick checked the time. Ten past midnight.

'Better get a move on.'

The coxswains triggered the outboards and the Rigid Raiders surged foward, aiming straight for the oncoming freighter.

The US Navy pilots would take no chances. The only defensive weaponry spotted on the *Baalbeck* was that shoulder-launched SAM. Infra-red, three miles range: they could handle that. But suppose there was more? Bigger weapons, with longer reach?

That's why the Prowler was up. Flying high above the *Baalbeck*, the EA-6B's receivers inside its bulbous tail fin listened for transmissions from the target.

There were four men on board, pilot, navigator, two Electronic Countermeasures Officers.

Underneath, five pods of electronics containing ten jammers. Immense sophistication designed for global war. An electronic sledgehammer to crack the nut of the *Baalbeck*.

There were no emissions from the freighter, except the pulsing sweep of its navigation radar. However, even that simple equipment would spot the attack aircraft.

Seventeen minutes past midnight. It was time. The Prowler's senior ECM Officer activated the jammers.

Ten miles to the north the two Intruders detected the jamming on their own antennae. Radar off, they'd been guided to the target by the Hawkeye.

Beneath the nose of the lead aircraft, the TRAM turret rotated slowly. Target Recognition and Attack Multisensor – a clumsy name for a clever device. The TV display in the bombardier's cockpit showed wide-angle thermal imagery from the TRAM's sensor head.

Even at ten miles the freighter was easy to spot, the heat from its funnel dark against a lighter background.

The pilot banked left to correct his course. The bombardier pressed the toggle to arm the Skipper missile. The TRAM lens zoomed to maximum magnification; now they could see the shape of the *Baalbeck*'s superstructure.

The bombardier shone a light on the recce photo he'd taped to his knee. It was the same ship.

Eighteen past. Range five miles. The gimbals in the TRAM turret kept the image of the ship steady, centre screen. The bombardier laid the cross-wires on the *Baalbeck*'s stern, dead centre, just below the bridge. The kinetic energy of the Skipper would slice through the thin steel of the hull above the water line, and explode in the engine and steering gear. With luck it'd kill the ship and the crew, and leave the hulk afloat for the Brits to board.

One minute thirty to go, and all's well.

MV Baalbeck
00.19 hrs

A shout from below sent Ellafi tumbling down from the bridge to the wireless room, his guts already churning from seeing the white-out on the radar screen.

'Uhhh?' he grunted to the operator, who flipped the loudspeaker switch so he'd hear the burble of jamming blocking every frequency the *Baalbeck* could use.

Without a word, Ellafi turned his back, and made for the open deck.

Out in the air, he looked up at the patch of silver-grey, where a veil of mist obscured the moon. The diesel thumped a deceptive, reassuring rhythm. As he walked forward he heard the swish of the glassy sea parting at the bow.

A sudden shout from the lookout at the stern told him the time had come. With his image-intensifier, the man had spotted fighter planes approaching from behind.

Ellafi paused by the companionway to the hold. He

heard the soft hiss of the missile seekers trying to get a lock on the approaching warplanes.

Pea-shooters against cannon, he thought.

Feet on the ladder. Down into the dark. In his hand, the torch, slippery with sweat.

There it was. The cylinder of evil.

It is Allah's wish, he told himself.

00.20 hrs

'Marking!'

The laser reached out to the *Baalbeck*'s stern. The beam painted an invisible circle just below the name-plate of the ship.

'Lock on!'

The seeker on the Skipper missile had detected the mark.

'Stand by . . . uuh? Holy shit!'

The TRAM screen went black.

'Oh, my God!'

Both men looked up from their instruments to see flames blasting skywards from the *Baalbeck*.

The pilot wrenched the control stick to the right, banking the plane into a 3g turn.

'Sheeit! That's the nuke!' yelled the bombardier.

The pilot slammed the throttle levers forward, aiming for height and distance.

'If it is, we're fuckin' dead men!'

Blinded by the flash, Brodrick wrenched the night-sight from his eyes. Paralysed with terror, he stared at the fountain of flame and water half a mile away.

He fell sideways as the Rigid Raider heeled and turned to the coxswain's frantic twisting of the wheel.

None of them could speak; every man's voice was frozen in his throat, in the belief a nuclear fireball was reaching out to engulf them.

Seconds after the flash came the sound and the shockwave.

Then nothing.

'Bloody hell!' Brodrick gasped.

No mushroom cloud. No oblivion.

The ship was still there – just. Her back was broken, flames and smoke billowed into the night.

'Fuck!' Several voices in unison.

'Bloody Yanks!' Brodrick screamed. 'Look what they've done! Sunk the bastard ship!'

The bows of the *Baalbeck* upended and slid under; the detached stern threatened to follow it.

00.22 hrs

Captain Second Class Nikolai Bonderenko watched the death of the *Baalbeck* through the periscope. It had been a textbook attack, the torpedo striking just forward of the superstructure, detonating under the keel to ensure the snapping of the vessel's spine.

The underwater shockwave had hit the submarine six seconds after the explosion. Now on the sonar loud-speakers they listened to the agonised grinding of steel, as the target's hull plates ruptured and tore.

A sobering sound, like the terrified cries of men.

For all of them it was the first torpedo they'd fired in anger. Chilled by the cacophony of death, they hoped it was an experience they would never repeat.

'Down periscope! Depth two hundred. Make course zero-nine-zero!'

As the oiled shaft slipped into its well, Bonderenko looked round at his men. None would return his gaze. Exhilaration at what they'd done was already turning to shame. He'd need to act fast.

He grabbed the public address microphone.

'Men. Comrades.' His voice was heard the length of the boat.

'My congratulations and my thanks. The orders we were given have been carried out correctly. This is not a moment for jubilation; the death of a ship and of the men on board is always a tragedy. But it is a moment for pride in a job well done, however terrible that job may be.

'You know the reasons why that ship had to die. On board were nuclear weapons stolen from our homeland. What we've done today will ensure they can never be used by one nation to terrorise another. That is all.'

A murmur of approval in the control room. He'd said the right words.

Time for them to run. The world was never supposed to know it was they who'd sank the *Baalbeck*. One hour to leave the scene, then they'd surface for air, and report to Moscow.

00.27 hrs

Brodrick held the UHF handset to his ear, hardly believing the words he was hearing.

'The bloody Yanks didn't shoot,' he told his incredulous crew.

He was talking with HMS *Eagle* on an encrypted

radio, relayed by a transponder on the Commando Sea King which was heading towards them.

The *Baalbeck* had disappeared, its hot metal and burning oil turning the sea into a cauldron as the stern went down. Now there was just darkness and the faint stirrings of a breeze.

'What the hell happened, then?' It was the Welsh corporal who spoke.

'Torpedo. An ASW Sea King was dipping and heard it run. Some bloody submarine. God knows whose!'

The two Rigid Raiders put distance between them. The helicopters would want five hundred metres separation when they winched the men and equipment out of the water.

Brodrick thought of the men on the *Baalbeck*. Could any have survived? Habib, perhaps? Hardly likely.

But shouldn't they look? Maybe there'd be someone clinging to a life raft. Someone to confirm who'd been on the ship, and the contents of the hold.

'Turn her round.'

'Eh? Thought we were to get the hell out of it, sir?'

That's what they'd been ordered. They all knew that.

'Change of plan. We're going back!'

The coxswain hesitated, then swung the wheel. The men were silent.

'There's a nookular weapon down there, sir,' Corporal Rees reminded him quietly. 'If it goes off while we're bobbin' around on top, it won't half make our eyes water.'

'Look,' Brodrick snapped. 'We don't know *what* was on that ship, or *who* was on it, do we? We'll never bloody know unless we find some clue. So, we're gonna eyeball the bits, okay?'

The coxswain opened the throttle wide. Better get it over with quick.

Brodrick supported himself in the bows and aligned the imager on the water ahead.

He imagined the wreck falling through the depths. Some of the water round here was over a mile deep. What would the pressure do to a nuclear bomb? Could it act like the explosive trigger and compress the plutonium to a critical mass?

He cowered inwardly at the thought. Maybe Rees was right, maybe they should turn back. Perhaps this was Lebanon all over again – with him leading his men to their deaths.

Then he saw it. Dark, black patches on the sea. Dark through the imager because they were hotter than the water around them.

'Slow down!' he yelled at the coxswain. Instantly the boat sank back from the plane.

They were amongst it. They could smell the stench of burnt oil.

'Get your torches on. Look for bodies, bits, anything.'

Under the beams of the lights they found themselves surrounded by flotsam. Splintered timbers, half a life-ring; rags and oil clots, still smouldering.

'Over there! Port bow!' Rees shouted.

They all saw it, the pinky-yellow of human flesh.

Gingerly the coxswain steered towards it.

A naked torso, scorched and headless, grotesque and revolting in the glare of their lights.

'Leave it,' Brodrick ordered. 'We won't get a word out of that one.'

The boat puttered on across the ring of debris, a hundred metres wide. They circled right and cut back through the meaningless wreckage. Nothing to tell them what they wanted to know.

'Hang on! To your left,' Brodrick pointed with his torch. 'Bit of timber. See it?'

As they got close they saw it was rough deal.

'A pallet, sir,' Corporal Rees observed.

Useless.

'Okay. Forget it. Let's go home . . .'

'Hang on, sir. What's it got on it?' Rees interrupted. 'Writing. Look.'

Brodrick stared. The corporal was right. Letters or numerals? He couldn't see.

'Let's get the bloody thing on board.'

The corporal leaned over the side and eased one end of the pallet into the boat while Brodrick lifted the other.

The grubby, yellow timber was singed and scorched, but the part where the Cyrillic lettering had been stencilled was untouched.

'I think you've cracked it, Corp. That's Russian.'

Forty-five minutes later the Commando Sea King winched the Rigid Raider down onto the deck of HMS *Eagle*, then landed close beside it.

As the rotors wound down, Brodrick felt an overwhelming sense of exhaustion.

He jumped down onto the grey, steel plating.

'Stay there, please!'

The muffled voice came from inside a mask. The man, fully clad in protective clothing, pointed a geiger counter at them. He ran it up and down Brodrick's immersion suit and over his arms and his hair. Then he repeated the procedure with the rest of the team.

'Okay. You're not too bad. But we're going to decontaminate you anyway. It's your hands mostly.'

'What d'you mean?' Brodrick demanded.

'Radiation. Something you've picked up. Some bit of timber you've got in the Raider. It's red hot. Set this counter ticking like a timebomb!'

'Okay. Let's have it straight,' Brodrick demanded.

He and his boat crew of six were sitting in the small briefing room, wearing fresh overalls and clutching paper cups of hot tea. They'd been stripped naked on deck and drenched with icy water to rid them of the radiation.

'Come on. You're the quack. What've we done?' Brodrick pressed.

The medic hesitated. It wasn't straightforward.

' "Don't know" is the short answer. Don't know what sort of dose you've had. Maybe your annual limit in one go. Keep away from plutonium for the rest of the year and you should be okay.'

'But there was no nuclear explosion,' Brodrick insisted.

'That's right. But it could be that the torpedo set off the explosive triggers in the devices. Those charges have to be detonated in a precise sequence to achieve critical mass. But an accidental bang could shatter the core and scatter the plutonium. That pallet you picked up was coated with plutonium dust. Nasty stuff. Particularly if you breathe it in . . .'

The marines looked darkly at one another. They'd all spent a good thirty minutes in close proximity to that pallet.

'They're shipping you back to Gib after sun-up. The medics there'll give you a good going over. I should think you could do with some kip by now.'

The door opened and in walked the PWO, Lt Commander Nick Brady.

'How are the happy heroes?' he breezed.

'Not so happy,' Brodrick replied, indicating the Surgeon-Commander.

'Take no notice of him. He's only a dick doctor,' Brady cracked. 'Look, I've got news for you. One of those Russians you brought in on the Yank Sea King – Papushin, is it? He's had a look at the plank you recovered. Says the writing confirms it's part of a pallet for transporting nuclear weapons.'

'Good. But has he told you why their submarine had to sink the bloody ship, so that all the real evidence is a mile down at the bottom of the sea?'

There were still questions to be answered, Brodrick thought. Vital questions.

' "What submarine?" is what Papushin said,' Brady snorted.

'They're admitting nothing. But upstairs,' – he nodded in the direction of the bridge – 'they've worked it out. They say the Russians were terrified the Americans would get at their nukes before they did. And also they wanted to deny Washington the pretext for having a bash at Libya.'

'Aha. So the big invasion's cancelled?'

'On hold, anyway. No doubt they'll try and fish the evidence up from the bottom of the sea, but that could take weeks.'

'Seymour Hoddle will be doing his nut!'

'I bet. Anyway, as you know, the excitement's over for you lot. At 09.00 you'll be cabbed to Malta, and a Herc'll fly you to Gib.'

'In a hurry to get rid of us, aren't you?' Brodrick said sourly.

Captain David Dyce sat on the swivel chair, looking anxious and worn, in the dim light.

'Can't sleep when there's a submarine about,' he explained wanly to Brodrick. 'The *Jackson* thinks she's got a handle on it, but she's not certain. Too damned noisy in these waters.'

340

'You wanted a word, sir?'

'Yes. Just wanted to know your thoughts. How're you feeling, by the way?'

'Okay, sir. No radiation sickness,' he joked.

'Good. But we'll not take any chances. You'll have a thorough check-up in Gibraltar.'

Brodrick nodded. Behind him one of the VHF channels chattered on a loudspeaker.

'Maltese coastguard,' Dyce explained. 'The whole world knows by now that a ship went down. They keep calling up to ask if there's any sign of survivors. The *Baalbeck*'s skipper and crew were Maltese, apparently.'

'We saw a corpse. Nothing living.'

'We'll have another look in daylight, to see if anything else has surfaced. Otherwise it's all rather inconclusive.'

'It would be nice to know who was on board the *Baalbeck*, sir,' Brodrick stressed.

The Captain eyed him uncertainly.

'Mr Abdul Habib, you mean? All we know is he left Lebanon by boat.'

Dyce sounded unusually diffident, as if he were trying to draw Brodrick out.

'There's two things that still puzzle me, sir,' Brodrick announced. Might as well plunge straight in.

'Oh, yes?'

'Firstly, what was the *Baalbeck* doing when we spotted her? She was heading north, not south. And secondly, why had she been firing off radar countermeasures?'

Dyce nodded. He'd had the same thoughts.

'Any conclusions?'

'Deception, obviously. The chaff could've been because she thought the Americans were already on her trail. Hoped to throw them off the scent. Heading for Valletta instead of Tripoli could've been part of that. . . .'

'But. . . ?'

'But the countermeasures could've concealed

341

something else, sir. A repeat of the trick they pulled on Wednesday. Transferring the cargo to another boat.'

'Ah, yes.'

Dyce looked away at the surface plot – hundreds of unidentified radar returns over thousands of square miles of sea.

'That plutonium dust you picked up seems to make a nonsense of that theory,' he stated, without conviction.

'There were two bombs, sir. We only found one pallet.'

Dyce stood up and thrust his hands in his pockets. Around him the operations room hummed. Millions of pounds' worth of sophisticated electronics, years of experience and training, yet maybe they'd been out-witted by a terrorist.

'I'm still expecting to bring the ship to Gibraltar by Good Friday,' he stated quietly, gazing blankly at the screens. 'The men have got families joining them there for Easter.'

Then he spun round and looked Brodrick squarely in the eye.

'You're not really going to Gibraltar for your health, Captain Brodrick. I want you to find Mr Ahmed Bizri.'

Twenty

Two full days had passed. Two days of utter frustration.

On Monday Brodrick and his marines had been peered at by radiation specialists, in a series of tests which had found no evidence of plutonium inhalation in any of them.

The doctor had cautioned them, however.

'One can never be totally sure with these things; wouldn't be a bad idea to look out for signs of lung cancer in about ten years' time.'

'Thanks very much, doc,' they'd answered.

Brodrick had spent Tuesday morning with Commander Camfield, the base security officer. The Spanish police had told him they still had not traced Ahmed Bizri, or 'Youssef Boukari', as his forged Spanish passport had described him.

A dead end, that's what it seemed. They couldn't begin to look for him without some sort of clue.

He'd spent the rest of Tuesday probing for weak points in Gibraltar's security. At the frontier he'd watched the faces of those crossing from Spain, in the vain expectation that Bizri's might be one of them.

It was in the harbour that he feared the real danger lay. With Camfield, he'd stood on the Gun Wharf and looked across to the South Mole, where HMS *Eagle* was due to tie up on Thursday.

'Just suppose there is a nuclear weapon, on a small freighter,' Brodrick had ventured. 'How close could it get to *Eagle*?'

'Too close,' Camfield had answered. 'Particularly if it's a suicide attack. Nothing to stop them just chugging along the other side of the Mole and pulling the trigger. They'd finish off *Eagle* and most of Gibraltar.'

'What about a cordon, then? To keep ships out of the bay unless they've been searched.'

'Have you any idea what it's like here, Easter week?' Camfield had retorted. 'People are on holiday. Come Thursday there'll be hundreds of boats charging in and out of the marinas. Ironically, some of them'll be protesting at the arrival of the *Eagle*! The Spaniards are paranoid about warships with nuclear weapons on board.'

He caught a quizzical look on Camfield's face, as if the man wasn't sure whether to treat the matter with total seriousness.

'Level with me, will you?' Camfield had said. 'How real do you think the risk is? Because if you know there's an attack planned, then to be safe HMS *Eagle* had better head back to Portsmouth without stopping here at all!'

'That's the trouble,' Brodrick had answered. 'We *don't* know. We only suspect. And the navy won't divert the ship without something solid.'

They turned away from the water, back to Camfield's car. Before climbing in, Brodrick stopped him.

'What you just said, about a suicide attack – that's a good point. I don't think it would be suicide. Abdul Habib's a born survivor.'

'In that case,' Camfield had concluded, sombrely, 'he'll have planned something more subtle.'

Now it was Wednesday midday. Unsure where to turn next, Brodrick returned to the wardroom of the shore base *HMS Rooke*, after a morning spent prowling round the marina. He was called to the reception desk.

'Telephone for you, Captain Brodrick.'

The CPO pointed him in the direction of a booth.

'Thanks.' He picked up the receiver. 'Hello? Captain Brodrick speaking.'

'Oh, very official!' A woman's voice, heavy with sarcasm. 'Hello darling!'

'Who. . . ? Jackie!'

'What do you mean, who? Who else calls you "darling"?'

He laughed.

'Everyone! You know what the navy's like! Hey, it's amazing to hear you. But . . . why?' he asked, suddenly concerned. 'Has something happened?'

'Yes. I've decided to take some leave!'

'Oh! You're going somewhere?'

'I've gone already. I'm at the Rock Hotel!'

'What? Here in Gibraltar? Bloody Hell! That's fantastic!'

'I was worried you'd think I was intruding.'

He laughed again, but there was something odd here.

'How did you know where I was?' he queried. 'Don't tell me it was the charms of Gibraltar that lured you!'

'Hardly! I. . . , I heard in the office that you'd be here,' she explained awkwardly. 'Now, when can I see you?'

'Well . . . now, I suppose. I'm on duty, but I can come up. Hey, that place costs an arm and a leg!'

'I know. I decided we deserve it.'

'We?'

'I've got a room with a huge double bed!'

The WRN driver swung the wheel hard left and the Cavalier ground up the sharp incline to the door of the hotel, where pots of bright, red geraniums adorned the porch.

'Could you wait, please?' Brodrick asked her.

Jackie stood at reception, wearing jeans and a black roll-neck sweater.

'Darling!'

She flung her arms round his neck and hugged him.

'I thought you'd be in uniform!' she exclaimed, holding him at arms' length.

'It's security. We all wear civvies here,' he smiled. 'You look great! New jumper, and you've cut your hair. Nice!'

She'd had it cut short.

She took his arm and led him up to the lounge.

'I've ordered some coffee. But since it's nearly lunch-time, perhaps we should make it G and T. Or even . . .'

She nuzzled up to his ear and whispered another suggestion.

He grinned and gave her a squeeze.

'That'll have to wait,' he smiled. 'I've got a car outside. For now, coffee'll do fine.'

He felt tense, his emotions in conflict. He should be concentrating on trying to find Bizri, not being distracted by Jackie.

'When did you get here?' he asked stiffly, puzzled by her sudden arrival.

'An hour ago. *Dreadful* flight. The plane was packed.'

They sat by the broad window overlooking the harbour and Algeciras Bay. Jackie saw grey bags under his eyes.

'It's such a surprise!' Brodrick exclaimed, awkwardly. 'You decided to come on the spur of the moment?'

'At the weekend. It took a couple of days to fix things. . . .'

She could see he was suspicious. She'd have to tell him.

A waiter set down the tray and hovered for a tip. Jackie signed the bill and gave him a few coins.

'The thing is, I could be in trouble,' she continued, when the waiter was out of earshot. 'They know I told you about the letter from the Turk. They say I've contravened the Official Secrets Act, and could be sacked – or worse. A friend advised me to get out of sight for a few days . . .'

'They?' he queried. 'Who do you mean?'

'Someone I know, in security.'

'Bit academic now, isn't it? he scoffed. 'The news-papers are full of speculation that the nukes were on board the *Baalbeck* when she went down.'

'I think there's something else they're worried about,' she added. 'Something to do with my former boss.'

'George Webster? What've you got on him?'

'Nothing! But maybe they don't know that.'

He drank some of the bitter coffee and glanced at his watch. She could see he was stressed and anxious.

'What happened in the Med?' she asked gently. 'You look pretty shattered.'

Her hand hovered for a moment, wanting to touch him but not daring.

'The papers didn't mention you, of course,' she continued. 'But I guessed you must've been somewhere nearby. They said the freighter just blew up and sank, and that the Brits and Americans had nothing to do with it. Is that true?'

She wanted to know if Alan had been right, to know if Peter really had been sent to Gibraltar to get him out of the way. She noticed his right knee jiggling nervously.

'It's not the whole truth,' he mumbled, so as not to be overheard. 'We were about to take her, when the Russians got in first. With a torpedo.'

'Take her? What d'you mean?'

He glanced sideways at her.

'Board her. We were in our raiders, a mile away.'

'My God!' she breathed. 'So . . .'

Alan *had* been wrong.

'So, if it had been a few minutes later, you'd have been on the ship when she blew up!'

'Yep.'

'My God, Peter! You'd have been killed!' she exclaimed.

He shrugged.

'That's right.'

She grabbed his hands, shaking slightly. Was that another of his nine lives gone?

'Is that the end of it, now?' she asked. 'If those two nuclear weapons are on the bottom of the sea. . . ?'

His expression clouded.

'If. That's the trouble; we're not sure,' he cautioned. 'We know one was on board. The other might have gone to another ship. Transferred by that evil bastard, Abdul Habib.'

'Oh.' She blanched. 'And?'

'It's possible it's heading for Gib.'

'Oh, shit . . .'

He nodded.

'Because *Eagle*'s coming here? He wants to blow up the ship with it?'

He nodded again.

'But – that'd be like Hiroshima! Why're they letting people in here, for God's sake? Shouldn't they evacuate the place?'

Peter shook his head.

'We're only guessing, that's the trouble. We don't know anything for certain. We mustn't start a panic without firm facts – that's what's been decided.'

'Can't they search the wreckage of that freighter?'

'They're trying to. But the water's a mile deep. It'll take ages.'

She frowned again.

'And is that why you're here?'

'Yes. You remember Ahmed Bizri? Dyce sent me to try to find him.'

'Of course. And have you?'

'No,' he grunted. 'The bloody Spanish police say there's no trace of him.'

'Well, they would say that, wouldn't they?'

'What do you mean?'

'Even if they had found him they wouldn't tell anyone here. This is Gibraltar!'

Suddenly it was as if she'd drawn back the blinds in a darkened room. They'd been using a direct approach with the Spanish authorities, the English way. No wonder they'd got nowhere.

'Jackie, you're brilliant!'

He stared at her intently. An idea was forming in his mind.

'You know this part of the world, don't you?'

'That's right. My parents had a farmhouse, a finca, about fifty miles from here. I spent all my school holidays here.'

'And you speak the language.'

'Yes. I was bilingual once.'

His mind was racing. No longer was the search for Bizri at a dead-end.

'I've got news for you,' he declared. 'You've just been hired, as an interpreter, by the Royal Marines!'

He stood up and pulled her to her feet.

Suddenly they were aware of another person, a few feet away, clearing his throat.

'Hullo, again!'

A young man was looking at them with intense curiosity. Jackie hooked her hand through Brodrick's arm.

'Oh, hello, Jeremy!' she began, her face flushing. 'Peter, this is er. . . , Jeremy . . .' She couldn't remember his second name.

'Baxter,' the young man offered, stretching out his hand.

'Jeremy's a journalist,' Jackie warned. 'We sat next to

each other on the plane from Gatwick. He's here to write a story about HMS *Eagle* . . .'

'How interesting,' said Brodrick, nudging Jackie towards the lifts.

'Yes,' Baxter replied, walking with them. 'You're not connected with the ship, by any chance?'

He could tell that Brodrick was military.

'No. Quite disconnected, really. I'm here on holiday. Rock climbing. With the apes. . . ,' Brodrick added flippantly.

'Really?' Baxter answered, coolly. 'Love to hear about it. Perhaps I could buy you two a drink later?'

'Maybe. But we've got to dash,' Brodrick continued. 'It was nice to meet you.'

He put his arm round Jackie's shoulder and hustled her away.

The lift doors opened. Jackie pressed the button for the second floor.

'You didn't tell him anything about me, did you?' he asked tensely.

'Of course not! Now what are we doing? Explain.'

'Okay. Look, get your passport, and whatever money you have. We're going to Spain.'

The WRN driver took them back to *Rooke*, where Brodrick grabbed his own passport and made a vital phone call to Commander Camfield.

Then they were driven to the frontier.

'We'll walk through and hire a car in La Linea,' he told her. 'It'll save hours trying to drive across.'

He pointed to the long line of vehicles queuing for Spanish customs.

'Peter, where are we going, exactly?'

'To see an old friend of mine. I want you to charm him.'

'You might've warned me! I'd have worn something sexier, not just jeans and trainers.'

'Just smile! He'll love it!'

They rented a Seat from the Avis office. While Brodrick signed the papers, Jackie went to a bar and bought bocadillos. They were both hungry.

'Where exactly are we going?' she demanded, as they headed west, eating the sandwiches.

'Algeciras. The port. We're calling on a man named Pepe Alvarez. He's a lieutenant in the Spanish customs.'

The road round the bay was lined with ugly industrial sites. Chimneys belched fumes that caught in the back of their throats. Algeciras loomed ahead, an urban sprawl backed by hills that had been temporarily greened by the spring rains.

Twenty minutes later they drew up outside the low, drab building which housed the Aduanas.

Brodrick led the way and pushed open the scuffed, wooden door. A uniformed officer at a reception desk eyed them suspiciously.

'You know what to say?' Brodrick nudged.

'Of course.'

She leaned forward so he'd smell her perfume, and asked to see Teniente Alvarez. The officer's eyes lit up. He was used to rougher trade in this part of town. He frowned uncomprehendingly when she gave Brodrick's name, so she wrote it down as he picked up the telephone.

She said something in Spanish that made him laugh.

A short while later, an anxious, middle-aged woman with her hair in a bun, emerged from a corridor and beckoned them to follow.

Pepe's office was small and drab.

'Peter, my fren'! This is a . . . an especial pleasure,' Alvarez stammered, reaching out his hand. The look in his eyes was cautious and suspicious.

'Pepe! How good of you to see us!' Brodrick beamed. 'This is my assistant, Jackie Bartlett. She's interpreting for me!'

Jackie spoke in Spanish for a moment and Brodrick thought he saw the suspicion in Pepe's eyes begin to disappear.

They sat down.

'The las' time we meet, you throw me off your ship!' Alvarez joked.

Brodrick grinned, then told him what *Eagle* had been doing for the past week. Pepe's eyes widened.

'Some of that I read in the newspapers, but not all,' he concluded. 'Nuclear weapons! That's very serious. More than smugglers . . .'

'Oh, did you catch them, by the way?' Brodrick wondered.

'Some of them. Not all,' Pepe replied grimly.

There was still some anger at being let down, Brodrick realised.

'Pepe, we need your help.'

It was time to come to the point.

'The ship's still in danger. Some sort of terrorist attack. We don't know what exactly. The key to it could be that Arab we found on the boat we boarded, remember?'

'Boukari. Youssef.'

'Exactly. Real name – Ahmed Bizri. I have to find him.'

'Attack HMS *Eagle?*' Alvarez queried, looking from Brodrick to Jackie and back again. 'What with? Not . . . nuclear?'

They'd entered a diplomatic minefield. The British in Gibraltar hadn't given the Spanish the full reason why they wanted Bizri traced. Too explosive – politically.

'As far as anyone knows for sure, those nukes are at the bottom of the Mediterranean,' Brodrick assured him, praying Jackie would stay silent.

Alvarez understood English well enough to sense there was ambiguity in his words.

'Mmmm. If Mr Boukari is still in Spain, the policia may know,' he shrugged. 'You must speak with them . . .'

He feigned a degree of indifference. This wasn't customs business.

'Of course. But Pepe, you know how it is. Official channels. It takes days, maybe weeks. I only have hours,' Brodrick pleaded.

Alvarez looked from one to the other. Boukari was still a source of friction between them. He remembered that Brodrick had tried to flout Spanish law when they'd boarded the *Medina*.

'I don't think I . . ,' he began regretfully.

'Por favor,' Jackie intervened. 'Es muy, muy importante.'

Alvarez swallowed, and moved a few papers on the top of his desk.

'Maybe they don't know anything, the policia.'

'But would you ask them for us?' Jackie begged, in Spanish. 'They might not tell us, but they'd tell *you*. *Please*, señor!'

Alvarez seemed to weigh up the implications of helping them.

'Okay. I – try. Please . . . you wait. Outside. My assistant . . .'

He stood up and opened the door to the next office.

'So far, so good,' Brodrick grunted.

'He's sweet,' Jackie whispered.

'But will he do anything?'

They didn't have long to wait.

When Pepe opened the door again his face betrayed nothing. Brodrick's heart sank. It looked as if they'd got nowhere. Then the Aduanero held out a small sheet of paper.

'This is the name of a village – not far from La

353

Linea. Mr Boukari has been seen there. You can ask, maybe.'

He shrugged as if doubtful it would help, but from the look in his eye, they knew that what he was giving them was pure gold.

'Is there a house name or a street. . . ?'

Pepe arched his eyebrows disdainfully. Such details were too much to expect.

'Look, I'm very, very grateful, Pepe. This may save a lot of lives.'

'Be careful, my fren',' he warned.

Their first stop was at a garage to buy a map.

'Why don't we talk to the police?' Jackie suggested, as they spread the sheet across the steering wheel.

'We just did. Through Pepe,' he told her.

'I mean officially. Explain things to them, and get their help.'

'Look,' he turned to her, irritated. 'In just one hour, we've achieved something on our own that the official channels couldn't hack in a week!'

'Yes, but . . .'

His eyes burned with obsession. A familiar look to her. She'd seen it after his return from Lebanon, when he'd been wild and irrational. Suddenly she remembered Alan's words in the cemetery. 'They think Peter's unreliable.'

'All I'm saying is, if you're going to drive up to this place and confront Bizri . . . you might need some help.'

'There's no time for that.'

He crunched the car into gear and drove out of the forecourt, sliding the map onto Jackie's lap.

'Here. You're navigating. We want Alcala de la Frontera. It's on the green road – a turning just before San Roque.'

Map-reading wasn't her strong point, but she found

354

San Roque and a green route, and then the pueblo. Not so hard after all.

Brodrick felt far from calm. Jackie was right of course; he could do with some back-up. He didn't even have a gun with him. But what could he do? Go to the Spanish police now, after they'd told the Gibraltar authorities they'd no knowledge of Bizri? Ridiculous! They wouldn't co-operate. They'd lock him up, more likely, or send him back to Gib and tell him to mind his own business. Have to take a chance. He'd call for reinforcements if he needed them.

They turned off the main road and climbed into the hills. By the time they reached the village it was after five.

'What's going on here?'

The road was blocked by police, and cars were being diverted into a field.

'It's Semana Santa,' Jackie explained. 'Holy week. They must have a parade here tonight.'

'That's all we need!'

They parked and got out. Families with small children wearing satin masks and conical hats drifted towards the narrow main street.

The centre of the village was perched on top of a hill, an old castle at its heart. The road petered out halfway up, continuing as a cobbled alley lined by humble white houses pressed close together.

'Where on earth do we begin?' Brodrick sighed.

'How about an ice-cream?' Jackie suggested, brightly.

Brodrick scowled. That wasn't what he meant. But why not? Everybody else had ice-creams. It'd make them less conspicuous.

They bought two cones at a shop selling refreshments and brightly coloured ceramics.

'The parade starts at six, according to the woman in the shop,' Jackie told him. 'There'll be floats with statues of the Virgin Mary, and bands . . .'

355

'With Ahmed Bizri marching at their head, I suppose!'

Jackie puffed out her cheeks. It looked hopeless. They had the name of this pueblo, but no other clues.

'What's he look like?'

'Shortish, pudgy, face like a lump of dough. Dark hair stuck down with grease over the bald part. Eyes are a bit bulbous. Olive skin. Aged thirty-five to forty, I suppose . . .'

'You've just described half the men walking up and down this street,' she mused.

'I know. Come on, let's recce the place.'

They walked briskly up the hill, weaving through the crowds, who were ambling about waiting for the parade to start.

On the steps of a freshly painted church an ornate, silver float with a canopy of purple was having adjustments made to the sprays of white flowers which exploded round the feet of the Virgin.

They came to the castle. Once it must've been a fine fortress; now its grey stones were cracked and overgrown. Brodrick took Jackie's hand to help her up to the top.

'That's quite a view,' she panted, out of breath.

'Beautiful. But not too big, thankfully,' he observed.

The red-tiled roofs fanned out from the base of the castle.

'There can't be more than three or four hundred people living here,' he guessed. 'But why would Bizri come to a place like this? If he wanted to be inconspicuous he'd be better off in a large town.'

'Perhaps he knows someone. . . .'

'Wait!' He turned to her. 'I remember, Bizri told Pepe he had a Spanish wife. But I'm not sure I believe it.'

'His friends could be Arabs,' she suggested. 'Moroccans, Tunisians, Libyans even. There are plenty around. They put their money in apartment blocks on the coast.'

'You're a mine of information . . .'

'I have my uses,' she grinned.

'Should be possible to find out if there are Arabs living here. A postman, perhaps? He'd know.'

'Yes, but he'll probably be carrying one of the floats. We could try a shopkeeper.'

He helped her down from their vantage point and they made their way back into the village.

The first shop they came to sold tobacco and magazines. Brodrick browsed the array of soft pornography, while Jackie went inside. General Franco would turn in his grave if he could see this lot, he thought.

Jackie came out shaking her head.

'Not very helpful,' she said.

'Perhaps you should've bought something,' Brodrick remarked.

Further down the street was a small grocery, grandly named 'Supermercado'.

Jackie dived in, picking up a wire basket on her way.

From down the hill, came the heavy thump of drums. The parade had begun.

Jackie emerged, clutching a striped plastic bag, grinning impishly.

'He called them Moroccans, but I don't think he really knew what they were,' she announced in a hushed voice. 'He said they've got a finca surrounded by a high wall on the other side of the village. Said we can't miss it. There's nothing else like it here. It's at the top of a twisty road that drops down to the sea. To the place where the rich keep their boats – that's what he said.'

They were getting somewhere. Boats. The sea. That would make sense. Brodrick flexed his shoulders to ease the tension in his neck.

'Come on! Let's go and look.'

'Peter! Stop a minute.' She pulled at his arm. 'You *will* be careful? You won't just go barging in, will you?'

'Don't worry.'

She wasn't reassured.

They walked away from the noise of the bands, up past the foot of the castle, and down the other side of the village.

'I seem to have bought some bananas,' Jackie remarked. 'Would you like one?'

Nerves made her flippant.

'Not now, thanks.'

On the left they passed a small, empty bar. Its owner peered hopefully from the darkened interior, leaning on the back of a rushwork chair.

Ahead, the cobbled street broadened into a road, wide enough for a car. On the right stood a tiny church, its door open, with a young woman in black attending to flowers in holders each side of the entrance.

Opposite the church was a high wall with a pair of panelled, metal gates set into it. Beyond, they could see the russet, pantiled roof of a large house. The finca.

Jackie clutched his arm.

'This is it,' she whispered. 'Just like the man said.'

They were on the very edge of the village. The potholed road fell away sharply and disappeared amongst arid foothills, dusted with the green of spring. They were facing east. The Mediterranean must lie beyond the distant ridge.

The sun had already dropped behind the old fortress. Long shadows darkened this side of the village.

Brodrick sensed in his gut that this was the place. Behind those walls was the man whose deception had caused the death of his comrades in Lebanon.

The finca was enclosed in a rectangle, about forty metres by seventy-five. He guessed the wall itself to be two metres high. It'd only take seconds to get over. The far corner would be best, where an almond tree in full blossom should hide him from the house.

'It'll be dark soon,' he murmured. 'Better if we come back later.'

He slipped an arm round Jackie's shoulders and felt her trembling.

'Don't worry,' he said, squeezing her. 'It'll be okay.'

They walked back up towards the banging of the drums, like a couple of tourists.

In the narrow main street, the blue of dusk was punctuated by the gold of candle flames, hundreds of them, held by villagers.

At the head of the parade came the drums and the mournful fifes. Behind the fragrant floats walked penitents dressed in white cotton robes, their eyes peering through slits in the green satin of their conical hats.

It's like the Ku Klux Klan, Brodrick thought.

Following the flower-bedecked symbols of Christ's suffering, women in black wailed solemnly, holding rosaries, their mantillas held rigid like fans.

'You should be here on Good Friday,' Jackie replied softly. 'That's when the fervour really gets going.'

Friday. Two days away. They might all be dead by then.

Suddenly Brodrick felt the skin crawl on his neck. It was as if he sensed Bizri watching him. He looked round. No one was there, of course.

The procession looped its way through the village, watched by the elderly from crowded balconies. Soon its head was back at the church. Then, in festive mood, the crowd broke up and promenaded through the streets, some grabbing seats in the restaurants and bars. The smell of grilled lamb filled the air.

'Aren't you hungry?' Jackie asked, clutching her stomach. 'We've only had a sandwich and an ice-cream all day.'

Brodrick looked up at the sky. There was still a glow from the setting sun. He'd need it darker than this.

'Okay. Let's see what we can find.'

It was quite dark when they returned to the finca, the only light emanating from the little chapel opposite the steel gates.

'Now look.' Brodrick held Jackie by the shoulders. 'I want you to hang around here, but keep out of sight. If I'm not back within half an hour, find a phone and ring Gibraltar – Commander Camfield. Here's his home number.'

He handed her the car keys and a piece of paper.

'I told him we were going to Spain, so he'll know who you are.'

In the spill of light from the chapel, Jackie could see the lines of tension on his face.

'Don't do anything crazy,' she whispered, her voice hoarse with fear. 'Promise?'

He kissed her and turned away, melting into the night.

Panic gripped her. She wanted to run after him and drag him back. Then she got a grip on herself. She walked steadily across to the little church.

Three small steps led up to the tiny doorway. Inside, there was a small plain altar, with four candles burning.

A face turned towards her, startled. The woman in black who'd been tending the flowers was sitting there.

'*Perdon*,' Jackie murmured, hesitating.

The woman gestured towards the other chairs, then returned to her prayers.

Jackie sat. She didn't often go to church, and seldom prayed. But there was no better time than now.

Brodrick reached the far corner of the wall, and crouched while his eyes adjusted to the dark. There was no sound from the other side, just a faint glow. Lights were on somewhere in the grounds.

He felt in his pocket for the small torch he'd brought from *Rooke*.

Then he reached for the top of the wall, and pulled himself noiselessly up until his eyes were level with the rim. Just as he'd hoped – it was dark the other side, and there was a tree for concealment. He swung over and dropped to the ground.

The old farmhouse was at the other side of the garden, lights showing from the windows. A gravel drive had been laid to the house from the steel gates. Light shone from a garage. Parked in front was a Range-Rover, its rear hatch open.

He heard the clink of metal. Hammering, someone using tools.

The sound of voices. More of a rumble. Low guttural sounds. Spanish? Arabic? He couldn't tell.

A man appeared, carrying a wooden box with a handle. This wasn't Bizri. Too young. The box seemed heavy; he needed both hands to lift and slide it into the back of the vehicle.

From inside the garage came a shout from another man. Grating Arabic, the timbre bitterly familiar. Brodrick felt a frisson through his body. He'd found him!

The young man went to help. Shortly, two of them emerged, carrying something white – a large, rounded container. The figure with his back to Brodrick was shorter, fatter, balding.

Ahmed Bizri.

His face turned sideways. There was no mistaking the pudgy features, the face Brodrick saw in his dreams.

Blood pounded in his temples. He wanted to spring forward and seize Bizri by the throat, to break his neck like a rabbit's. He clenched his teeth. He had to stay cool.

That object they were carrying – he recognised it now. A life-raft canister from a pleasure-boat.

The two men checked things were secure in the back of the Range-Rover, then turned for the house.

A life-raft container? If the boat sinks, the raft inflates

361

– that's how it worked. But here? Not the sort of gear you'd bring ashore for maintenance.

His mind raced.

Suddenly it hit him. Like a vision. He understood it all, with perfect clarity.

He knew now how *Mustadhafin* planned to destroy HMS *Eagle*!

Bizri had brought the container here to remove the raft. It was empty, now! The space inside would be just big enough to house a small nuclear warhead.

The woman in black glanced darkly at Jackie. She didn't want this tourist here, in her church. Jackie resisted the pressure for as long as she dared, then rose from her knees, crossed herself and walked quietly out of the door.

Just seven minutes had passed since Peter had slipped into the darkness. Already she was desperate for him to return.

She moved away from the pool of light by the church and blended into the shadows.

She held her breath, listening for sounds coming from beyond the wall. But all she could hear was laughter from the bar up the hill.

Brodrick sprinted across the coarse grass to the side of the garage. He crouched, listening.

Nothing.

He had to be sure. Had to look inside that container.

The men were still in the finca. He could hear their voices.

He'd have to chance it. If he got wind of them returning, he'd have a second or two to reach the wall and climb it.

Just ten metres to the open hatch of the Range-Rover. *Go!*

He sprinted forward. Two clips held down the cover of the white container. They clicked noisily. Damn!

The hinged lid opened easily. Empty, just as he'd thought. Two wooden jigs glued in place, with curved recesses. To hold a cylinder.

He'd seen enough. He closed the lid and pressed on the clips.

Suddenly his head jerked back and he choked. He grabbed frantically at his throat. A thin rigging cord crushed his windpipe.

From behind him there was a shout.

'Ahmed!'

There'd been a third man in the garage! Fool! He hadn't looked.

Brodrick struggled, lungs straining, trying to break free, but the line jerked tighter.

He thrashed with his hands, searching for his assailant, but something hard in the back of his neck held him at a distance.

Harsh Arabic rent the air. The sound of feet on gravel.

His head hummed. There was pressure on the artery – no blood getting to his brain.

The man who'd snared him swung him round at the end of a pole like a rabid animal.

Giddy, eyes blurring, Brodrick saw the doughy face of Ahmed Bizri closing with his own. Then the heavy pistol swinging wide.

He felt an explosion in his temple, then all was blackness.

Jackie heard the shouting. Her heart seemed to stop.

Scuffling feet. A struggle. Peter was caught! She knew it. Please God, don't let them kill him!

She flinched, anticipating the shot. She tried to shout his name, but no sound came.

What should she do? Had to get help.

Ring Gibraltar, Peter had said. But she needed help here and now!

There'd be police in the village, somewhere.

She heard an engine start. Then the clatter of bolts sliding back in the gate. She could see the steel panels from where she stood. Maybe they'd see her! She pressed back into the shadows.

The gates opened halfway. A man's face appeared, young and fearful. He looked up and down the dusty road, then, seeing no one, he pulled the gates fully open. An engine revved and a Range-Rover burst out into the road, headlamps blazing. It swept past her, pounding over the ruts that led down to the coast.

Two pairs of eyes in front shot her a glance. In the back, she saw a shape. It could've been a man, head covered, slumped against the side window.

Peter!

'Oh, help!' she whimpered, starting to run towards the village.

Suddenly she stopped again. More voices. This time from the little chapel.

Odd voices. One a woman's, urgent but restrained; the other a man's, metallic and fainter.

Jackie tip-toed up the steps and put her head inside.

The woman in black was talking into a portable radio!

'*Perdon*,' Jackie began, nervously.

The woman whipped round. She pulled a pistol from her carrier bag and pointed it at Jackie's head.

The jarring of the suspension on the potholes jolted Brodrick from his unconsciousness. He could see nothing. Rough cloth smelling of diesel oil covered his head. He tried to open his mouth, but couldn't.

Something hard and lumpy behind his back pushed him forward in the seat. As his brain cleared he realised what it was. His own arms, pinioned so tightly he could no longer feel them. The vehicle lurched to the right and he fell sideways across the seat.

'Ooof!' he grunted.

The pain in his head made him wince. There was a vicious bruise where Bizri had hit him. He tried to move his legs, but they too were bound. He lay there powerless.

His throat felt raw. He guessed they'd used a dog restraint. They'd bloody nearly strangled him!

A rough hand grabbed the cloth from his head, then grasped him by the hair and jerked him upright.

'So, mister! Different now, heh?'

Bizri's eyes gleamed viciously in the glow from the dashboard. He tore the tape from Brodrick's mouth, then growled an order to the driver.

The Range-Rover stopped; Bizri got out of the front and came round to the back, edging onto the seat. Brodrick remembered that smell of rosewater from Lebanon. It was cloying, vile.

'Different from last time,' Bizri repeated, prodding with the pistol as the vehicle started off again.

Brodrick didn't respond. He sensed a sexuality in Bizri's violence.

'Remember? Answer! What your name?'

'No name,' he replied, flatly.

The gun barrel jabbed into the swelling on his temple. He yelped at the pain and recoiled against the side window.

'You get from me same what you did,' Bizri snarled.

Got to concentrate, Brodrick thought. Survival. That's the first thing. Then fight back, somehow.

'Why you here?' Bizri demanded.

'I was curious.'

'You lie!'

Another jab to the head.

'Bastard!' he yelled.

Bizri gave a throaty laugh.

The little shit's getting a hard-on from this, Brodrick thought.

'Soon you will be happy that you die,' Bizri hissed.

'I'll bloody take you with me,' Brodrick coughed defiantly.

'Heh! Oh no. You make big mistake.'

Bizri pistol-whipped him across the wind-pipe. Brodrick gagged, his throat in spasm.

'Why you not on your ship?' Bizri demanded.

Brodrick rocked forward, mouth wide, gasping for air.

'I'm on leave,' he croaked eventually.

The pistol smashed across his lips.

'You answer! And how you find me? Eh?'

He turned his head away.

Bizri yelled in Arabic. The Range-Rover skidded to a halt. He and the driver got out, wrenched open Brodrick's door and pulled him onto the stony ground.

They dragged him like a corpse into the glare of the headlights, then jerked him forward onto his hands and knees.

Two of them! Better pray they're not both bent. He tensed his muscles to test the bonds. Tight as wire.

By his ear came the clink of steel as the pistol was cocked.

'Where is your ship?' Bizri grated.

'I dunno.'

The gunshot cracked beside his ear. The muzzle flash scorched his cheek. The bullet zinged, as it ricocheted off rocks into the darkness.

'Look, I don't know where the sodding ship is!' Brodrick yelled, ears ringing. Time to make a noise. The gunshot – a shout – someone might hear.

'But you know where it goes . . .'

'So do you . . .'

The gun barrel hot against the back of his neck.

'You tell me!'

'Okay. It's going to Gibraltar.'

'Tomorrow. What time?'

'I don't know. Look, I really don't know!'

Silence. He cringed, waiting for the next blow. He could hear Bizri's laboured breathing. Unfit. A ball of flab. Easy meat if he got his hands free.

'Why you come looking for me?'

Think. Think.

'To tell you you're all washed up.'

A hesitation in the wheeze from Bizri's lungs.

'What you mean, wash up?'

Another jab to the neck.

'That you're finished. You and Habib. Him and those nuclear toys. They're at the bottom of the Med.'

'Hah! You think so?'

'I bloody know it. Saw the ship go down.'

A gamble. A deadly gamble.

Bizri laughed again. He kicked a stone so it skidded off the track into the scrub.

'Big mistake, mister! You make big mistake! Soon you find out. But too late, because you die, and your ship!'

'Crap!'

Bizri smacked the barrel across Brodrick's face. Blood began to stream from his nose.

'You British! So arrogant! But so wrong!' Bizri's 'r's rolled like a tambour. 'Tomorrow your *Eagle* will be finish. Finish!'

'Bollocks! You can't do it. Habib's dead!'

The words spluttered out from his swollen lips.

'Hah! If he dead, then today he speak to me from heaven!'

That was it! His pulse throbbed in his neck. Proof at last! Proof that they intended to destroy the *Eagle*, proof that they still had the means to achieve it. But it was a proof that would die with him if Bizri put a bullet in his brain.

'What d'you mean?' Brodrick asked, his mouth bitter with the taste of blood.

'I tell you nothing,' Bizri sneered. 'Soon, you will know.'

Hands gripped his arms and pulled him back towards the Range-Rover. They bundled him across the rear seat and secured the door.

'So arrogant!' Bizri seethed as the vehicle resumed its bumpy journey. 'You think "Britannia rule the wave". You think you can tell Arab peoples what to do! You are wrong. People who betray the Arabs, people like your fren' Bicknell, they die.'

'Bicknell?' Brodrick exclaimed, raising his head from the greasy seat cover.

Bicknell betrayed *Mustadhafin*? What did he mean?

'That bugger was a friend of the Arabs.'

'Hah! He say that. Arab peoples don't say. Bicknell was a thief. He owe us.'

'Owed you? Money? What for?' Brodrick probed.

'What for? You not know? Drugs. Opium. That what for.'

Bicknell! Dealing in drugs? The man the British government had sacrificed a dozen men to try to rescue?

'Great British hero, yes? Hah! Great drug merchant! Big, big business! He buy all our heroin one year. Promise much money, but pay nothing. Nothing! That's why we take him!'

Brodrick dropped his head onto the seat, speechless.

Was that what it had been about? Why the government had sent him to Lebanon? To stop Bicknell talking?

Twelve men dead, to stop the world learning how Bicknell had made the millions that he'd paid into their party funds!

Peter felt his body begin to quiver. The smell of smoke, the stench of burning flesh, the images of Lebanon, all came flashing back.

Vomit rose in his throat.

Bizri ignored him. The Range-Rover leapt from pothole to pothole down the track. Brodrick retched onto the floor.

Minutes later, the wheels ran smoothly and tyres hummed. They'd reached the metalled road along the coast.

Brodrick felt numb, exhausted. So much death for so little reason. So much more to come unless he could stop it. He cursed his carelessness at the finca.

Jackie! Had she seen what happened? Had she got through to Camfield?

They drove for fifteen minutes, then the yellow glow of street lighting told him they'd entered a town.

Bizri dropped a cloth that smelled of diesel over his head and warned him to be quiet.

The vehicle stopped at traffic lights. Brodrick thought of yelling, but with his head towards the floor the chances of anyone hearing were slim.

They turned sharp right, then the wheels drummed on an uneven surface. They stopped and the driver killed the engine.

He heard a familiar sound. The slapping of rigging against metal masts. They were in a harbour.

The side door opened and hands reached in to pull him upright.

'Pig!' Bizri spat, smelling the vomit on him.

Brodrick felt his face swollen and stiff with dried blood. He looked round. They were in a marina at the far end of one of the piers.

No sign of life on any of the boats. The owners lived in Hamburg or Stockholm, he guessed. It was too early in the year for them.

'You walk,' Bizri ordered, untying the rope from his ankles.

They eased him onto the wooden boards of the jetty, then the driver punched him in the stomach.

Brodrick fought for breath as they hustled him along the boardwalk. If he'd thought of running for it, he couldn't now.

His feet stumbled over a glassfibre gunwale and they

bundled him inside a cabin cruiser. He was pushed onto seat squabs, and the rope whipped round his ankles again before he could resist.

The two men conferred in Arabic, glancing at him. Bizri pulled the pistol from his pocket and held it down by his side.

A new fear gripped Brodrick. Bizri looked ready to finish him off. The driver restrained him. He seemed to be warning that a shot could puncture the hull.

Reluctantly Bizri stuffed the gun back into his waistbelt, and the two stepped onto the jetty.

Brodrick looked around for something, anything that could cut the ropes binding hands and feet.

Within seconds the men were back, carrying the large, empty life-raft container. They positioned it on its stern mounts and bolted it securely in place.

Not a large cruiser, he thought. The sort a family might use for a day's outing.

The men went ashore again. Brodrick twisted his head to look on the shelf behind. A small, cardboard box caught his eye. There was just a chance. He wrenched his arms up behind his back, straining the sinews, until his fingers could clasp it.

He dropped the box behind him and scrabbled with its lid, then froze as the men returned, carrying the other cases from the car. They ignored him, absorbed in their work.

His fingers felt metal, thin and curved. They worked along the hard edge, until he found what he was looking for. The sharp points of a set of dividers.

Brodrick lay back against the cushions, straining to dig the points into the tape that bound his hands. He kept his eyes on the cockpit.

The driver puzzled him. He was doing something strange with the wheel. He'd clamped a grooved hoop over it and was screwing some sort of control box onto the floor beneath. There was a pulley on the box; he looped a rope from it to the hoop on the wheel.

Automatic steering gear!

Oh, Lord!

He saw Ahmed Bizri plug a rod aerial into a hand-held transmitter.

They were rigging the boat so it could be remotely controlled, to turn it into a guided missile. Carrying a nuclear warhead!

Suddenly the strands of tape loosened. He flexed his forearms and his hands burst free. They tingled as the circulation flowed again.

Bizri stepped into the cabin and looked at him. Brodrick returned the stare, arms firmly behind his back.

'You understand now?'

'I do,' he answered, praying Bizri would come no closer. 'So where is Mr Habib, then, if he's not dead?'

Bizri looked at his watch, holding it at an angle so he could see it in the dim cabin light.

'He is coming closer,' he replied enigmatically. 'Soon we will go to meet him. He will be surprised to see you.'

Brodrick eyed the gun in Bizri's belt. Too far away. Couldn't reach.

The driver grunted that he was ready. Bizri turned, picked up the transmitter from the cockpit and stepped onto the jetty.

Brodrick lifted his legs onto the seat, tucking his feet behind his back.

'Don't look,' he prayed, watching the driver like a hawk. His hands reached down and felt for the knots.

He heard a whirr from the cockpit and froze. The steering wheel spun one way, then the other. Bizri was testing the sytem.

The driver grinned with satisfaction, stepped up onto the deck and waved at Bizri to return.

The knots were tight. Damned tight. Brodrick tugged and teased, but his ankles stayed bound.

A starter motor whined. The diesel thudded into life.

Bizri returned with one more bag from the vehicle. He slung it into the cabin, giving Brodrick hardly a glance. Then he stepped onto the deck and moved to the bows to untie the warp.

Now!

Brodrick propelled himself forward, grabbing at the frame of the cabin hatch. He held fast and dragged his body upright.

Startled, the Arab at the helm swung menacingly towards him. He gripped the top of the hatchway, and took his weight on his arms, hunched his legs and kicked, striking the driver in the chest.

'Ooof!'

He swung his legs forward again and let go, landing on his feet by the steps to the deck. A glance to the bows. Bizri had seen him and was stumbling towards the cockpit, hand fumbling for the gun in his belt.

Go for it!

Hands on the deck, Brodrick vaulted into the sea. Water gurgled in his ears, drowning the sound of the pistol shot.

Down and to the left. Strong, wide arm strokes. A kick from his ankles, still locked together.

A stinging in his backside. He'd been shot!

Lungs bursting. He had to surface. Must be under the jetty by now.

One hand reached up. The cold of the air, then timber. His head emerged from the water. Just enough room beneath the boardwalk to breath.

The white hull swung away from the pontoon. The stern was free, the bow still held by the warp. Brodrick saw Bizri, standing on the prow, gun outstretched, searching the surface of the water for some sign of him.

Suddenly Bizri's knees buckled. With a yell, he toppled sideways into the water. As the boat swung, the bow rope had caught him behind the legs.

With a primaeval growl, Brodrick launched himself

towards the thrashing figure beyond the pontoon. Just metres away, Bizri saw him. With his left hand flailing the water to stay afloat, the right hand levelled the gun. Brodrick snatched a lungful of air and plunged his head underwater. The crack of the pistol shot merged with the burbling in his ears.

His goddam legs! He was bound like a mermaid! In the pitch black, he could see nothing. By instinct he swung first left, then right, calculating to put himself the other side of Bizri. Surface? Not yet.

Lungs bursting, he stretched out his hands, feeling for the other body. Gently, gently. There'd be one chance only. One chance to surprise.

The tips of his fingers felt cloth. Down a bit. Legs pumping, treading water. Bizri's legs. Gently. Feel the way up. Now!

Head breaking water. Gasp for air. Left arm round the neck. Right hand go for the wrist. Reach! Reach for God's sake! Christ! Where's his bloody arm?

Underwater again. Metal banged against his skull. Shit! The gun! Another second and he was a dead man. Scrabbling with his right hand, his fingers clasped Bizri's wrist, wrenching the barrel away from his temple. His ear exploded.

Alive! He was still alive! The bullet had missed. Bizri twisted beneath his grip. He was strong for such a flabby bastard! Brodrick jammed the hard muscle of his left forearm tighter against the Arab's windpipe. With his right hand he fought to squeeze the gun from Bizri's fingers. His head broke surface again.

'Randal!'

Brodrick's anguished yell pierced the night. Then he filled his lungs to the brim. Down, down they sank, into the black, Bizri kicking and twisting. Brodrick eased pressure on his throat, praying he'd gulp water into his lungs. With a sudden spasm, Bizri's right hand opened, grabbing for the air. The pistol tumbled into the dark depths.

Chest splitting with pain, Brodrick kicked up to the surface again.

'Singer! Blight!'

One by one in a frenzy of anger and agony, he yelled the names of his squad, all of them. A roll-call of the marines killed in Lebanon, killed by the man whose weakening body was trapped below the water by his own.

Suddenly there was no more struggle. The arms went limp, the head stopped butting for air. Brodrick relaxed his grip, but kept the body submerged.

Then came the roar of a marine diesel. The Arab driver had freed the cuiser from its bow rope.

Shit! They can still do it! The bastards still have their boat and their bomb! He watched forlornly as the powerboat headed for the sea.

Then came another sound, from the direction of the road. Police sirens! Blue lights flashing on the main pier and the sound of running on the planks.

He looked towards the mouth of the marina, where a spill of light from the town picked out the white hull of the motor-cruiser.

Then a sharp beam pierced the darkness from beyond the boat. Stentorian voices barked in Spanish. There was another craft out there. A police launch!

Brodrick threw his arms wide, lay back in the water and panted with relief.

'Arriba las manos!'

The click of rifle bolts. Two dark figures on the jetty trained guns on him.

'Okay, okay,' he shouted.

Gently he swam towards them, blinking in the light from their torches. With his left hand he towed the drowned body of Ahmed Bizri.

'Peter!' came a shout from the main pier. Jackie's voice!

'¡Es el marino ingles!' he heard her explain. '¡Dejenme pasar!'

He reached up and grasped the timbers, but with his legs bound, he was stuck.

'Gimme a hand, will you?' he coughed, calling to the black-clad policemen.

One of them put down his rifle and hauled him out of the water, while the other kept him covered. When they saw the rope round his ankles they finally understood.

'The other fucker's dead!' he announced to their uncomprehending faces.

He heard the pounding of feet along the jetty, then Jackie was there, flinging her arms round him.

'Oh, my darling,' she cried. 'I thought – I thought – !'

Suddenly he winced.

'You're hurt! My God! Your face!'

'It's my bum that hurts most,' he told her. 'I think I stopped a bullet.'

She babbled at the policemen in Spanish and they inspected him.

'Doesn't look bad,' she translated. 'Just a graze.'

'Jackie, you've got to tell these bastards.' He shivered with cold and shock.

He looked towards the harbour mouth. The cruiser had been stopped.

'They *were* going to blow up the *Eagle*! Tell these Spaniards. They've got to know! Bizri was on his way to meet Habib,' he babbled. 'The bomb was to go in the boat. All remote control.'

'Okay, okay. I've told them most of it already. They've been fantastic. There were half-a-dozen of them up in that village, watching the finca. There was a police-woman in the church! They knew about Bizri, knew about the boat down here.'

'Bet they didn't know he'd emptied a life-raft container to hide the bomb in!'

'They knew about the container; but they said it was to hide drugs in!'

'Drugs! Fucking drugs!' he growled. 'That's what Bicknell was into.'

'Bicknell? What d'you mean?'

'He bought heroin from *Mustadhafin*. Tons of it. That's how the bastard made his millions!'

Jackie gasped. So this was the secret that Alan had kept from her. The government's political party had been financed by drug money!

George Webster had once been a director of Bicknell's company. No wonder he'd resigned.

'That's incredible!' she exclaimed.

The sirens had faded to silence. The rumble of diesels got steadily closer. They turned to watch the motor cruiser close with the jetty, a police officer at the helm.

'But you've won now, haven't you?' Jackie whispered. 'It's over!'

Brodrick shook his head forlornly.

'No way!' he answered. 'Habib's still out there. On a ship, with his nuclear bomb. And every minute brings him closer to HMS *Eagle*.'

Twenty-One

The trawler wallowed in the sickly swell. The diesel thumped rhythmically, keeping the generator going, but they were stationary.

Abdul Habib sat in the small wheelhouse next to the high-frequency transceiver he'd used for communicating with his adjutant in the past few days. But Bizri was two hours late, and there'd been no word of explanation on the radio.

To his left the sky was already lightening, increasing the risk that someone might see them transferring the bomb to the powerboat.

That something was wrong was a certainty. He trusted Ahmed. If there'd been a hold-up, he'd have called by radio to tell him. He threaded the amber beads back and forth through his fingers.

They must not fail! Not now! Not after all the planning, all the struggles – all the deaths. His young brother, whose shattered body they'd dragged from the rubble in Beirut – he owed it to him not to fail!

The Maltese skipper leaned against the chart table like a stupefied rabbit. He was to be paid a handsome sum for transporting this Lebanese gang leader and his sinister cargo, but had begun to suspect that he wouldn't live to enjoy it.

Five days ago, when the canister sheathed in plastic was swung onto his deck from the freighter *Baalbeck*, he'd sensed it was some kind of bomb. When Habib had ordered him to secure it in his trawl net and trail it astern underwater, he realised it was a weapon that needed extraordinary methods to hide it from the prying eyes of the helicopters.

Not until two days later had he learned the truth. While Habib slept, he'd heard the BBC World Service tell of the stolen nuclear weapons and the sinking of the *Baalbeck*.

Since then, he himself had hardly slept, knowing that an explosive device that could wipe out a city was being towed just fifty metres astern of his trawler.

He knew he should tell someone, call on the radio, warn the world. He'd thought of cutting the trawl wire and letting the evil slip to the bottom of the sea. But Habib's men had noted his agitation, and were watching him night and day. The one called Samir had whispered what he would do to him and his family if he betrayed them.

Abdul Habib raised the binoculars again and swept them round the horizon. It was from the darkness to the west that the powerboat should come. To the south, the long, dark shape of a supertanker, its deck twinkling with lights, aimed for the Gibraltar Strait and the Atlantic. To the east the orange tinge of the dawn sky and another ship approaching, just a distant shape in the morning mist. But of the powerboat, there was no sign.

There'd only been one plan, with no fall-back if things went wrong. All he could do was wait.

Algeciras
06.35 hrs

'We've got to get out of here! Tell them, Jackie!'

They were at police headquarters in Algeciras.

There had been endless questions, going round in circles.

'I have,' she whispered. 'But the more you push, the more they'll resist. They're Spanish.'

'You're telling me . . .'

Back at the marina, a paramedic had applied first-aid to the bullet wound on his buttock, then they'd taken him to a telephone so he could call Camfield in Gibraltar. The Commander was shaken to learn of Bizri's elimination, but stunned by the confirmation that a nuclear bomb was still at large nearby.

'But what's the problem?' Brodrick persisted.

'Look, even if they accept that killing Bizri was self-defence, they say you're the only witness and you can't leave the country,' Jackie explained.

'But it's only to go to bloody Gibraltar . . .'

'Exactly.'

They sat in a dimly-lit waiting room that smelled of black tobacco. The police had been amiable enough, plying them with coffee, but when Brodrick had attempted to leave, they'd made it clear they'd stop him.

'What do they *want*?' he demanded.

'Evidence. Against Bizri and his accomplice,' she answered. 'Look. See it from their point of view. They'd been watching him for nearly a week, convinced he was smuggling drugs. They hoped to catch him in the act. Then we come along and spoil everything.

'There was I, half hysterical, babbling away about an atom bomb and a British marine whose life was in danger! It's amazing they believed me. But they did! And they were brilliant, Peter. They moved like lightning. That's why they stopped the powerboat.'

She clutched his arm and squeezed it.

'But the problem is they've blown their whole under-cover operation. And they've found no drugs! Just an empty life-raft container . . .'

'Converted to hold the bomb!' Brodrick erupted in exasperation.

'But they've only your word for that. And frankly they're finding that part of it hard to believe. They've been questioning the other Arab – trying to, anyway. But he hasn't said a word. You're their key witness, and they're scared that if you leave the country you won't come back.'

He held his head in his hands. Every minute that passed gave Abdul Habib time to make new plans.

'Get me to a phone again, will you?' he asked, standing up. 'This is crazy. I've got to get to Gib! Camfield had better pull some strings.'

HMS Eagle
07.15 hrs

Captain David Dyce stood tensely by the bridge window looking down onto the flight deck. Two more Sea Kings were winding up, ready to increase the patrols as they got closer to Gibraltar.

He could see the Rock clearly now, a great hump in the morning haze. Within two hours they'd be alongside the South Mole.

At each side of the bridge, the lookouts had been doubled, to report the merest hint of other vessels coming too close. Five miles was the nearest they'd allow. Any boat coming closer was being warned off by radio.

The signal from Naval Headquarters at Northwood had got Dyce out of his bunk two hours ago. To read in cold print the confirmation that *Mustadhafin* had planned to destroy them all with a nuclear weapon had sent a shiver down his spine. The suspicions, obsessions even, of Peter Brodrick – all had been confirmed in a few short words.

The attack had been planned to take place on the high seas, the signal had said, maybe in the very waters they were now transiting. But it had been foiled by Captain Brodrick and the Spanish police.

'Remarkable how Brodrick got the Spaniards to help,' Dyce mused, turning to Lieutenant-Commander Nick Brady, 'after we did the dirty on them by pulling out of the drug hunt.'

'Yes, sir. I can't wait to hear how he managed it.'

Brady was desperately uneasy, as were all of the officers in the small circle who'd been told of the threat the ship had faced. Out here in open water the helicopters could chase away any small craft that became too inquisitive, but as the sea traffic funnelled into the Strait, and they rounded Europa Point into the bay, such separation would prove impossible.

'I'm not entirely happy about the decision to proceed into Gib, sir,' Brady cautioned. 'Not my job to say it, but I thought I'd better anyway.'

'The only alternative's to steam straight through and head for Pompey,' Dyce prickled. 'I've considered that, but it'd ruin the weekend of three hundred families. They've flown out to Gib just to be with their boys.'

'Sir, if these bastards let off their bomb in Gibraltar harbour, it'll ruin more than their weekend!'

'Look! It's a question of risk assessment,' Dyce answered tartly. 'All the evidence from Brodrick is that the attack was planned for open sea. They want to kill us, not civilians. So Gibraltar harbour could be the safest place for *Eagle*.

'The search has started for the vessel carrying the bomb. The whole darned circus again. Nimrods, helicopters – all run from Gib this time. The Russians are still on the *Jackson* with their neutron detectors, but they'll be here this afternoon. It should be easier in a smaller area; and Habib's ship must be within a hundred miles of the Rock.'

Brady still looked doubtful. Even if the risk was infinitesimal, surely it should be avoided?

'It's gone to the top,' Dyce confided. 'PM was consulted an hour ago. He agrees we should go onto alert state Red, but stick to our plan.'

07.45 hrs

Abdul Habib's eyes brimmed with tears of frustration. The silhouette on the horizon south of them was unmistakeable. Twin funnels, ski-jump for the Harriers at the bows – HMS *Eagle* was passing them by.

'Ahmed! Ahmed!' he moaned. 'What happened to you? My friend, my brother!'

Bizri had been discovered. He knew that now. The carrier was on alert. In the past ten minutes they'd heard her call on Channel 16, warning other boats to keep their distance. Helicopters were flying out to identify the closest ships.

One had just passed over the trawler. Samir had held his long knife to the skipper's throat until it was gone.

Habib stepped out of the wheelhouse onto the narrow side-deck. They were underway again, just a knot or two.

Ahead of him in the hold, buried under the trawlnet that had earlier been used to tow it astern, was the weapon that had become the focus of his entire existence. He counted the cost of getting it to this point – hundreds of thousands of dollars' worth of heroin that would otherwise have made him and his organisation rich; numerous lives sacrificed to cover his tracks.

In his mind he pictured Farouk, crushed and dusty as they carried him from the smoking ruin in Beirut last year. A life so precious to him. To some extent he cursed himself for his brother's death – it was he himself who'd told the boy to stay at the headquarters while he went to search for Bizri. But above all he blamed the British.

And they'd still pay the price! He'd see to that.

No boat, no Ahmed. A disaster. Yet. . . , there had to be another way. His brother had trusted him. Now, in Allah's kingdom, he'd be watching, trusting Abdul to avenge his death.

Habib held out his hands in supplication, palms upwards for Allah to inspect. Vengeance, he realised, might now require the sacrifice of his own life.

So be it. Vengeance there must be.

Ahead lay the outline of the Rock of Gibraltar, a monument to the British colonialism that had helped plant the mark of Cain on the Arab world.

That's where HMS *Eagle* would be in a few hours' time.

It had not been his wish to destroy any but the guilty. But he'd come too far, committed too much to have anyone stop him now.

Innocent? Who was innocent? Not the people who lived in Gibraltar; they were part of the very foundations of British colonialism.

And the Spanish? Colonialists like the British, they clung to their stolen lands in north Africa that rightly belonged to the Arabs. Innocents? Not them.

His mind raced ahead. A moment ago he'd faced failure. Now he knew success was still within his reach.

What humiliation for the British if their *Eagle* were to be trapped and killed in its own nest! And what could then stop the angry Spanish expelling the smouldering remnants of the British Empire from Gibraltar! A double blow to those English, who still believed they could rule and cheat the poorer peoples of the world.

He pushed open the door of the wheelhouse.

'My friend,' he said menacingly to the Maltese skipper. 'I want you to catch me some fish.'

'The crazy bastards!' Brodrick howled. 'They're bringing *Eagle* into Gib!'

He'd caught a glimpse of the ship turning by the breakwater, as the Spanish police car headed down the broad highway to the border post in La Linea.

'Maybe they've already found Habib,' Jackie suggested.

'That I doubt.'

Camfield's efforts had won through in the end; the police had agreed he could leave Spain. He'd had to swear to return for Bizri's inquest in a few days.

The Seat they'd rented was still up at Alcala de la Frontera. The police had said they'd drop the keys into the Avis office, so the agency could go and collect it.

'¡¡Gracias! ¡¡Muchas gracias!' Jackie said over the driver's shoulder as they pulled up by the customs post.

Brodrick thanked him too and shook his hand. Then they got out.

It was a matter of minutes to pass through immigration. On the other side in Gibraltar, Commander Camfield was waiting, with an official navy car.

'Welcome. And congratulations,' he chirped, seizing Brodrick by the hand.

'Miss Bartlett, I presume,' he added, greeting Jackie. 'Bit of a hero too, by all accounts.'

'Not so sure about that,' she laughed nervously.

'First things first, Peter. You were injured, I think,' he hinted coyly.

'A scratch on the bum, that's all,' Brodrick assured him.

'Don't need a medic then?'

Brodrick shook his head.

'Right. Then we'll head for my office. The car can take you on to your hotel, Miss Bartlett. The Rock, is it?'

'Oh. I wanted to stay with P. . . .'

'I'll see you later,' Brodrick interrupted. 'When things are sorted out.'

She felt bruised. For the past few hours it had been him and her. A team. Now it was him and them again.

'Oh, all right,' she conceded. She hadn't been to bed for twenty-four hours, and a hot bath would be welcome. 'You'll let me know what's happening?'

'Of course.'

In Camfield's office overlooking the harbour, Brodrick accepted the offer of coffee this time. He'd need it to stay awake. Little chance of sleep for another twenty-four hours probably.

He stared through the window at HMS *Eagle* being nudged by the tugs against the Mole.

'We assumed from what you told us that they'd not try anything in Gibraltar itself,' Camfield explained defensively.

'The one thing I've learned about *Mustadhafin* is never to make assumptions,' Brodrick retorted.

Camfield jingled coins in his pocket.

'Anyway, they've begun the search,' he announced. 'Nimrods are up, producing a radar plot, and *Eagle*'s Harriers and Sea Kings are flying reconnaissance from the Gibraltar runway.'

'We don't even know what type of ship Habib's on,' Brodrick stated icily.

'Could be a small freighter, like the one that was sunk.'

385

This was crazy. The bosses weren't taking the threat seriously enough.

'You've got to keep stuff out!' he exploded, whipping round to face Camfield. 'Every bloody ship that doesn't live here. You've got to stop them coming in!'

'All right! All right. Calm down,' Camfield soothed. 'That's being done. There's a frigate and two mine-hunters out. They've created a cordon about two Ks from the Rock. The best we can do. And there's Royal Marines out in Zodiacs off the marina.

'Look,' he confided, 'we've put out a story that some mines fell off the back of one of our ships during the night, and they're bobbing around in the bay some-where. We're warning all the boatowners not to go out until they've been found. It's working a treat! They're all sitting in their gin palaces not daring to move!'

'Not bad, not bad. It's a start at least,' Brodrick smiled, somewhat relieved.

10.25 hrs

The trawler hove to, six miles east of the Rock. The winch clattered as the trawl net rose from the sea with its small catch of squirming fish.

The skipper and his crewman, a fellow Maltese, tipped their harvest into the hold, so that it covered the polythene-shrouded nuclear warhead. Then they secured the net.

'Over here!' Habib summoned. He was standing by the wheelhouse.

The Maltese, faces taut with fear, hobbled reluctantly across to him. The skipper stopped by the bulwarks, hands on hips, determined not to look cowed, but some sixth-sense gripped his crewman. The man began to flinch, a split second before Abdul Habib pulled the pistol from his pocket, and fired two shots into his chest.

'Ayee!' the skipper wailed, reaching his hands above his head in a desperate attempt to save himself.

But the shots he expected never came.

Samir grabbed hold of the skipper's shirt and pulled him into the wheelhouse.

'You okay! You okay!' he repeated in hoarse English. 'Habib say – you do! Then you okay! Unnerstan?'

Out on the deck Habib's men, Rashid and Ali, bound fishing weights to the arms of the dying crewman, and tipped his body over the side.

The skipper moaned with fear as Habib entered the wheelhouse.

'You listen me,' Habib barked. 'You talk on radio to Gibraltar. Say you have big trouble. Engine pooof!'

He gestured with his hands, indicating an explosion.

'Say need help. Understand?'

The skipper stared uncomprehending, mouth agape.

'Then, I not kill you.' Habib's mouth smiled, but his eyes didn't.

The skipper knew he was a dead man, whatever Habib might pretend.

'You understand?' Habib rasped. 'You call now. Engine broke. Need tow into Gibraltar.'

The skipper's eyes widened. He understood at last. He'd watched the aircraft carrier steam past, heard the warning calls on the radio, seen the anguish on Habib's face as it disappeared behind the Rock.

They wanted him to help arrange mass murder.

Without consciously willing it, he shook his head from side to side.

'No . . .'

He heard his own voice croak the word.

'You *do* it!' Habib howled.

The skipper shook his head again.

Samir elbowed Habib to one side. He held the knife before the skipper's eyes so he could see the keenness of the blade. With his other hand he pulled at the skipper's trouser belt, unfastening the buckle.

The skipper's eyes froze as he felt the buttons rip, his trousers slip, and Samir's cold, rough hand clasp his genitals.

Death when it came would be a relief. But before that, he knew now he'd be ritually emasculated if he defied them.

Samir lowered the knife.

'Okay . . .' the skipper trembled. 'Okay.'

Samir stepped back a pace. The skipper pulled up his trousers and turned towards the VHF set.

Down below in the cramped engine compartment, Rashid and Ali taped a small square of plastic explosive to the silent diesel, and sprinkled fuel oil on the wooden duckboards.

10.55 hrs

Outside the Ragged Staff Gates, a small group of pressmen and television crews crowded round the first of HMS *Eagle*'s sailors to come ashore for their Easter leave.

'Nothing to say,' they mumbled.

'Did you know about the nuclear bombs? Did you see the *Baalbeck* sink?'

'Nothing to say. Talk to the press office.'

They'd been well briefed and weren't in the mood to disobey orders. It might be different when they'd had a skinful.

Inside the gates, beyond the journalists' reach,

Brodrick stood by the water's edge watching the blue smoke from a tug, speeding for a gap in the breakwaters.

He felt powerless now. The security machinery had ground into action, controlled by Camfield, not by him. He'd done his bit. It was almost as if they didn't need him anymore.

Camfield had suggested he go back to *Rooke* and get his head down for a few hours. But there was no way he could sleep.

On the other side of the harbour, HMS *Eagle* gave the appearance of a ship winding down for shore leave, but deep below deck the Operations Room was fully manned. Screens glowed with the radar plot, linked down from the Nimrods, and controllers directed the Harriers and Sea Kings, flying from the runway of Gibraltar airport.

'Five degrees thirteen west, thirty-six, zero-six north.'

The air controller radioed a helicopter with the co-ordinates for a trawler in trouble. Engine fire, according to the coastguard. The Gibraltar Salvage Company had sent a tug and wanted clearance to bring the hulk into the harbour.

'Tell those booties to search it thoroughly,' ordered Nick Brady, who'd volunteered for the first watch as operations officer.

'And I mean thoroughly.'

One deck up from the Ops Room, Captain David Dyce had moved to his harbour cabin and was preparing for visitors. Whenever the ship entered port his first few hours were spent receiving guests. Gibraltar's Chief Minister was due in half-an-hour.

Corporal Rees looked down from the juddering Sea King and focused his binoculars on the smoking hulk below. The wheelhouse looked burned out. The paintwork round the stern of the steel-hulled craft was blackened and blistered, no name or port of registration decipherable.

On the foredeck, the crew huddled forlornly, keeping their distance from the heat at the stern. Fire extinguishers, empty presumably, lay on the deck. One of the crew waved pathetically.

Not long now, Rees thought. The tug was coming. Only a mile away.

He slipped the strop over his head, and pulled it tight under his armpits. A thumbs-up from the winchman, then Rees slipped forward off the ledge and was lowered to the trawler's deck.

He unlooped the strop and readied his SA-80. Thirty seconds later another marine had joined him.

'Speak English?' Rees shouted.

The men's faces stayed blank.

'Leetle,' one of them said eventually. 'Arabie . . .'

The man pointed to himself and his three fellows. Their faces were smoke-blackened, their eyes reddened and bewildered. They'd not moved from where they were, half-sitting, half-lying.

Half-dead by the look of them, Rees decided.

'Any-body-hurt?' he articulated.

Another blank stare, then one of them pointed to the stern.

'Watch 'em,' Rees ordered his junior, and turned towards the remains of the wheelhouse. The deck felt hot beneath his feet. He bent to touch it. Hand hot.

'Bloody hell,' he muttered to himself as he looked down the companionway into the engine space. It smelled of smoke and unburned diesel. The ladder had been destroyed by fire. No way to get down. He got on his belly and leaned in to get a better look.

'Bloody hell,' he wheezed again.

He spotted the crack on the engine block. Never seen anything like it, he thought. Must've been a fault in the casting, to go like that.

Everything was black. Everything. Including something lying against the bulkhead. Something about the size and shape of a man.

'Shit!'

The body was charred beyond recognition. A hand gave it away. Rees counted the stubs of five fingers.

He pulled himself up again. The accommodation space below the wheelhouse was the same – completely burned out. Rees returned to the bows.

'Your mate, back there?'

He gestured with his thumb. Blank stares, then one of them nodded.

'Where you from?' he shouted, concentrating on the man who looked older than the others and had made the attempt at speaking English.

'Algerie,' Habib answered weakly.

'Got any papers? Passports?'

Rees noticed a holdall the man was clutching. He pointed to it.

'Passports?'

Habib rummaged in the bag and brought out four well-fingered travel documents. Rees studied them, not too sure what he was looking for. Algerian, all right. Seemed genuine enough.

'Where you from? This boat? Papers this boat?'

Habib shook his head and pointed to the burned-out wheelhouse. Rees understood and nodded.

'Name of boat?'

'*Shelif*,' he replied. 'From Oran. Algerie.'

'Okay, okay.'

Rees had never heard of the place. No way of checking.

He glanced about him. Better look in the hold. He gestured to the men to help him roll back the canvas cover, but they gaped with exhaustion.

'They're bloody knackered. Here,' he said turning to the other marine, 'gi's a hand.'

Between them they pulled at the canvas, then quickly wished they hadn't. They saw the glint of fish in the hold and smelled what the heat of the fire had done to it.

'Okay. That's enough,' Rees decided. 'Here's the tug, look.'

He signalled to the helicopter, and the Sea King swung slowly back towards them, dangling the line that would winch them back into its comforting normality.

12.10 hrs

'Reckon I'll go back to the ship,' Brodrick muttered. Sitting in Camfield's office with nothing to do but drink coffee was making him twitch.

'I'll give you a lift round there.'

Camfield picked up his portable telephone, and led the way down to the quayside.

The driver headed south, past seldom-used dockyard cranes, and round behind the empty dry-docks.

'Not much business for the ship repair yard, by the look of it,' Brodrick commented.

'They're desperate just now,' Camfield answered. 'Nobody's building new ships, so the yards are all competing to repair the old ones.'

The car turned right, onto the mole heading north again. *Eagle*'s square, grey stern rose up ahead of them.

'Here okay?'

Camfield told the driver to stop by the gangway.

'Great. I'll see you later.'

Brodrick opened the door to get out.

'You've got this number?' Camfield asked, holding up his phone.

'I have. See you later.'

He closed the door, then froze, staring out to sea.

'Hang on!'

Brodrick slapped his hand on the roof of the car to prevent the driver pulling away.

'What's this? Look! I thought nothing was being allowed into the harbour.'

A tug was towing a blackened trawler towards the gap in the breakwater.

'Oh, yes. We know about that one. An S.O.S. case. Your guys have checked it already,' he reassured Peter. 'Algerian boat. Engine exploded. One crewman dead apparently. The others are pretty shocked.'

Brodrick watched the boats pass within a hundred yards of the mole. Two men were visible on the deck of the trawler, leaning on the bulwarks, staring blankly at HMS *Eagle*. He noted the burned-out wheelhouse and the charred paint round the stern. Was there something familiar about the cut of the bows? He frowned.

'Ought to have a look ourselves. Shouldn't we?' he suggested. 'Just to be on the safe side.'

'I'll do it,' Camfield nodded, 'on my way back round to my office.'

'Just as well.'

Brodrick turned to the gangway and waved.

Inside the aircraft carrier he made straight for the Operations Room.

'The hero returns!' Brady exclaimed, grabbing his hand. 'Are you all right? We heard you'd been hurt.'

'A scratch.' He put a hand to his backside, where the flesh-wound had begun to throb.

'How's the search going?' he asked.

Brady took him to the radar plot.

'It's the long process of elimination. No clues so far. Every ship we've identified couldn't have been anywhere near the *Baalbeck* last Saturday.'

'What about that wrecked trawler? The one I saw being towed into the harbour just now?'

'From Algeria. Haven't had confirmation yet, but your Corporal Rees had a look at it. Said the engine had definitely exploded. Things were in a right mess.'

Brodrick bit his lip. Time was slipping away. Habib would be up to something, he was sure of that.

'When do the Russians get here with their radiation kit?' he asked anxiously.

'Not until seventeen hundred.'

Brodrick shook his head. Too late. Too late.

'We've lost the initiative again, that's the trouble,' he worried.

'We're doing our best, old son,' Brady consoled him. 'We can't *all* be superman!'

Commander Camfield told the driver to stop the car by the ship repair wharf.

He could see the length of the harbour, and the jutting bows of the tug coming towards them.

On the quayside, dockyard workers sat on bollards, waiting to secure the damaged trawler when she came alongside.

Camfield's anxiety was increasing with every minute that passed. He sensed they'd missed something.

Was it a mistake to think that Habib was still out there with his bomb? Maybe his ship had put into Algeciras, or into Tangier across the Strait. Maybe he was waiting for *Eagle* to sail again before staging his nuclear ambush. In which case what Habib needed most was intelligence. Information about the date and time of *Eagle*'s departure from the Rock.

They'd better devise a deception plan.

The tug slowed and began to turn, bringing the trawler abeam of the wharf.

Four men on deck, Camfield counted.

His phone shrilled.

He pressed the 'on' button.

'Sarn't Roberts down at the border, sir,' the voice crackled in his ear.

'Oh yes. Got a problem?'

'Don't know, sir. There's a couple of Arabs we've stopped at immigration. Moroccan passports. But the police here think they're forged. Just thought, in the present circumstances, you'd best know about it.'

'Yes. Yes. Thank you sergeant. Umm . . , hang on a minute.'

Camfield held the phone away from his ear and looked at the trawler.

Priorities.

The boat had been checked already. He was just doubling up. The Arabs at the frontier – that was something new.

He put the phone back to his ear.

'Okay sergeant. I'm on my way to you.'

13.05 hrs

Brodrick had headed for his cabin. It'd been his intention to rest on the bunk for just a moment, but he'd fallen asleep within seconds.

Now the phone had woken him.

'Cap'n Brodrick,' he mumbled into it.

'Peter? Nick! Get to the ops room fast! We've news!'

He threw himself down the companionway steps and along Five Deck.

'What's up?' he demanded.

'Signal from Northwood. The bomb's on a trawler!'

'Jesus! How do they know?'

'The Maltese found two Russians drifting in a ship's lifeboat. Finally got them to admit they were from the *Baalbeck*. They said one of the bombs had been transferred to a trawler. And Peter – the bastards had fitted it with a simple time fuse!'

'Oh, my God! They've just towed a trawler into the sodding harbour!'

He barged along Five Deck and up to the brow. Two of his marines stood guard at the end of the gangway.

'I need that!' he yelled, snatching an SA-80 from the soldier's hands. 'Get another one from the armoury!'

He hurled himself down the gangway. At the bottom, an official car waited. He wrenched open the door and threw himself in beside the driver.

'Hey! What you doing?' the man protested. 'This car's for the Chief Minister!'

'Not any more, it isn't. Get down the end of the dock!'

The driver stared as if Brodrick were mad.

'Bloody get moving!'

Brodrick slid back the bolt of the rifle.

The driver turned the key in the ignition.

Dock workers were using the trawler's derrick to unload the stinking fish from the hold, swinging panniers of it across to the quay, where it was dumped in a lorry.

Brodrick jumped over the side and onto the deck.

'Have you searched this thing?'

Two men stood by the hold. Both turned bemused faces towards him.

'What you mean?' one of them asked.

'All over? There may be a bomb on board.'

At the word 'bomb', the labourers moved fast, swinging themselves up onto the dockside.

'Hey! Come back!'

He looked down into the hold, still silvery with fish.

'Yeah, I seen somethin',' one of the workers shouted. 'Something' wrapped in plastic sheet. Under the fish!'

They were still backing away.

'Come back!' Brodrick yelled. 'Get the sodding fish out! Look, if this thing goes off, it won't just be me and you dead, it'll be the whole of fucking Gibraltar!'

That stopped them.

'You've got to help!'

He cocked the SA-80 and swung it towards them.

'Quick!' he screamed.

They ran back, jumped into the hold and shoveled fish into the panniers. He leapt down beside them, feet sliding on skin and scales. He could see the grey film of plastic curved over a drum. With his bare hands he pulled fish away from it, trying to clear a space around it.

'Gimme a knife!' he yelled up to the deck.

A hand reached one down to him.

He slashed at the plastic, revealing a grey-black metal drum, less than one metre long, thirty centimetres in diameter. He ripped and pulled. Somewhere there had to be controls. Switches.

There. On the end. He cut round the polythene and folded it down like a flap.

A liquid-crystal display. Numbers counting down. He fumbled in his pocket and found the torch he'd put there last night.

The figures showed jet-black under the beam.

One-ten. One-nine. One-eight . . .

'Shiiit!' Brodrick breathed.

These were minutes. Minutes and seconds.

Fifty-nine, fifty-eight.

Oh, dear God! Less than a minute to go. Help me Lord!

Trembling, his hands reached for the panel. His fingers touched the combination locks. Must be for the access codes. Too late for those.

A switch. On/off. Try it.

Click.

Fifty-one, fifty, forty-nine.

Terror. Panic. Sweat, icy cold down his neck.

Try the locks. Spin the dials. Nothing.

Oh God!

Forty-three, forty-two.

Fingers round the edge of the panel. Wrench it out. Cut the wires.

It's set into the metal casing. Screws to undo? Four of them.

'Screwdriver!' he screamed.

Try the tip of the knife.

Thirty-one, thirty.

Point's too sharp. Just turns in the groove.

Twenty-six, twenty-five.

'We're getting a screwdriver,' came a voice from the deck. 'It's in the office . . .'

'Too late! Too bloody late!' Peter hissed.

He leaned back, hands out in front, rigid, powerless. Death. He could smell it like he'd smelled it in Lebanon.

Nineteen, eighteen.

Think, man! Think! Think how it works.

The panel. What's it made of? Some kind of laminate. Not steel.

Thirteen, twelve, eleven.

Behind the panel? Electronics. Switches. Krytrons.

Nine, eight, seven.

One chance. Only one.

He stood.

Five, four.

Finger on the trigger. Rapid fire.

Trrrrrat! Trrrrrat!

The hail of bullets shattered the timer dial. Steel and lead ripped through the laminated panel.

Trrrrat! Ricochets zinged round the hold.

Click! He'd emptied the magazine.

Eyes tight shut. Every muscle tensed like iron.

Wait. Wait for the end.

Wait.

Nothing. He opened his eyes again. Smoke from the bomb. Smoke and sparks.

It was dead. The primitive electronic brain needed to unleash its nuclear terror had been destroyed.

He turned to look up at the daylight. Faces lined the rim of the hold.

'You okay, Peter?'

'Two seconds to go,' Brodrick heard his own voice tremble. 'Two bloody seconds to go.'

A hand reached down to help him up onto the deck.

'Is that ... *it*?' asked Camfield, terrified. 'Is the damned thing safe?'

'Think so. Dunno. Never seen one of 'em before . . .'

'Peter!'

Jackie's voice.

He wiped the sweat from his eyes. He saw her standing on the quayside.

He stepped across the deck. The sight and sound of her was triggering an eruption of emotions long repressed.

He scrambled blindly onto the wharf and crushed her in his arms, his body trembling. Great sobs welled up from his throat.

Twenty-Two

14.10 hrs

They watched the police van swing past the Naval Headquarters and drive slowly towards them, along the line of dockyard cranes. Ahead of it came a police car, blue light flashing. Behind it, a Land-Rover from the Military Police.

'Extraordinary!' Camfield exclaimed, still quaking with guilt at his failure to search the trawler when it came alongside.

'Quite extraordinary! I'd had a call about suspect Arabs trying to get in to Gibraltar, and while I was down at the border, these characters were trying to get out. Two of them stank of fish, that's what got me thinking.'

The van halted by the edge of the jetty. From the escort vehicles police and MPs jumped out and spread in a circle. The rear of the van opened and four men were brought out, each handcuffed to a burly police officer.

Brodrick watched, hand on hips. So these were the men. So puny, so dejected, yet so lethal.

'See the one with the scar across his throat?' Camfield nudged. 'Pulled a bloody great knife on us when we nabbed him.'

Then the commander turned and beckoned to a soldier.

'Okay, Corporal Rees.'

The marine who'd boarded the trawler earlier that morning stepped forward and looked closely at the prisoners' faces.

'That's them, sir,' he stated quietly. 'No doubt about it.'

Brodrick saw the prisoners' eyes dart fleetingly to the right, and observe the crowd of bomb-disposal specialists crawling over the trawler. Then they looked away again, defeated.

Failure had a bitter taste. Brodrick knew that. He'd tasted it too.

'Okay. That'll do,' Camfield shouted. 'Take them away!'

The police began to push their prisoners back to the van.

Suddenly Brodrick propelled himself forward.

'Habib!' he yelled.

The four stopped in their tracks. At first none moved his head. Then one pair of eyes, blazing with hatred, looked to see who'd shouted his name.

Abdul Habib didn't speak. His look said all there was to say.

Brodrick quivered. Here at last was the devil he'd fought for so long but never seen. The man who'd broken him in Lebanon, and slaughtered his marines.

His eyes began to blur, his ears hummed with gunfire. In his nostrils, the tang of cordite and eucalyptus. They were back, the ghosts . . .

He felt his hands reach up, towards Habib's wiry neck . . .

'Okay!'

Restraining fingers on his forearm.

'Take them away, I said!' Camfield shouted to the Military Police.

The commander stood in front of Brodrick, fixing him with his sharp, little eyes.

'You've done your bit, old son,' he growled. 'Leave 'em to the law!'

The mists lifted from Brodrick's mind. The spirits slipped back into the recesses of his soul. But he doubted whether he'd ever be rid of them.

He nodded to Camfield and turned away.

'Come on, you lot.'

The police bundled the four into the van, locked the door, and the convoy drove off to the military detention centre.

16.35 hrs

The overweight WRN driver accelerated through the Ragged Staff Gates.

'If those buggers get in my way, I'll run 'em over,' she commented, indicating the crowd of pressmen clamouring to see who was in the car.

'You do that!' Jackie told her.

It was over. Twenty-four hours of tension and terror.

Captain Dyce had been humble in his thanks, almost as if he were apologising for having doubted Brodrick's convictions.

'I can't believe what's happened,' Jackie gulped, then pressed her forehead into his shoulder. Brodrick clasped her head with his hand.

'Is it safe now? Really safe?' she asked suddenly, lifting her face again. 'Makes me shudder to think of the bomb sitting there in the dockyard.'

'It's safe,' he assured her, taking her hand. 'And tomorrow it's being sent home. The Russians are flying in to collect it.'

The car swung round the corner by the cable-car station, and ground up the hill to the Rock Hotel. They turned their heads to look down at HMS *Eagle* in the harbour. So close. It had been so close.

'No need to wait this time,' Brodrick told the driver, as they stopped outside the entrance.

He eased himself out of the car and winced. Maybe the wound on his backside needed some attention after all.

Jackie noticed his pain. One more scar, she thought. One more of his nine lives.

She picked up her room key from reception, and they walked up to the mezzanine where the lifts were.

Halfway across the lobby, their way was suddenly blocked. Facing them was the young man they'd met the day before.

'Jeremy Baxter. Remember me? From *The Times*.'

'Oh, yes,' Brodrick sighed, wearily.

'Now look, Captain Brodrick . . .'

His voice was hushed and he kept peering over Brodrick's shoulder to check none of his competitors had followed him in.

'No more bullshit. I know who you are, and I know what you've done. I want to tell your story. The world deserves to hear it.'

'No thanks.'

Brodrick made to push past him.

'I know you can't talk officially. We'll do it anonymously. Totally unattributable. If you'll come to my room now, nobody'll see us; nobody'll know you ever spoke to me.'

Suddenly Brodrick thought of Richard Bicknell, the man whose corruption had triggered off the long trail of death.

He thought of the politicians in London, who'd unknowingly promoted their electoral prospects with the profits from Bicknell's drug dealings.

The world had yet to learn the full truth about these matters.

This young man was offering him the chance to reveal it. Perhaps he should speak out. Perhaps he owed it to the twelve who'd died in Lebanon.

He felt Jackie's tug at his arm.

But who'd thank him for saying his piece?

The families of his dead comrades? Hardly. 'Your boys died for no good reason' – that's the message he'd be sending them.

What about the nation he was paid to fight for? His revelations might bring down a government. But was it in the country's interests?

Maybe, if those politicians knew they were receiving drug money. But they couldn't have done.

And who'd rejoice most at their downfall?

Abdul Habib.

No. It was over now. Let it stay over.

'Thanks, but no thanks,' he said.

He pushed Baxter to one side, and slipped his arm round Jackie's waist.

It felt good there.

Also in Arrow . . .

SKYDANCER

Geoffrey Archer

PROJECT SKYDANCER

The brainchild of the Ministry of Defence – terrifying in its simplicity. New warheads had been designed that could evade the batteries of anti-ballistic missiles the Russians had set up in Moscow. For Aldermaston scientist Peter Joyce, it was the pinnacle of his career.

Until documents from the project turned up on Parliament Hill and he is left with two alternatives: write off a billion-pound project, or approve tests which could give Russia the power to wipe out the West at the touch of a button . . .

SHADOWHUNTER

Geoffrey Archer

HMS Truculent is a nuclear-powered, hunter-killer submarine, and one of the most deadly weapon systems in the world.

Phil Hitchens is its distinguished British commander – who has broken away from a NATO exercise and embarked on his own darkly vengeful and deadly mission.

SHADOWHUNT is the codename of the desperate sonar search for *HMS Truculent*, last seen heading for the Kola Inlet where the cream of Soviet sea power lies unsuspecting at anchor.

Shadowhunter is Geoffrey Archer's nail-biting, authentic thriller of undersea battle and international tension – a chillingly credible account of the world brought to the brink of catastrophe.

RINGMAIN

George Brown

A US state visit in the diplomatic diaries, a Labour MP freelancing as an IRA fixer; and a mole at the top of British Intelligence worth lorry-loads of Armalites to the dangerous men in Dublin . . . the high-explosive ringmain circuit is falling into place.

Its last connection is the world's most expensive death dealer who kills the highest placed for the highest price. Code-named Siegfried, he's in London to earn three-quarters of a million pounds with a job on the side.

Between the steel toe-cap going in and the ringmain triggering to detonate, the kill-master will find out which side . . .

THE DOUBLE TENTH

George Brown

Malaya, 1952 – The War of the Running Dogs.

They shot the Chinese courier and took the documents he was carrying. Then they cut off his hands and rolled him into a shallow grave.

Another act of barbarity in a savage jungle war, another dead Communist and another successful mission for the police and the SAS.

Thirty-five years later – members of the ambush party start dying unpleasantly. One of them has had his hands cut off. The past is catching up with the men who stood in that jungle clearing – the past in the form of a man with artificial hands and an insane rage to reclaim what was taken from him – at any cost . . .

MORE BESTSELLING FICTION
FROM ARROW . . .